A KISS
OF THE
SIREN'S
SONG

E. A. M. TROFIMENKOFF

A KISS
OF THE
SIREN'S
SONG

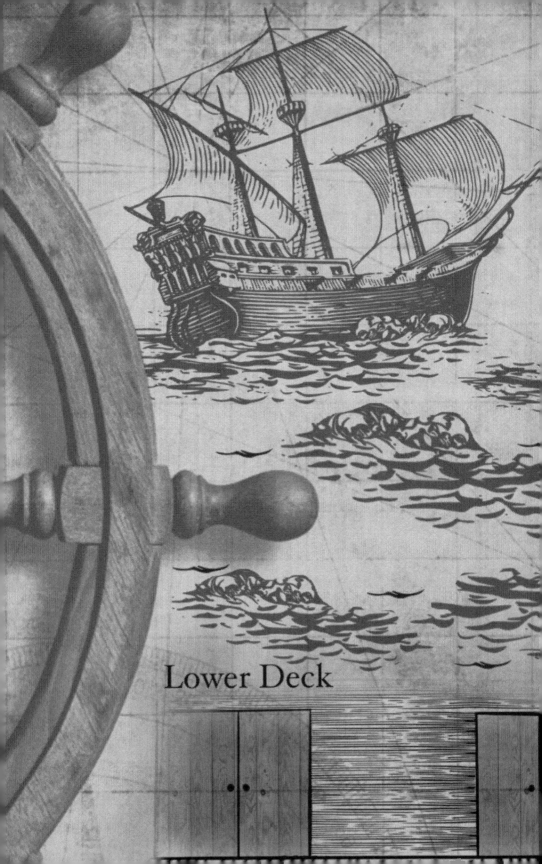

Lower Deck

Upper Deck

Content Warnings

- Violence
- Body mutilation
- Demons
- Human burning
- Sex (explicit and non-explicit)
- Drowning
- Blood
- Alcohol
- Gambling
- Murder
- Death (General)
- Death (of Parent)
- Death (of Partner)

First edition November 2023

Interior design by Cathrine Swift

Proofreading by Rebecca Scharpf

Cover design by Covers by Jules

ISBN 978-1-7380597-1-3 (paperback)

ISBN 978-1-7380597-2-0 (hardcover)

ISBN 978-1-7380597-0-6 (e-book)

Official Soundtrack

1. Siren Song - Lambia
2. Seven Nation Army - The White Stripes
3. Immortals - Fall Out Boy
4. Can You Keep a Secret - Ellise
5. Demons - Imagine Dragons
6. Everybody Wants To Rule The World - Lorde
7. Enemy - Imagine Dragons, Arcane, League of Legends
8. Centuries - Fall Out Boy
9. Bad Moon Rising - Mourning Ritual, Peter Dreimanis
10. MIDDLE OF THE NIGHT - Loveless
11. I'm Gonna Be (500 Miles) - Sleeping At Last
12. Stuff Is Messed Up - The Offspring
13. All I Ask - Adele
14. Way down We Go - KALEO
15. Let The Bad Times Roll - The Offspring
16. Kill Of The Night - Gin Wigmore
17. Queen of Kings - Alessandra
18. Hero - Martin Garrix, JVKE
19. Heroe - Il Divo

Available on Spotify

Author's Note

It goes without saying that this book is entirely a work of fiction. I must say, however, that it was not uninspired. I encourage the reader to read up on the stories of Anne Bonny and Mary Read, the two women pirates (and lovers) that were the spark of inspiration for this book. An honorable mention to all of the sapphic videos my friends have sent me through the years that resulted in an inescapable, but not unenjoyable algorithm change.

The first draft of this book was written in 21 days during my first ever NaNoWriMo experience. At the time, I was a PhD student studying computational and theoretical science (yes, I am aware I am a nerd, thank you for that astute observation). I was teaching undergraduate chemistry and tutoring; developing, supervising and marking midterms; volunteering for the PAW society; and trying to maintain some kind of work/life balance.

I do, after all have four fur babies and a husband I adore wholeheartedly. Oh, and I can't forget the trip to New York I took with my mom in the middle of all of that too. Don't ask me how I managed it. I do not have an answer. I must admit the five hour plane ride each way was great uninterrupted writing time, and perhaps that was part of my success.

Somehow the moral of this story is: watching Broadway musicals and taking long plane trips is somehow a recipe for creative writing success. But I digress.

Before you read this book, there are a few things you should know and understand about the lore of the "world" if you can even call it a world. The sirens in this book are not like the mermaids you might guess them to be. They don't have tails or fish scales, they definitely do not wear clam bras, nor are they birds. The word siren has a two-fold meaning to me.

First, a siren is loud. It grabs your attention, and it has the power to stop everything around it and command objects to move out of its way. In case it wasn't clear, I was referencing an emergency vehicle siren. These kinds of sirens are also vibrant. They are colorful and eye-catching. So how could I meld this contemporary definition of a siren, with the mythological siren I know and love? Enter Sinbad. Yes, the animated children's film which I still love and adore to this day. In the film, the sirens or mermaids or whatever they are, are essentially extensions of the water that have the potential to take humanoid form. They are whimsical and powerful, and they sing underwater, which can be enchanting, especially to male, horny sailors (who would have thought?). The sirens in this novel are human extensions of the water. They are shape shifters (water can adapt and conform to the container it is in, and it is often transparent, unless some kind of light is shone on or through it), and have powers of persuasion (water is the universal solvent, it can dissolve many things, but not everything; sometimes you have to understand what it is you're working with before trying to get it to do what you want).

So, although the powers in this book are fictional, they are all based in science for the most part. So, if you see someone blending in with their surroundings or turning water to ice, they are essentially turning themselves to liquid form (we are mostly water after all), or turning their surroundings into a different state of matter. Both require energy input or energy extraction. Either way, it's a laborious process, and I hope you appreciate the scientific perspective I took when it comes to super powers.

With that said, I should probably provide a disclaimer. At one point in this story, it is mentioned that one character downs an entire container of rum and then swallows a lit match so they can breathe out flames. DO NOT DO THIS AT HOME. This is a work of fiction. Please don't try it yourself. Okay? Okay.

I also want to point out that there is not enough sapphic fantasy in the world. As a queer person, I wanted to portray two very different queer characters that find a beautiful love despite less than ideal situations. This story is all too familiar for most of us. Although we may not have to battle physical dragons or demons, we do have to deal with the consequences of white supremacy and fascism which are still alive and well in our society today.

On most days, this feels like a demon looking over our shoulder at best, or like we are in the belly of the beast at worst. Be kind to yourselves, readers. We're all going through a journey. I hope you find some queer love to help you through it. The world would be a much brighter, safer and healthier place if we all embraced the power of queer love. Even if you are a cis-gender heterosexual individual reading this, I hope you can appreciate some of the real and figurative challenges we face daily.

While there is no queerphobia or transphobia in this book (we get enough of that in our daily lives, we don't need to live through that on the page too), I tried to depict our battles allegorically. Often, the queer community must band together to fight a power that seems invincible and indestructible. We face challenges, biases and real danger in coming out to our friends and family, let alone the public. Sometimes it feels like we have to carry the weight of the world on our shoulders, because there is no one else that will hold the sword or the shield for us. If that feels all too real for you, please know that you are seen.

You are respected, and you are loved. I hope you feel that when you are going through the pages of this book.

One last note before you embark on your epic journey. I have already mentioned it, but there is no queerphobia or transphobia in this novel. We see these actions and experience their effects enough in our real day-to-day lives. I wanted this book to be a place where queer love and queer joy can exist without having to overcome that obstacle (there are plenty others the characters have to tackle, trust me). It has never been and will never be wrong to be queer. You are not broken. There is nothing that needs to be fixed. You are a whole human with whole human experiences.

I hope this book reminds you that you can be you, whatever that is at the time. You are always evolving. You are always learning. You do not owe anyone any part of your identity until you are willing to share it. Be safe, my friends. Throw some compassion into the world.

Dedication

For anyone who is still trying to figure themself out.

And for my nana,
who always seemed to know me better than I knew myself.

"*The heart of [a person] is very much like the sea, it has its storms, it has its tides and, in its depths, it has its pearls too.*"

Vincent van Gogh

Prologue

Kaia

I should have known better than to think that I could marry for love without consequences. His eyes, pale and distant, stared up into an endless abyss. While he was lucky enough to drift away, I was stuck, seemingly forever, attached to this mortal plane.

I was helpless, bound and gagged and folded into myself. My swollen belly pushed against my legs and up into my chest, nearly cutting off my breath. A small pool of water had formed under and between our bodies from the ocean spray, and a frigid cold had seeped under my skin and into my bones. The low amber light from the setting sun peered through the gaps in our wooden crate, casting a slim halo of light around his face. There was only darkness between the damp wooden planks in front of me. No hint of the sea or the sky, and no light, just emptiness. The last fragment of my broken heart wondered if he could see the sky behind me, if somehow, he was still with me. I silenced the thought nearly as fast as it came. I had spent too long living a fantasy, unknowingly walking us into a nightmare. I squeezed my eyes shut as fury boiled in my chest. These men that killed my husband thought they knew the power of the sea well enough, but there was no controlling the storm brewing inside me.

Crimson swirls danced behind my eyelids as I let my anger take over. They had said they had been robbed of what should have been rightfully theirs. So be it. I would give them exactly what they deserved.

It might have been hours or days or weeks before I finally felt the unfiltered warmth of the sun on my skin again, but my resolve never wavered. One thought consumed my mind and one thought only, and it had nothing to do with survival. My hand clasped around the long tooth necklace my husband always wore. I tugged it off his neck with a sharp pull. The jagged edge pushed into my skin, and I felt a thin line of warm blood flow through the palm of my hand. I swallowed down the pain and clenched my jaw.

"We should have just dropped them offshore."

"Someone would have seen."

"She's too well known."

"You think she's dead yet?"

"Gods, what's that smell?"

"Just throw 'em overboard."

"You can't just drown a pregnant woman. There's bad luck to be found in that act."

"Compared to the luck we ought to have if we let her die from that stench?"

"Calm your worries, lads. Them are nothin' but a bunch of ghost stories."

The familiar voices swam around us. My fist tightened around the tooth in my hand, and my teeth ground together as I anticipated what came next. I knew I would likely only have one chance to strike, and once I did, I would no longer have the element of surprise on my side. I had to make it worth it. The image of their faces swirled beneath my closed eyes, and I pictured exactly where I would strike each one of them. Under the armpit and into the ribs, or across the throat, if I could get close enough. I had good aim, but I couldn't risk losing the grip of the only weapon I had. So close contact it would have to be. It would be an impossible task to take on all five of them, especially in my state, but there was no going back now. And there wasn't a bone in my body that was built for accepting defeat.

Something metallic clanged against the crate opening behind my head, and the stiff wood creaked as it finally gave way and lifted. Someone leaned down behind me, and I felt the hot, sticky breath of one of the men on my face. A familiar sense of hatred for him bubbled up from my stomach, and I tasted bile at the back of my throat. It took everything in me not to flinch away from his rotten breath.

"Hmm," he considered.

He reached in to touch the side of my stomach where my unborn child was still growing. I couldn't wait any longer. I quickly turned and forced the point of the tooth into the man's eye.

He flew backward with his hand over his face as a shrill scream pierced the open air. I slowly emerged from the casket, my damp hair pooled over my shoulders, and the once smooth and soft night dress I wore now clung to my body in salt-dried crisp, awkward angles. I knew I looked like a nightmare, and so be it. I was one.

I snarled at the beasts in front of me. These so-called men who only a year before had professed their undying love for me. Who vowed to never harm me. To always protect my honor and to never lay a hand on me. I made the mistake of believing them the first time, but never again would I trust a man's oath. The idea of taking all of their words away made the edge of my lips turn up. Yes, their tongues would make lovely decorations.

I reached down and grabbed the dagger the first man used to open the crate. Even with the fang in one hand and a dagger in the other, I knew I was still heavily out-armed. The odds were not in my favor, but if I knew anything, it was never to underestimate a woman hell-bent on revenge for the sake of her dead husband and her unborn child.

"You murderers," I hissed at them. My voice was hoarse from disuse, but it made my words no less potent.

"Put the blade down, Kaia."

I whirled around to face the man who had spoken. The edges of my wet hair splashed across my cheek. Mor—I stopped the name before it had a chance to fully register. I cast away their names like they were nothing more than a lilt on a wave. They meant nothing to me. In my eyes, they had no name. They served no purpose. They were monsters, all of them, and so I would see them and treat them like monsters. I felt my face heat with the fire I had been holding on to since I was first put beside my dead husband.

I swung the dagger through the air at him, and he took a step back.

"Now, lass, don't do anything hasty."

This voice was closer. I spun on my heel, and my elbow made contact with his jaw. Disoriented, he crouched down and brought his hand to his face. There was no hesitation on my part. I brought the blade down between his ribs at his back, and I felt as the sharp edge pushed through his beating heart. The man looked up at me, eyes wide and mouth open in shock.

"Kaia...." he whispered before he fell, lifeless, to the deck with a loud thump.

I grabbed the blade from his back, and his blood painted over my dress.

I looked up just as a force hit me from the side. I landed hard, and the breath left my lungs. Stars swirled around my vision as I gasped for air. Someone's foot crashed down on my side, and I heard more than I felt the bones break from the force. I tried to cry out, but my voice was broken, and even so, there was no one left to hear me now who would bother to help. This was it, I realized. All the moments where I had begged to join my husband in his blissful distance were washed away into an overwhelming sense of panic. I realized, in that moment, that it was not just my husband that I had lost, but I would soon lose our child as well. My heart shattered into a million pieces.

"Just throw 'er over."

"She's good as dead now anyway."

I heard a splash as they tossed my husband into the sea. I distantly felt two men wrap their arms under my shoulders and legs. Soon, we would both be in her eternal embrace.

The wind played through my hair as I flew down, weightless. The last thing I saw before the waves took me was the glint of a gold tooth almost winking at me mockingly.

The ocean swirled around me. As I looked to my side, I saw his body floating lifeless and still under the pale blue waves. I was suddenly acutely conscious as a cold resolve settled into my bones. I was a part of the sea just as much as she was a part of me. I swam to my husband and wrapped my hands around his face. Then, for the last time, I pressed our lips together, as my heart and soul split, cracking the ocean and earth in two. I was the sea, and she was me. We were powerful, and we would not let them die. From my will and my heart, I made it so, and so it was. From then on, and forevermore.

The Pirate

The Writing on the Wall

Sybine

Dim lights, dark eyes, whispered lies, and hidden knives. It was just as any other night at a tavern, and yet, I noticed the sparks in the air. A promise of something dangerous. A promise of adventure. And maybe, if I was lucky, a promise of escape.

The tavern door creaked open.

The first man that walked through was so tall, he had to duck his head to enter. The silver buttons on his dark coat seemed to sparkle in the low light of the room. His black hair dripped from the pouring rain outside, and his boots thudded against the worn wooden floor as he made his way to the bar bench. Several other men followed him, and when they too reached the bench, the tall man slammed his wrist down on the slab in front of him.

"Service!"

His voice boomed throughout the room. My stomach leapt at the sheer power of it. Several servers came to the front to address him. They exchanged hushed words before the mistress in charge ushered him to the back of the room. The man commanded so much attention that I nearly missed the woman on his arm. Her long dark hair fell in a curtain, giving the impression that she had just emerged from the shadows. She wore several knives at her back and one attached to her thigh on either leg. Although she was clearly trained and dangerous, she walked with a seductive grace that made several sets of eyes turn, including mine. She was clearly not a woman to be trifled with. The shadow woman and the large man turned and gestured for the rest of their company to follow. Together, they made their way behind the dark curtain at the back of the room.

I sat back in my chair and wrapped my hands around the partially empty mug in front of me, keeping my eyes on the curtain, but none of them returned. Something felt wrong about the interaction I had just witnessed, but I had seen and taken part in worse. Still, something inside me stirred. The window beside me rattled from the thunder outside, accompanied by the slight taps of the raindrops. A light streaked across the sky, illuminating the dark corner where I sat, and the empty plate in front of me.

A group of bearded drunks began laughing and throwing their fists against the table a few paces down from where I sat. I turned my head to see one frowning red-cheeked man pointing at the paper he was holding. Something about him looked vaguely familiar. I returned my gaze to the mug in front of me so I didn't draw any unwanted attention.

"I swear to you," he said between his slurred syllables, "this wretch took me for everything I own!"

The table erupted into laughter.

My eyes widened. I recognized that voice. I allowed myself another glance over. Sure enough, there he was. He was no one, really, just an easy target from a few nights ago. I didn't even remember his name. Now that I thought about it, I couldn't recall what I had stolen off him either. Still, the paper in his hand concerned me, and my stomach tightened at the sight.

"Which is little more than a compass and a soggy sandwich on a good day!" one of the others replied after he caught his breath.

"You don't believe me? Fine! Be gone with you all. I hope she strips you dry as well! Mark my words, she'll return! And when she does, I'll be having my riches back."

"Don't you mean your 'britches' back?" a man with a long scraggly beard jested. "You seem to have lost yours along the way!" He held his round belly as his low laugh filled the room.

I bit my lips closed at the last remark to stifle a laugh. I remembered the way he went running out of his room after me that night. Although he didn't lose his britches completely, they definitely weren't on his person as one would have expected, meaning I may or may not have tied them around his ankles to ensure an efficient getaway. His excitement at the restraint quickly turned to panic as he realized, far too late, what I was doing.

All the men at the table erupted in laughter again. The red-faced man stood up, slammed the paper on the table, and stormed out the door.

"Guess his ale's on us."

"Again."

"Wonder what he was on about with that wench from the west."

"Probably just some woman who got the best of him. He never does tie his purse or drawstrings tight enough, if you know what I mean."

I nodded to myself. I knew what he meant probably better than anyone else at that table. But they didn't need to know that.

"Ah, to hell with him! He's never paid his share anyway. He was probably just looking for an excuse to leave. He'll be back tomorrow with a new one, I'm sure of it."

With that, the men stood up, leaving their coins behind on top of the crinkled paper.

There was no one around us, save some quiet folk a few tables down, but they seemed too distracted by their own drinks and food to pay any mind to me. I made my way toward the men's table, only to find a nearly perfect copy of myself staring back at me. My long black curls swam around my face, and my chin tilted down, accentuating my large, round eyes. Still, there was something off about them. Fortunately, my gaze was something very hard to replicate. Unfortunately, it was still unmistakably me inked onto the parchment, along with a posted reward of fifty thousand gold pieces to whomever found me.

Fuck.

A bell rang from the curtain where the large man had passed through, and the room fell silent. I took a few steps back to merge into the shadows as a hoarse voice filled the room.

"The captain will now be accepting cabin crew and deckhands! Come place yer name among the strongest and bravest. Sail the seas with Captain Stormson, and you will be rewarded with riches beyond measure! Come! Sail to the Kraken's Cove!"

Excitement erupted around the room. The surrounding conversations picked up in both pace and intensity, and soon, a choir of voices filled the room again.

My heart pounded in my ears as I considered my options. I could continue my flight south, but how long would it be until I reached the southern peak of Elandia and had to board a ship anyway? These posters had followed me this far; they would surely continue. Something in me knew he would stop at nothing to get his hands on me again. I took a deep breath. There were two paths in front of me: continue south and hope that I wouldn't get caught, which would be ignorant at best, and detrimental at worst; or take the opportunity to flee now. I set my shoulders and my jaw and finally took a step forward.

2

Bound

Elora

I rolled my eyes.

Men. Fools.

It would have taken less than a minute for me to rid them of their tongues, but fortunately for them, this blade was meant for a different target.

I had visited the Stumbling Sailor every night of the last week, and it was always the same. The name of the tavern represented the demographic of the patrons well. Had I not been waiting for the crew announcement, I would have taken care of a few of these fools, but I couldn't afford to be kicked out of yet another tavern for a violent outburst. Especially when I was so close to my goal that I could almost taste it.

I focused on the plate in front of me. Only the gods knew how long it would be again before I had such a hearty meal. It would be a waste to let any of this go, and where I was headed, I would need as much strength as I could get. I was, after all, about to enter the dragon's den.

From the edge of my vision, I caught the person in the corner stand and make their way to the vacant table. The darkness clouded their features, and while I could not make out what it was they were looking at, they seemed taken aback by it.

Another fool, more than likely, I thought to myself. In my experience, they all were.

A loud bell rang beside me, and I clenched my jaw in anticipation.

"The captain will now be accepting cabin crew and deckhands! Come place yer name among the strongest and bravest. Sail the seas with Captain Stormson, and you will be rewarded with riches beyond measure! Come! Sail to the Kraken's Cove!"

A smile crept over my face. I had been waiting years for this moment, and finally I was about to get a sweet taste of revenge.

I wiped my face with my handkerchief and stood from my chair. The legs slid against the liquor-steeped floor slowly, and I nearly tipped over from the resistance.

"Stupid drunks," I muttered to myself.

I retrieved my bag and made my way to the back. Several people had lined up by the table, waiting, like me, to sign their lives away in search of that which they desired most. Aside from my body, there were other things that separated them from me: primarily their thirst for gold, and my thirst for blood. Glory and riches were all that drove these men, which is what I preferred. Those who focused on the coins in their pockets had a tendency to crave more of what they already had and were willing to do anything for it. I always found that those kinds of men speak a simple language, and I could always trust them to go against whatever they said. If anything, false promises were the only things they could truly keep, which made them reliable and, more importantly, predictable.

"Come all, to Drakkon's crew! Come sail to riches beyond measure!"

It was, unfortunately, clear that a few of the men in line had no other choice. Their tattered clothes and bony silhouettes did not make them desirable crewmates, and yet they were met with excitement and vigor.

In my experience, people barely regarded or welcomed sailors in their position. On the various ships I had sailed on, everyone had either been experienced enough that they needed no extra hand-holding, or so strong that they could immediately be put to work to do the heavy lifting...or both, like myself. Something about the interactions between the recruiter and these desperate men set my teeth on edge. The last thing I wanted was to be babysitting weak, unknowledgeable, greedy, desperate men. I had no time for pleasantries or mundane tasks. I was here for one reason and one reason only, and that had nothing to do with teaching folks about how to live on the sea. Still, I had waited years for this. I couldn't back out now. If I had to take out some unfortunate souls on my way, then so be it.

I assumed my position at the end of the line behind a wiry man with thin hair and thinner clothes. His frail frame hunched, and he struggled to move forward with the line. On a few occasions, I was concerned he wouldn't make it to the table, let alone the ship.

He stumbled forward, and I caught him at his belt loop. I couldn't have cared less if he landed on his face and made a fool out of himself, but I couldn't let that bring any unnecessary and unwanted attention in my direction. Luckily for him, I needed to remain in the shadows...for now.

"Ah, why...thank you...lad," he said. His voice was rough and low, and he spoke with a growl which could have only come from years on a pipe.

"Don't mention it," I replied shortly as I brought him back to balance.

"Don't suppose...you would have...some old weed...for an old man...?"

He took long wheezing breaths between his words.

"Afraid not," I said. "Can't say I enjoy the taste."

He chuckled. A low noise that started deep in his belly and made its way up.

"Ha! The young folk...not the same...as when I...was your age. Back when I...."

The man started the way they always do. A story of woe, followed by how they managed to luck their way through. Except that was rarely the case. There was no luck about it. Only their business in their pants, or the coins in their purse. You couldn't make your way through this world without the right junk in your pockets.

"That's quite...somethin'...isn't it?" he asked.

"Indeed," I said.

"Next!" the man at the table called.

The wiry man in front of me moved forward, and I followed.

"Name?"

"Harlan," the man in front of me said.

"You sure you're wantin' to sign up for another adventure, sir? Seems like you've seen yer share already."

Harlan took a deep breath and clenched his fist.

"Look here...laddie...I know...I don't look like much...but I've got more wits...and more balls...then the lot of you combined...and if you...don't want...me...you're gunna have...to say...it straight."

The man at the table smirked.

"Right then," he said, "sign here."

He turned the page toward Harlan, along with a long pen and ink. Harlan signed and began to step away.

"Not so fast there. One more thing," the man behind the table said, and he moved the knife from the edge of the table toward Harlan.

"The crew of the *Vindicta* bind in blood."

I raised an eyebrow at the mention of this ancient form of commitment. I hadn't heard of a blood binding since before my father's time, and even he had only heard stories. Pirates didn't have laws, but they tended to abide by an unspoken set of rules. The last pirate conclave was held nearly a hundred years ago, after the pirate king Laraghan sacrificed his crew in a fit of madness. No one knew what was said in the conclave, but no blood oaths had been sworn since then, not even to some of the most bloodthirsty, ruthless pirates since. As far as I knew, requesting blood binding of a crew was at least frowned upon, and at most outlawed. That Drakkon had such a request set my teeth on edge. I didn't like this at all.

Harlan tilted his head to the side, and the man behind the table smirked.

"Just a drop will do. Yes, there, next to your name is fine."

Harlan eyed the knife and hesitantly stuck it to his finger. A small pool of blood accumulated, and after a few moments, he pressed it to the paper beside his name. He had now been bound in blood.

"Next!" the man behind the table called.

Harlan moved to the side and disappeared behind the curtain.

"Come on! Step up!" he called to me, ushering me with his hand.

"Name?"

"Loren," I responded.

"And what are you applyin' for there, lad?" he asked me. "You seem a fair bit stronger than yer old man." He gestured to the curtain behind him that Harlan had just moved behind.

"He's not," I said sharply, "my old man."

"Very well, sir. I meant no offense." He waved his hands in front of his face as if to wash away his words through the air.

"Any guard positions left?" I asked.

The man squinted his eyes at me hard and looked me up and down.

"The captain likes to choose his guards himself, if it pleases ye. But, I think in this case—" he paused to scan my body one more time— "he might make an exception. You look like you could take the guards single-handed!" He laughed, his deep boom echoing across the room.

He was right. But I wasn't about to tell him that.

"You honor me, sir." I bowed my head slightly to him.

"Sign here," he said to me, handing me the pen and ink.

I signed, and when he passed me the knife, I didn't hesitate. I looked him straight in the eyes, and when the blood began to drip from my hand, I smiled and swiped it across the paper. As much as I hated the idea of the bond, I had to get on the ship, and there was no way I was allowing the man to see any kind of weakness in me.

"Bound in blood." I repeated the words Harlan had said before me.

With that, I made my way through the curtain and stepped into the dragon's den.

3

New Name, New Life

Sybine

I quickly wove my hair together at the back of my head and repositioned my hat to cover my face. Fortunately, I had worn my large jacket and britches. They hid my curves well. I only hoped it would be enough to get me past the table.

When the old man stumbled, I was surprised to see the man in front of me catch him by the loops of his pants. I could see the muscles of his neck tense and then relax under his black shirt as they both steadied. I wasn't surprised when he volunteered as a guardsman. Loren stood at least a head taller than me, and his broad shoulders looked strong and fit. In short, Loren looked like he had been training his entire life for this job, and I agreed when the man behind the table said he looked like he could take the guards single-handed. No doubt he had been told this before, but he accepted the compliment with grace and followed through with the signing.

"Next!"

I stepped forward. I spared a look behind me to make sure no one had recognized me from the posters. Fortunately, the tavern had mostly emptied, and those that remained seemed more preoccupied with their own business, drinks, or both. The rain came down harder and seeped through the crack under the door.

"Name?"

I turned back around to face the man behind the table.

"Syb—" I cut myself off. New name, new life. "Sebastien." I replied.

"Well, Sebastien. It's your lucky day, I reckon. Fancy some riches, do we?"

That's what got me into trouble in the first place, I thought to myself.

"Something like that," I said.

He stared at me through thick eyebrows, studying my face and body.

"Have we met before?" he asked me. "There's just...something about you. I can't quite put my finger on it."

"I tend to frequent the land," I said behind gritted teeth. "It is only recently that the sea has called my name."

The man stroked the stubble on his chin.

"Still," he said, intrigued, "there's something about you."

The wind burst open the door, shaking the windows and causing my hat to fall off and reveal my face.

He sighed.

"Shove off, lass. We don't take women on the *Vindicta*...wait...."

His eyes suddenly widened in recognition.

"Blimey—" he chuckled— "looks like it's my lucky day, not yers. I know someone who will pay a pretty price for yer pretty face."

I had hoped I wouldn't have to resort to this. It was so much more rewarding when people handed things over of their own free will. But this was different. This time, I had no choice, and unfortunately, that meant neither did he.

The man stood up and made his way around the table to me. I closed my eyes and took a deep breath, calling a power deep within myself. A familiar sense of calm washed over me, and I could feel the energy crawling over my skin. I opened my eyes to meet his and placed my hand on his cheek. Immediately, he stood still. I had him in my trance. Like a fly caught in a web.

"You will accept me as a deckhand," I began. My voice was soft and smooth, like a mother consoling a babe. "You will forget my face and this encounter, and you will return to your master with your complete roster."

The man's eyes glowed a faint silver as my spell took over. He relaxed under my palm and let out a gentle exhale. I took my hand away, and he blinked a few times before returning to his chair.

He looked up at me with fresh eyes.

"Name?"

"Sebastien."

"Well, Sebastien. Looks like it's yer lucky day, I reckon. We have one spot left as a deckhand. Welcome aboard."

Fear at First Step

Sybine

The boards creaked under my feet as I walked up the plank ramp. My fingers methodically fiddled with the buckle on my belt bag. The familiar tension around my thigh from the leather strap helped keep my mind grounded as I made my way onto the ship. I kept my head down as I boarded. The crewmates were lined up at the edge of the deck, waiting, hands folded behind their backs.

Not for the first time, I wondered what I was doing. Not an hour had passed since I saw my face on the wanted poster. I had not even an inkling of knowledge about what it meant to be a deckhand or what life at sea was like. What was I thinking? What was I possibly going to do on a boat in the middle of nowhere, surrounded by pirates? Did I really think I could get away with hiding myself on deck...for how long? I had never tried to influence more than one person at a time, and certainly never in a crowd. If I was to be found out, I would be completely and utterly screwed. I mentally scolded myself. I hadn't even asked where we were going or how long it would take to get there. I had never made a less calculated decision, and I had spent most of my nights trying to empty the pockets of men, which was admittedly not the safest or most planned out career choice.

A loud bang behind me interrupted my thoughts, and everyone turned around. Fortunately, they were staring at the figure behind me, rather than having their attention on me. I scurried up the rest of the way and joined the end of the line.

I squinted through the rain in the night to see the large man from the tavern walk up the plank to the ship's deck. Two men followed behind: a nasty looking, bulky brute with choppy black hair and a stubble beard; and the man from the table with his list in hand. I noticed that the woman was missing from them. A part of me wondered where she had gone, but before I continued with the thought, a commanding voice interrupted me.

"So," the large man said, his voice low and raspy, "this is my new able-bodied crew."

"Yes, Captain," the man from the table responded.

Captain. So this was the man I had signed my life away to.

The brute of a man, presumably the first mate, made his rounds around us. We all kept our heads down respectfully as he inspected us. My heart thudded in my chest, and it rang in my ears, echoing the rain pouring on the deck.

"You, there," the brute said, and pointed toward a tall man who I recognized as Loren. "Step forward."

He took a single step forward but did not raise his head. Even from here, I could make out the sharp line of his jaw and the hollows under his cheekbones. I could tell from the way he narrowed his eyes that he hated having to lower his head to them. The muscles in his neck and jaw tensed as he moved. His black shirt rippled around him from the wind. In the dark, it was like he was clouded in shadows.

"What is your name, sailor?"

"Loren, sir," he responded.

"You look like you're fit for the guard," the man said. "Brandor!"

The man from the table made his way toward the two.

"Aye, Rhyker, sir."

"Is Loren under the guard crew?"

"Yes, sir."

31

"Excellent." He seemed to hiss the words from beneath his teeth. A sneer spread across his face.

Slowly, he made his way down the line until he reached the old man at the end.

"I thought we weren't taking charity on this sail, Brandor."

To my surprise, the old man straightened his back and met Rhyker's eyes with the same intensity.

"I've been misnamed before, sir, but that one is new," he said defiantly.

The words rolled off his tongue with a lilt that reminded me of how my Gramps used to speak. He even had the same white hair. My heart gave a longing thud in my chest. If only I could turn back time.

Rhyker's eyes flashed with something that resembled amusement. Then a soft smile tugged at the side of his mouth.

"Good to know you have more life in you than you look, old man," he replied.

"The name is Harlan."

"Very well, Harlan. Welcome aboard."

The rain continued to pour, and lightning cut through the dark night. The gods rumbled restlessly in the sky as Rhyker finished his rounds. I relaxed and let out a long breath after he passed me.

"Well, some of them look half-starved, but I believe we have a fit enough crew for our voyage, Captain."

The captain made a loud grunt from behind us, and my muscles immediately tensed again. I had been so focused on Rhyker that I had forgotten all about the captain. I clenched my jaw but kept my head down, making sure my face was as hidden as it could be. The captain's footsteps echoed through the night, each one strong and deliberate. He stopped in front of us, and I chanced a slight glance under my hat at him. His dark curls fell just below his shoulders, and his short beard looked more like a shadow on his skin in the night. Two small scars seemed to glow silver on his face; one split the eyebrow above his left eye, and the other swept across his cheekbone on the same side. A vein pulsed at the side of his temple as he flexed his square jaw. Everything from his dark, nearly black stare to his rigid posture screamed danger, and I had to force myself to swallow the fear he instilled in me from his presence alone. His deep breaths were low. Each one seemed to stretch impossibly long, and I watched what looked like smoke dance in the air from his nose and mouth.

"This is the *Vindicta*," he grunted. "You sail for more than just glory and riches. If we are successful, you will be the crew of a captain who will rule the seas with the power of the Kraken's Fang." He ran his eyes down the row of us. "Now get to your bunks, you restless dogs. We set sail at dawn."

Slowly, everyone broke formation and moved toward the end of the ship.

"And I better not see or hear any mischief tonight. The consequences of such actions would be...severe."

The hair on the back of my neck rose, and something in my stomach turned over. But something else flickered in the back of my mind. A small tug that I couldn't quite place. Something familiar and foreign at the same time. Before, I had thought it might have been fear of the unknown, but no. This was something much more akin to excitement and anticipation.

5

Stranger

Elora

I was surprised at how easy it was to make rank on this ship. Drakkon only chose those who were competent and learned sailors. Yet, half of the crew seemed like they had seen either too many sunrises or too few meals. Still, the training I endured over the years had paid off. I was an appointed guardsman, and completely unsuspected.

During my studies, if I could call them that, I gained much more than skills with blades and words. My muscles that were once lean had grown. I could carry more than any man I knew. My breasts that were once soft had changed to fit the rest of my toned body. I was tall too, which gave me a distinct advantage when it came to fighting. It, unfortunately, also meant that I had to be wary of lower attacks. Besides the time I spent training with my daggers and shivs, I also practiced balance. In a fight, sometimes it came down to who could literally hold their own weight the best. It had been ages since I lost a fight, but I still remembered how it felt to fall.

Unlike the other ships I had sailed on, there were no bunk designations on the *Vindicta*. After the captain's words, everyone else scattered like rats. In my experience, it paid to be composed. No room or bunk designations meant one of two things: either this was meant to be a brief trip, or not everyone was expected to make the return journey. Of course it was possible that Captain Stormson or Rhyker, his first mate, had made an error in organization, but something told me that this chaos was not only anticipated, but also deliberate. The fact sent a prickle of energy up my spine. If I wanted to achieve what I'd set out to do, I would have to remain vigilant.

When the upper deck had mostly cleared, I made my way down the short set of stairs near the hull of the ship. Various echoes of voices rang out from down the hall to my right, and I turned to follow them. All the doors were closed except for the one at the end of the hall. Perfect. The further away from the chaos, the better. The room was dark. The candle had long been extinguished. I pulled out a match and lit it again.

The room was small. A bunk with two narrow beds on top of one another was pressed against the inside wall. Two wooden chests lay side by side on the opposite wall, which left just enough room to walk in between to reach the beds.

A loud thud behind me caught my attention, and I turned around to find the source of the noise. A petite man stood just outside the door, not even an arm's length away from me.

"Sorry about that. I didn't realize this room was taken. I'll just...." He trailed off as he looked down the hall. I didn't need to follow his gaze to know what he saw: a row of closed doors and occupied rooms.

The man turned back to me, and I barely had enough time to notice how he bit his lips together before he tilted his chin down for the tip of his hat to cover his face again.

I had hoped for some space for myself. Being on the same ship as pirates was dangerous. Sleeping in the same room as one was a death wish. Yet, something told me I had nothing to physically fear about this man. He was short and scrawny, and his clothes were far too big for his frame. He kept his head down, so he clearly had something to hide, or didn't want to be noticed, and his fingers fiddled with the bag at his side even as he stood in front of me. He was nervous.

The ship shook slightly as we set off from the dock, and he stumbled.

"Sorry, I'm still getting used to walking on a ship."

I studied the man up and down. He had no more balance than that of a newly born horse.

"Why apply as a crewman on a pirate ship if you have never actually been on a ship?" I asked, pointedly.

He lurched again as the waves rocked us. A bolt of lightning lit up the room through the small circular window, and I recognized him as one of the men from the tavern.

He shrugged.

"No choice," he responded as he strolled past me and into the room. I hadn't invited him in, but I guessed he had come to the same conclusion as I did: there was no other choice. Unless he wanted to sleep out in the hall or in the rain. I swallowed down my annoyance.

I studied him as he shuffled over to the bunks. It was obvious that he had never boarded a ship before, and even more obvious that he was uncomfortable with being on one.

I raised an eyebrow at him and crossed my arms over my chest as I leaned against the doorframe.

"I doubt someone held a knife to your back or throat to get you on board. So you are either lying, or you're completely incompetent."

The man stopped wobbling for a few moments to straighten his hat, and removed his hand from his bag. He turned around and took a deep breath before he responded.

"Listen, you're not the captain, and I'm not your servant. My business is my own. Let's...let's just get through this night, okay?"

But it's not just this one night, I wanted to tell him. He would find that out tomorrow when everyone returned to their bunks. You didn't dare enter someone else's space after it had been claimed. Not if you valued your life and fingers. These folks preferred to ask questions after lashing out with their blades, not the other way around. Sometimes people just had to learn that the hard way.

"Very well."

The man nodded his head at me in anxious agreement.

I ran my tongue along my teeth under my lips as we stood in what could have been an uncomfortable silence. I could never tell for myself. But the man started fidgeting with the bag at his side again.

I lifted my chin and stared down my nose at him.

"What's your name, sailor?"

The man swallowed, but to my surprise, stood up slightly straighter and squared his shoulders.

"Sebastien."

I smirked at him.

"And what is your role on this ship, Sebastien?"

"I...uhm...." He trailed off.

I tilted my head to the side slightly. He was nervous again, but not because of me.

"Well?" I asked again. "Are you a deckhand? Star reader? Map maker?" I paused and then smirked again. "Or are you just a thief looking for a convenient getaway?"

Sebastien went as still as a rock, and I bit back a laugh.

"Relax, we're all liars and thieves here. You would hardly be the first."

He let out a nervous chuckle.

"Deckhand. I'm a deckhand."

I scoffed.

"Good luck with that." I had put in my time as a deckhand many years ago. It wasn't a role I was eager to return to anytime soon. I swore I could have felt the phantom calluses on my hands ache from the memory of scrubbing the deck every day.

It was Sebastien's turn to tilt his head at me.

"You'll find out in the morning. I'm Loren, by the way. Not the captain, like you so generously pointed out earlier."

"You're a guardsman." He nodded, as if putting two pieces of information together. "You were in front of me in line at the Stumbling Sailor."

So he was more perceptive than he seemed. Interesting.

Sebastien nodded again as he unbuckled the bag at his side.

I grunted in agreement.

He threw his bag onto the top bunk. Then he paused and turned around.

"I hope it is not rude of me to assume the top," he said.

I shook my head.

"Be my guest." I gestured to the top bunk.

We stood there awkwardly, staring at each other for slightly too long. Sebastien exhaled, and his dark hair in front of his face moved with his breath. His eyes glistened green in the flash of lightning.

Sebastien rocked back and forth on his heels, and then he let out a nervous breath.

"Well, goodnight then," he said.

I tipped my head towards him.

"Goodnight."

I pushed myself off the doorframe and closed the door to our room as he climbed up the small ladder that brought him to the top bed. He was quick. By the time I had turned around, he was under the blanket and rolled facing the wall.

It could be worse, I thought to myself, and let out a deep breath.

I sat on the lower bed and took my boots off, followed by my coat and knives. I tucked one under my pillow. Couldn't be too safe when you were surrounded by pirates. Then I made myself as comfortable as I could be. It wasn't too long until my eyelids grew heavy and my body relaxed. Tomorrow would be the start of my life. The life I had been waiting years for.

Vision

Elora

Lunge. Twist. Retract.

Calm your mind, I told myself.

Repeat.

Lunge. Twist. Retract.

I took a deep breath to slow my heart rate. I had practiced these steps since before I could hold a proper sword, so much so that they came almost too easily to me. It allowed my focus to slip and other things to enter my mind. I couldn't afford the distraction.

I jumped back and forward from my empty fade into a low lunge that would take anyone out at their knees. Most people were good at protecting their chests and faces, but unless you were expecting a lower blow, most didn't see it coming until it was too late.

Good, little sword. I heard David's voice in my head encouraging me, just like he had all those years ago. *Now finish the job.*

I pictured Drakkon's face in my mind as if he were right in front of me. I pictured him falling to his knees, completely at my mercy, which, fortunately for me, and unfortunately for him, I did not possess. White fiery rage flooded my veins and filled my body with a familiar fury. I crouched down and swiped my leg around my body in a half circle, a move that would knock my enemy to the ground after I wounded him. I brought my sword up over my head, and with both hands on the hilt, I plunged it toward the ground, toward his head.

"What are you doing?"

On instinct, my blade changed its course. In one swift motion, I had Drakkon pinned to the wall of the hall with my blade against his throat.

Suddenly, the vision in front of me dissolved. Drakkon's skin fell, and the victory I had earned slipped through my fingers like water. I blinked in confusion as I finally registered that there was no one else between me and the wall. I held my blade against the wood panels and nothing else.

Sebastien stood at my side in the doorframe of our room. His round eyes were wide, and I could have sworn I saw a flash of silver spark through his green irises before he disappeared into thin air.

"What?"

I shook my head and closed my eyes for a second. When I opened them again, Sebastien was staring at me, concerned.

"I'm sorry, I...." He trailed off.

I pushed off the wall and took a deep breath as I ran a hand through my short hair.

My sudden loss of grip on reality made me feel sick. My lungs felt heavy and full of water, and there was a strange prickling sensation at the nape of my neck.

"It's dangerous to interrupt someone in the middle of a training session, Sebastien." My voice came out low and hoarse.

He looked at me in disbelief and scoffed.

"This isn't a training ring, Loren. This is a hallway where people walk, filled with rooms where people sleep."

He was right about that. This wasn't a training ring like I had ever been in. But it's not like I could practice on deck where Drakkon had the opportunity to study my moves. Even taking the time to practice in the hall was risky, but there wasn't enough space in our room for any kind of intense maneuvers. I obviously couldn't tell him I was training to kill our captain, and that I had been training for that single purpose for over a decade, so instead, I went for a killing blow, this time with my sharp tongue instead of my blade.

"This isn't a sailboat, Sebastien. And we're not destined for some faraway enchanted fantasy land. This is a pirate ship. And trust me when I say that no matter where we land, it will be far less than peaceful. So yes, this is a hall, but make no mistake, the second you walked on board, you entered the most formidable training ring of your life."

Sebastien swallowed and flexed his jaw. It looked as if he might say something, but before the words came out of his mouth, the meal bell rang.

"Get dressed. I'll see you at breakfast." I kept my tone low and sharp. I sheathed my sword at my side and made my way down to the dining hall, hoping that somehow the heaviness in my chest would subside.

Dirt for Disguise

Sybine

Loren was a prick. Unfortunately, that made him no less correct about my circumstances. I recalled Loren's haunted glance, and my stomach turned. It wasn't just vacant; it was completely overwhelmed, like someone had put a spell on him. I would know. I had seen that look too many times to count now. And yet his spell wasn't from me. Something told me it was completely self-made.

I walked over to and opened my chest at the side of the room. It was filled with extra shirts and trousers of all sizes. I held up one of the white tunics. It was far too large for my frame, but it would hide my curves well. I pulled last night's jacket off and tucked it away at the bottom under the extra trousers. Luckily, I had worn one of my tighter chemises the night before. The men I saw usually preferred my form-fitting attire, but since last night hadn't gone according to plan, I found myself now on a pirate ship in a top made for seducing men, surrounded by dangerous men. Fantastic.

Fortunately, the chemise held my breasts relatively close to my body, so as long as whatever I wore on top wasn't form fitting, I would be able to hide them relatively easily. Unless, of course, a wave splashed me, in which case, everything would be available for everyone to see. But no chances of that on a pirate ship, right?

I shook my head at myself. I had no choice. If I wanted to blend in, I had to put on the white shirt. It wasn't like I could walk around in my skin-tight chemise all day. That would draw far more attention. For now, at least, it was safer to play the part of a pirate, or at the very least, sailor.

I brought the soft shirt over my head and let it fall loosely over my shoulders. Two strings wove back and forth through the V-neck, and I tied them up tight so that my chest would be as covered as possible. At least this way, if anyone asked, I could argue that I was just protecting myself from the sun. No one would question me trying to cover up my pale skin.

I looked at myself in the small mirror above the chests. I could not look more out of place. My scrawny frame didn't come close to filling out the arms of my shirt or the legs of my trousers. My skin looked as if it had never seen the sun, and my sage green eyes seemed to shine even brighter than they usually did. I sighed. This was going to be a long and exhausting journey. I was used to playing a part for other people, but never had so much rested on my ability to put on a convincing performance. At least, if I had to, I could count on my powers of persuasion, as long as we were alone, and I could touch them and they didn't hurt me, and oh gods my head was swimming again.

I sat down on the bottom bunk and threw my head into my hands. How the hell was I supposed to pull this off? In what world did I think I would ever be able to pass for a man, let alone a sailor, when I had never spent a single day on the sea? I gripped my hair at the base of my skull and pulled. I sat there until my fingers ached from holding them so tight. The pain grounded me until my heart rate slowed.

Whether you think you can do this doesn't matter anymore. You're already here. You have to do this.

I took a deep breath and ran my fingers through my long curls.

One step at a time, I told myself.

I methodically wove my hair together into a long braid down my back. I had seen men with long hair before, and most of them wore it like this to keep it out of their face. I stood up and looked at myself in the mirror again. In the dark, it was hard to tell, but in the daylight, my features gave me away. My nose was too short, my cheekbones too high, my chin too round, and my jaw too soft. The features that once allowed me to rule the night were now completely working against me. I looked down and tried to swallow the pit that was rising in my throat. My eyes fell on the dirty crevice between the floor and the wall. I recoiled slightly, knowing what I must do, knowing that I had little time to do it. I took a deep breath and reluctantly bent down to dip my fingers in the grime.

I lifted my chin up to take one last look at myself in this form. After this, I would truly become Sebastien. With one last deep breath, I brought my finger up under my eye and smudged. Then again, under my chin and cheekbones, and finally under my eyebrows. By the time I finished, my features were sharper, and although it looked like I was slightly dirty, from a distance, it wasn't noticeable. I gave myself a small smile in the mirror as I placed the hat back on my head.

"Hello, Sebastien," I said to myself before finally stepping out of the room and into my new life.

For the First Time

Sybine

I didn't see Loren at breakfast after all, which, if I was being honest with myself, was quite a relief. In my experience, men didn't like to discuss their surface feelings, let alone the nightmares that haunted them during the day.

"All deckhands to the upper deck immediately!" a voice called from the end of the dining hall.

I quickly stuffed the last bits of food from my plate into my mouth and made my way past the long line of tables back to the hall. After a few paces, I found myself at the bottom of the stairs, looking up at the clear blue sky. I gazed in awe at the clear crystal quality of it as I ascended the stairs and ran straight into the back of one of the other sailors.

"Oi! Watch it."

"Sorry," I said under my breath.

The man wasn't much taller than I was, but he was much broader. His thick muscles made it look as if he had some kind of boulder between his shoulders and his neck. It looked like he was permanently shrugging. As he turned around to face me, his long, braided sandy hair smacked me under my eye.

"Ouch." I brought a hand up instinctively to cover the patch under my eye that he struck.

"Mind your space, will ye?" He rolled his eyes at me and mumbled something about a fang before he turned back around.

I moved past him and took the last few stairs until I was finally on the upper deck. It looked so much bigger during the day than at night. There was a large wooden mast in the center of the deck that supported a sail as wide as some of the houses I had seen growing up. There were ropes everywhere, tied to beams and poles of various sizes, and some of it was attached to the railing at the edge of the deck. I made my way over to the rail and ran my fingers along the smooth wooden grain, and that's when I finally saw it: the sea.

Something in me seemed to unleash. It was as if I had lived my entire life forced to walk because of a chain around my ankle, only to find myself freed and able to run. It was like living in the dark, thinking that a candle was the only source of light, only to find myself finally able to stand in the sun. It was like sinking my teeth into a fresh strawberry after only eating stale bread. In a word, it was like life. It was like I finally knew what it was to truly live.

"Pretty amazing, isn't it, kid?"

The old man from the tavern came to stand beside me. He looked out at the horizon as if admiring a long-lost friend.

"It is," I said, a little breathlessly.

Harlan's grip strengthened on the railing as he closed his eyes and took in a deep breath.

"It never changes, you know," he said. "The draw of the sea, and the magic she holds. Even after all these years, she still takes my breath away."

He opened his eyes again, and I studied his face as he longingly searched the horizon. The white stubble of his beard reflected the sun, as did his ashen hair. His eyes were a pale blue, like the crest of a wave on the sea. Despite his age, he looked strong, which was a large contrast to how he had been last night.

"You seem to be feeling better."

He turned and smirked at me.

"I always feel better when I'm home, don't you?"

Although the words weren't meant to wound me, I felt a pain in my heart all the same. I hadn't had a home since Gramps passed all those years ago.

Harlan's face fell.

"I'm sorry, kid."

I looked up into his clear blue eyes.

"What for?" I asked.

He reached out and put a hand on my shoulder.

"Grief is like a specific color only you can see. The world never looks the same after. And when you've lived for as long as I have, the world is plenty colorful. I'm sorry to see those same shades reflected in you."

A familiar warmth spread through my chest. The tension in my shoulders ebbed slightly, and for the first time since I set foot on this ship, I felt like I wasn't alone.

"I'm not," I said, "sorry, I mean." I gave him a sad smile. "I can't imagine a world without the color of that love, and I wouldn't want to."

Harlan squeezed my shoulder and then returned his hand to his side. A smile played across his face.

"I'm glad to hear it, kid."

"Deckhands! Report for duty!" a voice called from behind us.

"I guess break time's over."

Harlan turned and made his way toward the crowd of people assembled near the center mast. I took one last glance out at the sea before following him over.

"I want every inch of this deck scrubbed to within an inch of its life every morning immediately after the final breakfast bell. The quicker you complete your section, the more time you will have for waxing and polishing...don't make that face at me, sailor, you knew what you were signing up for."

Rhyker's voice carried over us. I stood at the back, behind Harlan and the man with the long blond braid. I could just make out Rhyker from a small space between their shoulders, and his eyes were pinned on someone in the front. His face was a mask of fury.

"But I—"

"But nothing," Rhyker hissed back. He took a strong step forward, and all of us instinctively took a step back. I tried to swallow, but my throat was dry as sand. Although he wasn't nearly as tall or broad as the captain, Rhyker was a force all on his own. It was as if he commanded fear, and my body had no choice but to oblige. His dark eyes narrowed as he scanned us. His face pinched up in disgust when he reached the end.

"Pitiful," he mumbled under his breath. Rhyker turned his head and spit onto the deck beside him. His jaw flexed as he returned his gaze to us. He raised one finger, then another, and then another as he gave us a short-itemized list of duties.

"Wash, wax, polish. Simple, even for you pea-brains." He scoffed and rolled his eyes. "Get to work."

The deckhands scattered. There were lots of mumbles of "aye, sir" and "right away, sir" as people made their way back down the stairs to the lower deck. Unfortunately, because I was at the back, it meant I would be last in line. I tried to shuffle as closely as I could to Harlan, but it didn't matter. A wave crashed against the ship, and just like last night, I stumbled to the side awkwardly.

"You there, sailor with the black braid."

My heart dropped, and a numbness spread through me.

Think, think, think, think, think. Okay, if he approaches you, you might have a chance before anyone else notices.

I took a small glance at either side of me. No one was there, but I noticed Harlan stiffen slightly in front of me as well. He slowed his pace considerably. I swallowed again, took a breath, and turned around. I kept my eyes trained on his feet. Hopefully, with my head down and my hat covering my face, it would be enough for him to just give me whatever order or tongue lashing he needed to and then let me continue on my way.

My heart pounded with every step he took toward me. It echoed in my ears until I lost the sound of the waves and all I could hear was the drum in my chest and Rhyker's firm steps on the deck.

"You dare not address the first mate?" His tone was cold and sharp. It took everything in me not to wince back from it.

"Sorry, sir. I mean, aye, sir?" It should have been a statement, but my voice trailed off in a higher pitch at the end, making it sound more like a question, and making me sound more and more like I had no place here.

"This one's with me, sir."

I closed my eyes and let out a long breath as I recognized Harlan's voice behind me. I sent up a silent thank you to whatever god was listening.

"Hmm," Rhyker grumbled.

"Still in training, but we'll get it sorted, sir." Harlan put a reassuring hand on my shoulder and I relaxed slightly under his grip.

Rhyker let out another low hum.

"See to it he doesn't take an early departure off this ship, old man. We need all the hands we can get."

"Aye, sir."

Rhyker turned on his heel away from us, and I counted each step he took away from us.

...12, 13, 14-

Harlan's grip strengthened on my shoulder. I felt him lean down next to my ear.

"Stick with me, kid. I'll make sure you're safe. Now, come on. Let's get scrubbing. Don't want to draw any more attention."

9

Cost

Elora

My mind continued to whirl from the events of this morning. It had been a long time since I lost control like that. It was no doubt an effect of the sleepless night from before.

I leaned onto the table with my elbows and ran my hands through my short hair. It had seemed so clear at the time, so real. I had had him in my grasp, and then it just slipped through my fingers.

Someone pounded their mug against the table a few places down from me, interrupting my thoughts. I looked up and saw...him. I felt the same heat of anger rise and flush my cheeks. My eyes darted quickly to the side, and I noticed we were not alone. Four others had joined me at the table.

Drakkon stood at the end. His dark curls framed his face almost like smoke. He looked down at us under his thick brows. The two silver scars seemed to wink at us menacingly. I clenched my fists together. If I focused hard enough, I could remember the feeling of his flesh under my fingertips and how his blood had run over my palm after. I had failed all those years ago, but things were different now. I was stronger, more patient, and much smarter.

He placed his hands down on the table with a loud bang to get all of our attention. His black coat swung forward, the golden embroidery at the edges pressed against the table. The soft tap of the buttons against the wood starkly contrasted the sound of his other movements.

He tilted his head slightly to the side, and a stray curl moved past his dark eyes.

"Well, I suppose you five could be worse," he hissed through gritted teeth.

My fists clenched the fabric of my trousers so hard that I thought I might tear right through them. But now was not the time to act rashly. I needed to be careful, strategic, and precise. Just like I planned. And the plan did not include me lashing out in front of the rest of the heavily armed men on this ship.

The man across the table from me lounged back in his chair. His black shirt was unlaced at the collar like mine, but his thick chest hair filled the space where his dark skin should have been showing. His full lips turned up into a smile.

"Something amusing to you, sailor?"

The man raised his eyebrows slightly, but not in surprise. No, this was more like the hint of a challenge.

"Not at all...Captain."

The man sitting beside me chucked slightly under his breath and then hiccupped loudly. It was barely midday, and he was already drunk. Blades and ale were rarely a good mix, in my experience. And even though I hated the captain with every part of me, even I wasn't foolish enough to act out in front of him. There was a reason he had the reputation he did, and it wasn't because he was keen on giving free passes and forgiveness.

Drakkon slammed his wrist down on the table, and all of our eyes darted over to meet his narrowed gaze, which was solely focused on the drunk man beside me. Slowly, like an animal stalking his prey, Drakkon sidestepped and gracefully moved around the table until he reached the man who had chuckled. I couldn't see his face, but I didn't have to. His blond curls shook around his head in panic, and his body stiffened.

"Have you not heard the stories? Do you think me...merciful?" Drakkon's tone was low and dangerous. I had done more than just hear the stories and the horrors that fell upon the crew of the *Vindicta*. I had witnessed some of them firsthand. That's why I knew that there was no way this man was walking away from this altercation unscathed.

"N-n-n-no, sir. I mean, yes, s-s-sir."

"Well, w-w-w-which one is it, lad?" Drakkon mocked.

I heard the man swallow loudly, and his body trembled.

"I-I've heard, sir."

Drakkon cocked his head to the side and raised an eyebrow at him. Then he leaned over to whisper in the man's ear. It was a surprisingly intimate gesture, and it caught me completely offguard, especially when, seemingly out of nowhere, Drakkon's eyes landed on mine.

I clamped my teeth down hard, but held his gaze.

"Then perhaps you should have listened more closely, lad."

Drakkon began his retreat, a cruel smile across his lips, and with a sharp cut up, he sliced the man's ear clean off. He held it up proudly, as if displaying a trophy or a crown.

An ear-splitting cry rang out from the man in front of me as his hand came up to cover the space where his ear had been. Within moments, blood poured through the gaps in his fingers.

I didn't flinch. I had seen worse. Gods knew I had inflicted worse. That didn't mean I relished in the man's pain like Drakkon did. If anything, it was the opposite, but I definitely couldn't show that. So I sat back in my seat instead and pretended like I was as comfortable as I would be in front of a fire on a cool winter day.

"You're lucky I still need you alive, lad, or I'd be holding more than this in my hand right now."

The other three men at the table sat upright and tense, their eyes firmly locked on Drakkon. They clearly thought that was the best way to gain the respect of their captain. And while that might have worked before his display of power, it was surely going to get them nowhere now. Drakkon respected, if respected was even the right word to call it, people who didn't shy away from violence. Sure, he wanted obedience, but more than that, he wanted to be surrounded by people who had strong stomachs and sharp blades. People who wouldn't second-guess or flinch at an order to maim or kill. And while that was dangerous company to keep, most people who fit that criteria were predictable. Unfortunately for him, that assumption would not work out in his favor when it came to me. But he didn't need to know that. At least, not yet.

"Go get to the surgeon, you useless drunkard," Drakkon hissed.

The man beside me nearly jumped up from his chair and ran out the door to the medic's room beside us.

Drakkon turned around and took a few steps to one of the support beams in the room. He held the bloody ear up and pinned it to the beam with his knife. When he returned his gaze to us, there was a sick grin across his lips.

"Now that we've dealt with that little scene, I can finally finish what I came here to tell you. You will find your job duties posted under that—" he gestured to the ear on the post— "every morning. You will not hesitate, and you will question nothing written or asked of you on this ship. Do I make myself clear?"

The other three nodded so enthusiastically that I thought they might crack their necks with the force. I just gave a low nod in understanding.

"Good. You have the day to introduce yourselves and monitor the rest of your crewmates. The first day is the worst, but try to keep everyone alive, if you can."

He was right. There wasn't a single ship I had been on that hadn't seen a casualty before the first night at sea. It was the price of pirating. Considering his penchant for blood, his request to keep everyone alive was perplexing and concerning. But, regardless of how I felt, I needed to follow through on the orders if I wanted to gain his favor. If I had to save a few lives in order to take his, then so be it.

10

A Line of Truth

Sybine

I wiped the sweat from my brow with the back of my hand. The sky was perfectly clear, leaving the sun open access to burn me on the spot. I could feel its intensity through my shirt as well, and I hoped that I would be able to push through the last few hours before our shift was over.

"She's a scorcher today, isn't she?"

Harlan walked up the stairs behind me with a fresh bucket of soap water. He dropped it on the deck to my right and kneeled down beside me.

"I think I might burst into flames right here," I admitted.

"You 'n' me both, kid."

After a few scrubs, Harlan began to whistle a low, eerie tune. It sounded familiar, but I couldn't quite place where I knew it from.

"What's that song?" I asked him.

Harlan's lips pinched together, and his eyes turned down slightly.

"That be the Siren's Song," a familiar voice said to my left. He walked over to us slowly. I brought my gaze back down to the deck in front of me as a rush of nerves exploded all over my body. I would know the sound of those boots and that tone anywhere: Rhyker.

He stopped a few paces ahead of me.

"Would anyone care to educate our rookie on the dangers of the ocean?" he asked.

I swallowed down the lump in my throat and hoped that he couldn't see my arms shaking underneath me.

Several men laughed, including one with a bandage across his head, before one of them hummed in a low baritone. The laughter settled, and then slowly, one by one, they brought their voices together.

Her skin so pale and eyes of green,
More beautiful than I'd ever seen.
My heart so wished
For the Siren's Kiss.

A Kiss of the Siren's Song

More enchanted than I'd ever been.

Across the sea of memory,
They called our souls to be free.
My heart so longed,
For the Siren's Song,
And its haunting melody.

Behold! What sight had caught our eyes?
A monster in disguise!
My heart so shocked
By the Siren's wrath.
A murdering temptress of lies.

Alive today and gone on the morrow.
Heart full of sin and eyes full of sorrow,
My heart turned death
From the Siren's Breath,
No more sand in the hourglass to borrow.

My eyes stung from the tears that threatened to escape them. I knew the song, or at least the melody. But the words were nothing like what Gramps used to sing to me.

The song felt like a betrayal. I dug my nails into the deck boards beneath me. Something in me rose to an intolerable level. It threatened to burst out of me like a tidal wave, but I couldn't risk lashing out. I had nowhere to go and no one on my side. I was alone, and I had never been more painfully aware of that truth.

An icy silence fell over us. There was not even a whisper of wind or a cry from a bird overhead. It was as if everything had stilled, like the life of the world around us had been stripped away just from voicing the lyrics.

Rhyker bent down and reached a hand toward me. His fingers squeezed my jaw to tilt my head up. I slammed my eyes shut, unable to look at him without revealing what was in my heart.

"Now you see," he sneered. "There are horrors you can't possibly imagine in these waters. And unless you'd like to meet them, I suggest you get back to work."

My mind was a mess of stories and lies.

The sirens from the song couldn't have been the same creatures that Gramps used to tell me about. They were fierce, yes, but also gentle and kind. They helped care for the sea and everything that lived and breathed within Her. They weren't monsters...they couldn't be. Could they?

Gramps used to always say there was a line of truth to every claim. But how could two diametrically opposed perspectives both be true?

"You seem a bit lost, kid." Harlan's voice interrupted my thoughts.

My hands felt raw from scrubbing the deck. How long had I been in this spot? The muscles in my shoulders and arms ached from the back-and-forth motion. My lips were dry, and I was suddenly aware of how parched I was.

As if reading my thoughts, Harlan bent down and placed a mug of water in front of me.

"Here."

I greedily downed the entire mug in a few seconds. Almost instantly, the fog that had clouded my mind dissipated, leaving behind a sense of clarity I hadn't felt in a long time.

"Thanks," I said, passing the mug back to him.

He sat down on the deck beside me, resting an elbow on his knee while he leaned against his outstretched arm.

"What's on your mind?"

It was quiet on the deck, but it wasn't the same frigid silence that had accompanied us earlier. After a quick look around, I realized that Harlan and I were among some of the last few still working, and the sun had moved well past its midday point.

I looked out to the horizon and let out a breathy laugh.

"I guess I'm trying to figure out what to believe."

Harlan hummed in agreement.

"Was it the song?" he asked.

I returned my gaze to him. There was no hint of mockery on his face. He tilted his head to the side as if genuinely interested.

"I only ask because you seemed to disappear right after."

I nodded.

"Rhyker didn't help either," I admitted under my breath.

Harlan leaned forward slightly.

"Something tells me that his bark is worse than his bite."

I raised my brows at him. I would be a fool not to fear someone in Rhyker's position, given the rank and nature of mine, even if I wasn't lying about who I was.

"Something tells me that his bite is still plenty strong."

Harlan sat back again and let out a low chuckle.

"Perhaps," he said as he studied me.

Harlan eyed me as if asking a silent question.

"Can I tell you something?"

He moved an arm out in front of him as if gesturing to me to continue.

"I've...I've never sailed before."

Harlan smirked.

"This is your grand confession? I'm afraid you're a few days too late, kid. That ship has sailed." He extended an arm out in front of him as if drawing a line through the air.

I scowled at him.

"No, that is not my confession. What I was going to say was that I grew up on the mainland, in an old cottage away from the castles and cities. I didn't...I mean, of course I heard about sirens, but not...like that," I finally managed to say.

Harlan's eyes widened slightly, and he pinched his lips to the right side of his mouth.

"Songs are like stories, kid. It depends on who's tellin' them." He tilted his head to the side and rolled his eyes slightly. "And it depends on who's writin' them."

I shook my head.

"But then...who do I believe? What do I believe?"

He shrugged.

"That depends, I guess."

"On what?" I asked.

"On you," he said simply.

I groaned.

"I know you're trying to be helpful, Harlan, but I just don't understand."

He gave me a soft smile.

"Tell me, if someone were to ask you to describe a siren before you set foot on this ship, what would you have told them?"

His question surprised me.

"Don't worry—" he chuckled— "this mind's a bit more open than theirs." He pointed to his temple.

"Oh," I said, still a little off guard, "well, I suppose I would say they are sea creatures."

Harlan nodded.

"And?"

I ran my tongue over my lips before continuing.

"They have certain abilities...and they take care of the sea."

Harlan sat back slightly.

"Interesting." He hummed. "Why would they care for the sea?"

What an absurd question.

"It's their home. Why wouldn't they?"

Harlan raised a hand up in front of him in apology.

"That's a fair point, kid." He brushed his fingers through his short silver hair. "You have my apologies. I had no stories of sirens when I was a child, so you'll have to forgive this old man for his curiosities." He paused and stroked his chin slightly. "Abilities, you said? Seems a bit fantastical, don't you think?"

I scoffed.

"More fantastical than luring men to their deaths and eating out their hearts?"

He raised a shoulder.

"Well, that would depend on the ability, I guess."

"I guess," I agreed.

As I ran a finger over the smooth wood in front of me, my mind wandered back to the tales Gramps used to tell me. He always described the sirens like something out of a dream: real and not real all at the same time. They were like an extension of the sea in a way that made their forms fluid and flexible. And because they were so intimately linked, they were able to communicate in ways that, as a kid, I couldn't possibly imagine. As a grown woman, however....

"That song everyone sang earlier. Is there another version of it?" I finally asked.

Harlan thought for a moment.

"That's the only one sung on ships like this."

I sighed, and Harlan gave me a curious glance.

"Do you know another?"

I nodded.

Harlan looked around the deck. It was just the two of us now. Everyone else had presumably gone down to the dining hall for dinner.

"Would you sing it for me?" he asked.

"Oh," I said, surprised.

He shook his head slightly.

"After you've lived as long as I have, you grow bored with hearin' the same songs, laughin' at the same jokes, and tellin' the same stories. I admit, I yearn for somethin' different."

I sucked on my teeth.

"I'm not much of a singer," I admitted, which was true, but I was also concerned that he would note the natural high pitch of my voice if I sang.

He waved a hand out in front of him, as if to brush off my concerns.

"Can't be any worse than I've heard. And I've heard more than my share."

Harlan had agreed to help me, and thus far, he hadn't given me a reason not to trust him. Still, I wasn't ready to expose this part of myself.

"I'm sorry…I don't remember all the words," I lied.

Harlan's face softened. His eyes fell slightly, and his mouth turned into a sad smile. I had been deceiving him from the start, but something about this lie felt much worse. Guilt bubbled up in my stomach, and my chest tightened.

I quickly changed the subject.

"Harlan…can I ask you something else?"

He nodded.

"When we first walked on board, the captain said something about a fang. I've heard some of the others mention it as well. What is it?"

Harlan pinched his lips together in a line.

"The Kraken's Fang? Did you know there was a crown too? People always forget about that one. Always so focused on the weapon, but never the actual power." He sighed and looked around to see if anyone was listening to us. "It's just a legend, not unlike your sirens, I guess. It's a powerful weapon rumored to brew storms and decimate lands. And one cut from the fang would untether anything and break any barrier."

I flinched.

"But it's also been rumored to encourage new life and create homes for all kinds of creatures. It depends on who you ask. Some just say it has unparalleled power."

"And what do you say?"

"I say...that if you need a mythical weapon to inspire loyalty, you must not be a very good leader."

A bell rang from the lower deck. If we didn't go soon, we would miss dinner entirely.

"Don't worry about it, kid," Harlan said as he stood. He reached out a hand to me to help me up, and I took it gratefully. "Come on. Let's go get our food before it goes cold."

E. A. M. Trofimenkoff

As we walked across the upper deck to the stairs, all I could think about were the last two stanzas from the song how I knew it.

The rumors now spread on the ocean of red,
Of a creature worse than the dead,
Of our skin that shifts,
And our minds that rift,
Now monsters that sailors dread.

Gone today and reborn on the morrow.
Ready to surface, condemned to the shadows.
Now tarried we rest,
In the low, dark depths,
Ne'er to return to the shallows.

Fighting for Scraps

Sybine

It was terribly difficult to avoid someone when they were literally staring you in the face. Were the gods laughing at me? Was this some kind of divine justice?

We were all asked to stay after dinner for some evening revels. I had hoped to slip away, but I wasn't that lucky. My name was posted on the wall next to Loren's for the Scraps tournament. If I left now, he would know, and I had a feeling that I was already not in his best graces.

Loren sat leaned to the side with his head slightly rested against his loose fist. A finger traced over his lower lip. When his eyes locked on me, something flashed behind his eyes. Something...hesitant? Worried? Was he...embarrassed? I didn't even have time to blink before his relaxed demeanor returned.

"I see you've survived your first day."

I gritted my teeth together and gripped the back of the wooden chair to pull it out and take my seat.

"Did you expect me not to?"

Loren shrugged as if nothing could have meant less to him.

"You're steadier on your feet." He nudged his chin toward me, and his eyes swept down my legs.

"Oh." I hadn't noticed, but he clearly had. Now that I thought about it, I had only stumbled a few times today. The slow rock of the ship felt almost normal now, although my hips ached from the constant strain from trying to stay balanced. But he didn't need to know that.

"Kind of you to notice."

Another shrug.

I took my seat. The rest of the men in the hall sat in sets of twos down the tables. A single deck of thin wooden cards sat between us. The edges were black, as if they had been burned. A thin, black line outlined the back of the cards. The center had a dagger etched and burned into it. I stared in awe at the delicate spiral pattern on the hilt. All around the blade were jagged lines, like the bolts in the sky during a storm. Whoever made the cards must have been incredibly skilled and patient.

"Never seen a deck of cards before?" Loren raised an eyebrow at me and studied me curiously.

I shook my head.

"No, it's not that. I mean, of course I have. But these...are beautiful." I ran my finger along the carved ridges. "I've never seen their equal."

Loren smirked and gave me an almost disbelieving look. As if his studying had come up with something puzzling.

"What happened to your face?"

Heat immediately rose to my cheeks. No one had noticed the dirt under my eyes and chin all day, but I had kept my head down and my hat on. In the low light of the hall, I had hoped it would be more...inconspicuous? Less noticeable? Clearly, I had been mistaken. But I had been working on scrubbing the deck all day. Perhaps that would be a good enough excuse?

"Oh, I—"

Loren's brows furrowed. He pinched his lips together and reached over the table.

"May I?"

I bit my lower lip.

"Oh, okay."

He gently swiped his thumb over my cheekbone, just under my eye. His touch was light, almost hesitant, as if he were afraid of hurting me.

I swallowed. His touch sent tiny sparks under my skin. The rest of his hand slightly caressed the side of my face. Loren's eyes were dark as he studied me. When his gaze landed on mine, something caught in my throat.

"Did someone hurt you?"

He sounded genuinely concerned. I remembered the man's braid hitting me earlier this morning. The skin was tender under my eye, but I didn't think it had left a mark. Apparently, I was wrong.

"Oh, no. I just walked into someone this morning. It was my fault." I let out a nervous giggle.

His hand lingered on my skin, just a touch too long. He looked at me like I was worth taking the time to see. I felt a soft heat rise from my chest.

"Begin!" Rhyker called from the front of the hall.

Loren shook his head and blinked. He cleared his throat as he reached over to take the cards from between us. And as if the last few moments hadn't happened, he asked, "May I?"

I nodded slightly and brought my hand down to my side, where my bag was always attached to my leg. I ran my fingers over the cool metal of the clasp and reminded myself that I was fine. No one was attacking me. This was just a simple game of cards.

Loren shuffled the deck with ease. His movements were almost rhythmic. The toned muscles in his forearms tensed as he moved the cards forward and back in his hand. When he was satisfied, he placed the deck in front of me.

"Care to split?"

I reached over and lifted the top quarter of the deck up to reveal the Six of Earth. I scowled at the card. Loren took the bottom part of the deck. The last card was the Two of Water. He placed the cards back on top of mine.

He looked amused and expectant as he sat back in his chair with his arms crossed.

"Well," his voice was low and smooth. "Shall we begin?"

A small burst of energy ran up my spine.

Relax, he's just toying with you, I reminded myself.

Loren gestured to the deck of cards between us, a silent invitation for me to deal. He looked at me as if he were challenging me, which I supposed he was, but this was different. This was something deeper than the surface-level competition we had entered.

"Wait," I realized, "you think I don't know how to play."

He smirked at me.

I squared my shoulders and grabbed the deck from the table. I rolled my eyes and scoffed.

"Oh please. I've been playing Scraps since I was a child. Don't be so quick to bet against me, Loren."

He raised an eyebrow at me, and I could have sworn I saw the edge of his lips twitch up just slightly.

I dealt us both our five cards, making sure to dramatically snap his down in front of him every time. Agitation grew in me with every card. Surely, this wasn't just a pirate game? Gramps and I used to play every night when I was younger. He always said it was a great lesson in strategy, because it wasn't only about making your moves based on your cards. You had to know your opponent as well. You had to be able to guess what risks they would be willing to take. Would they play it safe? Or would they go all in? It paid to be attentive and study your—

Oh.

It dawned on me that Loren had been playing me since before I even sat down. He was measuring every move I made, every word I said, every blink, every pause, every gesture.

"What?" he asked.

The realization made me accidentally pause my deal on his last card.

I shook my head and dealt the final two cards. Then I placed the deck between us and flipped the first card on the deck face up beside it. King of Fire. How fitting.

"Nothing." I smirked at him. "Let's play."

Loren eyed me from across the table. His gaze drifted down to the cards between us. He paused a moment before making his move. His fingers tapped against the top of the playing deck three times before he finally took the top card. He examined it carefully, looked at me, and then back down at his row of five cards. He replaced the first card of five with the one in his hand, smirked, and then placed the replaced card face up on the discard pile. Two of Water.

"Nice move." Sarcasm dripped from my words as I reached to take the two.

He shrugged and sat back in his seat as he placed a coin on the back of his first card, showing his turn was over.

"A calculated risk."

We traded turns back and forth. He made the most unpredictable moves: taking fives, trading threes, and sometimes just moving his coin over without even looking at the card underneath. By the time we got to our last cards, I was so confused by his moves that I almost missed the Two of Air in front of me. I shook my head slightly and took a deep breath to clear my thoughts. I replaced the last card in my line with the two. It was a good trade. I placed the Ten of Fire on the discard pile, and moved my coin to my last card, signaling the end of my turn, and therefore the end of the game.

We both flipped our cards face up and tallied our points. I had the two of water, Three of Air, Six of Water, Ace of Earth and the Two of Air. That made nine points from the three and six, minus the four points from the twos. This was the best hand I'd had in ages, and I couldn't help the smile that played across my face.

I looked up triumphantly. Based on the cards that Loren picked up, I knew I had won. Sure enough, when I looked over at his cards, I saw his tally was much higher than mine.

"Five points," I said, my chin high and shoulders square.

Loren smiled at me as if he were the one that won the game. My feeling of triumph ebbed. Did I miss something?

"Twenty-three points," he said. "Well done, Sebastien. It seems you have won this round."

I looked at him curiously. All around us, people rose from their chairs. The winners walked over to the paper on the wall and they marked down their victories literally by scratching out their opponent's name. Loren relaxed back in his chair again, arms behind his head as he watched each person walk by, as if he were taking inventory of all the winners and losers.

"Wait...did you...lose on purpose?"

The corners of his lips turned up into a wry grin.

"You said not to bet against you, so I didn't. But don't think for a second that meant I wasn't betting on me."

12

Bet

Elora

Everything was going exactly according to plan. This tournament was an excellent opportunity for me to show my strategic aptitude. When I pulled this off, Drakkon would have no choice but to bring me into his conversations. After all, it was much better to have a cunning person planning with you instead of against you. Or so he would think, anyway.

Poor Sebastien. He didn't know I had played him until it was too late. David always told me it was easier to beat a man with a broken ego than one on the high of winning, and he was right. I won my next few games easily. The closest score was

9 to 13, and that was only because the man across from me got lucky and drew a Two of Earth at the end.

I crossed out the name of my opponent on the paper in front of me and turned back around. I leaned against the wooden post and crossed my arms, studying the room. There was a group of people around the last table. They were quiet, studying the looks on the faces of the men playing. One of them I recognized as the old man from the tavern. What was his name? Harvey? Baron? I shook my head. It didn't matter. What did matter was that I would play either him or Radrhim in the final round.

Someone cleared their throat beside me. I glanced over. Sebastien stood with his hands in his pockets, watching the game.

"Smart play," he said.

I gave him a half smirk.

"That's what you get when you're raised around pirates, I guess. A win is a win. It doesn't matter how you get there."

He frowned at me.

"That doesn't seem very honorable."

I scoffed.

"Who told you there was honor in piracy?"

He opened his mouth and then closed it as if he were about to say something and then thought better of it.

I smirked and returned my gaze to the game.

Several seconds passed before he spoke up again.

"Are you okay? This morning, I mean...you seemed...distracted?"

I clenched my jaw. I had, admittedly, reacted poorly after trying to cut the wall to pieces. It wasn't his fault that I hadn't sleep last night, and it certainly wasn't his fault that I'd mistaken him for Drakkon. The least I could do was apologize.

The things I do in the name of my father.

"Yes." I cleared my throat. "Sorry...for how I reacted...and for what happened before."

I could feel the heat in my chest and cheeks. I may have had a penchant for death, but that didn't mean I had to be cruel and lifeless. I sighed. I hated apologizing. Especially when I had something to apologize for.

Sebastien shuffled awkwardly beside me.

"It was...I mean, you were...." He sighed. "I was scared."

I swallowed.

"I understand."

I could feel his gaze on me, but I couldn't return it. All I could hear was my father's voice in my head telling me he was disappointed, that he'd taught me to protect those who needed it, not attack them.

I closed my eyes and finally turned back to him. When I opened them again, I was surprised to see that he was looking up at me with concern, not fear.

"Listen, I—"

He held his hand up to cut me off.

"I can tell there's something else going on. Look, that's your business, and I understand if you want to keep it private. But if you find yourself wanting a friend, or at least something other than a sword to talk to, you could try to talk to me."

I blinked in surprise. He was offering me a kindness that I knew I didn't deserve. But there wasn't anything to discuss. At least not with him. Not without potentially risking everything.

He gave me a sad smile, as if knowing I would decline his offer.

An uncomfortable silence stretched between us. There was a tension in my shoulders that I had not felt for many years. Disappointment, especially in myself, was by far my least favorite feeling. That's why I had spent so many years training. A part of me was always afraid that I would let my father and myself down. Until now. I had nothing left to lose, and everything to gain.

"My money's on Harlan," Sebastien's voice interrupted my thoughts.

That was a quick change of pace. Right, Harlan. That was the old man's name. My shoulders relaxed slightly. It was nice to change the tone back to normal pirate banter. I decided to follow Sebastien's lead.

"Oh? Care to put your money where your mouth is?"

Sebastien placed a hand in the bag he always wore at his side and retrieved a single piece of wood shaped like a coin.

"What's that supposed to be?"

He shrugged.

"I got it from some man who was threatening a barmaid once." He paused and looked down, as if unsure of whether to add anything. "I, uhm, made him think better of his choices."

I nodded. I could relate to that. I had many experiences threatening men over less noble causes.

I put my hand in my pocket and brought out a plain black handkerchief. I always kept one on me in case I needed to...clean up. Black never showed blood. That was the reason I always chose black shirts as well. It was always better to make sure your enemies didn't see you bleed.

Sebastien wrinkled his nose at the fabric.

I laughed.

"Relax, it's not used. Plus, I thought we were making bets using unorthodox objects."

Sebastien tilted his head to the side.

"At least mine looks like a coin."

"I'm going to let you in on a little secret, Sebastien." I folded the handkerchief carefully as I spoke. "The value of something rarely depends on its appearance. Who's to say this isn't woven from the finest silks that kings and queens can only dream of?"

His eyes widened in surprise.

"Is it?"

I let out a low laugh.

"Of course not." I fought the urge to roll my eyes. "Do you really think a pirate would walk around with an invaluable nose rag in their pocket?"

Sebastien looked up at me, confused.

"I, uhm, I guess not?"

I turned the fabric over in my hands.

"Then again, perhaps this was once the handkerchief of the Sea King. Or maybe it was torn from the cape of the Moon Goddess herself. It's such a silly little concept, don't you think?"

I could tell by the vacant look in his eyes that I had lost him.

"...handkerchiefs?"

I finally rolled my eyes.

"Value."

Sebastien looked up at me through his round green eyes, and something in my stomach turned. It had been a long time since someone saw me, and I thought perhaps Sebastien had taken a small peek. It was an unsettling feeling: foreign and strange. Thankfully, it was over almost as soon as it started.

Harlan stood from the table and placed a hand on Radrhim's shoulder as he walked by. He made his way over to us with a smile on his face.

"Well, I guess we know who I'm playing next."

I placed the folded handkerchief in Sebastien's hand.

"Make sure you take care of that precious silk, okay?"

I could have sworn I saw a slight smile play across his lips as Harlan came up and scratched off his opponent.

"Well, looks like it's the two of us, lad."

"It would seem so."

We walked to the table in front of us, and I gestured to the seat across the table from me. We both sat.

"Shall we break to shuffle?"

I nodded.

"After you then."

I reached over and placed my hand on top of the deck.

"Low card shuffles?" I asked.

He nodded.

"High card deals," he agreed.

I ran my fingers along the burnt edges of the cards slowly until I reached almost the bottom. It was a trick David taught me. The further down you broke the deck, the fewer opportunities your opponent had to outdraw you. Of course, it limited your options as well, but not as much as it limited theirs. He was always picky about the calculated risks. But I was relatively certain this one would pay off in my favor.

I lifted the deck and revealed my card. Ace of Fire. I smirked. The only card that could beat that was the wild card, The Ocean, and the likelihood of that being the bottom card of the deck was extremely slim.

Harlan gave me a wide grin. His eyes seemed to sparkle in the candlelight.

"Well played, lad."

He flipped over the last card. King of Water.

That was far too close for comfort. I let out a small sigh of relief.

"Rotten luck," Harlan said, shaking his head. The hint of a smile still stretched across his lips.

"Better luck next time."

Harlan took the rest of the cards and shuffled. I watched every move he made. He seemed calm, but reserved. His shoulders were slightly hunched forward, but not from any kind of injury that I could tell. He shuffled the cards in an almost too-controlled rhythm. It was like—

"Are you playing me, Harlan?"

He gave me a wry grin. He sat back in his chair and pointed a finger toward me.

"You're a perceptive one." He shrugged. "It was worth the try."

"No honor among pirates, remember?" Sebastien whispered from behind me. "A win is a win."

I choked back a laugh. No honor indeed. Harlan gave the deck one last shuffle before handing it over to me.

A group gathered around us as I dealt our cards. There were a lot of whispers and handshakes, but I didn't take my eyes off the man in front of me. The gods only knew what other tricks he had up his sleeves. He met my gaze with equal strength.

"Nothin' gets past you, does it?"

"Not usually," I admitted.

He pushed his lips together and nodded almost respectfully as I dealt the last card and placed the deck between us. The first card flipped over was the Four of Air.

"Alright," he said, "let's play."

Harlan looked at his first card, pinched his lips together, and placed it back on the table face down. He moved the coin over to indicate that he was going to keep his card.

I looked back and forth between the four, Harlan, and the cards in front of me. There were still so many cards in play. The likelihood of the card in front of me and the one at the top of the deck being lower than a four was very small; even so, it was four points. Reluctantly, I took it from the discard pile and exchanged it with my first card. I wanted to kick myself when I turned over the Three of Water. I placed the coin on the back of my card to show the end of my turn.

Harlan tutted.

"Rotten luck."

He grabbed the three and replaced it with his second card: the Jack of Air. His was a much better trade.

I peeked at my second card. Nine of Fire. I bit my lower lip and glanced back and forth between our cards three times. Any more than that, and it would seem like I was putting on too much of a show, any less, and I would look too desperate. I ran my tongue over my teeth and narrowed my eyes before pushing my card toward Harlan.

"A trade then."

I nodded.

We traded cards. And it was a good trade. He got my nine, and I got his Two of Water. I kept my face still and emotionless. I kept my breathing steady and my posture as normal as I could.

A half smile turned the corner of Harlan's mouth.

"You're very good," he said.

I looked down at the deck of cards.

"Your move."

"Hmm...." He grumbled, before picking up a card from the deck. It was the best choice he could have made, aside from trading me back my nine. But he didn't know what I had under my fingers, or what I had traded him. My bluff had worked, after all.

Harlan took the card and replaced the Nine of Fire with it.

I did a mental tally. I had two points, and Harlan had one at the least, and twenty-three at the most. But based on the cards I had seen, it was more likely that his score was somewhere between eight to fifteen. Even though we likely had a wide point difference, it would be foolish to replace my next card with anything higher than a five.

"Good trade," he said. "You?"

I gave him a shrug that gave nothing away and reached to take the top card of the deck.

Ten of Earth. Shit.

I placed the card on top of the Nine of Fire and looked at my next card. I could have screamed. The King of Water, the fucking King of Water was staring back at me. I kept my face neutral as I carefully placed the card down.

Harlan's eyes narrowed slightly, as if trying to peek through my mind. Too bad for him. I had years of practice hiding my secrets, and I would not break that streak over a stupid game of Scraps.

Harlan took a quick glance at the next card in front of him.

"I think I'll keep it," he announced.

Voices chittered around us. Usually after the third round, the big bets started, so it did not surprise me when someone yelled, "A gold piece in favor of the old man!"

"And one for the young buck!"

Young buck? Really? That was the best they could come up with?

I rolled my eyes. I had twelve points. It was the most I'd had all night, aside from the game against Sebastien, and I was only three cards in. These next moves would be crucial. At the least, Harlan had zero points, which would definitely be a worst-case scenario for me. But the probability of him having twos back-to-back was small. At most, he had thirty-three points, which was just as unlikely. I estimated his count to be around fifteen, which would put us in a three-point difference. Although that was the most favorable case, I was trained to fight as if you were against the worst possible outcome. In other words, I desperately needed to find a two or an ace this turn.

The last trade I made worked out well in my favor. I took a peek at the card in front of me: Six of Water. Fuck. Not an ace or a two, and not low enough to keep. My only option was to switch my card with Harlan's and hope it was anything less. I used the same prescription: look back and forth three times, bite lip, run tongue along teeth, then trade.

"Another trade...interestin'," Harlan said as we exchanged cards.

When I lifted it up, my heart sank. King of Fire. The fucking King of Fire. Not only was it a horrible trade, but I was now sitting with twenty-two points in my hand. Unless....

94

I let a false smirk twitch at the edge of my lips. I widened my eyes slightly and took a deep breath.

"Don't waste your energy, lad."

I looked up and met Harlan's amused gaze. That's when I knew it. He was just as good at reading people as I was. And worse, he had many more years of practice than I did.

"I don't know what you mean." I made an effort to tilt my head slightly and pinch my brows together in fake confusion.

Harlan bit his lips together, and the twinkle came back in his eye. Was he...mocking me? It took everything in me not to clench my jaw and fists. Instead, I relaxed and let him make his move.

He took a card from the top of the deck and immediately put it on the discard pile. The Ten of Water. Harlan placed his coin on the back of his card with a smirk.

"Last turn, lad. Make your move."

A familiar voice rang out from behind me.

"Two gold pieces in favor of Harlan."

Sebastien reached around me to place the two golden coins on the table.

So much for wood and handkerchiefs, I thought to myself.

"Any last bets?" someone called out.

As I reached for the deck between us, a few other men tossed their silver and copper coins on the table. Some on my side, some on Harlan's. Although, many seemed to favor him over me, and honestly, I couldn't blame them. If I were able to bet right now, I'd be putting money on his side as well. I was fucked. The only way to come out of this would be to draw the—

Gasps echoed around me as I froze. The card I drew from the top of the deck was—

"The Ocean!" a man behind me squealed happily.

I gawked at the card. The soft swirls of the wave crashing in on itself were so lifelike that it almost took my breath away.

"You did it!"

Someone shook my shoulder, and I shrugged them off. They didn't seem to mind much.

I could barely believe it. I won? The Ocean was a guaranteed win. It brought your score down to zero and trumped any ace or two in the deck. And I had drawn it.

Harlan relaxed back in his chair and slowly clapped his hands. But it didn't seem insincere at all. It felt like the opposite. I had done it. The next step in my plan was complete, and I hadn't even had to draw blood for it. I allowed myself a moment of pride.

"Good game, lad."

I smiled back at Harlan.

"Good game."

I stood from the table and made my way through the group of men to the post at the back. I scratched off Harlan's name, leaving mine completely unscathed.

"I think Harlan would call that rotten luck. On his part, of course."

Sebastien stood beside me, looking at the table I'd just come from. The men were distributing the winnings based on their bets. They wouldn't notice two gold pieces missing from the pot.

I turned to Sebastien and took out the coins from my pocket.

"Like I said—" I pushed one of the coins into his hand much more confidently than I felt— "just because I wasn't betting against you didn't mean I wasn't betting on me."

Proposal

Elora

The celebration ran long after night fell. It seemed this crew loved an excuse to drink and tell loud, obnoxious stories that were likely entirely fabricated. I only had to stop about six fights, and only one person lost a finger. But that was mostly their own fault. One of the deckhands stupidly accepted a bet that he could stab between his fingers with his eyes closed. He was probably too drunk to remember it, so tomorrow morning was bound to be a fun wake-up call. Still, overall, I considered it to be a successful evening.

I pretended to sip at the mug of ale in front of me like I had all evening. I hated the taste of it on my lips, but it was better than having a clouded mind, especially after the events of the morning.

"The captain will see you now." Rhyker's voice was low behind me.

I had waited all night for this.

I set the mug down on the table and pushed back my chair. "It's about time."

Rhyker grumbled something under his breath as I stood.

"What was that?"

"Nothing. Come on, let's move. The captain doesn't like to be kept waiting."

Rhyker led me to the end of the dining hall through a narrow passage, which turned into a tight corridor with two rooms. One, presumably, was Drakkon's quarters, and the other was likely Rhyker's. The hallway was dark, save for the faint candlelight flickering through the open door at the end.

I knocked three times and waited for the invitation to enter.

"Come in." Drakkon's low voice boomed through the door and echoed around us.

Rhyker pushed open the door and motioned with his hand for me to walk through. Drakkon's room was much larger than the one that Sebastien and I shared. There was an enormous bed surrounded by a wooden frame to the left of the room, just beside the window. Curtains draped the frame, although I couldn't tell whether they were crimson or black in the dim light. Drakkon sat at a sturdy wooden desk on the opposite end. A map was strewn across the top with various items on the sides to keep it from rolling up. It looked quite old, based on the yellowing of the paper and the faded print.

"Ah, Loren, correct?"

"Yes, Captain."

His dark curls bounced slightly as he nodded.

"Good. Come. Sit."

I followed the orders, despite not being his dog on a leash. My time would come. For now, I needed to gain his trust.

I pulled out one of the chairs on the other side of the desk and took a seat. Rhyker followed and did the same.

Drakkon sat back in his chair and linked his fingers together over his stomach.

"So, Loren. How does one come to win a tournament in such a way?"

I crossed a leg over my knee and relaxed into my chair as well. I picked at my fingernails, not making eye contact with either of them.

"On purpose," I said matter-of-factly.

"Is that so?" he asked.

"Quite."

I let the silence wrap around us. Drakkon needed to know that I would be tight-lipped if it ever came down to it. So I waited for him to ask me to elaborate before sharing any other details.

"Tell me, then." It was more of an order than a request, but I obliged him all the same.

"Captain, is it not easier to make a final blow when your opponent is on his knees?"

He gave me a small, lopsided smile.

"Indeed."

"Then I think I've made myself clear."

Another twitch of his lips.

"Indeed," he repeated.

He sat forward in his chair and rested his head on his hand as he studied me.

"How have I not heard of you, Loren?"

Now was the time to lie.

"My family lived on the mainland of Elandia. I grew up training to be a soldier. The lifestyle...let's just say it wasn't a good fit."

Drakkon chuckled at that.

"Too many rules. I prefer to make my own."

"Indeed," I echoed.

He eyed me curiously again, and I knew what question would come next.

"So, what brings you to the *Vindicta*? Aside from the glory and riches."

I had been practicing this response for years. I knew he wouldn't buy the typical story of greed when it came to me. No matter how hard I tried, I could never pull off that particular persona. But my ego. That I could lean into.

"Captain, I'll have you know I am the best."

"At what?"

"Everything."

Drakkon raised his eyebrows and nodded slightly.

"Go on."

"My mind is as sharp as my blade. I am a weapon in every way. One day, I will captain my own ship, but until then, I need experience. I could be very useful to you."

"Hmm," he grumbled.

I felt Rhyker's eyes burrowing into me from the side. He had been silent until now, but I guessed he knew where I was going with this.

"Rhyker is your first mate. Make me your second, and I'll show you just what kinds of skills I have."

"Hmm."

He bit his lips together and squinted his eyes at me as if just by looking closely enough, he would be able to identify a lie if there was one. But there wasn't. It was all true. I was extremely well trained. I wanted a ship of my own one day. This ship, to be precise. And I wanted it at the bottom of the ocean. I could be very useful to him if he gave me the right orders, and of course, if he made me his second, he would experience exactly what skills I had firsthand.

I sat in my chair, calm and stone-faced. I gave no emotion. No hints at my motives. I gave him a blank slate. Inside, I begged him to agree. This was the simplest way, with the fewest casualties.

Rhyker shifted in his seat beside me.

"Captain, if I may."

I turned my head to him and met his gaze. I was used to getting my way through force. I hated relying on others to make decisions, but it wasn't like I could loosen his tongue here in front of Drakkon. So instead, I maintained my composure and waited for what he had to say.

"Later, Rhyker," Drakkon said sharply.

Rhyker opened his mouth, but then thought better of it and closed it. He nodded his head slightly, but I saw his frustration in the way his jaw worked and his brows furrowed. He was not happy with my proposal. Not in the slightest. Fortunately for me, the decision was not in his hands. Unfortunately for me, Rhyker had Drakkon's ear.

"I admit I brought you here to test you, Loren."

Obviously.

"You've given me a lot to think about. We might have a use for you in our ranks."

Rhyker shot Drakkon a sideways glance, but Drakkon either didn't care or didn't notice. Likely the former, which was good news for me.

"The other sailors don't know this yet, but we're on route to make port on Tamarine. If everything goes according to plan, you'll have my decision by the night after."

No other tests or trials? No demonstrations of devotion or allegiance? Something was off about this entire voyage. First it was the blood oath, then the crew choice, and now this? There was definitely more going on than Drakkon and Rhyker let on, and I had to make sure I had all the information before I made my move. The last thing I needed was to be blindsided after striking him down.

I nodded.

"Thank you for your consideration, Captain."

To Feel the Sea

Sybine

My ears rang from the overly enthusiastic drunk pirates around me. What was with all the singing and banging and yelling? I sighed and let my head fall down on the table. There was a split in the wood that pinched my forehead, so I shuffled slightly to the side. Right into someone's arm.

I rolled my head to see who I'd run into. Harlan was staring right back at me with a look of amusement.

"That drunk already, kid?"

I groaned.

I hadn't had a sip of ale all night. I didn't like the taste, and I didn't like the way it made me feel. But for all the ale I hadn't drunk, I still felt sick. My body ached from the work that morning, and my head felt like it might split in two at any second. I was exhausted from just a single day on the sea. I still had no idea what I was doing, where we were going, or what I was going to do when we got there. I was so tired of overthinking and rethinking, of shrinking myself and hiding myself, that I thought I might break if I had to form another thought or pretend to be Sebastien for another second.

Harlan placed a hand at the top of my back and gave me a reassuring squeeze.

"If you can believe it, my first trip on a ship was much worse. That's not to say this hasn't been tough for you, but at least you haven't been tossed overboard."

I sat up and tensed slightly.

He laughed.

"Don't worry, I'm not threatenin' to toss you in the sea, kid."

"Oh...good." I gave a nervous laugh.

Several people started pounding their fists against the table, and I winced at the noise. Harlan gave my shoulder a light tap.

"Come on, kid. Let's call it a night. They're not goin' to miss us."

I had no energy to fight him. I had been wanting to leave for a few hours, but I didn't want to leave alone, and Loren had left with Rhyker and had yet to return. And anyway, Harlan had said he would watch over me. If I could trust anyone on this ship, it was him.

"Okay." I pushed myself up from the chair and followed him out of the dining hall. When we finally left, I took in a deep breath and let out a long sigh. The soft light of the moon illuminated the stairs to the upper deck in front of us, making it look like a shower of silver cascading down from the heavens. I felt myself called to it, and before I knew it, my feet were leading me up the stairs.

"Where did you go, kid? Oh."

Harlan's footsteps echoed behind me as he followed me up.

When I reached the top of the stairs, I paused to take everything in. The salt breeze was crisp and cool. It played through the hairs of my braid that had come loose throughout the day. The moon sat high in the sky, a perfect half circle against a curtain of black. The sea was calm, barely rocking the boat for the first time all day.

I walked to the railing where Harlan and I had stood earlier that morning. The moonlight shone over the small waves like liquid silver. The night stretched on for as far as I could see. An energy pulsed under my skin. It was the same pull I'd felt earlier. I could feel it spreading from my fingertips through my arms, until it finally found its home in my chest. It felt warm and familiar. It was comforting, like a lover's embrace. It was like the world opened up to me, like I had finally found the key to unlock all of her secrets. Everything was clearer and stronger. I felt like the power that I'd known always existed within me was finally willing to break free.

"You have the same look as this mornin'."

I let out a long sigh.

"I can't explain it, it's like—"

"Findin' yourself even though you never knew you were lost?"

I let out a low chuckle.

"Something like that."

"Me too, kid. Me too."

The low sounds of laughter echoed up the hall into the night air.

"I wonder if any of them feel this way," I said under my breath.

Harlan took a few seconds before responding.

"I don't think so. They're not like us. They don't feel the Sea the same way we do. And they aren't here for the same reasons either."

I turned to him.

"Why are you here, Harlan?"

He gave me a sad smile and looked back out at the sea.

"Same as you, I suppose. Running."

"Oh, I—"

"Don't bother, kid. I know that look. Hell, I've worn that look. I just hope you didn't get yourself into too much trouble."

I bit the inside of my cheek nervously.

"Nothing I can't handle."

I *hope*.

He laughed lightly.

"Glad to hear it."

I ran my fingers along the smooth wood of the rail. It was calming, being in the open air under the cover of night. In the shadows, I didn't have to pretend. I didn't have to put on a show or wear a face that wasn't mine. I didn't have to stand a certain way or hold my shoulders in the right posture. I could just be me.

"Harlan?"

He nodded.

"Yes, kid?"

"What are you running from?"

He leaned over and rested his elbows on the deck while he looked out at the sea.

"I made a mistake a long time ago. I've been trying to fix it ever since, but...people aren't always cooperative."

I let out a low laugh. I knew that all too well. But my options weren't always as limited as others'.

"So you're...running away from a mistake?"

He shook his head.

"Not this time. Hopefully, I'm runnin' toward a solution." He tilted his head toward me. "Now, we could sit here all night going over all our regrets, or we could go get some rest and try again tomorrow."

The rush of energy slowly ebbed, and the same exhaustion I'd felt in the dining hall settled into my bones again.

"I don't think I'll be able to stay up all night at this rate."

Harlan gave me a small smile. The skin at the edge of his eyes crinkled, and something in my chest tugged. It had been so long since I'd had a friend, but I felt the familiar bond between us.

A strong pulse of guilt raced through me at my deception. If we were on land, and I wasn't Sebastien, this would be real. I sighed. I was exhausted and defeated. Harlan didn't know I was a fraud, but I still felt horrible for deceiving him.

"Thanks for tonight."

He put a hand on my shoulder.

"Anytime, kid."

Below the Surface

Sybine

I couldn't remember the last time I had slept that hard. It was completely dreamless, just a void that held me down. I opened my eyes slowly. My eyelids were still heavy, and somehow, despite sleeping through the night, I felt completely unrested. The sun blinded me through the window, and I reached my hand up to block it.

Shit.

I was late. I was really fucking late. Somehow I had slept through both breakfast bells, and then probably for some time after that. Rhyker was going to kill me.

The frame of the bunk beds made a protesting screeching noise as I practically threw myself off it. I landed on the floor with absolutely zero grace and nearly twisted my ankle in the process. I quickly replaced my shirt with a new one from my chest and took a quick second to look at myself in the small mirror. I had dark rings under my eyes that made them look sunken, but the dirt from the day before had mostly been brushed off during my sleep.

"Shit, shit, shit," I mumbled to myself as I frantically applied an extra layer to my chin and cheekbones. It looked rough, but it would have to do. I quickly twisted my hair into its normal braid and put my hat on my head as I raced out the door, down the hall, and up the stairs.

The upper deck was filled with people of all ranks. By the look of things, they had all been working for well over an hour. Rhyker was at the helm, and he was staring at me with a raging intensity.

I quickly broke our eye contact and focused on the deck again. I found a spot near the starboard side. When I reached my position, I realized I had completely forgotten my bucket and scrub brush.

Not wanting to draw any more attention to myself than I already had, I slowly turned around. To avoid making eye contact with anyone, I focused my gaze out onto the sea.

Just like the first time, an energy exploded within me. I was overwhelmed by the scent of the ocean in the breeze. It filled me with an unimaginable force so quickly that it took my breath away. I was so distracted that I ran straight into someone. I lost my footing and fell hard down onto the deck.

Loren stood above me, looking down at me under his large dark eyes. He extended a hand out to me. I took it immediately and gratefully. He pulled me in close and whispered into my ear. Again, the energy hummed over my body, and he seemed immune to its power. That same rush of confusion and intrigue washed over me.

Just when I thought he was about to offer me some advice on how to move forward, he surprised and confused me again.

"Your shirt is untied." He gave me a sideways glance and continued walking with another guard.

I felt heat rush to my face, and I stood there shocked as I watched him descend the stairs in front of me.

In my rush to leave, I had forgotten to tie up the laces, leaving my chemise slightly exposed at the top. Fortunately, I was facing the sea, and people were paying more attention to their own work rather than my shirt. I quickly did the laces up and raced down the stairs to the lower deck.

I hadn't made it four steps down the hall before someone grabbed my shirt and tugged me backward. I ran into them hard, and I couldn't help the grunt that left my lips as I did.

"What—"

A muscular arm wrapped around my neck, while his other held me close to his body.

"Don't fight, lad," a low voice whispered in my ear.

I shivered. It was one of the other guards. I pressed against his arm at my neck, but it didn't move. I clenched my jaw and tried to push my elbow into his stomach, but he sidestepped easily out of the way of my blow.

"I said, don't fight."

His grip tightened, and my face went hot. He was trying to cut off my air supply.

"What...do you...want?" I managed to squeak out.

His laugh shook my body.

"A lesson from the first mate."

Rhyker.

I took a quick glance down the hall in front of us. We were alone. I could make this stop. I could make him stop. Even better, I could make him regret it.

I let myself go limp in his arms, and predictably, he let me fall to the ground. Before I hit the floor, I twisted and jumped backward, just far enough so I was out of reach.

The man's eyes were wide with surprise. I knew from experience that I had a very narrow window of time before the shock wore off and he came back at me with double the ferocity. I struck first.

I grabbed his arm and let the familiar energy run over my skin. Before, it was like reaching into a well, but this felt like a tidal wave. I could have bathed in the power for days, and I still would have more left over.

"You did exactly as Rhyker asked. You gave me a scare and a warning, and something to remember the lesson by."

The man's eyes were blank and dazed. A small ring of silver outlined his brown irises. He was now completely under my spell. I reached to his side and brought out the knife from its sheath. I pinched my eyes closed as I brought the blade down across my forearm. It wasn't deep enough to cause any permanent damage, and I made sure it was short enough that it would heal as quickly as possible. Despite all that, I winced from the pain, and stars speckled my vision. But I wasn't finished with him yet. I put the knife back in the sheath at his belt and continued.

"When he asks you what took you so long, you will tell him that the sight of my blood made you sick." I paused for a moment. I always hated this part. I hated making people forget. I pushed my chin up and looked into his eyes.

"You will forget this interaction ever happened. You will forget that I have given you these instructions." I took a breath. "And you will never lay a hand on me again."

I let go of his arm and placed my hand over mine where my blood was soaking through my shirt. The man's eyes cleared, and he looked at me blankly before his eyes fell on my bloody arm. His face turned a pale shade of green. He turned on his heel and ran back toward the dining hall.

I let out a long sigh of relief.

I was finally alone again.

I ripped a piece of the bottom of my shirt off and tied it around the wound at my arm, using my teeth to tug on the other side. I would have gone to change my shirt and clean the wound, but there was no telling where Rhyker's patience and thirst for blood would end. I would take care of it later. Better for him to see me bleed, anyway. If I was lucky, maybe he would leave me alone for the rest of the day.

I rounded the corner into the supplies room where the soap and wax were. I stopped dead in my tracks when I saw Loren standing there, waiting for me. He grabbed me by the arm and pulled me inside the room before I had a chance to even decide whether to enter or turn back. He glanced outside the door before closing it and locking it with a set of keys from his belt. Then he turned around and studied me.

My stomach jumped to my throat. I found it very difficult to breathe, and I could feel a cool sweat running down my back.

But rather than looking at me with disappointment and disapproval, he looked at me like I was...human.

"Well, I certainly wasn't expecting that," he said.

I was speechless. Why was he with me and not the captain?

He studied me curiously.

"Who are you?" he asked.

My question, precisely, I thought to myself.

"I—uh," I hesitated. "Sebastien?" My tone was not at all convincing.

His brows furrowed, creating a small crease in his forehead.

"What were you doing with Waldreg?"

I swallowed nervously. He had seen me. Even worse, he had seen Waldreg after my spell took hold. If the knowledge of my power got out, it would spread like wildfire. The crew would have me cast overboard...or worse. People hated having their minds meddled with.

I took a deep breath and reached down into my gut. Instantly, I felt the familiar power rush over my skin. Every part of me radiated with energy. I reached out and took his hand in mine.

"You're going to forget what you saw."

"Why would I forget?" he asked, pulling his hand away from me. He was instantly put on guard. "In case you haven't noticed, I believe I'm quite a lot stronger than you, and significantly taller. If you're planning on making me forget by hitting me in the head, you would definitely need the element of surprise to succeed."

I stood there, shocked. No man had ever been able to break my enchantment before. Never. There was something more here than he was letting on.

"I—uh—no. I mean, I would never. I'm not dull."

"Nor eloquent, it would seem," he responded.

A heat rose in my cheeks, and I said my next words with barely any preliminary thought.

"Why am I under interrogation? I could easily ask who you are."

He was taken aback slightly at my response.

"I am not the one going around trying to tell people what they do or do not know, or what they have or have not seen. Don't put me on trial just because you're on the defense."

"You're deflecting."

"And you're being a hypocrite."

Voices began to slowly echo from down the hall.

His jaw worked. He put a hand over my mouth and pressed his body against mine, effectively pinning me against the wall.

His dark gaze was fierce, and his voice was low.

"Not a word."

I swallowed. My stomach did a little flip, and a warmth spread over my skin. Loren caged my body, and all I could do was stare up at him. He was...beautiful. There was a slight hint of gold in his dark eyes that flickered in the candlelight. The sharpness of his features was dulled from this angle, and his thin lips that were usually pursed together were parted slightly, as if he too were taking me in for the first time. My eyes trailed back up to his as the voices died off again, and my breath caught in my throat. He was looking at me, and I mean truly looking at me, peeling back all of my layers until he could finally see me. My heart gave a loud thud that echoed through my ears.

Loren closed his eyes tightly and exhaled softly as he pushed himself off me. He cleared his throat and put a hand on the door handle. He kept his gaze down, as if deliberately trying not to make eye contact with me again.

"We've already been here too long. If you would like to discuss this more later, we can. If not...that's your business, I guess."

With that, he opened the door and disappeared down the hall. Not for the first time, I was left completely stunned and speechless.

Tales

Elora

Sebastien had caught me completely off guard. The way he'd looked at me...it was like he'd actually seen me. And worse...I'd wanted him to. It was the first time I had wanted anything else in so long that I'd almost forgotten what it felt like. The warmth, the uncertainty, the thrill...it was all so overwhelming.

And his lips....

Fuck...the caress of his lips against the palm of my hand had been electrifying. I could still feel them. I could still feel the spark. And there were those eyes, green like the sea on a clear day, hypnotizing, drawing me in, drawing me down.

I clenched my fist, as if squeezing the life out of my hand would make the feeling disappear. It only made it worse. It felt like the boards of the ship had given out beneath my feet. I was free-falling, plummeting toward a dark unknown, grasping at anything to pull myself back up again. Those few seconds we'd shared had felt like a lifetime, like the birth of a star or something bigger.

I ran a hand through my hair.

Get a grip, I told myself.

So what if his eyes are the most captivating thing you've ever seen?

So what if his lips felt like the kiss of a rose petal between your fingers?

So what if his warm breath over your hand sent a current down your spine?

I leaned against the wooden panels of the hall as if they would help steady me from the waves crashing in my mind. I closed my eyes and let my head fall back against it.

Fuck.

"Rocky morning?"

Waldreg walked past me with a smirk on his face.

"You have no idea."

He lifted the bucket in his hand.

"Looks like you might be needing this more than I do."

I eyed him curiously.

"What are you doing with that?"

He pinched his lips together and lowered his eyes, embarrassed.

"I felt a little sick, myself. I'm not sure what came over me."

I did. I opened my mouth to tell him, but immediately closed it.

Think strategically. You have information. Use it wisely.

As far as I could tell, I was the only one who knew about Sebastien and his...persuasive techniques. If I said something now, it was possible I would miss out on the opportunity of a lifetime.

I stood up straight and adjusted my shirt.

"Feel better, Waldreg."

The rest of the day went by relatively smoothly. If anything else minor happened, I paid it no attention. My mind was caught in a loop from the events of the morning. I played the situation over and over again. Whenever we caught sight of each other on deck, Sebastien would turn around and put his head down.

The day lasted a second and an eternity all at the same time. The dinner bell rang and my stomach growled. I made my way to the dining hall on the lower deck. The hall was filled with drunken sailors. Some were singing while others were screaming at each other to communicate over the noise, which only elevated the sound in the room.

I took my dinner from the serving station and looked for an empty table. They were all mostly filled, save one in the far corner with two people. I made my way over only to find Sebastien and Harlan sitting there staring at me. I paused and looked over at the other tables.

"Come, join us," Harlan said.

Sebastien and I made awkward eye contact as I put my food down on the table and sat in my chair. I cleared my throat.

"Thank you."

We sat and ate. No words were exchanged between the three of us until Harlan broke the silence.

"I could freeze with the ice in the air between you two," he said. "Tell me, lads. Have I missed somethin'?"

Sebastien and I eyed each other.

"Nothing," we both said at the same time. This, of course, drew more suspicion towards us.

Harlan made a grunting noise between his lips. Then he smiled and sat back in his chair.

"You know, lads, there is nothing wrong with two sailors gettin' along, if you catch my meanin'."

Sebastien's water caught in his throat, and he coughed some of it up into his hands.

"Oh, uh, no. It's not like that," he said.

I rolled my eyes. This was not helping.

Harlan raised an eyebrow.

"We'll see," he replied.

I jumped as one of the crewmates slammed his pitcher onto our table. He had clearly had a few before this one.

"On the wide wide wide wide wide," he took a breath, "wide wide ocean!" he exclaimed. "How exciting! Drinking! Treasure! And maybe a few ladies too, eh?" He nudged me in the arm, and I flinched. There were few things I hated more than drunk men.

"Yes, how wonderful," I said dully.

"Oh, come on! Cheer up, mate!"

I stared at him blankly. I had no tolerance for drunken fools.

"Ouch," he said, pretending to be stabbed.

When I still didn't respond to his theatrics, he bent down close to my ear. I could smell the rum on his breath.

"Maybe the only thing that will excite you is the Kraken's Fang, or...I know! The Dragon's Breath!" His voice rose in pitch as he turned around and exclaimed to the rest of the room. Several people took up his chant.

"Dragon's Breath! Dragon's Breath! Dragon's Breath!"

The chant went on for several rounds before it was interrupted by Rhyker.

"Enough, you dogs!"

The voices calmed.

"The captain is a very busy man. He has no time for parlor tricks."

With that, he stood up from his table and left the room. It wasn't long before the voices started again.

Fools, I thought to myself.

"What do you think they meant by the Dragon's Breath? And what does that have to do with the captain?" Sebastien asked.

"Come now," Harlan said disbelievingly, "you can't be serious. Surely you have heard the tale of the captain? Every person who ever wanted to sail under Captain Stormson has heard the tale."

I, of course, knew the tale by heart. Every day I trained, I thought about how infamous he was based on one serendipitous event.

When Sebastien continued his blank stare, Harlan sighed. After a moment, he straightened his back as best he could and lowered his voice. He ushered Sebastien in close, as if telling him a secret only he could know. Which, of course, was ridiculous, because as Harlan had mentioned, everyone who wanted to sail with the captain knew his story. But I could appreciate his efforts.

"Drakkon Stormson is his name, the captain. Folks say he was hatched under the light of a great storm. The gods fought in the heavens, and when their fists clashed, a great bolt was sent down from the sky. It was said that this bolt struck a large dragon egg, and the captain was born."

"That's ridiculous," Sebastien said. "Dragons aren't real."

Harlan flashed him a look.

"Oh, my dear, I think it would surprise you to find out exactly how much is real in this world."

Sebastien's eyes lit with an unearthly green, so fast it was nearly imperceptible. An energy seemed to hum around him. Something that I was noticing with him when he felt threatened or scared.

Harlan continued after taking a sip of his ale.

"After he became captain of his ship, rumors grew he could actually breathe fire. Some of his old crewmates would come on land from time to time and tell stories of how he burned his enemies to the ground with his breath. Eventually, some of them became so paranoid that they would fall victim to his fire that they ran away inland, never to be seen again. Some say they can still hear the screams of the dead echoin' through these halls if you listen closely at night."

Sebastien's eyes widened at that last statement, and I rolled mine.

A playful smile took over Harlan's face, and a low laugh emerged from his belly.

Sebastien looked between the two of us.

"If you believe in those kinds of ghost stories," Harlan finally added after catching his breath.

Sebastien chuckled nervously.

"Come on now, old man. You'll scare him half to death if you continue with that kind of talk." I reached over and grabbed Sebastien by the shoulder, shaking him slightly.

"There are worse stories than fire on these seas," Harlan said under his breath. I thought I caught a look in his eyes that was almost as sad as it was nostalgic.

Sebastien looked at him, confused, but before he had a chance to ask, Harlan picked up his dishes and made his way from the table. We sat there for a moment in awkward silence before Sebastian cleared his throat.

"Well, I think I'll be off to bed," he said. "It's been a long day."

"Indeed," I agreed.

I was far more tired than I expected to be after only one day at sea. Sebastien took his dishes away, which left me alone with my thoughts. The only thing that brought me peace was knowing that one day, Drakkon's screams would haunt these halls, too. That day could not come soon enough.

17

Trust

Elora

I awoke to a large crack, followed by a sharp pain in my back and a heaviness over my body.

"Ugh," I grunted.

I blinked, trying to get the fog to clear from my eyes.

"Ow," a muffled voice said above me.

I turned my head slightly to see what the weight was. My eyes adjusted to find the top bunk, and presumably Sebastien, on top of me.

"Get...off...." I grumbled.

I could feel the bed shift as Sebastien made his way off it. His feet made a loud thud when they hit the floor. He bent over to look at me, one hand on his head, holding his hat.

"Are you okay?" he asked.

"Do I...look okay?" I responded.

"No, not really," he said, and he stood back upright.

I rolled my eyes.

"Well, are you going to help get this off me?"

"I'm...trying...." He grunted.

A deep breath escaped me as I tried to roll over. Fortunately, the bed wasn't too heavy. I propped it up with my elbow, which allowed Sebastien to get his hand underneath and hold it while I rolled out.

My body landed on the cold wood with a thud, and I grunted again.

Sebastien held out his hand to me to help me stand. I hesitantly took it. A slight tingle made its way up my arm. My chest tightened, and I suddenly became very aware of every feeling in my body. My shoulder hurt from landing on it, and a large section of my back was tender from my rather rude awakening.

"Thanks," I said. I released his hand and brushed off the dirt from my clothes. "Are you okay?"

He paused for a moment, looking over his body.

"I think so," he said.

In the low candlelight, I could make out where the frame had snapped. I traced the splinters with my finger. It had snapped right in half. I wasn't surprised. From what I could see and feel, the wood had rotted. I was only surprised that it hadn't broken sooner.

I looked out the window. There was no hint of sunrise. When I turned back, I saw just how exhausted Sebastien was. His face was as pale as the sails on the ship, and there were dark rings around his heavy eyes. For a moment, I thought he might fall asleep on the spot.

"We still have a few hours before dawn," I said, "so we might as well try to get some more rest if we can."

The muscles in Sebastien's neck tensed.

Sebastien let out a nervous laugh. He fiddled with the clasp on his bag again.

"I can sleep on the ground," he said. "We can just push the mattress between the wall and the bunk."

I looked back and forth between him and the narrow space he was talking about. It was barely wide enough to step through sideways. There was no way the mattress was going to fit there. And there was no way we were going to be able to fix the frame, either. That left two options: one of us on the cold, hard wooden floor, or both of us in my bunk.

Under normal circumstances, I wouldn't have hesitated to make him sleep on the ground. But these weren't normal circumstances, and he wasn't just some other random man. My mind was screaming at me to forget about the closet and move on. To keep my focus without any distractions. And yet here he stood, small, cold, and tired. I knew he would sleep on the floor if I asked him to. I set my resolve. I wouldn't let this become a distraction. We'd had a single interaction that had been charged with the tension from the conversation and our proximity.

I opened my mouth, but my tongue wouldn't wrap around the words.

I could hear my father's voice in my head like a nagging echo against my own internal thoughts.

What's the harm? We help people, remember?

I mentally rolled my eyes.

"The mattress won't fit there. You can sleep on my bunk until we figure something else out."

Sebastien's body went rigid.

"Oh, no, I can't—"

"Don't worry," I said, "I only sleep with one knife under my pillow. Now come on. Help me clean up this mess."

Sebastien was exactly as weak as he looked. Either that or he was much more exhausted than I thought he was. His face pinched, and he groaned as he helped me push the top bed up and off the bottom one. Once we had stacked the wood planks and leaned the mattress against the wall, we both looked at the narrow bed in front of us.

"It's a good thing you're small."

I lifted the thin blanket and Sebastien inched towards the side of the bed closest to the wall. He rolled over, facing the wooden panels. In the dim light, I could barely make out the outline of his braid and narrow shoulders. It was as if he disappeared into the shadows. I crawled in after him, making sure to stay as close to the edge of the bed as possible.

I felt every dip in the mattress as Sebastien adjusted himself to move closer to the wall. The space between us felt charged somehow. Even though our bodies weren't touching, I was painfully aware of every movement he made and every breath he took. My skin felt like it was on fire. I closed my eyes, but all I could see was him staring back down at me in the closet before. My mind and body felt like we were preparing for an attack of some kind. My heart rate increased, and I felt a cold sweat run down my back.

I hated nights like this. I used to have them frequently as a child. It was like I was some kind of energy sponge that absorbed too much throughout the day and was then forced to expel the excess at night. Usually I would take a walk or practice some steps for close range fighting. When neither of those options were available, sometimes I would just shake my hands above my head as if I could flick the extra energy off of my skin. Tonight was unfortunately abnormal in that I couldn't go for a walk around the ship without it seeming suspicious, and I didn't want to repeat what had happened with Sebastien in the hall, either. And since we were now forced to share the same bed, something told me that me shaking like a person possessed might not send the best message.

I resorted to tapping my fingers to my thumb on each hand in the same pattern, starting with my forefinger and ending with my pinky. After what felt like a hundred rounds of it, I sighed. It would take me all night to finally relax, at this rate.

I felt a dip in the mattress as Sebastien adjusted again.

"Are you okay?" he asked.

"Yes, sorry for waking you." My response was more like a reflex than an actual answer.

"I wasn't asleep," he replied. "I'm exhausted, but I can't rest."

"Me either," I admitted.

I sighed and rolled over. I wasn't expecting him to be facing me. His green eyes almost glowed in the dark. The sight of them caught me off guard. They were both beautiful and haunting all at once.

Although his back was pressed against the wall and my body was teetering on the edge of falling off the bed, our faces were only inches away. We weren't physically as close as we had been in the supplies room, but there was something about sharing this space together that felt intimate and raw in a way that I had never experienced before. I couldn't tell if the tension spreading across my skin was from the residual energy or...something else.

I swallowed.

"What's bothering you?"

A muscle in Sebastien's neck twitched as he moved his head back, giving us slightly more space.

"I keep thinking about something Harlan said."

I thought back to Harlan's rendition of Drakkon's rumored origin story, and I tried my best not to let out a groan of annoyance.

"Don't let the old man's stories keep you up, Sebastien," I told him. "They're just stories."

Sebastien let out a long sigh.

"I've heard worse."

A low laugh escaped my lips.

"Have you now?"

"I grew up on stories worse than him, trust me."

Trust me. The words echoed in my ears. It had been a long time since I had trusted someone. Could I trust him? I wasn't sure.

"Consider me intrigued," I said as I leaned my head in my hand. "Come, Sebastien. Tell me a ghost story."

He hesitated for a moment and took several deep breaths with his eyes closed. It was such a long time before he spoke again that I thought he had fallen asleep.

"Do you believe in sirens?" he asked.

I laughed.

"Like people with tails like fish that lurk at the bottom of the ocean waiting for lonely fishermen to lure down to the depths where they pick their teeth with the bones of their victims?"

Sebastien's eyes flew open, and he stared at me in horror.

"Relax." I rolled my eyes. "I don't think their mouths are big enough to pick their teeth with the—ouch!"

Sebastien elbowed me in the ribs before I had a chance to finish my sentence. I grimaced.

"Fine, yes, I was born and raised a pirate, so of course I have heard stories of sirens. And, no, before you elbow me again, I don't think they are man-eating monsters of the sea."

Sebastien seemed satisfied with that answer and continued.

"My gramps used to tell me stories about the sirens," he said, his voice low and full of melancholy. "He said they were forced out of their homes and nearly all killed. I was too young to understand that the horror wasn't the act itself, but the intention behind it. The sirens weren't killed and hunted because they did anything wrong, they were killed and hunted because they were different, and that made them a threat."

"Interesting.... I grew up on stories of how they would attack every ship that approached them, and sometimes would even hunt them down."

I paused, because that wasn't strictly the whole truth. I grew up on stories of sirens essentially being equated to monsters. That was until David showed up. Then everything changed. Even though he was only with us for a short time, he became like a second father to me, and he taught me more than I cared to admit.

"But then again, I remember an old friend telling me something similar once. I admit, I never really stopped to think about it too much," I added. "Even though we grew up on different stories, I heard some similar to yours. Not to mention I have witnessed the violence some men are capable of firsthand. I know the lengths they will undertake to cover up their wrongdoings."

Sebastien relaxed slightly beside me. Oddly enough, some of the tension I had been holding ebbed as well.

"Are you worried that we are going to be attacked?" I asked him.

He shook his head.

"No, it's not that. It's just a...I don't know...it's like a nagging feeling at the back of my mind that I can't quite place. I don't think I'm worried about being attacked. At least not by Sirens."

I leaned forward slightly.

"Listen, I know it is not always easy working on a ship, so if you get into trouble, you can always come find me, okay?"

Why was I offering that? Had someone dunked my head in seawater? Only hours ago, I was hoping to distance myself from him so he would not draw attention to me. And now, here I was, essentially offering to be his bodyguard. I mentally scolded myself. The exhaustion and this residual tension had clearly gone to my head.

He mumbled something under his breath that I couldn't quite understand.

"I beg your pardon?"

He propped himself up on his elbow like me and closed his eyes. He took a deep breath, and when he opened them, I recognized the same light in them I'd seen earlier at dinner, and twice before as well.

"Do sailors always use their true names?"

I froze. Where was he going with this?

I shook my head slightly.

"No, not always. Why do you ask?"

He pinched his lips together and carefully considered me.

"Can I trust you?"

No. I will always put my needs before yours. And I will not go down with your ship.

"Yes."

I mentally scolded myself again. What was I promising?

"My name isn't Sebastien."

The tension in my shoulders eased slightly. For a moment, I had thought he was going to ask if I had given my real name, or ask who I really was. I held back a sigh of relief.

I waited patiently to see if he would elaborate, or if he wanted to leave it as it was.

"You don't seem surprised," he said.

I thought about this for a moment. In a way, I wasn't surprised. But that wasn't because I suspected Sebastien's identity to be false. It was because I hid behind a false identity as well. People hid things all the time. No one ever really showed their true face, in my experience. I always expected everyone to be lying about who they were.

"I knew you weren't a sailor," I responded.

"That's not what I meant, and you know it."

I paused again, letting the information sink in further.

"I suppose I knew there was more to you than meets the eye. You're not like anyone I've crossed paths with before."

He pinched his lips together slightly.

"But...why are you telling me this now?" I asked.

He let out a small laugh.

"Really? That's your question? You're not going to ask me what my real name is?"

I shrugged.

"I've always been far more interested in what motivates people."

His eyes looked over my shoulder as he contemplated his next words.

"I just...want something to be real, I guess."

I swallowed. Suddenly, my deception felt slightly wrong as well. A prickle of discomfort nagged at the back of my mind. I pushed it away. Now wasn't the time or place, and I still wasn't sure if I could trust Sebastien, or whatever his name was, at all, let alone with something so important.

"And how do you not know I won't tell the captain the first chance I get?" I asked.

He ran his teeth along his lower lip.

"You've had every opportunity to tell him about Waldreg, and yet here we are."

I ground my teeth together slightly. He thought I held my tongue out of kindness, and not because I was planning on using that knowledge to my advantage eventually.

"So I figured if I could tell anyone, I could tell you."

I was used to tricking people into trusting me, but I had never felt this way after. The others were always a means to an end, but this time? This time was unintentional. For once, the person in front of me expected nothing of me in return. I didn't have to make a grand gesture in any form. There was no trade or barter or demonstration of devotion. It was just this: a simple moment of truth.

"Do you want to know my real name?" he asked.

There is power in names. Even though David only told me this once, it somehow had crawled under my skin. It was partly why I kept my true name so close to my chest as well.

"Only if you're willing to give it." If I had learned anything over my years of pirating, it was that information rarely came freely. If there was an ulterior motive to this confession, I would not be responsible for paying a debt that I had no agency in agreeing to.

He thought about this for a moment.

"I'm Sybine."

Sybine.

The name rang through my ears, smooth and light. Everything seemed to fall into place. Her soft features, slight frame, and high voice I had originally attributed to mere feminine features that a man possessed. It wasn't the first time I had observed them on a man. I had come across all kinds throughout my travels, and the bulky, bearded, low tone class of men were often the minority. More often than not, they were just average people: some tall, some short, some narrow, some broad, some soft, some toned. I was usually far more focused on their movements, how they carried themselves, and what kinds of weapons they possessed. Their gender never mattered to me, so I never paid it any attention.

"Sybine," I echoed, and I could feel the hint of a smile on my face as well.

Sybine tipped her head down slightly, no longer meeting my gaze.

"You're not angry? You're not surprised I am a woman?"

I let out a sharp breath.

"I have no right to be angry," I said simply. "You don't owe me, or anyone else, for that matter, any private information about your identity. Thank you for trusting me with it, though. I can't imagine that was an easy decision."

I took a breath.

"As for you being a woman..." I trailed off.

Sybine trusted me with her name. But I couldn't say I held the same trust with her. No one knew my true name, and for a good reason. I wouldn't jeopardize my mission for it.

"I knew there was more to you than what meets the eye. But I'm in no position to make any assumptions. Am I surprised you're a woman? Not entirely. I am much more surprised by your presence on this ship. What brought you here?"

Sybine bit her lower lip.

"That's a bit of a long story."

"Well then. It's a good thing we have all night."

Full of Surprises

Sybine

I was still completely shocked at how well he'd taken the news of my identity. He continuously surprised and impressed me. I had never met a man so conscientious and aware before. It was a refreshing change from the greedy and extremely self-assured men I was used to.

"My story—" I paused to gather my thoughts— "is one that I am not necessarily proud of."

"You don't have to share anything you're not comfortable with," Loren said. "I understand. I've done things I'm not proud of either."

I relaxed slightly and took a deep breath.

"As you have already guessed, and seen, I have certain...talents. In the past, I have used these to my advantage to...uhm...get what I want from people. Specifically, men."

He nodded.

"I am actually quite a successful thief, despite the evidence of the last few days. I am usually far more dexterous and balanced, but something about being on a ship for the first time, surrounded by open water that stretches far beyond what I can see, has had me on edge, I admit.... And then there are the pirates."

Loren chuckled softly.

"I remember my first time on a ship," he said. "I was quite small, but I remember spending most of my time on my ass instead of my feet."

I chuckled at that image. A young Loren, probably with legs like sticks, trying to balance on a rocky ship.

"So compared to that, I think you're doing well," he said.

I felt a slight rush of heat in my cheeks, and I pulled the blanket down to my waist so I could breathe easier.

"That makes me feel a little better," I said, slightly relieved. "As I was saying, I actually have somewhat of a reputation on land. The men I target are usually rich assholes that have more money than they know what to do with. So I help them with that by taking some off their hands and giving it to people that need it more."

His gaze drifted for a moment, as if a memory shadowed his thoughts.

"That doesn't sound like a terrible reputation to have," he finally said.

I pinched my lips together and moved my head from side to side.

"You'd think that, but rich people really love their money."

Loren gave me a knowing look, as if I had said "the sky is blue" or something equally indisputable.

"Pirate, remember?"

"Right." I let out a small, nervous laugh. "Well, that night at the tavern, I was sitting across from a table of men, one of whom I had robbed a few nights before. The one was pointing at a wanted poster that had my face on it. When they left, I walked over to the page and saw my face looking back up at me. I panicked. Usually I'm much more careful. Like I said before, I have certain advantages that other thieves do not. I can make people forget they saw me."

Loren paused in thought.

"Wait," he said, "is that what you did to Waldreg? Is that what you tried to do to me?"

I nodded.

"Yes," I said. "Only, it didn't work on you, obviously, because here we are, having this conversation."

His eyebrows furrowed, causing the line in his forehead to show again.

"I wonder why it didn't work," he said. His eyes drifted in thought.

I shrugged.

"I don't know," I replied. "It's always worked in the past."

A wry look crossed his face.

"So, you're saying I'm special, then?" Did I detect a hint of playfulness in his voice?

I rolled my eyes.

"Are you going to let me finish my story, or are you going to steal the spotlight?"

He just smiled and motioned with his hand for me to continue.

"As I was saying, I panicked. It wasn't the first wanted poster I had seen. A few weeks ago, I saw one in a town to the north. I thought that by moving south, I would be safe, but it seems my reputation has caught up with me."

"How much is the reward?" Loren asked.

My eyes widened slightly, and he must have noticed.

"What?" he asked. "If this adventure goes dry, I'm going to need some kind of retirement plan."

"50,000 gold pieces," I said.

Loren darted up beside me.

"50,000 gold pieces!" he exclaimed. "What did you do, rob the prince?"

I hesitated.

"Sybine, you didn't!"

"It wasn't my fault!" I said. "The crown was sitting there, right in front of me. Anyone would have done it."

"How on Earth did you get close to his crown?" Loren asked me, genuinely impressed.

I hesitated again.

"Sybine!"

"Don't judge!" I said. "I needed a break from the rain, and he was courteous enough to bring me to some lodgings for the night."

Loren laughed.

"Oh, I am sure he was very courteous."

I nudged him.

"Look, I didn't know he was the prince. I just thought he was another thief like me. I woke up in the middle of the night, and there was the crown, sticking right out of his bag, practically begging for me to take it. When I was absolutely sure that he was asleep, I took the bag and ran for it. A few weeks later, my wanted poster started appearing at every tavern in the north. That's when I knew I was in trouble."

"And that's what led you to enroll."

"Exactly."

Loren absorbed the story and let out a few deep breaths.

"Well?" I asked.

Loren chuckled.

"I just can't believe you slept with and stole from the prince, all in the same night."

"I told you, I'm not proud of it."

"I would be," he said, chuckling to himself. "So how much money did you make off selling it then?" he asked.

I hesitated for the third time, and my eyes made their way toward my bag on top of my chest on the other side of the room.

Loren followed my gaze.

"No. Sybine!"

He practically jumped out of bed to inspect my bag.

"Loren, wait."

But it was too late. He already had his hands around the crown, which glistened in the moonlight from the window.

I sighed.

"I meant to sell it. I really did. I just...couldn't. I never intended to carry it across the sea."

Loren studied the crown in front of him carefully, twisting it around slowly as if to take in every detail. The sapphires and diamonds shimmered in the low light of the candle, while the black base seemed to disappear into the darkness of the night, leaving Loren looking like he was twisting gemstones through the air with some kind of magic.

"I don't think I would make a very good prince or king."

"I don't think anyone can be a good prince or king," I replied.

Loren turned around and looked at me quizzically.

"Think about it," I said. "The role of a king is to do what, exactly? Protect the people? Provide for the people? Rule the people? But let's be honest, that is not a one-person job. That is a job fit for an army or an entire population. So either you run a militant society, or the society runs you. Either way, you are nothing more than a fancy piece on a chessboard."

Loren thought about that for a moment before turning back to look at me again. Something flashed behind his eyes.

"You are full of surprises, Sybine."

'Under the Skin

Sybine

Something heavy pressed against my side when I woke up. I opened my eyes groggily to find Loren's arm pinning me down. He must have rolled over at some point in his sleep and wrapped his arm around me. My cheeks flushed, and I gently placed my fingers around his wrist to remove it from my waist. A long, deep breath escaped his lips to dance along the back of my neck, sending a shiver down my spine. My heart made a small leap in my chest. I had slept with so many men before, but never anyone like Loren. And we had only slept together in the most literal sense of the word. Still, I had never slept beside someone after having such an intimate moment like we shared last night. There was something magical in the space that we shared, and I was selfishly glad to know that he felt comfortable enough to properly rest in my presence.

The muscles in his arm suddenly tensed, and before I had a chance to say anything, Loren rolled over in a single frantic movement. He froze, and his breaths came slow and steady, as if trying to figure out if I was awake or not, and whether I was aware of where his hand had just been. I felt the stinging heat in my cheeks again. What was the proper protocol for moments like these? Usually I was long gone before the men I was with ever had a chance of waking. But not Loren. Here we were, both feigning sleep, a growing tension between us. I finally decided to clear my throat and roll over as if just waking up.

"Good morning," I said, trying to make my voice sound as groggy as possible.

"Good morning." His tone was flat and emotionless. He clearly felt embarrassed about waking up so close to me.

"Did you rest well?"

"Yes."

I was acutely aware of his apprehension to conversation. Or maybe he was just concerned I would ask him about something else.

"Do you know what the crew will be doing today? Rhyker said something yesterday about making port. I've never made one before, though," I admitted nervously.

I hoped it wasn't as laborious as scrubbing the deck. My body ached all over from the constant bending and pushing. It had been a long time since I had to perform any kind of manual labor to that extent. And that wasn't exactly the form of exercise I was used to.

"Yes."

I rolled my eyes under my closed lids.

"You're a man of few words this morning."

This time, all I received in reply was a grunt as he got out of bed. He turned around and raised an eyebrow at me, as if expecting me to turn away so he could preserve his decency.

I sighed and rolled over, facing toward the wall once again. Once I heard the chest close and the slow clack of the heels of his shoes on the wooden floorboards, I returned to my original position facing him. This time, it was my turn to raise an eyebrow in expectation. He was holding some kind of white piece of clothing in his hands. His body went rigid the moment our eyes met, and he ran a hand through his hair slowly.

"Here."

I sat up and moved myself toward the edge of the bed. I took the cloth from his hands. When I held it up, my breath caught.

A corset?

No. I took a closer look. From first glance, it appeared to be a corset, but there was nothing to suggest whatever this was, was meant to support and accentuate my breasts. If anything, it looked like it was meant to compress them. Was that even possible?

"What is it?" I asked.

Loren sat on the top of his chest. He left one leg stretched out, and rested his elbow on top of the other that was bent at the knee. He gestured to me with his other hand.

"Put it on."

I gave him a shy glance, and he turned to look out the window.

I carefully removed my shirt and chemise and let them drop to the floor. I slipped my arms through the corset-like thing like I would a coat and began working at the clasps down the front. After what felt like an eternity, my fingertips were raw and sore, but my breasts were firmly being held against my chest. While it restricted my movement slightly, I found it set my shoulders back straighter, giving me the impression that I was a proud man, which, for the purposes of this trip, I guess I was.

"Okay."

Loren turned around and evaluated my work. My cheeks flushed and my skin prickled under his gaze. When he was done, he twirled his finger in the air.

"Turn around," he ordered.

I turned my back to him and brought my braid over my shoulder. I heard him stand and make his way over to me. His breath on the back of my neck sent a ripple of energy down my spine. My toes curled in my boots.

"May I?" His voice was low and breathy. He placed a hand on my lower back. I could feel the warmth of his skin through the fabric.

I nodded, no longer confident in my ability to form words.

I heard the soft sound of the laces being untied at my back, followed by the slight release of pressure. My throat went dry and my body tensed slightly against my will.

"Relax, Sybine," he whispered. "Let out your breath."

I closed my eyes and let out a long exhale. As I did, he tightened the laces at the top, pressing my breasts even closer to my body. My eyes flew open at the sudden jolt, and I stumbled back into his chest. This was not where I had thought the morning would bring me.

Loren adjusted the fabric at the top, letting loose a wrinkle that was pinching me. His fingers brushed the sensitive skin near my spine, and I had to fight to not let go of another breath that might give me away. My skin felt impossibly hot, and it burned from where his fingers had been only a moment ago.

Slowly, he tightened the laces until he reached the bottom. I was barely breathing by the time he finished and tucked in the loose strands.

"That's better."

He took a step back from me, and I became very aware of the space between us. I ran my tongue over my lips before turning around to face him again.

Loren tilted his head, examining me. He nodded once and brought his eyes up to mine. He cleared his throat, and a muscle tensed at his jaw.

"We'll be back on land today, at least for a few hours. That's what it means to make port. The captain has some business to attend to on Tamarine before we continue on our voyage."

Loren walked to the door and placed his hand on the handle.

"Wait," I said before he could leave. "What is this?"

He hesitated, his hand tensed around the steel of the handle.

"It's a shape holder. Some people call it a binder."

I had figured as much, but there was another question on my lips, begging to be asked.

"Why...why give it to me?"

He let out a low breath. The muscles in his neck tensed as he tilted his head back slightly. I wished I could see the look on his face so I didn't have to guess what he was feeling.

"People have helped me get where I am. Consider it a debt repaid."

He hesitated again before twisting the handle.

"Listen, this isn't my first time working with a crew like this. At some point, we will probably end up at a tavern. When that time comes, keep your head down. Don't draw attention to yourself, okay? Even if by some miracle the wanted posters haven't reached this island yet, they will eventually, and when they do, you don't want anyone to be able to point in your direction. Do you understand what I'm saying?"

I nodded, but then realized that he wasn't looking at me, so I added, "Yes, I understand."

Loren took a deep breath and finally opened the door.

I quickly changed into a fresh shirt and followed him around the lower deck and up the stairs to where the crew was gathering. I tucked my braid under my hat and kept my eyes down as I joined in line with the rest of the deckhands. Within a few minutes, everyone had made their way up, and we waited for instructions while Rhyker paced back and forth in front of us.

"Days off on the sea are limited. So make the most of it while you can. I know we just set sail, so don't be expecting any more gifts or leniencies from here on out. You hear? After this, you'll be lucky if you're not woken up in the middle of the night to change our chamber pots. And get your pathetic asses back here by sunrise, or it might just be the last one you ever see."

I tried to hide my wince. I might have hated my job scrubbing decks, but at least I didn't have to clean up their piss.

Within a few hours, we were back on land. The men around me cheered and grunted and nudged each other. They made bets on who was going to come back the most drunk, the most broke, and the most lonely. I heeded Loren's advice and kept my head down, following the crowd as they moved along the trails to the town.

"Don't worry, kid," Harlan said from behind me. "Have some fun, but stay out of trouble."

I attempted an easy laugh, but it came out as more of a croak, so I tried to cover it up by having a cough, which only seemed to make the situation worse.

Harlan made his way up beside me and frowned at me.

"Well, you won't be warmin' anyone's bed tonight if you keep actin' like that." He paused and stroked his gray-stubbled chin as if in serious contemplation. When his eyes met mine again, they twinkled with mischief. "Unless you already have a certain someone."

My eyes widened, and I felt a rush of heat move through my chest up to my face. My thoughts raced back to waking up with Loren's arm draped over me. I could feel a phantom pressure from the memory of his touch against my side that made my heart give a jump in my chest.

"No, I mean...uhm...I don't have someone, and I don't want someone either."

Harlan gave me a playful wink.

"Don't hold back, kid. This old man's seen it all. And although these eyes have had their share of years, I always know what I see."

What the fuck was that supposed to mean?

I just nodded in response.

"One day, you'll see too." Harlan's gaze shifted to behind me before he gave me a full, crooked-toothed smile and continued on ahead. For an old man, he was certainly in better shape than I had given him credit for.

"What was he on about?"

I nearly jumped out of my boots.

"Sorry, I didn't mean to startle you...are you okay?" He gave me a concerned look.

"Yes," I said a little breathlessly.

"Using my own tricks against me?" he teased. "Look, I'm sorry I wasn't particularly talkative this morning. I just woke up feeling strange. But it's settled now. Nothing a little sea mist couldn't cure."

I woke up feeling strange, too, I wanted to say, but I held my tongue. If he had sorted his feelings out already, then this morning must have just been an awkward coincidence that I was reading far too much into. It wasn't like I enjoyed being in his arms more than anyone else's. It definitely wasn't as if the warmth from his body was like sitting next to a fire on a cold winter's day. And it definitely wasn't as if I felt safe and cherished in his embrace. Everyone enjoyed being held from time to time, right?

"Are you okay, Sebastien?" he asked again. I almost felt disappointed hearing my false name from his lips.

I blinked and tried to push down the knot in my stomach. I nodded and gave him as genuine of a smile as I could.

"Yes, sorry, I was just feeling a little nervous." At least that wasn't a lie.

He nodded, as if completely understanding. Even though I was sure he didn't.

"Oh, good." I hadn't noticed Harlan's slowed pace until I almost ran straight into the back of him. "Some of these islanders can be a bit rough around the edges, so I'm glad you two are plannin' on staying together. If anyone approaches you, he can fend them off."

He pointed at Loren, whose face had slightly flushed.

"I'm sure you can," Harlan said confidently. He turned and flashed a smile at me.

"You don't think anyone will be suspicious?" I asked. I immediately scolded myself. There was nothing to be suspicious about. Plenty of the other sailors were probably going to part off in groups. Why would we together draw any more attention than them?

Loren was infuriatingly quiet.

Harlan furrowed his brows at me.

"At two fellows who happen to be bunkmates walkin' together through a town? What's so suspicious about that?"

I shrugged my shoulders and tried to fight off the sudden tightness and flutters in my chest.

"Nothing, I guess," I admitted.

"Great, now that that's settled, I think I'll find myself a quiet place for a drink."

Harlan turned off the path toward a brick building with a wooden sign above it. I couldn't read the name from here, but there was a mug of ale clearly etched into it.

"I guess that means we will be together today," I said nervously.

"Hmm." Loren's face was a mask that gave nothing away. "The old man was right about one thing. If anyone approaches us, I can take care of them."

I let out a small sigh of relief.

"I'd like that, thank you."

"Don't mention it."

20

Debt

Elora

I spent most of the night lost in a memory I had nearly forgotten. It was a cold winter evening, and I had come back to the inn empty-handed, bruised, and exhausted. It was the last fight I had lost at the Broken Spoke over five years ago. Everyone, including myself, had bet on me to win. No one had come close to taking me down in over a dozen matches, so naturally, I was favored to win the next one.

What I had not anticipated was who stepped into the ring with me. Her hair was tucked behind her head in a tight wrap held by a thin silver pin with a bird on the end. Her dark eyes were accentuated by the sharpness of her cheekbones, and her olive-toned skin seemed to glow from the light of the torches on the walls. The most surprising thing about the match wasn't that she was a woman, or even that she was smaller than I was. It was that I had shared a meal with her not an hour before the fight, and she'd never once mentioned who she truly was.

"I'm Ren," she said between bites.

"What brings you to the Broken Spoke?"

"I'm here for the fight. I'm sure it will be one to remember."

I cringed at the memory of how ill I felt standing across from her. I hadn't even lasted five minutes in the fight before I buckled over and emptied the contents of my stomach. She had ruthlessly kicked at my side, knocking me over, before straddling me and hitting at my face and stomach before I finally lost consciousness. She had poisoned my food, knowing who I was, knowing that she was going to fight me, knowing that she would have the advantage. That was the last time I ever underestimated a woman, and the last time I ever trusted anyone.

I had been starving and parched by the time I made it back to the inn. I could remember how it felt to be wasting away all too well. I didn't have any money to pay for food or a room, but I was prepared to trade my knives or anything else I had on me if I had to. When I had walked up to the bar bench, the woman tending it looked me up and down, nodded her head, and brought out a small leather pouch. The coins in it had clinked as she set it down on the smooth surface.

"Someone dropped this off this mornin'. Said to be givin' it to someone who be needin' it. Yer the roughest one I've had all day. Go on, it's yours."

I never got a description of the person who brought the purse, but a part of me wondered if I was now walking with them after all these years.

"You seem distracted," Sybine said as we turned a corner.

"A little," I admitted.

I lifted my head up to check and make sure we were still following Drakkon and Rhyker. After identifying them, still walking at the front of the group, I let myself come back down to a normal posture.

She didn't press for any other information, which I was thankful for. But I couldn't let go of the nagging feeling in my stomach. I had to know if it was her.

We reached a point in the road that branched off in four different directions. Most of the men took the left path that led to a series of sturdy-looking brick buildings, but Drakkon and Rhyker continued forward. So forward we would go as well.

Sybine's steps slowed as she looked at me.

"What is it?" she asked.

"Have you ever been to Navryn? It's a small village on the mainland of Elandia."

Sybine pushed her lips to the side of her mouth as she thought. Her eyebrows pinched together, creating a small line on her forehead.

"I'm not sure...maybe?" She shook her head. "I've been traveling around for so long that I don't really remember the names of places I've stopped in." She paused and looked at me curiously. "Why?"

We came to another fork in the road and paused. I looked from side to side, as if taking my time to decide where to go next. After a few seconds, I finally led us down the path to the right, still a healthy distance away from the two men.

"After what you said last night...I was just curious. Someone helped me there once."

She raised her head as if realizing something.

"Is that what this—" she gestured to her midsection— "was about?"

I nodded.

She gave me a playful smirk.

"I think I'd remember you."

I shook my head.

"I don't know who it was. We never met. And the only description I got was that the person wanted to give the cash to someone who needed it."

Sybine tilted her head to the side, considering my words.

"Sometimes if I couldn't find a person or family to help, I'd just leave a purse of coins at the door of a tavern or inn with a note that said something like that."

I hadn't thought much about the source of the money over the years. No one seemed to know who it was on that first night, but I had hated that I might never have known whose debt I was in. Until now. Maybe it was Sybine, maybe it wasn't. But my debt was either paid to the owner, or paid forward. Regardless, it was off my shoulders.

"If it was you...thank you."

Sybine's smile was genuine. Her eyes lit up, and the skin at the edge of her eyes folded a little.

"You know, Loren, it's not weak to need help every once in a while."

David said something like that once.

"What is it?" she asked.

I shook my head.

"Nothing. Just a ghost from my past."

We came across a series of merchants selling all sorts of goods, from clothing to jewelry and carved ornaments. Sybine's attention was caught by one to our left selling dresses and tunics in all different shapes and sizes. I let her examine them as I kept my eyes on Drakkon and Rhyker.

The two of them continued down the path, looking behind them every once in a while. It was like they didn't want to be followed, which, of course, meant that I would absolutely keep track of them. If I could get them alone and surprise them, it was possible I would be able to execute my plan without having to risk everyone on board finding out. Misfortune fell on people all the time during stops like this. No one would suspect a deliberate attack, much less one from me. All I had to do was get away from Sybine.

I looked over at her while she talked to one of the men selling tunics. He was clearly trying to sell her on something she didn't need, but she didn't seem concerned or affected by his charms—a fact that started to clearly bother the man. I had to bite my lips together to hold in a laugh. She had no idea the effect that she had on people. Sure, she had some unearthly power of persuasion, but this was beyond that. This was something completely her own that had no name. Or maybe it did. Maybe that was just Sybine.

She turned around, catching my stare. The moment our eyes met, I felt her under my skin. The feeling that I thought I had washed away this morning returned like a tidal wave, and I found myself fighting for breath.

I gestured to the side of her head.

"Your...hair's undone." My voice was much rougher than I intended.

165

Sybine's cheeks turned a light pink.

"Thanks," she said, reaching her hand up to tuck the stray hair behind her ear.

I nodded and forced my eyes to look at something else. Anything else. My vision was cloudy, and all I could see in my mind were her big, beautiful green eyes staring deep into my soul. I was suddenly scared of what she saw there. Would she be afraid of the darkness that I held? The darkness I purposely let fester? Would she be saddened by it? Or worse, what if she hated me for it? I pushed the thoughts away, closed my eyes, and took a breath. When I opened them again, I saw Drakkon and Rhyker at the edge of the path past the merchant tents. As they looked around again, I bent down as if to fix my pants or shoes. Satisfied with what they saw, they rounded the corner into a thick brush of trees.

I stood up so quickly that I nearly knocked over a rack of clothing. The owner gave me a disapproving look, but I ignored him.

"Stay here. I'll be right back. Don't do anything...foolish."

I took off down the path, staying as close to the edge as I could, and turned right when I made it to the trees. I immediately caught sight of them again and tucked behind a thick trunk.

The two men made a last look around before ducking into a shop at the end of the road.

"What was that ab—"

I whirled around, grabbing the source of the noise by the waist and pinning them up against the tree.

I nearly rolled my eyes.

Of course, it was Sybine. Of course, she had followed me and not listened to me. Of course, she had done something foolish.

It was too late to turn around now. I didn't know how long I would have until the two men emerged again, and with every passing second, the opportunity was slipping through my fingers.

I could tell her to go back, but that would waste time trying to convince her I wasn't up to something, which, of course, I was. Telling her to stay where she was would probably work just as well as it had last time. So that left me taking her with me and hoping she wasn't too squeamish around other people's blood.

In fact, maybe this was a better option after all. After I took care of Drakkon and Rhyker, there was still the merchant to contend with. And although I wasn't completely against collateral damage, I tried to avoid it where I could. Sybine could prove useful in erasing their memories of us if it was necessary.

I held a finger to her mouth, effectively silencing her.

"Do you trust me?"

Her eyes widened, but she nodded.

"Good. Keep quiet and don't leave my side."

Power

Elora

I wasn't sure what I expected to see when I peeked through the curtain door of the shop, but it certainly was not Drakkon and Rhyker sitting across a table from a woman dressed in deep purple robes holding a crystal ball. The edges of the tent were decorated with woven red ribbon that upon first glance looked like blood dripping down the walls.

My original plan was to wait until everyone was distracted, and then strike from behind. I would need to take Drakkon down first. Rhyker would be easy enough to fight, but I knew from experience that Drakkon was much stronger, quicker, and smarter than he let on. The scar across my chest burned from the memory.

Unfortunately, the opening of the tent would only give me access to Rhyker. Drakkon sat on the other side of him, and there was only one way in or out. I would have to wait until they left to make my move. But that didn't mean I couldn't gain some information while I waited.

"Varix," Rhyker purred, "lovely as always." He reached over as if requesting one of her hands. She looked at his gesture with barely veiled disgust.

"A pleasure, as always." Her tone was anything but genuine. And she did not agree to his unspoken request. Her voice was high and unpleasant. It had a ringing quality that set my teeth on edge. I could tell it had the same effect on Sybine. She winced every time a word left Varix's mouth.

Rhyker brought his hands back to his lap, and I struggled not to laugh as I watched his jaw flex. There were few things that gave me more joy than watching men be put in their place.

"What brings you back to my shores? You already have your ties—" she gestured around the room— "what more could you possibly want?"

"You know what we want, Varix. Don't play coy," Drakkon hissed.

Varix shook her head, causing her long white hair to twirl through the air.

"You men and always assuming things. I know a great deal about what you want." She pointed her gaze toward Rhyker. "You, Rhyker, desire belonging. You seek what you have been promised, but you are too afraid to take action. You want to be known, to be seen, to be loved."

Rhyker's fists clenched.

"You know nothing, witch," he spat back at her. "I do belong. I am first mate to the greatest captain that has ever sailed these seas. I have everything I could ever want and more."

Varix ignored his words and moved to address Drakkon.

"And you, Drakkon. You seek what so many before you have failed to acquire." Varix leaned forward and rested her elbows on the table. "You seek true power. A power great enough to tame oceans. But more than that, you crave status. Isn't that correct?" She tilted her head to the side, a sly grin sweeping across her face.

Drakkon sneered at her.

"No."

The single word boomed throughout the tent.

Varix's lips pulled up, exposing her yellowed teeth.

"We shall see."

"Just give us the chains, witch."

Chains? What use could these two possibly have for chains?

Varix frowned.

"I warned you of what would come, Drakkon Stormson. And yet here you are, back at my table, despite everything that you know will come to pass."

The lines between Drakkon's brows darkened as he pinched them together. The light of the candle flames danced across his features, making him look every bit the demon I knew him to be.

"You said that I would yield a power most men would never dream of. You said I would be one of the greatest forces the sea has ever seen, one that would rival the power of the Sea King himself." Drakkon stood, his impressive frame towering over Varix. If she was threatened by him, she didn't show it. "And yet here I am, no closer to the power than I was six months ago. So I ask you again, witch. Give me the chains." He held out his hand directly in front of her face.

My stomach knotted. Powerful enough to rival the Sea King? There was much more at stake here than I had anticipated. The only weapon I knew of that could possibly grant a man such a power was...the Kraken's Fang.

Drakkon was serious. This wasn't just a trip for glory and riches. He hadn't lied when he'd told us all that he was going to rule the seas with it. He had every intention of chasing the legend, and with the Fang in his hands, there would be nothing to stop him.

Raise Hell

Sybine

A shiver ran down my spine. What could Drakkon possibly want with so much power? Nothing good, I guessed. I had never met a power hungry man with altruistic motives.

With each passing moment, I felt my resolve slip. This was not at all what I had expected when I'd followed Loren. He was sneaking around and trying to hide, which, in my experience, meant that he was trying to steal something. I never thought that the two of us would be spying on the captain instead. Something felt very wrong about this entire situation.

"Who told you of the chains, and what makes you think I have them?" Varix asked calmly. I admired the woman. She was maintaining her composure much better than I was, and I wasn't even the one being directly interrogated by the captain.

"My contacts are my own, and none of your business," he hissed.

"Your business is my business, Drakkon. Don't forget who put you where you are."

Drakkon scoffed.

"You give yourself far too much credit, Varix." His voice dripped with venom.

Varix's eyes narrowed.

"I could say the same of you."

This was too much. We were not supposed to be here. Some things were better left alone. Why was Loren so intent on listening? What could he possibly gain from this? If they found us, I knew they wouldn't hesitate to strike us down. And then what? This was not worth dying for.

I went to take a step back, but Loren's body caged me. I glanced up at him. He flinched and pursed his lips together. He looked as if he might go through and take them all on by himself at any second. He shook his head at me, silently telling me to stay where I was. There was a pit in my stomach that refused to settle.

"Your place in this story is nothing compared to mine, witch. If you don't want to hand over the chains, then so be it. I will burn this tent to the ground. I will raise hell where I stand. I will walk over your rotting corpse and take what is mine, if I must."

Varix stood to meet his gaze and leaned over so there was little more than a hand's width between their faces.

"Do. Your. Worst." Her glare held the power of a thousand suns, and I was suddenly overwhelmed by the fiery frost emanating from her.

A small gasp escaped my lips.

I dropped the cloth to the tent as I watched the three heads from inside turn in our direction.

Loren stiffened. Panic surged through me. Loren grabbed my elbow and pulled me to the side. I heard footsteps approaching us, and my fingers went numb. The world began to tilt and swirl in odd patterns. There was a fuzziness to my head, and my thoughts came in crashing waves.

I couldn't make my legs move.

Run! Run! Run! I screamed at myself, but they wouldn't budge. Loren shook me, mouthing the same words, but I couldn't hear him. I could barely make out his face. My vision blurred at the edges, and I was relatively certain that I was going to lose consciousness at any moment.

Loren grabbed me by the waist and pulled me around the back of the tent behind the trees. There was a small shrub in front of us, and my eyes caught on the dewdrops that speckled its leaves.

There was a loud drumming in my ears that completely drowned out the words he was trying to say. Loren twisted my head to look at him, his grip strong on my jaw. His eyes were wide with urgency. I couldn't understand what he was saying. I was vaguely aware of him removing my hat and combing his fingers through my hair. He kept looking over my shoulder and then shaking me and then looking again. I couldn't stop my mind from racing and my heart from jumping in my chest. He slammed his eyes shut, shook his head, and—

He kissed me.

The act was so unimaginable that it shocked my soul back into my body. A new life sparked in me. A fire of awareness spread across my body in a tidal wave. His lips were much softer than I imagined them to be. I felt myself relax in his embrace. It was as if his kiss breathed the air back into my lungs. I could finally taste the air again. I could finally see again. I could finally think again. Oh gods, what were we doing?

His lips moved with an urgency I didn't expect. His hands trailed down my back toward my hips, where his fingers gripped my tender flesh. With one swift motion, he picked me up and pressed me against the thick tree stump. I wrapped my legs around his waist as his hands moved up my back and through my undone hair. I let out a low moan just as the footsteps finally came around to find us.

"Take your whore business somewhere else, sailor." Rhyker's voice called out.

I stiffened, but Loren kept his hands exploring up and down my back, pulling me in closer to him. I could feel his heart beating through his shirt, an echo of my own pounding in my chest.

"You hear me, sailor?"

Loren removed his lips from mine, and to my surprise, I felt something in my stomach sink, almost like disappointment.

"Yes, sir," he said breathlessly.

The footsteps retreated, and Loren finally relaxed. He closed his eyes and put me down. My legs were shaky underneath me, and I held onto the tree for balance. Loren raked a hand through his hair.

My face flooded with heat.

Loren's eyes flew open as I took a hesitant step forward. I was suddenly aware of his absence between my legs. I adjusted my trousers and dusted off my shirt.

Neither of us said anything. We stayed there in an awkward silence that seemed to stretch into an eternity.

A faint shade of pink dusted his cheeks under his warm, dark eyes.

"I'm sorry if that made you uncomfortable. I tried to ask if it was okay, but I'm not sure you heard me. I tried shaking you, but you looked so distant. I...panicked."

I shook my head.

"It's okay, Loren. You don't have to apologize."

He ran a hand through his short hair again.

"I don't want you to think that I was...I don't know what I'm saying."

I grabbed his hands in mine and looked him in the eyes.

"Loren, it's okay. You don't need to apologize," I reiterated.

He let out a long breath, and his shoulders relaxed. He nodded his head slowly.

"Let's go. We need to get out of here before they come back."

A Storm of Flames and Smoke

Sybine

I heard the loud crack of fire splitting wood before I saw the smoke from the flames. Drakkon had followed through on his promise.

"Come on." Loren ushered me down a narrow path to our right.

"Loren, wait—"

I bent over and tried to catch my breath. I had finally recovered from the shock of everything, including the kiss, and my thoughts and questions caught up with me.

"We can't just...leave her...to die..." I said through gasps.

He shook his head.

"We don't have time for this right now, Sybine. We need to get out of here."

I looked up at the billowing smoke. My heart sank. We hadn't gone that far. If we turned back now, there was a chance. I turned around to face the way we came. Loren grabbed my elbow.

"Don't." His voice was low and commanding.

I twisted my arm free from his grasp and whirled around to face him. I balled my hands at my sides.

"I'm not leaving her!"

Loren's eyes widened, seemingly shocked. Then they narrowed just as quickly.

"Don't be a fool, Sybine."

His words stabbed me, and I winced.

"Better a fool than a coward."

I turned around and took off before he had a chance to stop me again. I flew down the path and through the trees, following our tracks from just moments before. When I rounded the last corner, my eyes widened in horror. Varix's tent was completely overwhelmed by flames.

A loud wailing noise came from inside. It was a shrill shriek that would paralyze any normal human.

There was a loud crack from behind me, and Loren came crashing through the trees. His lips were pinched together, and there was a firm crease between his eyebrows. He was furious.

He stopped a few paces in front of me, the muscle at the side of his jaw twitching.

"Did you buy that tunic?" he asked me.

I reached into the sack attached to my leg and pulled the shirt out.

Loren quickly took it from me and ripped the fabric in half. Before I had a chance to protest, he wrapped a portion of it over my nose so that it covered my mouth. He tied it around my head and then placed another piece of fabric over his mouth as well.

"Don't breathe too quickly. The fabric will help with the smoke, but it's not perfect. If you start to feel lightheaded, get the fuck out. Do you understand?"

I nodded.

"Good. Let's go."

He brought his arm up to cover his eyes, and he threw himself into the flames.

I followed a second later. Searing heat ran over my skin. I squinted through the storm of flames and smoke. I tried to take slow breaths, but I felt like I was choking. Everything was hot and dry. My heart raced, and my vision hazed around the edges.

Get the fuck out. Loren's voice echoed through my ears. But I couldn't. Not without them.

I took as deep of a breath as I could and held it. Then I slowly blinked the ash from my eyes and scoured around the tent. I could make out a dark shape in the corner, bent down close to the ground.

"Loren!" I called out.

"Here!" he called back.

I shuffled my feet forward until I hit something heavy. No, not something. Someone. I bent down beside Loren.

"Help me get her up," he said.

Still kneeling beside her, he wrapped his arm around Varix's back and pulled her into his chest as if in a lover's last embrace. I positioned myself behind her and put my hands under her armpits, ready to help lift her.

"No, grab her waist," he ordered.

I nodded and placed my hands just above the dips of her hip bones.

"On my count of three, we're both going to lift, and you're going to help push her over my shoulder, okay?"

"But Loren she's too—"

"Three!"

There was no warning, and no time to debate. I had no choice but to push her up as far as I could. She barely made it over his shoulder. He stood up on hesitant legs and made his way toward the opening again. His steps were slow. Too slow. I heard the snap of the wood above us, and the tent came crashing down.

"No!"

I threw myself at them as hard as I could. I sent Loren flying outside the blaze when my shoulder collided with his lower back. Varix tumbled to the ground in front of him. I landed hard on my stomach. My breath was completely swept out of me. I couldn't do anything but watch in horror as the flames descended on me.

I threw my hands out in a hopeless effort to save myself. My skin was suddenly alive with power. It thrummed through me in crashing waves. There was a loud crack as a board came down on my leg. But the pain I expected to feel was startlingly absent.

I looked down and froze. There was a small layer of ice on the board from where it touched me. The frost climbed up, engulfing the flames like a spiderweb, until all that was left was a small pile of wood and ash. Steam rose from it, not smoke, and it sizzled instead of crackled like from the fire. I was completely untouched. There was no mark on my skin. Not a burn. Not a scratch. I gasped, finally able to take a breath again. Was that...me? I looked down at my hands and turned them over, inspecting both sides. Nothing looked any different. There was still dirt caked under my fingernails, and my smooth skin was untouched.

Loren moaned beside me and Varix let out a long howl. She made indistinct, guttural sounds that seemed to come from deep within her soul.

I rolled over and scrambled to my feet. I would think about it later. I grabbed both of their wrists and dragged them an extra few paces away from the rubble.

In the short time it took for me to move them, Varix's cries went from being pained to something more like a plea. But a plea for what?

Death, my mind whispered back to me in response. I shivered.

The two of them were lying on their sides facing each other. I didn't know what else to do. Loren's clothes were torn and burnt, and Varix looked inches away from death. We were too late. And worse, I had risked Loren's life in the process. I had guilted him into following me. It was my fault that he was here, in front of me, coughing, bleeding, and torn to shreds. I was a swirling vortex of fear, shame, and despair. It was all my fault.

"Varix." Loren's voice was low and hoarse from crying and from the smoke billowing around us.

Varix moaned in response and her nearly colorless blue eyes fluttered open. She rolled onto her back and looked up at me. She raised a hand to my face as if consoling a babe.

"Do not...blame yourself...."

I flinched. Her skin was rough and chapped. The tips of her fingers were black and charred. It was like being embraced by thorns.

"Drakkon...he...the chains...." Varix's eyes shoved shut in pain, and she let out a low, grinding cough. I finally looked down to inspect the rest of her body. Her robes were frayed and torn and blackened from the flames and smoke. Her skin was red and blistered where it was exposed, and the tissue at the edges was beginning to turn a grotesque shade of purple. I swallowed down the bile that threatened to come up from my throat. I let the fabric covering my nose and mouth fall down so I could properly speak to her.

Instinctively, I took her hand. Her eyes opened to meet mine.

"Princess..." she muttered.

My brows knit in confusion, and I shook my head. Her mind was clearly fading. We did not have much time until she passed on.

"Shhh," I hushed her. I brushed a hair from her blistered face. She calmed in my embrace. "You are on a peaceful shore.

The waves dance between your toes. The sun shines down on you and kisses your skin. Birds fly in the clear skies above."

Varix heaved a quiet sigh of relief, but quickly became tense once I mentioned the birds in the sky. I continued, hoping to guide her away from whatever was causing her the mental pain.

"Your spirit is calm, and your mind is clear. Tell me, Varix, what is on your mind?"

"The wren...the calling bird...she..." Varix coughed again. "She is a shadow...the master...do not trust...the wren."

I frowned. Sometimes I had the ability to add clarity to people's last moments, but this was not the case with Varix. It sounded like I had accidentally brought up a painful memory, so I tried again.

"You are on a peaceful shore. The waves dance between your toes. The sun shines down on you and kisses your skin. The sky is clear above. Your spirit is calm, and your mind is clear. Tell me, Varix, what is on your mind?"

Her eyes closed and her shoulders fell back.

"Peace," she whispered.

A small tear tracked down my cheek as I watched Varix let out her final breath.

Peace

Elora

I watched in awe as Sybine's eyes glowed a piercing green. Her words were like a lullaby in the air. It was as if she was trying to sing Varix into her last peaceful slumber. I felt myself relax in Sybine's presence as well. There was something about her, something magical and pure, something beautiful, something kind. At that moment, I truly saw her for the first time: powerful and perfect. My breath caught in my throat. The horrors of our surroundings disappeared until the only thing was her. There were no cries of pain or suffering. There was no fire around us. There was only this perfect moment of peace in front of me. I had seen so much death in my life, but never had it been so warm and calm. Despite the events leading up to this, there was nothing but complete and total acceptance and peace on Varix's face as she passed into the next world in Sybine's arms.

I groaned as I rolled over. I pushed myself to my knees and reached out to Sybine.

"Come on...we have to go," I told her as I grabbed her arm.

She placed a gentle kiss on Varix's forehead before wiping her face with the back of her hand. She steadied me as we stood together. My head suddenly felt foggy, and my lungs were heavy and dry from the smoke.

I stumbled slightly, and Sybine wrapped an arm around my waist to help me regain my balance.

"It's okay. You can lean on me," she said. For the first time in over a decade, I let myself rely on someone else for support.

Sybine tightened her grip as I reached my arm around her shoulders. My steps were wobbly, like I'd had too much to drink, and my vision was clouded. My eyelashes were thick with ash, and it stung my eyes to blink. Sybine hesitated as we came to a fork in the path.

"Turn left here," I told her, and we rounded the corner to a tall stone building. "This one."

Sybine pushed open the door, and the pungent smell of liquor and the sound of rowdy men assaulted my senses.

"Are you sure this is a good—"

"Come on," I interrupted her before she could convince me out of this admittedly bad idea.

We walked up to the counter, and I reached in my pocket to pull out the gold piece from the other night. I placed it on the bench, and even though my vision wasn't quite clear, I could still make out the barmaid's eyes widening at the sight of it.

"Your best room," I ordered.

The woman nodded and came back a few moments later with a key in hand. I took it and left. Sybine and I walked past the drunken patrons toward the staircase at the end of the room. She helped me as we slowly ascended to the next floor. The key was for the last room at the end of the narrow hall. It was the only one with a decorated door with swirls of gold and black iron around its metal frame. I handed Sybine the key, and she unlocked the door easily. We stumbled into the room, which was, fortunately for me and unfortunately for my pocket since I'd spent an entire gold coin on it, small. Face down, I crashed onto the bed at the center of the room and let my eyes flutter closed. I focused on the breaths in and out of my lungs. They burned with the effort, but even since moving away from Varix's tent, I could feel my breaths improving.

"Can I get you anything?" Sybine asked.

I shook my head.

"Just need some rest for right now. Give me a minute."

Sybine sat on the edge of the bed beside me, and her weight shifted mine so that my hip was slightly leaning into her leg. I felt Sybine stiffen at the touch, but I did not have the energy to adjust myself. She cleared her throat.

"Can I get you some water?"

I let out a long sigh and nodded my head. I knew it would burn, but eventually it would help flush out the ash coating my throat.

A few minutes later, Sybine came back into the room with a large mug filled with an amber liquid, and a small glass filled with something clear. I didn't have to guess which one was for her, and which was for me. I rolled over onto my back to meet her gaze.

"Planning on getting me drunk too?" I tried to tease, but my joke fell flat.

"This isn't for you," she said, holding the mug up and taking a large gulp from it. She wiped her mouth with the back of her hand, and her face pinched from the taste. "I'm not sure I will ever get used to that."

I let out a low laugh.

I sat up as Sybine approached me with the small glass of water. I took a hesitant sip. It tasted like old dust. Although, I considered, that was perhaps just the taste of anything I could ingest at the moment. We sat in silence as we both nursed our drinks. Finally, when I couldn't stomach any more,

I poured the rest of the liquid on my face and scrubbed at my eyes with the backs of my hands. The water felt cool, and I was thankful to finally have the ash out of my eyes.

"How do you feel?" Sybine asked me.

I sighed.

"Like I just walked through hell and lived to tell the tale."

She laughed.

"Well, I guess you did, in a way. The captain did say he would raise hell to get what he wanted."

I smirked.

"I guess so."

A loud knock at the door made us both jolt up in alarm.

"Relax, lads, it's just me," Harlan said from behind the door.

Sybine walked over to let him in. He raised his hands, which were both holding jugs of water. There was also a new set of clothes on each of his arms.

"I saw you two walk in like you had just bathed in ashes."

Sybine and I exchanged a glance.

Harlan shook his head.

"I don't need to know the specifics. But I brought these in case you'd like to wash off any of the, uhm, evidence. Most people don't pay a gold piece for a shit room like this." He tutted disapprovingly.

"It was a last-minute decision," Sybine said coolly. "Next time, we will size up the market before buying a private room."

My breath caught. Next time. Would there be a next time? Or was that a slip of the tongue? Maybe I was just tired and overthinking everything. I sighed.

"Thank you, Harlan," I said, motioning for him to properly step into the room.

He shook his head and pushed the jugs into Sybine's chest.

"Don't worry, I won't be stickin' around to do any interruptin'. You just take these and get yourselves cleaned up."

With that, he turned on his heel and left.

I fell back onto the bed, exhausted. My eyes fixed on the knots in the wood that planked the roof of the room. Their dark swirls twisted and turned, and my vision twisted and turned with them. The last thing I remembered before drifting off into a restless sleep was the sound of Sybine's smooth and melodic voice telling me to close my eyes and rest.

25

Apologies

Elora

A few hours later, I awoke to Sybine nestled against my side. I looked down. Her hands were tucked delicately under her chin as she buried her face in my ribs. Her knees were curled up into her stomach, and her legs were braced against my hip. My stomach twisted, my skin flushed, and my mouth went dry. At the same time, my muscles tensed as I remembered her words to me in the woods.

Better a fool than a coward.

A stream of opposing emotions bombarded my mind. And here she was, resting peacefully beside me. I was furious with her for manipulating me, but even more so with myself for letting her. And yet, as soon as the anger rose in me, it seemed to settle. Could I blame her for wanting to help Varix? No. Was it worth the risk? Also, no. Was I the one who dragged her into it in the first place? Yes. I sighed and stared up at the ceiling. I reminded myself that I was in control of my actions and no one else's. It brought me a moment of peace.

I tried to sit up, but my head throbbed from the effort, and I eventually decided that a few more moments lying down was the better option.

Sybine stirred beside me. I looked down to see that her hair, which was always in a tight braid before now, was sprawled out around her head in cascading curls like waves about to crash onto the shore. She took a long breath and extended her limbs slowly. It was still dark outside, so I knew we hadn't slept through the entire night. I sighed in relief. We were supposed to be back by morning to make sure we were on the ship when it left. We still had some time.

I ran my fingers through my hair and found it slightly damp. When I pulled my hand out and inspected it, I found it was no longer covered in charcoal or dirt.

"I hope you don't mind." Sybine's soft voice pushed through the space between us. "I cleaned you up a bit, since you were quite dirty from the fire. And there was so much ash in your hair." She bit her lip. "I didn't take off any of your clothes or anything," she hastened to add.

"Thank you," I said.

Her face relaxed and gave me a shy smile.

"Oh good. I was scared you might be mad."

"For washing my hair?"

She sat up and shrugged. She wrapped her arms around herself nervously.

"...or for calling you a coward." She bit her lips together and cast her eyes down. "I didn't mean it. I never should have said it. I never should have goaded you into following me. I..." she let out a low exhale. "I'm sorry."

"Oh."

She turned around; her face held a look of confusion.

"Oh?"

I blinked and shook my head.

She helped me up to a sitting position, and I winced.

"I...I don't know how to do this," I admitted. I braced my elbows on my knees. My shoulders were so heavy, and I was exhausted.

"Do what?" she asked.

I gestured to the space between us.

"Apologize, I guess. And accept apologies. I've never...it's not something I do."

"Oh...me either. I usually make people forget when I've done something, but...."

"That doesn't work on me."

Sybine nodded as her fingers fiddled with the clasp of her bag. There was a thick, awkward tension that grew between us. I swallowed as I considered my next words.

"Listen, I—"

"Why were you outside of their tent, Loren?"

Sybine's question caught me completely off guard. She had every right to ask, of course, but I had hoped I would have more time to come up with a more believable lie.

She sensed my hesitation, and her gaze intensified.

"What happened?"

I searched my brain for something, anything, that might help me get out of this situation without revealing the cards I held so close to my chest.

"Drakkon said he had business on the island. He never gave me any details, so I thought I would get them myself."

It wasn't a lie, but it also wasn't the whole truth.

Sybine didn't look convinced. She loosened her grip around herself and folded her arms across her chest.

"To what end?" she asked.

Drakkon's.

It was a good question. Perhaps too good of a question. And one I wasn't ready to answer.

I clenched my fists. It was time to move the conversation away from my motives and toward theirs.

"I don't know what they have planned, but since they were willing to kill for it, I'm sure it's not a party trick. We need to be vigilant."

Sybine didn't seem pleased with my answer, but let me continue anyway.

"I shouldn't have dragged you into this. It wasn't fair of me."

Sybine let out a sharp breath.

"You didn't force me into anything. I'm the one who followed you after you said not to, remember?"

Yes, and I'm the one who wanted you to stay so I could use your powers for my own benefit after.

"I guess so."

She sighed and fell back onto the bed. Her arms extended out beside her as if she were flying.

"Some mess we're in."

I nodded. At least we could agree on that.

The tension in the room dissipated. For now, Sybine seemed to be finished with her questions. She didn't appear interested in pushing the conversation any further. I relaxed and leaned back on my hands with my head tilted toward the ceiling. After a few moments, Sybine rolled over and grabbed a glass from the bedside table.

"Here."

I didn't realize how parched I was until I saw the clear liquid. I drank it as quickly as I could without spilling it all over myself.

"Thank you," I said, a little out of breath.

"You're welcome. How are you feeling?"

I did a quick mental check around my body. I was still tired, and my body still ached. My head was obviously swimming in pain, but my breaths were coming easier, and my throat didn't feel as raw anymore.

"Better."

She smiled.

"Good. Because I think we are almost out of time." She glanced out the window where a hint of pale yellow was beginning to paint the dark sky.

Sybine walked over to the chair at the end of the room where the two extra sets of clothes were resting, courtesy of Harlan.

She ran her fingers over my black shirt. She held it in her hands as she turned to me. Her grip was so tight that her knuckles were white under her skin.

"I still have a lot of questions, Loren."

I nodded. So we weren't done talking about this yet. I readied myself for another round.

"But I also know what it's like to keep a secret that your life literally relies upon. And I know the cost of sharing it."

She relaxed slightly as she took a step forward and held out the shirt to me.

"I don't know what it is you're hiding, or how important it is, but I'm in no position to demand it from you, so I won't." She rolled her eyes up to the roof. "I guess what I'm saying is that if you want to talk about it, you can...with me, I mean." She let out a nervous laugh. "It's not like it could be any worse than what you know about me."

Oh, you sweet, innocent woman. You have no idea.

I scanned her body language for any hint of an ulterior motive. By the curve of her shoulders and the way she held her arms, I could tell she felt awkward or nervous. She shuffled slightly on her feet, which only reinforced the fact. Her eyes were round, but there was no hint of deception in them. What was her end goal? I couldn't figure out what kind of game she was playing. One of my gifts was being able to discern people's intentions and motives, but with Sybine, I always came up blank.

When I didn't reply, she swallowed and nodded.

"Consider it an open offer."

She quickly braided her hair back and walked to the door. She hesitated as she placed her hand on the doorknob.

"I'll wait for you outside."

After the door closed, I sat on the edge of the bed with my head in my hands. Not only had I failed to kill Drakkon and

Rhyker, I had also failed to save Varix, and failed to figure out what the hell Sybine wanted with me. The trip to Tamarine was completely unfruitful. All I had to show for it was a scratchy set of lungs and an ache in my back from where Sybine had forced me to the ground. The other scratches and bruises could be easily concealed under my shirt.

Despite the overwhelming failure of the night, I had gained some valuable information, even if I didn't know what it meant yet. I had every reason to suspect that Drakkon had the chains he wanted from Varix, but I had no idea what he meant to do with them. I couldn't ask about the chains without letting them know I had been spying on their conversation, but there was a chance they would tell me on their own time. They did say that if everything went according to plan, they would have a use for me. Even if they didn't, it was possible I would be able to convince Sybine to do some digging for me. Given her talents, it would be a much lower risk if she ever got caught.

After I changed, I met Sybine outside the door. We wandered back down to the bar counter, where I gave the key back to the same barmaid. She gave us a curious glance.

"Enjoy your stay?" she asked.

"Actually, about that coin—"

Sybine's grip around my elbow tightened, and she gave the woman a dazzling smile.

"Best rest in ages, thank you." She tugged on my arm and spun me around before I had a chance to ask for my money back.

When we exited the building, Sybine once again did not allow me to get the first word in.

"She just works there, Loren. She doesn't make the rooms, and she didn't make you give her a gold coin last night. Sometimes it pays more to be kind. Just let it go."

I raised my eyebrows, taking in this woman who only days ago set foot onto the first ship she had ever been on, dressed as a man, who only hours ago lulled a stranger into her peaceful last breaths, and who was infuriatingly difficult to read.

"Come on," she said, not acknowledging my glance, "let's get back to the ship."

Final Requests

Sybine

We weren't the only latecomers to get back to the *Vindicta*. About a dozen or so crew members stumbled off of the row boats after we returned. All of them were in worse shape than we were. Most of them were still drunk.

Loren and I stood in our respective places as the captain inspected the crew to make sure we were all accounted for. I let out a sigh of relief when Rhyker and Drakkon passed us by. A handful of the crew were chosen to stay on deck to help with the undocking process, but the rest of us were released to take care of our own business for the next few hours.

There was no choice in my mind where I needed to be. After yesterday's events, I needed some proper rest and a change of clothes. Loren and I made our way back to our room. He collapsed onto the bed and almost immediately fell asleep. His soft snores echoed around the room as I made my way over to the chests by the wall. I opened mine and grabbed a new binder. I glanced over my shoulder to make sure he wasn't watching before I lifted my shirt over my head and undid the clasps at the front of the tight cloth. I set the new holder on top of the chest for when I woke up and tucked the old one under the clothes. There was no point in wearing it to bed now. Loren already knew who I was. I brought my shirt back over my head and made my way over to the bed.

I crawled over him as gently as I could, trying not to wake him. Unfortunately, my knee caught on his leg, and I took a slight tumble down onto my side of the bed. Loren grumbled.

"Sorry," I whispered.

"S'fine," he mumbled back.

The pale morning light shone through our window and danced off his tan skin. His features were much softer in this light than when I first saw them. His cheekbones were less prominent, and his jaw wasn't as sharp. In this light, he was simply beautiful. I flushed as soon as I realized what I was doing and thinking.

You're only thinking about these things because he kissed you, I said to myself.

And because you liked it, I argued.

Shut up.

I sighed and leaned back. I admired him. That much was clear. He was strong, courageous, and willing to fight for what he believed in. Who was I in comparison? Some lost girl who stole a crown and somehow found herself trapped on a pirate ship with at least two people who were willing to brutally murder someone to get what they wanted.

Don't forget about Harlan. He helped you.

True, Harlan was probably the only man aside from Loren that I was not concerned would murder me in my sleep. But that felt like a standard that was far too low to evaluate someone's character on. Still, there was a familiarity about Harlan. Something that had made me trust him from the moment I'd met him. Perhaps it was because he didn't feel like a threat to me. Or perhaps it was something deeper and more instinctual.

"You are thinking very loudly," Loren grumbled from beside me. "Get some rest, Sybine. You're going to need it."

"You can read my thoughts?" I gasped.

Loren grunted and rolled over to face me just so he could make sure I was looking when he rolled his eyes.

"There is only one of us in this room with special powers here, Sybine, and while I have my talents, it's not me. But I can tell your mind is busy, regardless. Go. To. Sleep," he ordered before rolling over to face away from me again.

I closed my eyes and tried to clear my head. But there was something in the back of my mind that I couldn't let go of. If Drakkon and Rhyker had truly caught us, there was a good chance it would have resulted in a fight. And although Loren was obviously fit to handle himself, the only thing I could rely on was my ability to get into people's heads. That, unfortunately, required me to get close, which was more likely to end in me being stabbed than them forgetting why they were swinging at me in the first place.

There'd been whatever frost thing had happened back on Tamarine, but I had no idea if that had truly been from me, and if it was, how I had channeled it to happen. No. For now, I needed to focus on what I could control.

"Loren?"

He grunted in response.

"Can I ask a favor?"

He sighed.

"What can I do for you, Princess?"

I rolled my eyes at him even though he couldn't see me.

"Varix was confused, Loren. I'm no princess."

He laughed.

"I don't care if you are or if you aren't, Sybine. I just like the way it sounds. Besides, it suits you."

I sighed.

"Would you train me?" I finally got the words out.

He rolled over to face me again.

"Train you?"

I nodded, a little embarrassed.

"I don't want you to feel like you have to protect me all the time...not that you do, of course. I mean, I don't want you to feel obligated to...that's not what I'm trying to say..." I trailed off, flustered.

Loren smirked at me and raised an eyebrow.

"What I am trying to say is that I don't want to have to rely on anyone, and I would like to learn how to protect myself from swords and knives and things." I mentally scolded myself. By the sounds of it, I was in more need of training from a wordsmith.

Loren laughed.

"Fine, Sybine. I'll train you."

I swallowed the dry lump in my throat.

"Thank you."

He rolled over again. I thought the conversation was over, but before I could close my eyes and drift off, he said, "But don't think for a second that I'll go easy on you, Princess."

27

The Training Ring

Sybine

"You're standing wrong again, Princess."

Loren lunged at me, and I stumbled backward. I wasn't fast enough to catch myself, and I ended up landing hard on the floor, almost hitting my head on the wall of our small room in the process. Loren hadn't even touched me. He stopped himself a good arm's length away from me. After an eye roll, he reached down to help me up.

We weren't even using weapons. The only thing we had covered so far was how to stand and how to walk. Two things I thought I used to be relatively good at.

My skin chafed against the binder, and I winced as I brought my arm up to meet his. I tried to push the pain out of my head.

This did a much better job than the chemise, and if I had to put up with a little blistering, then so be it.

"Stop locking your knees," he said as he helped me to my feet again. "Keep them bent slightly. You'll be able to move faster that way...unless your goal is to end up on the flat of your back?" His tone was mocking, as if he was amused by this.

"Of course that's not my goal." I scoffed as he folded his arms over his chest. "You are enjoying this far too much."

He shrugged, but didn't deny my claim. Gods, he was infuriating when he wanted to be.

"Again," he said, giving me almost no warning before taking a few firm steps toward me. This time I sidestepped. I crossed my left leg over my right and—

Loren's arm connected with my shoulders across my back, sending me down to my knees.

"Don't turn your back to your opponent." He reached down. My knees stung from the impact. Heat flooded my body, and I couldn't tell if it was from embarrassment or anger.

"Well then, how the hell am I supposed to move away?" I raised my voice slightly, but not loud enough, hopefully, to wake our neighbors.

Loren's head rolled back, and he let out a long sigh.

"Watch."

Loren stood in front of me, arms slightly outstretched, as if ready to take or strike a blow at any moment. He stood on the balls of his feet, his heels hovering over the ground.

"If someone comes at me from my left, I open my body up and roll my shoulder back like this." He moved his left leg behind his right and made a slight jump to the side. "If you time it right, you might even get a chance to get them in the side or back. If nothing else, give them a good shove and get the hell out. It should buy you some time at least. Here. Now you try."

I tried to copy his stance, but I felt unsteady on my toes, like if at any moment I was going to tip over. Thankfully, we had moved the chests onto the bed, so if I did fall, at least I wouldn't crack my head open on the side of one of them.

"This feels really awkward," I admitted. "I have no balance like this."

He nodded.

"The more you practice, the easier it will get. You're training more than just your muscles. You're training your mind to know where your body is and where it needs to go next. Now I'm going to attack your left side just like I did before. I want you to do what I just showed you. Are you ready?"

I swallowed.

"Let's just do this."

His lips twitched to the side slightly, and he made another lunge forward. I tried my best to replicate Loren's footwork. Because I was already on my toes, it was surprisingly easy to make the transition. A surge of confidence ran through me, and I kicked my leg out to push Loren, just like he had said I could do if I were in that situation. I almost made contact when he threw his arm out and grabbed me by the ankle. I didn't even have enough time to register what was happening before I was twisted in the air and thrown back on the ground, this time on my stomach, with Loren holding my foot to my backside. I tried to push myself up, but Loren held me down with his other hand between my shoulder blades. He knelt between my legs, and for a brief moment, I was worried what someone would think if they were to walk in on us right now.

I grunted.

"I told you I wouldn't be easy on you," he whispered in my ear. "Next lesson: how to get out of an impossible situation." His grip tightened around my left ankle, and he pushed down harder on my back. "If you're pinned like this and your opponent is stronger than you, you only have a few options: words or leverage." He shifted slightly between my legs. "Right now, you have one advantage over me. Your weight is distributed evenly, and mine is not. That means, if you move correctly, you might be able to shift me off balance. Try rolling to your right."

I pushed up with my left arm and tried to rotate my body around, but I barely moved.

"Good. With how I'm holding you, most of my weight is being focused toward the left side of your body. That means that it will be difficult to work against. So instead, use that to your advantage and try to roll to your left."

This time, I pushed up with my right arm and found that although there was significant resistance, I could actually get myself to a point where I might be able to make a sudden move to flip over. So I did.

Loren fell onto his left shoulder and rolled onto his back. Somehow my leg had latched around his, bringing me with him. I stopped, straddling his hips. My hands hovered in front of me, and I froze. I had no idea what to do now. I could feel his heat everywhere our bodies met, and it sent tiny sparks over my skin. His eyes widened as he looked up at me, and I could have sworn I saw his pupils grow slightly. I might have been on top of him, but that in no way meant that I had the advantage in this situation. Loren reached up and grasped my wrists with one hand so fast that I barely saw it happen. In one swift movement, he twisted us around again so I was on my back, looking up at him. He held my hands over my head, and with his other hand, he traced a line across my throat. I shivered and arched involuntarily.

"Never hesitate." His voice was low and sharp, and I couldn't help the flutter that it sent through me. Slowly, his eyes drifted down. They settled on my slightly parted lips. I let out a sharp exhale as a blush of warmth spread through me. I was suddenly reminded of how his lips felt against mine and their soft, yet commanding, pace. I wondered if he felt the same way I did. If this thing between us was more than just some fantasy or figment of my imagination.

The breakfast bell rang before I had a chance to find out.

Loren let out a sharp exhale and released his grip on my wrists. Every part of me was thrumming with energy, and I couldn't help but feel a little disappointed as he raised himself off of me.

"Looks like we're done for the day," he said, as if whatever that moment was between us had never happened.

28

Second

Elora

What the fuck was that? I mentally scolded myself. I agreed to train Sybine for two reasons: so she would be less of a liability to me if we ever found ourselves in another Drakkon/Rhyker situation, and so that I knew what she knew. In other words, I wouldn't have to split my attention to try to keep her alive, and if she decided to betray me, I would always have the upper hand, since I knew her training. I had not agreed to train her so we could have moments like that.

"Somethin' on your mind, lad?"

Harlan had somehow materialized beside me. My heart stuttered for a moment as I came back to my senses.

I shook my head.

"Not at all."

"Hmm." His eyes narrowed, and his skin crinkled around the sides of them.

"Save your suspicions for someone who deserves them."

Harlan chuckled.

"Sure thing, lad, as soon as you tell me why you're hiding down here in the supply closet, lost in thought."

I looked around, as if seeing my surroundings for the first time. I was in the supply closet, but why? And how? I didn't remember walking in here. I grabbed the first thing on the shelf in front of me.

"Just looking for this."

Harlan raised an eyebrow at me.

"And is there a reason you're needin' oil like that?"

I looked down and read the label. "Doyle's Oils: For Skin Tensions and Other Sessions."

Fuck.

I cleared my throat.

"Dry skin. You know, from the salt water."

"Uh huh." Harlan crossed his arms over his chest.

The old man was taunting me. And even worse, I was letting him. I shook my head. I refused to feel embarrassed about something that there was no shame in, even if I was using it for...other things. Which I wasn't.

"Loren?" Rhyker stood in the doorway behind Harlan, who visibly stiffened at Rhyker's rough voice. He eyed the container in my hands curiously for a moment before returning his gaze to mine. "Come with me. The captain and I would like a word."

I nodded my head and made my way out the door to follow Rhyker. Harlan turned his body to let me through, and as I passed by him, he whispered, "I hope your skin feels better soon." I couldn't help the flush that spread through my cheeks. Harlan chuckled to himself softly as I turned the corner down the hall.

I tried to put Harlan's words and the events with Sybine out of my mind as I followed Rhyker down the familiar halls to Drakkon's quarters. I needed to be as clearheaded as possible for this conversation, regardless of whether I was promoted.

There were three potential outcomes to this meeting. First, I could be promoted to second mate, which was the best-case scenario. It required much less work on my part, and would likely result in the least amount of bloodshed. Second, I could be ordered to remain at my station with no promotion. It wouldn't be impossible to get close enough to Drakkon if that were the case, but it would make everything a hell of a lot harder. And third...if they knew it had been me outside Varix's tent, then it was likely I was walking to my execution.

Rhyker knocked twice on Drakkon's door.

"Enter."

Rhyker gestured for me to enter first. He held the door open, and I stepped through. The pale afternoon light shone through the windows, making the room look much more welcoming than it felt. Just as he was the first time we met in this room, Drakkon sat behind his desk. There was a book open in front of him he was keenly studying. The bloodred binding starkly contrasted the pale, yellowed paper, and there was something about all of it that made my skin crawl.

Drakkon snapped the book back together as I approached. Before I saw any other details, he had tucked it into a drawer to his right and locked it away. He took the key out and placed the chain that it rested on around his neck. It dangled just above the loose ties of his black shirt. He sat back and laced his fingers together, while his elbows rested on the arms of his chair. His coat was open, and it fanned around him, giving him the appearance of sitting on a throne rather than this old wooden thing.

"You wanted to see me, Captain?"

He nodded and gestured to the two seats in front of me.

If he was going to kill me, he probably wouldn't have asked me to sit first. Although, it would be convenient for him to have Rhyker attack me from behind first. Just to be safe, I chose the chair facing the door, near the left-hand side of the desk. Although it was further away from the exit, it would be easier to see an attack, not to mention that it would be a straight line to escape.

I pulled out the chair and took my seat. I made eye contact with Rhyker, who was smirking by the door. He took out a key and gave the door a quick lock before turning around to join us a few moments later.

My stomach twisted. Maybe this was an execution after all. With the door locked, I would have no choice but to fight my way out. And without the element of surprise, that was going to be a very hard battle.

The scars on Drakkon's face seemed to shine as his lips turned upward with what looked like amusement, as if he was mocking me for my past failures and potential future ones. Those damn scars. I wanted to rip them off his face.

I let my left hand fall to my side as if to rest it on my leg. My fingertips brushed against the dagger there, and I waited to see who was going to have to make the first move.

"The last time we were all in this room together, you petitioned me for a higher rank on this ship. I know what it's like to be young and driven, and I see that in you."

I wanted to vomit. We were nothing alike. I resented him for even considering it. Driven? No. He may have wanted to appear disciplined and driven, but I knew what he truly was. He was everything cold and ruthless, willing to stop at nothing to get what he wanted. He didn't care about anyone or anything. My father had taken him in like a son, and Drakkon had repaid him by stabbing him in the back. He was exactly the vicious monster he had based his reputation on.

"You honor me," I lied.

He eyed me carefully, and my fingers gripped the hilt of my dagger as I waited for his reply. Rhyker once again was completely silent and unmoving, but he kept his feet firmly placed on the ground and never relaxed in his seat. I spared a quick glance at him, and just as I suspected, his hand rested on the hilt of his blade at his side.

My best option would be to throw my first dagger at Rhyker to immobilize him. He would likely expect a shot to his face or chest, which meant aiming for his groin, thigh, or foot would have a better chance at landing. My eyes darted back to Drakkon, who was studying me with a cold intensity. I would have to be quick and precise. There was a small lantern lit at the corner of his desk nearest Rhyker. Perhaps if I threw that at him, it would give me enough time to get the key off of Rhyker and get out of here. That still left me stranded on a ship with them, but hopefully it would buy me enough time to come up with a better plan.

"Relax, Loren," Drakkon said. "I didn't summon you here to kill you."

Yet. The unspoken word hung suspended in the air between us.

"Then why am I here?" I asked.

Drakkon ran his tongue over his teeth, under his lips.

"I've considered your proposal. And I accept. Under one condition."

He...accepted? I could barely believe the words. It seemed...too easy. My stomach knotted.

Rhyker leaned forward, his face a stony mask of incredulity.

"Sir, I thought we agreed—"

"Enough, Rhyker!" Drakkon's voice boomed through the room as he slammed his fists down in front of him. "You do not have the authority to speak against or undermine me," he hissed.

Rhyker flinched as if Drakkon had delivered a physical blow to his face.

Drakkon turned back to me, his hands now flat on the surface of his desk.

"I still have use for you, Loren. But first, I need to know whether I can trust you. I'm sure you can understand."

I nodded, unsure of whether the tone of my voice would give away my confusion or hesitation.

"Good. Tomorrow morning, you will be given an order. If you accept and fulfill this order, the position is yours. If not..." He sat back in his chair. "Well, I don't think it takes too much imagination to figure out the consequences."

I nodded again. Something felt wrong about Rhyker's outburst and Drakkon's insistence, but I wouldn't find the answers by sitting here with them any longer.

"Thank you for the opportunity, sir."

My scar burned across my chest. Despite the warning in my mind, I was happy to be one step closer to my goal. I had waited a long time for this.

The
Dragon

29

Blade

Elora

"Are you sure you're ready for this?"

Sybine's neck tensed against the blade I held to her throat as she nodded.

Her body squirmed between mine and the wall. I braced my knee between her legs, and I held her arm down to her side with my left hand so she couldn't move.

"Okay then," I said, "next lesson. If someone ever had you against the wall like this, you need to think quickly. What do you have access to?"

She thought for a second.

"Nothing," she admitted. "My bag is on my right leg, and it's not like I carry anything other than the crown and a few coins in there anyway."

I rolled my eyes at her. Annoyance bubbled through me.

"What do you have access to?" I asked again. "Think, Sybine. You have one free hand. Pushing against me would be useless, so you need to come up with something else."

Her left hand trailed up and down the side of her body. She let out a frustrated sigh.

"There's nothing, I—wait."

She moved her hand from her body to mine. I tried to ignore the fire that sparked under my skin from where she touched me. Finally, she made her way down to my leg and wrapped her hand around the hilt of my other dagger I kept there.

"Good. What next?" I said a little breathlessly.

She swallowed.

"I use it?"

"Is that a question? Or are you actually going to do something?" I was surprised at the hoarse tone of my voice.

She pulled up quickly with a jerking motion, unsheathing the blade. The movement was so obvious that had I not basically told her to do it myself, I still would have seen it coming from a mile away.

I removed my dagger from her throat, stabbed it into the wall next to her head, and grabbed onto her wrist. She let out a startled gasp as I threw her hand against the wall, and the dagger went tumbling to the ground. It landed with a soft clink next to my boots.

"Good. You've partially disarmed me. Neither of us have weapons in our hands, but I still have the advantage with you against the wall. From here, you can try two things: hit their nose with the front part of your head, or bring your knee up between their legs as hard as you can. Both require you to know your enemy and yourself."

Sybine let out a shaky breath.

"And what should I do with you?"

I laughed.

"Hope that I'm not your opponent."

I released my grip on her wrists and pushed myself off her. There was a faint blush that painted her cheeks. The low light of the morning sun beamed through the window and highlighted her face. She was beautiful, and despite my best efforts, I couldn't push down the flutters that rose in my stomach when I looked at her.

I leaned forward to grab my dagger from the wall. She stared up at me. Her eyes were dark pools with a ring of silver green around them. Her lips parted slightly as she let out an uneven breath. Was she tired? Or was it possible she was...turned on by this? The signs were there: the flushed cheeks, the darkened eyes, and just a hint of bumps along the skin of her arms. We had shared one kiss, and that had been a life-or-death situation. Still, I wondered if it would feel the same with her against this wall, legs wrapped around me, calling my name into the darkness as I drove her wild with desire.

I pushed the thought aside. That was not going to happen. We were training. She was going to learn so that I didn't have to worry about her slipping up and making me choose between protecting her and killing Drakkon. The last thing I needed was for him or Rhyker to use her against me.

"What are you thinking?" she asked softly.

I grabbed my dagger from the wall and forced all thoughts of leverage and emotions for Sybine out of my mind. I needed to focus on what I knew. And what I knew was how to fight.

"Again," I said, and she shivered.

"Again?"

I took a few steps back, putting some much needed space between us. It was easier to concentrate that way.

I gestured to the ground with my blade.

"Pick it up."

"Okay," she said shakily. She bent over and took the knife from the ground, holding it awkwardly at the hilt as if it would bite her without any notice.

"There are a few different ways to hold a knife. Most people use a grip like this." I placed my dagger in my palm with the blade pointing out toward my thumb. "Wrap your fingers around it as if you're going to make a fist."

Sybine followed my movements.

"Good. What's nice about this grip is that it gives you the opportunity to strike easily when you're in close quarters. Like if I had you against the wall again. You'd be able to either stab me in the leg, side, or neck, or if your aim is good, through my heart if you wanted to."

"Through your...heart?"

I nodded.

"Come here."

She closed the space between us.

"Give me your hand," I said as I reached out to her.

I was forced to take a deep breath as she placed her hand in mine. My skin burned under her touch. It sent sparks all over my body, accumulating in my stomach.

I cleared my throat and lifted my arm up.

"There's a spot just between the ribs right here."

I guided her fingers over the small bumps of bones at my side until I found the right space. Sybine swallowed, and she ran her teeth over her bottom lip. Her eyes were focused on our hands, but I couldn't take my gaze away from her. Her touch felt good. Too good. And once again, the intrusive thoughts came racing back.

"Here?" Her voice was so soft that I barely heard it.

She pressed her fingers into my side, and although my shirt separated us, it felt like she had sunk deep into my skin.

"Yes," I said, a little breathless. My skin was burning hot and she was so close. So close that I could just-

"This is how I'd pierce your heart?"

I nodded, trying desperately to think of anything else other than wanting to feel her lips on mine again.

"Just...one thrust. Aim for the opposite shoulder. You'll never miss."

Sybine tilted her chin up to meet my gaze. It was like a shockwave through my body. Gods, what was happening to me?

I brought my arm down and let go of her hand. She took a small step back and trained her eyes on the window behind me.

"It'll be breakfast soon," she said as she held my knife back out to me.

I took it from her grasp and re-sheathed it at my side.

"I was thinking maybe we could—"

Two loud knocks at our door interrupted her. A small white envelope slid underneath.

"What's that?" she asked.

"I'm not sure," I admitted as I walked past her to pick it up.

The envelope was sealed with blood red wax containing a skull in it. No doubt it was Drakkon's seal. I turned it over in my hand and saw "Loren" written on the front.

Keeping my back to Sybine, I opened it. I quickly skimmed the contents to myself, and I clenched my teeth together when my eyes landed on the last order at the bottom.

Attached here is the crew registry for the Vindicta. *As you can see, Sebastien has not officially committed himself to the crew, the captain, the ship, or this journey. Your order is to rectify this immediately.*

Sincerely,

Rhyker, First Mate of Drakkon Stormson, Captain of the Vindicta

Bile rose in my throat. I had been right to have my suspicions from the beginning. If he had no intentions of using the blood binding for his own purposes, he would have never requested this. I had no idea what he could do with this power, only that the thought of it made my stomach feel like it was full of rocks.

"What is it?" she asked.

I kept my back turned to her and thought about the best way to ask my question.

"At the Stumbling Sailor, when you put your name down for the crew, did you...did you bind yourself?"

Sybine was suspiciously quiet behind me. I finally turned to face her. She bit her lips together and shifted her weight on her feet.

"No, I didn't," she finally answered.

I sighed and ran a hand through my hair.

"What is it, Loren?" she asked again.

I re-opened the note and read it out loud. When I finished, Sybine looked at me confused.

"Why does it matter if I did or not? I'm here, aren't I?"

I crushed the paper in my hand.

"It matters."

"But how? My name is there, and I am here and—"

"You don't understand, Sybine. It matters!"

I let out a low grunt of frustration. I turned around and threw my fist against the wall. I rested my forehead against it and closed my eyes. How could I have been so stupid? I should have waited longer. I should have never bound myself this way. And now...now it was too late.

"It matters," I said again, my voice low and defeated, "if he wants to control you."

Bound in Blood

Sybine

"My father once told me a story about a captain that went mad and sacrificed his entire crew. He used the blood binding to do it. He didn't even have to get any blood on his hands. They all just...killed themselves."

I sat beside Loren on the bed, wide-eyed at the story.

"That kind of power exists? But why? How?"

"The blood binding," he said simply. He held the crew list in his hands and stared down at it. "There's a reason it's so frowned upon, even by a pirate's standard. Binding yourself to a captain, the crew, and the ship is like handing over your fate to whoever holds the spell."

It was too much for me to process. My mind spun with the sudden information. I looked down at the paper, at Loren's name and his bloody fingerprint beside it.

"Is that...the spell?" I asked.

"It's part of it. But I don't think this is the original paper we all signed. Sure, it looks the same, but I doubt Drakkon would just hand it over to me freely. Whatever he has planned must rely on the blood binding."

I sighed with relief.

"So I don't have to use my blood on that thing?"

He looked up at me. His eyes were sad and glossy.

"I don't think it's that easy, Sybine. Feel it."

He held out the paper to me, and I touched the corner. Instantly I felt something, an odd and foreign, yet familiar, energy within it. I pulled my hand away, afraid of what it might do to me if I lingered too long.

"You feel that?" he asked.

I nodded as I held my hand to my chest.

"It's enchanted," he said before I could ask. "My guess is that it holds the same binding magic the original did."

We sat in silence for a moment, neither of us wanting to ask the obvious question: what comes next?

Loren's eyes drifted to the window longingly. It was a look I hadn't seen on him before. He was usually so confident, so smart, so aware. And now I saw something, a small crack in the armor he wore. It made me want to throw my arms around him and console him, but something held me back. I didn't know him...and he didn't really know me either. And this...this was far too much for me to handle. I wouldn't put my fate in someone else's hands. That was the whole reason I agreed to board this ship in the first place. But a part of me was terrified about what that would mean for Loren. If he didn't do what the captain and Rhyker wanted, what would they do? Would they punish him? Punish me? Worse?

Loren turned back around to face me. The sadness that plagued him before was washed away, and I recognized the determination behind his eyes. I swallowed nervously, scared of what he might do next. Would he force me to do it? He could if he wanted to. I knew that. Two days of defense training would get me nowhere with him. I wanted to disappear, to hide, to fade away, to never confront whatever this was again.

"Sybine?" Loren stood abruptly and looked around the room. "Where did you—" His eyes landed on me again.

He blinked and rubbed at his eyes and then blinked again.

"How did you do that?" he asked.

I gave him a nervous glance and leaned back, away from him.

"Do what?"

"You just...disappeared...and then...you were back."

"What?" I looked down at my arms and hands. I turned them over, but they seemed real to me. "I didn't do anything." I brought my gaze back up to his.

Something like a flash of realization crossed his face.

"I thought my eyes were playing tricks on me, but I've seen you do this before."

"What? When?"

"In the hallway when I was practicing. That first morning on the ship, and you scared me. And I think...I think I scared you too."

I remembered feeling scared that he would turn on me. That I would do anything to just slip away. I remembered thinking that all I wanted to do was just...disappear.

I looked down at my hands again. They still seemed the same. But there was an energy humming inside me, just at the edge of my mind. Something that had felt dormant for a long time and was just beginning to wake up.

"I...I don't know how I did that." As soon as the words came out, I knew they weren't the whole truth. Even if I wasn't completely sure what the actual truth was.

Loren nodded his head, as if deciding something. He brought his hand to his side and retrieved the dagger from it. At first, I thought he might attack me after all, but instead, he sat back down on the bed and slowly bent over to take his boot off. We both winced as he sliced the corner of his toe, drawing a thin line of blood.

"Give me your hand," he ordered.

I was too confused to do anything but obey. He wiped the blood from his toe and placed it on my index finger. Then he nodded to the paper sitting on the bed between us.

"Sign it," he said.

"But I...you—"

"Just do it."

Without thinking about the consequences, I placed my finger on the paper, smearing the blood beside my name. My eyes widened as I realized what I had done.

"Loren, why did you do that?"

He reached into his pocket and grabbed one of his black handkerchiefs. He held it to his toe and put pressure on the place where he had sliced his skin. He let out a long sigh.

"I'm already damned, Sybine. You saw my name. You saw my blood." He turned to face me. His gaze was so intense that I nearly couldn't hold it. "But you...you could be the key that gets us out of this."

31

Secrets in the Shadows

Sybine

"It's not your blood. It's not even your real name. You are as safe as you can possibly be. I was already bound. It was a logical decision."

"A logical decision?" I threw my arms in the air. "You cut your toe open. On purpose!"

He nodded as he put his boot back on.

"Yes, because when I bring back this paper to Drakkon and Rhyker, they are going to check to make sure that there are no scratches on my hands or arms. And they are going to check to see if your fingerprint matches mine. When they don't see any fresh cuts and they confirm our fingerprints are different, they will have no choice but to think that you have been bound as well."

I crossed my arms over my chest and fought a wince as the binder ran across my chafed skin.

"How do you know they won't check your feet as well?"

He gave me a sly grin.

"I don't. Consider it a...calculated risk."

I rolled my eyes.

"That barely worked out for you last time," I pointed out.

He shrugged.

"But it did work out for me, didn't it? Now come here and give me your hand."

He took his other dagger out and placed it on the bed.

"What's that for?" I eyed it suspiciously.

"If they check your hands right now, they're going to see smooth skin. Would smooth skin leave a mark like that?" He gestured to the paper. "Now be careful. Don't press too hard. You don't want to cut your whole finger off."

I sighed and took the blade from the bed. I held it to my pointer finger on my left hand and slowly pushed in. There was a sharp almost-snap as it pierced my skin, and a small pool of blood appeared. I immediately removed it from my finger and gave it back to Loren.

"Here, use this and put some pressure on it," Loren said as he handed me a clean handkerchief.

I wrapped it around my finger and held it tight. It throbbed so hard that it felt like it had its own heartbeat.

Loren reached over and grabbed the paper from between us.

He hesitated for a moment. The energy around his body shifted. The confidence retreated slightly, and a flash of uncertainty crossed his face.

"What is it?" I asked.

He looked up at me and ran his tongue over his lips.

"If you learned anything from Varix's tent, you will say no to this," he said.

I met his gaze, confused.

"Say no to what?"

Why the hell had I said yes to this?

Drakkon's room was much larger than ours, and for a moment, I allowed myself to be spiteful. Training in our small space was only useful if I came across a scenario that required me to attack or defend in close quarters. If we had a space like that, we would be able to do so much more. I could learn how to hold a sword, not just a knife. I could learn how to aim, how to run, how to lunge. But we didn't have the space, and it wasn't worth the time dwelling on it.

I moved over to the desk. Loren had mentioned a book with bloodred binding, but the only things on the wood surface were an old map with torn edges, an oil lamp, a compass, a few scattered pieces of paper, and some kind of steel device with its two points stuck into the map in different places. I figured I wouldn't find the book lying wide open, ready for me to inspect the pages, but I was still disappointed when I didn't find it there within easy access.

I bent over to inspect the locked drawer that Loren had said Drakkon put the book in. The keyhole looked to be similar to the others I had broken into before. All I needed was something long and thin. And I knew just the thing.

I grabbed the steel contraption from the map and placed it in the keyhole gently. After a few seconds of tapping and twisting, the lock clicked open. I twisted the lock around and pulled the drawer out.

The book wasn't there. The drawer was empty, filled with nothing but shadows.

"Shit," I cursed under my breath.

What was I supposed to do now? Where was I supposed to look? I sighed and closed the drawer again before taking a long look around the room. The only other furniture in the room, besides the bed and desk, was a large wardrobe a few paces away from me.

I carefully set the points of the steel device where I'd originally found them. I wedged them back into the two small holes on the map and pressed down so they would stay upright, just as they had been when I'd walked in.

My focus returned to the wardrobe, and I made my way over to it. Aside from its sheer enormity, it didn't look any different from the ones I had seen before. There were no intricately carved patterns in the wood, and no decorations of silver or gold around it. It was simple, with two black handles to open it. I wrapped my fingers around them and pulled.

The inside was just as plain as the outside. Drakkon's coats, shirts, and trousers hung from wooden rods. Three sets of boots sat at the bottom underneath the clothes on the left-hand side.

I carefully sorted through the pockets of his jackets. Aside from a stray piece of cloth, there was nothing in them either. Frustrated, I crouched down and checked the bottom of the wardrobe. There was nothing behind his boots, and nothing else on the floor of it, from what I could tell.

I balled my hands into fists. There was nothing here. Or, if there was, I had no idea where to look for it. The bed maybe? I took a quick peek underneath it and saw only the smooth surface of the wooden floor.

He wouldn't keep anything hidden in his sheets, would he?

Just as I finished asking myself the question, voices began to echo through the hall. I had already been here for far too long.

Shit.

There was only one way in and out of this room, and if they were in the hallway, it meant that I couldn't leave without being caught.

Shit, I said to myself again.

The voices were getting closer. My heart began to race as I panicked. Where was I supposed to go? There was the wardrobe, but if I closed it and he locked it, how long would I be stuck in there? Under the desk? That seemed like the worst option. All it would take was for him to sit down and he would discover me immediately. The bed? I scoffed.

Yeah right. Not in a million years.

So where?

Think. Think. Think.

Where would Loren go? He would have likely never gotten himself into this situation in the first place, but if he did, what would he think? What would he do? Where would he go?

What do you have access to? His words echoed through my head. I took a quick inventory. I had my bag at my side, as I always did, but that would be less than helpful. I stood and looked over at the desk. There was whatever I had used to pick the lock. I could use that as some kind of weapon if I needed to. I shook my head. There was no way I would get close enough to make that work, and even if I did, there were two of them. Whoever I didn't stab would be bound to make me pay for it, likely immediately,

What do you have access to?

There was my ability to get into people's heads, but that took time, and I had never tried it on more than one person simultaneously. And, once again, I needed to get close enough to touch them in order for it to work. I could hide behind the door and wait for them to come through, but if they were too far apart, or they saw me before I had a chance to make my move, I would be in trouble.

There was a gentle tug at the edge of my mind, just like earlier this morning. Something caught my eye, and I looked down. I held my hand out in front of me. It flickered in and out of sight.

The voices were at the door. I had no choice. I closed my eyes and called on the power that rested deep in my chest. Just like before, I focused on my overwhelming desire to disappear. I hesitantly opened an eye and glanced down at where my hand should be. It was strange. When I looked closely enough, I could see small ripples where my skin would have been. My form ebbed and flowed just like...water. It took an extraordinary amount of focus and energy to maintain.

"Leave us." The sound of the captain's voice nearly paralyzed me. The door opened, and Drakkon and Rhyker stepped through. My heart sank when Rhyker turned around and closed it behind him.

I froze, terrified that I wouldn't be able to hold whatever this liquid form was, and that I might do something that would give me away. I didn't make a sound or a move as they both walked toward the desk. Drakkon sat behind it, and Rhyker pulled out the chair to the right. From where I was standing, I could see both of them clearly, and I prayed to all the gods that they wouldn't be able to see me.

Drakkon pulled the key off his neck. Its smooth, gold surface glinted in the afternoon light coming through the windows. He reached down to his right and placed the key in the lock. He hesitated, and his eyes narrowed before he finally opened the drawer. I was surprised to see him lean over further and reach below the drawer. Was there a second lock that I had missed? Another key? When he sat back up, he was holding a thick, red leather-bound book in his hands. I ground my teeth together. It had been there this whole time? But how? It didn't matter now.

"We're getting close," Drakkon said as he placed the book on the top of the map on his desk. He flipped it open to a page near the back.

I took a hesitant step forward. When the floorboards didn't creak under me, I took another, and another, until I was against the wall beside the door, hidden in the shadow. I forced myself to take long, smooth breaths.

You can do this, I told myself.

Rhyker sat forward in his chair, leaning his elbows on his knees.

"Have you found a way into the lair?" he asked.

Drakkon hummed in response as he flipped a page over. He ran his finger over the black drawings and stopped near the bottom.

A torrent of questions raced through my mind. What lair? And why did they want to go there? What did it hold? And what the hell was in that book?

"And Loren? Are you going to tell me why you changed your mind?"

I held my breath to keep from gasping.

Loren?

"I don't need to explain myself to you." Drakkon's tone held a warning.

Rhyker tensed as if struck. My eyes darted back and forth between them. A muscle twitched at Drakkon's jaw, and he let out a soft sigh.

The captain stood and moved around the desk to Rhyker. He placed a hand on his face and ran his thumb over his cheek.

"But I do need you. You and Keldroth will get us through the trials. That's what I want. Have I not given you everything you wanted?"

My eyes widened. What the hell was I watching?

"I would..." Rhyker paused, and his head fell slightly. His fists clenched at the fabric of his trousers. "I would do anything for you. You know that."

Holy shit.

It was a good thing I was so well hidden, because I was relatively certain nothing else would be able to mask the look of complete bewilderment and shock on my face.

"I know." Drakkon's voice was the softest I had ever heard him use, but something about the way he held himself and the way his gaze hardened told me that there was something else behind his words.

The captain moved to stand in front of Rhyker, and he tilted his first mate's chin up to look at him.

"I need the boy alive. For now," he said simply.

Rhyker and I both swallowed at the same time.

"Soon," Drakkon purred, "we will have everything."

He let go of Rhyker's face and returned to his seat on the other side of the desk.

"But until that time, I need you to continue with your duties." Drakkon returned his focus to the book in front of him.

"Yes, sir." Rhyker stared at the captain with wide eyes.

Several seconds passed before Drakkon looked up from his pages again. He let out a long breath and interlaced his fingers together before placing his hands on the open book in front of him.

He looked at Rhyker expectantly.

"There is one other thing, sir," Rhyker said finally. "Some of the men are getting...restless."

A low rumble began in Drakkon's throat. The sound sent a shiver up my back.

"What harm would it be to take on a few wome—"

Drakkon slammed his hands down on the table so hard that it sent the compass beside him toppling to the ground.

"Don't finish that thought," he ordered.

"But sir, it's been fourteen years; surely that's long enou—"

Drakkon stood and leaned over the table. Rhyker shrank in his chair as the captain towered over him.

"You think I would rather have these brainless oafs than women on board?" Drakkon hissed. "My wife was worth five of them. Maybe more. You presume everything and know nothing."

Rhyker and I both flinched at his words.

"Twelve years," he scoffed. "Not even if I lived for another hundred years would I let another woman on board. The gods will not make a mockery of me." Drakkon sat back down in his chair with a deep scowl on his face. "You think I don't know their value, but you're wrong, Rhyker. It's precisely because I know their value that they do not sail with us. Never. Again."

I swallowed the acid in my throat. So that was why Brandor wouldn't let me board at first. What would he do if he knew who I truly was? Or worse, if he discovered me listening to this interaction? A sense of unease flooded my veins.

"It's time for you to leave."

Rhyker's fists clenched as he ran his tongue over his lips. Without another word, he stood and made his way toward the door.

I looked down at my hands. I still couldn't see my skin, but I also couldn't completely make out the floorboards beneath me. A cold exhaustion crept up my arms from my fingers. I didn't know how much longer I would be able to stay like this.

I caught a glimpse of the two open pages of the book and frantically tried to take in as much as I could from it. There were words I couldn't read from this distance, but I could make out the five drawings. Each of them was circled, and there were complex designs linking them, but the actual illustrations themselves were relatively simple. I tried my best to commit them to memory. They didn't look like they described a ritual involving chains and blood, but if Drakkon was studying them, they had to mean something. Maybe Loren would have a better idea.

Rhyker pulled the door open and glanced over his shoulder again before leaving. Grateful for the fact that he didn't immediately close it again, I followed him out into the dark hall and stayed a few paces behind him until we turned into the dining room. I let him continue through as I leaned back and fell down the wall. I brought my knees up to my chest and buried my face in my hands.

Every part of me ached. My muscles were sore from training, my skin was raw from the binder, and my mind was overstretched to the point where it felt like snapping.

I left the captain's quarters with more questions than I went in with. My head was swimming, and all I wanted to do was curl up and sleep for days. The edges of my vision blurred, and I couldn't fight the heavy weight in my limbs. I decided to rest against the wall. Just for a few minutes. Just until some of the exhaustion wore off. As I began to doze off, I heard my name being called by a familiar voice.

Gramps?

32

Exposed

Elora

Sybine was deathly pale. Her petite frame looked even smaller, curled up on the bed as she was. A part of me wanted to wake her to find out what she had seen, to learn how she had escaped, but she looked so peaceful. It felt wrong to disturb her.

Fortunately, I didn't have to. She stretched out her arms, and her eyelids fluttered open.

I sat down on the bed beside her. It dipped under my weight, and she shifted slightly toward me.

"Loren?" Her voice was still shaky from sleep.

I nodded.

"How did I...did you bring me back to the room?"

I pinched my eyebrows together in confusion.

"No. You didn't get here on your own?"

She shook her head. Her eyes drifted off in thought.

"Are you okay? You weren't at dinner."

She slowly pushed herself up to rest on her elbow.

"I slept through dinner?" she asked. Her eyes widened. "Oh gods, Rhyker is going to kill me."

I shook my head. I had told them that Sebastien had felt sick after seeing his blood on the paper that morning. The lie was a simple exchange of favors. At least that's what I kept trying to tell myself.

"Don't worry about him."

She eyed me curiously.

"But if you're ever around Rhyker and blood, pretend to faint or look sick."

"Uhm...okay," she said hesitantly. "Thank you...I think."

"Don't mention it."

Sybine pushed herself the rest of the way up and twisted around to hang her legs over the edge beside me.

She flexed her toes, and I could hear the soft tapping noises from her grinding her teeth together.

"Is everything okay?" I asked her.

She took a deep breath and tilted her head back slightly. She refused to meet my gaze.

"I'm sorry," she said.

My stomach twisted. That was not a good start to her telling me what had happened earlier.

"I...I didn't find the book," she admitted.

She told me about how she had searched through Drakkon's desk and wardrobe and couldn't find anything. And then Drakkon had retrieved it from the drawer she had looked through.

"It must have had a false bottom," I told her.

A thin line appeared between her eyebrows, and she tilted her head at me.

"It's a simple illusion to keep things hidden. To make sure people like us don't find what we're looking for."

"Oh, that's...clever."

I shrugged, but I couldn't help the sinking feeling in my gut.

"Were you able to read anything?" I asked.

She bit her lips together.

"I'm sorry, Loren. All I saw were a few drawings, and that's it. They didn't even make any sense. There was some kind of rock frame around them and waves crashing against the outside. Then, in the frame, there was a sketch of a ball of fire with a hand over top of it. Another one had three doors. Then there was one with two hands pushing into a head, one with stairs, and the last one was a book with smoke coming out of it. Does any of that make sense to you?"

It all sounded mad to me.

I shook my head.

"There's...something else," she admitted.

She took a few long breaths. She brought her hands up and adjusted her shirt under her armpits. She twisted her body around as if she were stiff and needed to stretch.

"They said something about keeping a boy alive...for now. And Loren...I think they meant you."

Fuck.

"Why would you think that?" I kept my voice steady, careful not to reveal my emotions, despite their attempt to drown me.

She kept her eyes down.

"You said that Rhyker wasn't happy about the captain naming you second if you followed the order. And then, this afternoon, Rhyker asked why Drakkon had changed his mind, and he said something about keeping the boy alive for now. Who else could it be?"

She finally looked up at me. Her sad eyes were wide and round, as if she were terrified.

I clenched my teeth and pinched my lips together in a hard line.

"Fuck," I said under my breath. "Did they say when?"

"When?"

I nodded slightly.

"When they were planning on...killing me."

She shook her head.

"I...I'm sorry. They didn't say anything else."

I slammed my eyes shut as the weight of it hit me. I knew that there was a chance this vendetta would claim my life, but I had hoped I would be able to take Drakkon down with me. Now that I was forced to confront it, I wasn't sure I was so ready to face my death.

How would he do it? Would he parade me in front of the crew like an animal? Butcher me like he had my father? Or would he make me do it myself?

A shiver ran down my spine. Fear was no longer familiar to me. It made me feel sick and out of control. I closed my eyes and tried to channel it into anger. Anger toward Drakkon for killing my father. Anger toward my mother for dying. Anger toward David for abandoning us. Anger toward myself for not saving us. I tried and tried and tried, but all that rose to the surface was an overwhelming sense of grief that I had held down for my entire life. I was flooded with it like a burst dam that was beyond repair. The bricks that I had so sturdily built up around my heart came crashing down all at once until I was stripped bare. I had never felt so exposed, so vulnerable, so weak...so tired.

When I opened my eyes again, Sybine was staring up at me, her eyes wide and glossy. Warm tracks of tears trailed down my face in a heavy stream I had no control over. I let out a shaky breath and ran the back of my hand over my face to wipe my tears, but it was useless. They just kept falling. And worse, I had broken in front of her.

"Are you okay?" her voice was light and soft, as if approaching a wounded animal.

I finally snapped.

"What is your game, Sybine? What do you want?" My voice came out harsher than I had intended, and she flinched back slightly.

"My...game?" Her brows pushed together. "I don't understand."

"Stop. Playing. What do you want?" I stood up, fists balled at my sides, ready to unleash the torrent of pain and agony crashing into me.

"I'm not playing, Loren." She shook her head. "I don't understand.... What's going on? Please."

She leaned forward as if going to reach for me. Her lips were slightly parted, and not an inch of her trembled or flinched. Her hands rested on her legs, but she didn't make the move to fiddle with the latch on her bag. Her feet planted firmly on the ground as she stood and took a step toward me. And her eyes...it was like she was trying desperately to see through my mask. If only I would let her.

Gods, I was a fool. I couldn't figure out her motives or what game she was playing because I was looking for something that didn't exist. Sybine was perhaps the first genuine person I had met my entire life.

"You're...not lying," I finally said.

She shook her head.

"I'm not."

"You're real," I sobbed.

She nodded.

"I am."

"There's no game," I admitted.

She took another step toward me.

"Loren, who hurt you so deeply that you believe everyone has a corrupted heart?"

I closed my eyes again and another wave of tears fell down my face. This was a lie. It was all a lie. But it wasn't hers. It was mine. A carefully constructed facade that had only kept me isolated my whole life. I couldn't bear to hear that name from her lips again.

"It's Elora," I said under my breath.

"What?"

I swallowed and brought my eyes up to meet hers.

"My name...it's Elora."

33

Scars

Elora

"I don't want to die without at least someone knowing who I am."

Sybine's eyes widened and her lips parted softly. Her eyes looked up and down my body, as if seeing me for the first time. She blinked and slowly made her way back up to my face. There was a soft smile on her lips, and I felt a warmth blossom in me.

"Elora," she murmured softly. My name was like honey coming off her tongue. I had never heard something so sweet and tender. My heart gave a slight flutter in my chest.

"Elora," she said again. "Elora. I like the way it feels to say your name, Elora."

My breath caught in my throat.

"Thank you," I whispered. "I think I need to sit down."

I perched myself on my chest and kept my knees up. I rested my elbows on them and ran both of my hands through my hair. Thankfully, my tears had slowed, and my mind was beginning to clear.

Sybine knew who I was now. Or at least she knew my name. There were still far too many secrets I was holding for her to truly know me. And although a part of me still felt uneasy about sharing my name with her, it was nice to know that if anything happened to me, I'd had one last moment of honesty. My father would be proud of that.

"Are you okay?" Sybine asked. She fidgeted with her shirt under her arms slightly before resting her hands back in her lap.

I lifted my head to meet her gaze and nodded.

"I think so. It's just...strange, I guess. Now that there's a sword hanging over my head, it puts a few things into perspective."

She laughed nervously.

"You could definitely say that."

I realized that Sybine probably had a sense of at least some of the panic I just went through.

"I can't imagine how you felt when you first saw those posters with your face on it."

She knit her brows together, and then her eyes widened.

"Oh, yes…that was scary." She hesitated for a moment and then asked, "What's been put into perspective for you?"

Everything, I wanted to say. But that somehow seemed both too simplistic and too complex all at the same time.

"Even though my father was a pirate lord, he had a big heart. He trusted people too easily, and it's what got him killed. And me…well, I did the opposite, and somehow ended up in exactly the same position."

She shook her head slightly, and a small crease formed between her eyebrows.

"The same position?"

She already knew my name. And I was marked for the grave anyway. It would do me no harm to let go of this now.

"Drakkon killed my father, and now he's going to kill me too."

Sybine gasped and threw her hands over her mouth. When she lowered them, her lips were still parted with surprise.

"What? Wait, then why are you here?"

I gave her a knowing look.

"You really can't guess?"

Her eyes widened so far that they looked as if they might bulge out of her head.

"You came here to kill him, didn't you?"

I nodded.

"And that day on Tamarine, when you went to the tent, that wasn't just to support them and get information. You went there—"

"Yes. I went there to kill him. And Rhyker too. He was Drakkon's first mate when they attacked our ship. He's been on my list ever since."

I would never forget that day. I wouldn't forget their voices or the sounds my father made while they cut out his tongue. For as long as I lived, those memories would be permanently imprinted on my mind.

Sybine looked down for a moment, and her fingers twisted in the sheet.

"How long has it been?" she asked.

"Ten long years." I looked out our small window at the sea. The sky hadn't quite turned red with the evening light yet, but I could see a slight hint of dark blue on the horizon.

"Ten years," she echoed under her breath. "He really is a monster, isn't he?"

I hummed in agreement.

"He was no better when he was younger, either," I said. "I was only twelve when my father took him under his wing, but even then there was something wrong about him. I was brushed off. Drakkon's wife and child were killed in an accident, so my father kept making excuses for him. I think...since he'd lost my mom giving birth to me, he felt like he could help?" I sighed. "I never understood."

"So you knew him," she said. "You knew him before the attack?"

I nodded.

"He was with us for almost two years."

Sybine's eyes flashed back up to mine.

"Two years? Why? How?"

I shrugged.

"Those were the same questions I had. The same questions I still have. One day, they just got into a huge fight on deck, and the next thing I knew, Drakkon was gone. My father said that Drakkon's ambitions outgrew his own and that he wasn't a good fit for the ship anymore, but I don't know, Sybine. I never got a genuine answer. And two years later, Drakkon came back to finish what he started."

I put my hand on my chest over the thin silver scar. I rubbed it gently, remembering the bite of Drakkon's blade.

You claimed to know my pain, Lire. You didn't then, but you will now.

I closed my eyes and tried to push Drakkon's voice from my mind.

"Fuck," she whispered. I heard her shuffle on the bed.

I sighed and dropped my hand back down to my side to grip the edge of the chest.

"That's some heavy shit."

Despite everything, I let out a low laugh.

"Yeah...it is."

She adjusted herself again. When I looked up, she squinted her eyes and pinched her lips together. She looked like she was in pain.

"Are you okay?"

She nodded.

"I'm sorry. I'm just a little uncomfortable. Do you mind?"

At first, I thought she was emotionally uncomfortable after hearing my story, but my assumption was obviously proven wrong when she began to take her shirt off.

My eyes immediately landed on the patches of red skin under her arms and across her back.

I sucked in a breath.

"Sybine."

Her jaw tensed.

"Is it that bad?"

I traced a finger along her sensitive skin. She flinched under my touch.

I moved my hands to her shoulders and turned her around to face me. Her blisters were bad. Although she had looked uncomfortable from time to time, I had no idea it had gotten to this point.

"How long have you been wearing them?" I asked.

She shrugged.

"I'm not sure. All day, I suppose. I put it on before breakfast and take it off before going to bed."

I swallowed and pinched my lips together. Then, realizing I was still touching her bare shoulders, I dropped my hands back down to my sides.

"That's too long, Sybine. You can really hurt yourself."

Her face flushed.

"I don't have a choice, Elora." She put her hands over her breasts. "These are a bit too obvious."

Heat rose from my chest and rested in my cheeks. I suddenly didn't know where to look, so I darted my eyes from place to place around the room.

I cleared my throat.

"It's still too long, Sybine. You have to find a way to take breaks, otherwise you're going to hurt yourself."

"Okay," she sighed. "I'll try."

"Good," I said, turning my back to her to look out the window. "Starting now."

"Now?"

"It's okay. I won't look."

There was a long pause before she replied.

"Okay."

I heard her fingers work at the soft fabric and tried not to think about what it would look like, or how it would feel to watch. Each sound of her undoing the clasps and laces sent a wave of heat through my body.

The soft thud of the lid of her chest closing echoed through the room.

"I'm finished now."

I turned around. She was back in her white shirt. The laces in the front were undone, revealing more of her chest than I had ever seen before, and below that....

My breath caught in my throat.

I could make out the soft points of her nipples poking through the fabric.

Sybine seemed to catch my gaze, and she hunched her shoulders over slightly so her shirt was no longer in contact with her chest.

"Sorry, that was rather indecent of me."

I cleared my throat and shook my head.

Three loud knocks at the door interrupted us.

Sybine instinctively crossed her arms over her chest, and her eyes squinted slightly with the movement.

"Come in," she said as she turned around to face the door.

Harlan poked his head in the door almost like a child who was afraid he was going to get caught doing something he wasn't supposed to.

"I don't mean to interrupt."

She shook her head.

"It's fine, Harlan. What do you need?"

A smile spread across the old man's face.

"The crew's starting a dice tournament in the dining hall. Morale hasn't been where Rhyker wants, so he's offered ten gold pieces to the winner as some kind of incentive." He waved his hand out in front of him. "The money doesn't matter to me. I just want an excuse to wipe the floor with these fellows."

Sybine grinned.

"Sevens?" she asked.

He nodded, his eyes glinting with mischief.

I had heard of the game, but never played it. I preferred cards. They were much more predictable. I hated the chaos that came from games of chance.

"I don't think gambling is a great idea tonight, Harlan. Sybine is very tired." I stepped forward and looked at Sybine. She was in a lot of pain, I could tell. Putting on the binder again was out of the question. So what was she going to do? Hunch all night?

Harlan looked back and forth between the two of us as if trying to see something that wasn't quite visible.

She scoffed.

"It's fine, Loren."

I shot her another knowing glance, hoping that she would understand what I was trying to convey. She dismissed me with a hand out in front of her.

"Thank you for the invitation, Harlan. We will be there in a few minutes."

34

Sevens

Elora

"It might give us a chance to tell the rest of the crew about the blood bond," Sybine said.

Mutiny: a desperate man's last resort. And we were desperate. But there was no guarantee that they would listen or even care. It wasn't a gamble that I was prepared to make yet.

"I'm not sure mutiny is the best course of action, Sybine."

"What other choice do we have?" Sybine said as she rose her hands in the air.

Her shirt brushed over her breasts from the movement. My mouth went dry, and my face flushed. I immediately turned my gaze away to focus on the light of the evening sun out the window. I didn't need this distraction. Especially not now. I tried to blink the racing thoughts out of my head.

"We don't have to stay for long," she continued. "But people will get suspicious if we aren't there."

I sighed. She was right. And I didn't need any more eyes on me than there already were.

"Fine," I conceded. "But let's start small, with someone who won't cause a scene. And once the sun sets, we will say our goodbyes and come right back."

Sybine sighed but reluctantly agreed.

"And when we get back, you will let me take care of those, okay?" I gestured to the space under her arms. I knew all too well the pain blisters like those caused. And if Sybine wanted to continue to train, she needed to take care of herself.

Sybine's face went red, but she nodded in agreement. She moved to the side of the room and lifted the lid of her chest. When she stood back up, she was holding a thin shirt that resembled an old nightdress in her hands.

She stared at me expectantly.

"Do you mind?"

My throat went dry, and I coughed to clear it.

I shook my head and turned around to look out the window again.

As I watched the sea breathe in front of me, I allowed myself a moment to pause and think. There were two things I was

267

certain of. At any moment, Drakkon would be able to control the crew. And at some point in the near future, he would make an attempt on my life. That didn't mean my efforts were futile, and it didn't mean I was hopeless. All it meant was that I needed to improvise. It was unlikely that I would be able to attack him and win with force, which meant I would need to think of something else. Poison? No. I had never seen him eat or drink with the crew, which meant he had his own personal stores. I hadn't seen them when I was in his quarters, which probably meant he had the cook prepare everything for him independently. Intercepting Drakkon's meals and drinks before they made it to him would be next to impossible. None of the men on this ship would be foolish enough to accept a bribe that might implicate them in his murder either. And although they weren't the sharpest crew I had ever sailed with, none of them would accept such a bribe without asking a few questions first.

That meant I had two other options: strike in his sleep, or have someone else do it for me without them knowing.

"Everything okay?" Sybine asked from behind me.

I turned back around and nodded. I would take the night to think of the best approach and figure the rest out on the morrow.

"Let's go."

The dining hall was already full by the time we arrived. The men sat in lines up and down each table. There were a few crowds around the ones at the front, and I instantly recognized Harlan sitting at the head of it. I motioned for Sybine to follow me, and I made my way through the sailors.

I scanned the room, and just as I had suspected, Drakkon and Rhyker were nowhere to be seen. I swallowed the lump in my throat.

"Try to relax and enjoy the moment." Sybine's voice was low and soft beside me.

How was I supposed to relax when, at any moment, we could all be forced to be Drakkon's puppets? Or worse, his human pincushions. Still, I took a long breath and tried to clear my head. With neither Drakkon nor Rhyker here, there wasn't much I could do. There was only one way in and out of Drakkon's room. I would have no advantage if I barged in there now, and the last thing I needed was to give him an excuse to kill me sooner.

As we approached Harlan's table, the men erupted into cheers and moans of disappointment. A group of men exchanged coins across the table.

Harlan's eyes fell on us.

"Ah, good to see you, lads! Come to play?"

We both shook our heads.

"Well, sometimes the bettin' is more fun anyway, innit?" He looked around at the group of men surrounding him.

Some of them pounded their fists into the table, others lifted their mugs in the air, but the message was clear: they were all in agreement, and they were all drunk.

"Actually, could we have a word with you?" Sybine asked.

"Alone," I added.

Harlan took a quick look around before nodding and leading us to the far corner of the room.

"What is it, lads? I'm on a roll here."

Sybine and I exchanged a nervous glance.

She cleared her throat.

"Do you remember the paper you signed before getting on the ship?" she asked.

"Aye," he said as he folded his arms across his chest. "What of it?"

"Do you remember…signing with…blood?"

Harlan's eyes widened and then returned to their normal shape nearly instantaneously. It happened so fast that I wasn't sure I had actually seen the change, or if I had imagined it. Before I had a chance to read the rest of his body language, he let out a loud laugh that seemed to come straight from his core.

"You think—" he cut himself off with another round of laughter.

I balled my hands into fists at my side. How was he not taking this seriously? Surely he had heard the stories and dangers of committing such an act. Yet here he was, laughing like we had just told him the worst joke in the world.

"Lads, you hear that?" he called out.

My heart dropped. We had chosen Harlan specifically because we thought he wouldn't cause a scene.

"We've signed our lives away like puppets!"

Everyone around us burst into laughter as well. Sybine's face flushed pink. Her fingers played at the clasp on her bag, and she bit her lips together.

Harlan reached out and grabbed us both by the arm, pulling us in close to him.

"Be careful who you say those things to," he said, his tone deadly serious. All hints of mischief and playfulness were washed from his face. "That enchantment works on the mind in other ways as well." He nodded his head toward the crowd that was still laughing behind us. "These fools don't remember anything, trust me. And you should try to forget it too, if you know what's good for you."

Harlan let us go and pushed between us as if he had said nothing.

"Now, who's my next challenger?"

I looked over to Sybine. Her lips were parted slightly, and her eyes were round saucers. I felt the same disbelief.

My mind raced with a thousand questions. What was the extra enchantment? How had Harlan escaped it? How had I escaped it? What did that mean for everyone else? How had this all come to pass? And the most important question: if it didn't affect me, would the general enchantment still work on me, or did I actually have a sliver of hope of making it out alive?

Sybine opened her mouth to say something, but I cut her off.

"We'll talk about this later," I whispered over to her. "For now, try to look normal. We can't afford to appear suspicious."

She nodded slightly and took a long breath before we turned around and made our way back over to Harlan.

Waldreg confidently strode up to the other side of the table.

"This should be interesting," Sybine whispered to me.

I nodded in agreement. Of all the guards on the ship, Waldreg had the worst temper. I briefly considered him as a candidate for Drakkon's execution and immediately pushed the thought aside. He was strong, but I would sooner trust a barnacle on the side of the ship to strangle Drakkon before I put my faith in Waldreg. With a heavy heart, I realized that there was no person on the *Vindicta* that I could trust to make the last strike. They were either too unpredictable, too greedy, too weak, too old, or too nice. I was delusional if I thought I could trust anyone other than myself to act in my best interest.

Harlan and Waldreg stared at each other from across the table.

"I've never lost a match, old man."

Harlan gave him a wry smile.

"I haven't either. And I have many more years under my belt than you, son."

I cleared my throat to keep from laughing. Maybe Sybine was right. Maybe this would be fun after all.

"Let the betting begin!" someone called from beside us.

Some of the men huddled around and whispered into each other's ears. Once all of them had shaken hands and returned their gazes to the two men, Harlan reached into his pocket and retrieved two small dice. He handed one to Waldreg and kept the second for himself. Waldreg did the same.

I knit my brows in confusion.

"Why are they trading dice?" I asked Sybine.

Her eyes sparkled up at me.

"Have you never played?"

I clenched my jaw and shook my head.

She practically bounced beside me.

"In Sevens, you never use one set of dice. To make sure no one cheats, you trade one."

I looked down at her skeptically.

"How could you possibly cheat?"

She rolled her eyes and laughed at me.

"Not everyone is as honorable as you are. Trust me."

I frowned at her. Sybine laughed and brushed my shoulder with her hand. An energy swept over my skin where her touch lingered for just a moment longer than normal. She brought her hand back to her side and cleared her throat. Her gaze returned to the game in front of us.

"People load dice all the time. This is to make sure that everyone has the same advantages and disadvantages."

I nodded even though my mind had wandered from the game. Another round of cheers and moans brought me back to my senses.

"Are they done?" I asked.

Sybine shook her head.

"No, that was just the preliminary round. That was to decide who rolls first. Seriously, have you never even seen a game of Sevens before?"

I shrugged.

"I don't care for games of chance."

Sybine laughed and shook her head.

"I guess I shouldn't be surprised."

I frowned.

"What's that supposed to mean?"

She gave me a disbelieving look and raised an eyebrow. Her eyes traced me from head to foot.

"I mean no offense. It's just that...you are very you," she said matter-of-factly.

I paused.

"Am I supposed to be someone else?"

She shook her head, a smile playing across her face.

"Just forget about it."

But how could I forget about it? Sybine saw me in a way that so many before her hadn't, and I couldn't shake the feeling that she had dove much deeper than I had ever intended to let her.

"There are seven turns. Since Harlan won the preliminary round, he gets to roll first and last."

Harlan tossed the dice. Three carved lines were face up on the first die, with four dots on the other. He gave Waldreg a proud grin before gesturing for him to take his turn.

"The only other rule is that you need to roll a seven to get a point."

"And you win if you have more points than your opponent, I presume."

She nodded.

The dice fell from Waldreg's fingers with a thump against the wooden table. This time, there were two carved lines and two dots facing up.

He looked across the table at Harlan under his thick eyebrows. The muscles in his shoulders tensed, and I couldn't tell if it was just a trick of the low candlelight or if a muscle at the side of his face twitched.

"Your turn, old man," he hissed.

Harlan sat back in his seat and gently rolled his dice. Five lines and six dots appeared.

Grumbles echoed around us. I looked up from the game to find many of the men standing around the table with their arms crossed and lips curled in sneers.

"I don't know why they are so surprised," I whispered to Sybine. "There are only six ways to roll seven, and—" I did a quick mental count of the other combinations— "thirty other possible results. The odds aren't—"

"Don't talk about the odds," someone from behind me scolded.

Sybine and I exchanged a side-eyed glance.

"Ha!" Waldreg exclaimed. Sybine and I both looked back to see a die with one slash, and another with six dots facing up.

Someone shoved between us to get to the table, hitting my shoulder hard on the way by. I clenched my fist by my side. I was ready to show him the mistake he had made, when Sybine grabbed my hand.

I froze.

Despite her icy touch, I still felt the heat rising within me. A flutter rose in my stomach, and a light rush filled my head. I looked down at where her fingers enveloped mine. Her pale skin appeared even lighter against mine. When I brought my gaze back up to meet hers, she shook her head at me.

"Don't. It's not worth it."

I ran my tongue along my teeth and looked back down at our hands. Sybine released her grip on me, flexing her hand slightly before returning it to her side.

I tried to bring my focus back to the game, but I could still feel the ghost of her touch on my skin. It was like a kiss of the sea breeze that sent a chill down my spine.

"So what now?" I asked her.

She cleared her throat.

"Well, if Harlan rolls a seven, he wins."

I nodded.

"Yes, I get that part, but what if he doesn't? Is it a tie?"

Her braid swayed across her back as she shook her head.

"No. If he doesn't, then Waldreg wins."

The last roll, Harlan's roll, would determine the winner. Either way, one of them was about to lose their streak.

"Se-ven, se-ven, se-ven!"

A chant rose around us as Harlan shook the dice in his hands.

I watched with nervous anticipation as he let them loose across the table. Waldreg's dice stopped first, three dots facing up. Harlan's dice spun around and around and around until it finally landed with an assured thud.

Four lines faced up.

Sybine let out a loud cheer and clapped her hands as everyone exchanged coins in front of us. For the first time in a long time, I felt a lightness in my chest. I looked down. The skin around Sybine's eyes folded together as her smile grew across her face.

Suddenly the lightness in my chest turned to flutters.

I swallowed and looked out the small window near the back hall. The sun kissed the horizon, illuminating the sky with brilliant shades of red and orange. Somehow, the evening had passed by in the blink of an eye.

I took a few steps forward until I reached Harlan. I put a hand on his shoulder and bent over to whisper in his ear.

"Congratulations, Harlan. You wiped him. That floor is spotless."

He smiled back and winked at me.

"Aye, that it is." His eyes shifted between Sybine and me, and he gave me a look that seemed to insinuate something that I should have known, but instead left me swimming with questions. "You two enjoy your evening."

With that, he turned back around and called out for his next opponent.

I moved back to Sybine and took her gently by the arm.

"Time to go, Princess."

35

Sunset

Elora

Sunset was always my favorite time of day. Although I had seen thousands of them, nothing quite compared to the extraordinary beauty of this one. A part of me knew where the extra magic came from, and another part of me was desperately trying to ignore the source. Despite all that, I still led us away from the drunken chatter and toward the bow.

"I thought we were going to bed for the night," Sybine said from beside me.

Our hands gently brushed together as we walked side by side, and something powerful shocked through my chest.

"I want to show you something first."

We made our way up the short flight of stairs to where the front of the ship met at a sharp point. I brought her over until the only thing separating us from the kiss of the sun on the horizon was the railing and the sea below us.

"Wow," she exhaled.

I felt her sentiment in my bones, and a chill ran down my spine. The amber light from the setting sun played across her cheeks and the narrow bridge of her nose, giving her a mask of gold that highlighted her brilliant green eyes perfectly. Soft wisps of her hair had fallen from the braid at her back, and they blew under her hat like small tendrils of her spirit set free at last.

I took a quick glance around the deck below us. There wasn't a sailor to be seen. It seemed everyone had taken to the dining hall for the festivities.

I leaned against the railing and looked out at the horizon.

"We need to talk about what happened back there," I said.

She sighed and leaned on the rail next to me.

"That didn't go as expected," she admitted.

"No," I agreed, "it didn't."

"It's strange though."

I looked over at her. Her brows pushed together, creating a line on her forehead. She turned to face me and tilted her head to the side slightly.

"Why did everyone else forget except for you and Harlan?"

I shrugged. I had asked myself the same question earlier, but the answer seemed fairly obvious.

"I don't know about Harlan, but that part of the enchantment probably didn't work on me in the same way that yours doesn't."

Sybine thought about it for a moment before finally nodding.

"So no mutiny," she said.

"No mutiny," I echoed. "I'm going to have to take care of things myself, after all."

"So what next?" she asked.

I let out a long breath.

"I'm not sure...I'm still figuring that out," I admitted.

She looked back out at the sea. The sound of the waves crashing against the boat soothed me. It was the sound of my childhood, and it filled me with a sense of peace.

I couldn't help but trace the line the pale light of the setting sun cast on Sybine's skin with my eyes.

"You're not alone, you know," she said.

The comment shocked me, and I froze.

I had always been alone. Every day of my life. For the last ten years.

My chest tightened.

The truth that I had believed for so long was slowly beginning to feel like I lie. Maybe I wasn't so alone after all.

"You should let your hair down," I told her.

Sybine turned around to face me, her eyes wide and shining. My gaze dipped down to her lush, pink lips that softly parted in protest. My throat suddenly felt as if it were filled with sand. I swallowed the dryness, trying to clear it.

"I used to climb up to the front of the ship when I was a kid," I told her. "I would sit with my legs dangling between the posts of the railing and let the wind comb through my hair. It was the closest I felt to flying."

She gave me a shy smile.

"That sounds...magical."

I nudged my head toward her.

"You should try it."

"But won't they see?" she asked.

"It's just us," I said as I gestured around the deck. "And we're behind the mast. No one will see."

My heart pounded in my chest. The image of our shared kiss on the island behind Varix's tent flooded my mind. Her flushed cheeks, her darkened eyes, the way her breath played over my skin, the strong thud of her heart against mine.

Despite my best efforts, I couldn't stop my attraction to her any more than I could stop the sun from rising, or the sea from breathing. Somehow, she had found a crack in the stone defenses of my heart and was beginning to take root there. I had been in countless fights, seen death firsthand from both my blow and others, I had watched my life as I knew it burn down and sink into the depths, and I had just found out that the sand in my hourglass of life was about to run out. Still, nothing had ever felt as terrifying as finally accepting and understanding the source of the flutters in my chest when I was around her.

Sybine reached up and unwound her hair from the braid. Her eyes fluttered up and she caught my stare. She bit her lips together, a soft pink blush extended over her cheeks. She tucked a stray hair behind her ear. Slowly, her lips parted again as a wide smile spread across her face.

"You know," she started, "you're not nearly as hard around the edges as you make everyone believe."

My stomach twisted.

"I am far from soft."

Sybine tilted her head to the side slightly and let her eyes fall down my body, studying me. When they returned to mine, she smirked at me.

"Maybe. But you're not made of stone."

She reached out a hand to meet mine.

I squeezed my eyes shut. Half of me was begging for more, to feel the rise and fall of her heavy breaths against my chest as I claimed her mouth and the sting of her nails as they scraped across my back. I wanted her body arched into mine. I wanted to twist my fingers in her hair and kiss down her neck and commit every curve of her body to memory. The other half of me was screaming to run away, to forget her and focus on Drakkon, to save myself, to save...her.

I turned my head away from her and looked at the floorboards of the ship.

I knew the dangers of dark clouds on the horizon. She was everything unexpected and alluring. She was a storm, and I was in uncharted waters.

"We shouldn't." My voice was much lower than I intended.

Sybine let go of my hand immediately, and my stomach sank.

"I'm sorry. I didn't...I didn't mean to...make you uncomfortable," she stammered.

I swallowed and closed my eyes again.

"It's not that," I said as I ran a hand through my hair. "I destroy things. I fight things." I paused for a moment and looked back over at her.

To my surprise, her gaze didn't harden at all. She didn't flinch away from me or expand the space between us. If anything, she softened.

"You don't have to push me away, you know."

I looked out to the sea and let the sea breeze breathe into my lungs.

"I'm not pushing you away, Sybine. This is just who I am." She was a thief. I was a murderer. By all means, we were not meant to be together in any capacity.

"No one can be defined in such binary terms, Elora. You don't give yourself enough credit."

I scoffed.

"What credit, Sybine?"

She took me by the hands and forced me to look at her.

"You care, Elora. I see it in the way you look at Harlan and the way you look at—" she paused for a moment and closed her eyes, as if saying the next words would be impossible while maintaining this intimate connection— "the way you look at me."

I removed a hand from hers and placed it under her chin to tilt it up. Her eyes opened again, meeting mine. So many emotions raced behind them, I couldn't keep up, but none of them were what I was used to. There was no fear, no apprehension, no anger, no malice, no pain. No, what I saw in her eyes was far more dangerous.

Something in my chest tightened.

I dropped my hand and turned around, eyes down, thoughts warring. I clenched my fists at my side.

"There's a darkness in me, Sybine. Whatever light you bring out in me can't erase that. It will stain you."

I heard her take a step. A shock went through my body as she placed a hand on my shoulder, her fingers giving me a gentle, reassuring squeeze.

"Then it stains me. I will wear it with pride."

Something in me snapped. I threw my head back, my eyes staring up at the golden sky.

"Fuck it."

I whirled around and took her face in my hands. I tilted her chin up and pressed my lips down to hers.

A Dangerous Creature

Sybine

This kiss was nothing like the one we shared previously. On the island, our moment was shared in an act of survival. Here, there was an energy between us that begged for release, a desperate charge of life.

My hands instinctively wrapped behind her neck. I gently swept my tongue over her parted lips. She tasted of sweet oranges and salt water. It exploded in an unquenchable euphoria in my mind. It was as if she was made to set every inch of my body on fire and consume me.

Her tongue softly brushed mine, as if gently testing my limits. Our lips danced across each other's hungrily, as if we were both starved for air, and we were each other's only source of oxygen. My hands worked their way up her neck, and I twisted her short hair in my fingers. The moan that escaped Elora's lips sent a shock of heat down through my chest and further still, until it accumulated low in my belly.

Elora quickly reached down and lifted me up. I wrapped my legs around her waist as she placed me on the railing. I pulled her in close, but still not close enough. I wanted to breathe her in. I wanted to taste every inch of her skin. I wanted to drown in those low, delicious noises that floated up from her chest. I wanted her. All of her.

I was vaguely aware of the danger the position put me in. There was nothing except her grip on me that kept me from falling down into the dark depths below us. The feeling invigorated me even further, and I quickened my pace. My heart pounded in my chest and ears, and my skin hummed with energy. I had never felt more alive in my life. Nothing felt as right as we did together at this moment.

No partner had ever made me feel like this. I knew she was battling something of her own, but she never broke from me. Whatever internal struggle she'd had before was gone, obliterated the moment our lips touched. I sensed a new resolve in her, something that made me clench my thighs together with anticipation.

We parted from each other slightly, both breathless, both overcome with this energy between and surrounding us. She pressed her forehead to mine, and I felt a small smile spread over her face.

"You are a dangerous creature, Sybine."

I smirked.

"You have no idea."

Elora closed the door to our room and turned around. She crossed her arms across her chest and leaned against the doorframe. It was just like the night we first met, and yet everything had changed. A nervous flutter began in my stomach.

I smiled awkwardly at her.

"Hi," I said, breathlessly.

She smirked at me.

"Hi."

I bit my lips together as my eyes shuffled around the room. The tension grew between us until it threatened to choke me.

"That was—"

"Incredible," Elora interrupted.

I felt my face flush and a familiar heat stir within me. Elora's eyes were dark. She looked at me with a desire that made my heart jump. But not with fear, like it had in the past with specific men. No, this desire made me feel seen and powerful and wanted.

Elora pushed herself off the frame and traipsed toward me. My breaths came heavy and fast. My chest was hot and my skin felt like it was on fire. The only thing that could possibly save me was her.

A silence spread across the room, save for her boots on the floor and my heavy breaths. It felt like it took an eternity for her to reach me. By the time she slid her hand up my arm to my face, I was ready to melt into her embrace. I quivered under her touch.

"Is this okay?" she asked.

I met her gaze with equal desire and nodded.

"Yes," I said, more than a little breathless.

"Good."

Elora moved her head beside mine. I could feel the warmth from her cheek against my skin. She placed a gentle kiss on the side of my throat, and I finally let go of the tension I was holding. Light sparked around the edges of my vision as she made her way down my neck to my collarbone. My back arched, and I breathed out a low moan. Sparks of energy traced her lips as she moved over my skin.

Elora let out a sharp exhale and wrapped an arm around my waist to steady me.

"Gods, Sybine," she groaned into my skin, "those sounds will ruin me."

Her words sent a rush over my skin, and I gasped. Although her motions were gentle, there was a palpable hunger that emanated from her. The same desperation rose in me. I felt it crawl through my chest and up my throat before finally tasting it on my tongue.

I snapped my head back up and reached for her. Elora's dark eyes met mine for only a second before I pressed our lips together. I parted her lips with my tongue, drunk on her taste again. Still, I wanted more. I craved her smell, her taste, her touch. My entire body thrummed with the need to have more of her. I reached down to the bottom of her shirt and twisted my fingers in it.

Elora tensed. She brought her hands down to meet mine.

"Did I do something wrong?" My chest heaved up and down from my heavy breaths.

She shook her head.

"No, it's not you. It's...I'm not I don't know how to say this but...I have scars. They're not...pleasant to look at. I'm not beautiful like you are." Her eyes fell to the ground as she spoke.

I released her shirt and reached up to brush her cheek with my thumb.

"Elora, do you really think I was trying to seduce you just so I could see you naked and judge you?"

She shifted awkwardly on her feet. I reached up and tilted her chin so she could look at me.

"I don't know who convinced you that beauty can only exist in one form. The setting sun is beautiful, and so is dim candlelight, and they are nowhere near the same. The beauty of the world, and everything in it, does not take away from or distract me from yours, because make no mistake, Elora, you are beautiful."

Cracked

Elora

I felt a rush of tears sting my eyes.

"No one has ever said that to me," I whispered. "I've never had this—" she gestured between us— "before. The people I have been with, they...well, they never made me feel like this."

Although my experiences were limited, they had all almost exclusively been the same. They never wanted to hear what I had to say. They never truly saw me. All they saw was a means to an end. Eventually, I numbed myself. I closed myself off, forsaking any kind of connection. It was easier that way. It was less complicated. It gave me time to focus on myself and my training. Until Sybine. Despite everything, I couldn't stop myself from feeling this way around her.

Sybine pressed her cheek to my chest. I placed a kiss on the top of her head and rested my chin there. Something cracked under my skin. Something I had kept hidden and protected for so long.

A familiar crackling energy stretched around us. My skin hummed to life. Sybine reached down to the end of my shirt again. This time, I didn't stop her. I knelt before her and raised my arms, as if offering myself to her. I longed to reach out and trace my fingers along her skin, to watch her body tense and relax under my touch, for her to anticipate my every move.

Sybine looked down at my exposed skin. I knew what she would see: a pattern of silver scars over my muscles; my proud, broad and defined shoulders; and tight nipples from my aroused state.

She gently ran a finger over the long scar across my chest. It sent a chill over my skin. No one had ever touched me like this. No one had ever made me feel like this either.

Her hand hesitated when she reached the end of the silver line.

"Who did this to you?"

A heat rose in my chest and took root in my cheeks as I met her gaze. The answer caught in my throat, and my tongue refused to taste his name. Not here. Not now.

Sybine's eyes widened.

"Oh, Elora. I'm so sorry."

She knelt down in front of me and placed a kiss on my chest. This time, a pulse of warmth spread through me. Her lips were like a prayer on my skin, blessing me with her light. I didn't know if I deserved it, but it felt too good to question.

Her lips moved from my chest to my collarbone and up my neck, until she placed a final kiss on my ear that set my skin on fire.

"Like I said," she whispered, "you are beautiful."

Those words were all I needed to send me over the edge. In an instant, I was standing with her in my arms. She jumped up and wrapped her legs around me the same way she had before. I took the last few steps to the bed and laid her down on it. Her hair fanned out around her like black rays of sunlight. Something desperate stirred in me. I wanted to devour every last piece of her skin. I wanted to feel every curve, every bone, every hair on her body. I wanted to caress her and consume her all at the same time.

"I want you. I want you to feel what you do to me, Sybine."

She squirmed underneath me. She traced her hands up and down my back, making a shiver run down my spine.

"What do I do to you, Elora?" Her words sounded as if they were breathed from the mouth of an angel. Too bad for her. I had no such heavenly convictions.

"You make me mad with a hunger I never knew I had."

I kissed her throat. She moaned, and I felt the noise through her skin.

"You make me feel like I've never tasted air before."

Another kiss. Another moan.

"You make me wild, Sybine."

"Show me," she said breathlessly.

I crashed our mouths together as I desperately tried to close the space between us. It wasn't enough.

My hands went down to her shirt, and I wrapped the fabric in my fingers. Then, in one swift motion, I ripped it off her body.

I was met with the thin white fabric of her chemise.

A low growl erupted from my chest. It wasn't enough. Seeing her perked nipples through the soft silk seemed to be driving me mad. I needed more.

I gripped the bottom of her undershirt and pulled it up over her head leaving her beautifully exposed.

Sybine gasped, and her back arched with pleasure as the cool air played over her skin. I sat up and tried to take every part of her in, trying to commit every inch of her skin to memory.

Something snapped in me. I could wait no longer for our skin to touch again. I lowered my lips to her stomach and let my teeth graze her. She gasped again and pushed up against me, as if the space between us was also too much for her to bear. I swirled my tongue around her skin, now marked by my teeth. She whimpered and moaned under me. I felt as if I might burst apart. The feelings inside me were too great for my body to contain.

I flipped her over onto her stomach and ripped the rest of her shirt off. It was already ruined, and it was in my way. I pulled her chemise off the rest of the way and tossed it into the dark abyss of our room. The muscles in her back tensed as I gently blew up her spine. Finally, when I reached her neck, I placed a trail of kisses back down. She relaxed and sank into my touch. My fingers traced down the side of her body, leaving a trail of goosebumps behind. I loved the effect my touch had on her. It mirrored her effect on me.

"Don't stop," she begged once I reached her trousers.

"Are you sure?"

She nodded.

I quickly pulled the pants down past her ankles and threw them on the floor to accompany the jacket there. I bit my lip as my eyes raked down her naked body. She was something from out of this world. Each of her soft curves melded into the next like a wave on the sea. I found myself wanting to drown in them.

I reached out to caress her soft skin. She melted under my touch.

"You are, without doubt, the most beautiful being I have ever seen."

I thought the words were kept in my head, but I felt them flow from my lips in a gentle cascade.

"Let me see you," Sybine's voice was like a gentle caress through the night.

I turned her back around so she could face me. She reached up and stroked my cheek.

I closed my eyes and leaned into her touch. For the first time in years, I felt safe. A sense of peace washed over me. I relaxed. My breaths came easier. My mind was clearer. Everything felt right.

A loud bang from the room beside us broke our trance.

I immediately darted up, retrieving the dagger under my pillow and thrusting it in front of me.

"What was that?" Her voice was hoarse.

Raised voices echoed around the room from the cracks in the walls. They were accusing each other of cheating. There were loud footsteps and slamming doors that continued for long minutes until finally, there was only the low hum of conversation on the other side of the wall.

I looked over at Sybine, who had propped herself up on her elbows. She had pulled the blanket up to cover most of her body. Her long hair cascaded in waves over her pale shoulders and down her back.

"I guess that's it for the night," she said. She tried to laugh, but I could sense the disappointment coming off her in waves.

"Yes, I guess so," I agreed.

We had gotten carried away. I had been so swept up in the moment that I had forgotten all the horrors around me. They came flooding back like a tidal wave. I swallowed the lump in my throat and ran a hand through my hair. Frustration rippled through me.

I reached down to grab a fresh shirt for her from her chest.

"Here," I said, holding it out to her, "sorry about the old one."

"Don't be." Sybine stood up and brought the shirt over her head. "I'm not." She gave me a gentle kiss and rolled back into the bed.

The Stories We Tell

Sybine

"There you go," Elora said after she finished putting the healing oil on my back and under my arms. "That should help with the irritation."

The relief was nearly instantaneous.

I let out a soft sigh.

"Where did you even find that magic?" I asked her.

Elora quickly wound the lid back on the container. I could have sworn I saw a light pink dust her cheeks.

"Supply closet," she said simply.

"Oh—" I laughed nervously— "of course."

Something had changed in the air between us. Did she regret what happened last night? I had fallen asleep under the impression that she was comfortable, but I wasn't as sure anymore. Then again, I wasn't the one marked for death either. Well, at least not on this ship.

"Thanks," I said shyly.

"You're welcome."

I ran my teeth over my lower lip. What was I supposed to do now? What were we? Should I kiss her goodbye before leaving for my shift? Would that be weird? Maybe a handshake would be better.

I mentally scolded myself. A handshake would definitely not be better.

"I'm going to...uhm...go and...scrub the deck?"

I wanted to bash my head against the wall and then maybe throw myself off the ship.

Really, Sybine? Scrub the deck? It was all I could do not to roll my eyes at myself.

"Yes, of course. Good luck," Elora said. She bit her lips together, and she shuffled her weight awkwardly from one foot to the other.

"Thanks." I gave her a small wave and spun on my heel to turn around.

As I walked out of the room, I pinched my face together with embarrassment. I'd had plenty of awkward interactions after spending the night with people before, but nothing had ever quite been that uncomfortable. Then again, I had never been with anyone I had growing feelings for either. It was safer that way. Gods, what was I doing?

I turned to go into the supply closet and ran straight into Harlan. Or, more accurately, straight into his full bucket, which fell to the ground with a loud bang and proceeded to spill its contents onto the wooden planks.

"Fuck, I'm sorry," I said as I bent down to right the bucket.

"Everything okay?" he asked.

I nodded slowly as I stood again.

"Rough night?"

"No—I mean, this morning—wait." The events before the Sevens game came racing back to me.

I took a quick look down the hall. It was empty, save for a few people going in and out of the dining room. I turned around and closed the door.

"What are you—"

I raised my hand to cut him off.

"What the hell was that last night, Harlan?" I kept my voice low, but my tone firm. I didn't want anyone to overhear us, but I also needed him to know that I was serious, and he had some explaining to do. "How are you so calm about all of this? And how come you're not affected by the spell?"

His pale eyes seemed to age with every question I asked.

"I'll start with your easiest question," he said as he began to undo the laces at his chest. He opened his shirt to reveal a small, nearly translucent, sky-blue stone on a thin band of rope. "It's sea glass," he said before I could ask. "Many think that stones like this carry protection enchantments from Kaia herself. I figured there wouldn't be any harm in me carrying it, and it seems to have paid off."

Sea glass? It seemed like such a small thing to have such power.

"You seem skeptical." He noted my silence.

Maybe because I *was* skeptical.

"It just seems a bit...I don't know...easy?"

He frowned at me as he tied the laces on his shirt again.

"Don't be so quick to judge, kid. You should know better than anyone that there is sometimes more to things than what meets the eye." He gave me a knowing look.

My blood went cold.

"You...know?" I took a step backward and wrapped my fingers around the door handle.

Harlan stepped toward me and placed a hand on my shoulder. His face softened.

"I'm sorry, that came out wrong." He sighed. "I've known for some time. But don't worry, kid. Your secret's safe with me."

"H-h-how long?" I stuttered.

He raised an eyebrow at me.

"Long enough."

Harlan let go of my shoulder and put some more space between us.

"Why not tell the captain?" I asked the question that was burning in my mind.

He scoffed.

"I have no love for him, trust me." Harlan took a breath and softened his tone. "And I would never do that to you, kid. I promise."

The tension in my chest eased slightly at his words.

Harlan leaned against the shelf beside him.

"As for your other questions...I'm calm, but I'm not indifferent. I don't want to see these men suffer any more than you do...I'll do what I can, but I don't have much power in this situation. And until we know what the captain is plannin', there's not much we can do."

I nodded. Elora and I had come to the same conclusion. There were only so many eventualities that we could prepare for, and even then, we were bound to miss something. It was better to expect something unexpected, and that, unfortunately, had limitless possibilities.

"Thank you," I finally said. "For not telling anyone about me."

He bowed his head toward me slightly before opening his arms out beside him.

"We best be makin' our way back to the deck before anyone finds us missin'."

Harlan pushed himself off the shelf and took a few steps toward me before leaning down to retrieve his bucket. I moved to the side to make way for him. He paused before opening the door and turned back around to me. He reached into his pocket and took out a yellowed piece of paper. Before I had a chance to ask what it was, he pressed it into my hands.

"I had some time on Tamarine to look up those siren abilities you told me about. I found it quite interestin', so here. Maybe you will too."

He turned on his heel, opened the door, and made his way down the hall. I glanced at the piece of paper in my hand and thought that it might just hold the answers to the most important question I had been asking myself my whole life: who was I?

The Siren's Call

Sybine

Harlan's writing on the old piece of paper was scratchy and tricky to read. There were words scattered all over, which made deciphering anything on it extremely difficult. Despite the relative illegibility, I was still able to make out a few words: shape-shift, water–ice–steam, mind link, and flow.

Really, Harlan? You couldn't have written these things down in sentences? I groaned to myself.

"I don't think I've ever seen you so focused, even with my knife pressed to your throat."

I looked up to find Elora leaning against the door, studying me.

"What's that?" she asked, nodding toward the paper in my hand.

A warmth rose from my chest and settled in my cheeks.

"It's nothing. Just some instructions from Harlan."

I quickly folded the parchment and placed it in the bag on my leg.

Elora hummed in what sounded like a disbelieving tone, but she didn't press any further.

"What are you doing here?" I asked.

She pulled out the jar of oil from behind her back.

"Just returning this."

She took a few steps toward me, and my breath caught as she reached around to place the jar on the shelf behind my head. Her black shirt shifted to the side, and I caught just the tip of the silver scar that I now knew stretched across her chest. Nothing could hide the flush that spread across my face as I thought about her, bare and exposed to me, just hours before.

I purposefully averted my gaze to instead focus on the shelves in front of me, trying to read the labels of the various cans and jars, but unable to retain any of it.

"Is everything okay?"

I tried to swallow, but my throat was dry and my voice came out scratched and hoarse.

"Yes," I coughed, "fine."

I could feel her gaze on me like the sweltering heat of a hot summer's day. My skin burned and tingled, and it was all I could do to keep myself as composed as I could possibly be.

"Okay, well, I'm on shift now. I guess I'll see you later."

Elora hesitated for a moment before finally removing her arm from around me and walking out the door.

My shoulders relaxed, and I let out a long breath. It was all I could do not to pull her into me so we could finish what we started last night. But was that something she wanted?

The question hung in my mind like a shadow.

I shook my head and scolded myself. I could guess all I wanted about her intentions and feelings, but I wouldn't know anything until we had a proper conversation. There wasn't anything I could do about us for the time being, so I returned my focus to the note at my side. It was time to put myself to the test and see what I was made of.

Gramps once told me a story of a woman who could change water into ice and steam with just a flick of her wrist. She was worshipped as a water goddess for many generations and was often sought after in the extreme months of winter and summer for what she could provide. When a traveling vagabond wandered through their village, he branded her a witch, a demon of the underworld, and an unearthly creature that should be banished back to the depths of the sea. Slowly, he changed the minds of the villagers, and the woman, despite her assistance and care for her community, was cast out and never returned.

When I was younger, I thought she was just a myth, but after Harlan's note, I wondered if there was more to the story than I had originally thought. Was I like her? Were my games of make-believe as a child actually the truth? Was this power that grew inside me with every waking minute something more than a magic trick? And if so, what did that mean for me? Would I too be abandoned? Cast out? Forgotten? Banished? Condemned?

I looked around the empty dining hall I was assigned to wash and wax. The isolation threatened to suffocate me. The chairs rested upside down on the tables, which made the room look crowded, but all I could sense was an overwhelming emptiness. I had already been abandoned, whether he meant to or not. To survive, I had cast myself out. I had made countless people forget me, and now here I was, banished and condemned from my life on land, running for my life, and praying that my mistakes would not catch up to haunt me.

The bucket of crystal-clear water reflected the pained look on my face. What would Elora think if she saw me like this, weak and uncertain? And worse, what if what I thought was true? What then? Who would I be to her? Who was I now? Would that change? Would Harlan understand? Did he already suspect? Why would he give me the note? And why now?

I closed my eyes and reached up behind my head to wrap my fingers around the back of my neck. The sea of questions flooded my mind. What if...what if...what if—

A loud crack brought me back to my senses. When I opened my eyes, I found that the bucket in front of me had snapped down the center. A thick layer of ice had formed on top of where the water was. It had forced the iron band holding the curved wood together apart, causing it to snap. A thin trail of water ran out from underneath the ice, coating the floor beneath it. I reached my fingers down into the small pool that was forming and felt the icy tendrils under my skin, calling to me.

A rush of something that almost felt like relief passed from my head all the way through my body and accumulated at my fingertips. Curious, I pressed them further into the water. My eyes widened as thin lines of ice formed like the roots of a tree burrowing into the earth.

My breath caught. The ice spread further and further. It reached all the way up into the stream that was feeding it and then down into the small reservoir. The wood swelled and cracked again until it was split all the way from the top to the bottom, exposing the clear crystals.

Wave after wave of energy continued to surge through me. I couldn't control it.

Panic gripped me.

I tried to pull my hands away, but they were stuck in a frozen grasp that I could not break away from. It slowly crept up my arms. I watched in horror as the silver streaks snaked their way up my pale arms, spinning webs of ice across my skin.

Two low voices began to echo through the hall to my right where the captain's quarters were. Another wave of horror swept through me. If they caught me here like this, stuck in these frozen manacles, there was no telling what they would do. No part of me wanted to find out.

I could feel my heartbeat in my fingers, and my skin almost felt like it was burning from the intense cold of the ice.

Burning....

Steam.

As their voices and footsteps came closer, I closed my eyes and tried to focus on the frozen mass beneath me.

It's just water, I told myself over and over again until I believed it. An image formed in my mind. The sea at night, its calm rise and fall, like it was alive, like it drew breath, like it had a form. I focused on that image with all the energy I could.

There was another crack and a rush of water over my hands as the bucket completely burst. The iron rod holding it together clanged on the ground next to the wooden splinters. I gasped with relief and pulled my hands free. I squeezed my fists together and ran my fingers over my wrists. They were red and swollen, but as far as I could tell, I wasn't hurt. The ice hadn't made it past my skin.

"...power...tonight. The feast must be filled." Drakkon's voice was much closer now. A few more steps, and I guessed they would enter the dining room.

I quickly shuffled under the tables to the corner and rested my back up against the wall.

"Everything is in place. All we need to do now is make sure the sailors are prepared for the sacrifice."

Sacrifice?

Drakkon and Rhyker made their way into the room and paused. I held my breath as I stared at their black boots under the table.

Slowly, one of them turned to face in my direction. He took a quiet step toward me. I squeezed my eyes shut and tried to grasp at the energy inside me. I needed to hide. I needed to disappear.

Another step.

It was like trying to hold water in an open hand: it kept slipping through my fingers.

Another step.

I reached for anything, any drop of power I had left.

Another step.

I couldn't do it. It was there, but I couldn't touch it. Each time I thought I was there, it pulled back.

Please, I begged. *Please.*

Another step. One more and he would be over top of me.

My head spun, and I dug my fingernails into the floorboards beneath me. With one last desperate push, I threw my mind into itself.

A flurry of stars danced in the darkness. They slowly pushed themselves together until they resembled a woman with her arms outstretched and long hair flowing behind her.

Her eyes opened to reveal two glowing, silver-green pools staring at me.

Stop fighting...let go....

She exploded into a thousand tiny fragments that surrounded and swirled around me. They crept in closer and closer and closer until all I could see was a golden haze. The darkness was gone. They pulsed around me like a heartbeat, and they swelled up to my mouth like the rising tide.

I let out my breath and allowed myself to be completely enveloped in them. It was unlike anything I had ever felt before. I was everything and nothing. Connected to all, yet bound to none. My heart burned in my chest. I was just as much a part of the sea, I realized, as she was a part of me.

"What is it, Rhyker?" Drakkon asked.

I hesitantly opened my eyes to find Rhyker staring down at me. No, not at me, through me.

"Nothing," Rhyker snarled. "Just some water a useless deckhand didn't clean up."

I didn't dare breathe.

"Deal with it later," Drakkon ordered.

Rhyker's face twitched slightly before he turned and made his way back to the captain.

"Go get everyone ready. I need them here before sunset."

"Yes, sir."

Rhyker stepped away.

"And Rhyker?"

His footsteps paused and turned around.

"Yes, Captain?"

"Don't disappoint me."

40

Duty

Elora

Giving in to temptation last night was possibly one of the most reckless things I had done in my life. And I had spent the better part of a decade in a fighting ring.

And yet, I couldn't get the image of her, breathless, wanting, and trembling in my arms, out of my head. The feel of her lips, the warmth of her skin, and the way it bumped and rippled under my touch...it was all too much.

It was like my own personal ghost, haunting my every step and every breath.

But the way she looked at me...like I was whole...like I was human...like I was more than the tool I had sharpened myself to be.

And our moment in the supply closet. The way her breath slightly caught as I moved around her to return the jar of oil, and the way she couldn't meet my eyes. All I wanted to do was take her jaw in my hand so she would look at me. I could have. I could have satiated the part of me that was starved for her gaze.

Gods.

How was it that on a quest for blood and on a ship full of liars, thieves, and murderers, that I would find the one person in the world that saw me for who I really was and didn't run the other way? A person who, despite all odds, cared about my well-being and my ambitions. A person who I never expected to trust, let alone care for.

I could have turned her head, but despite everything, I was still destined for death. I had seen enough of it in my life to know its pain. I wouldn't wish it on her, not for all the wealth or power in the world. If I could do one good thing in my life, it would be to make sure that Sybine never felt the weight of loss the same way I did.

So, like the self-sacrificing fool I had always been, I resolved to commit her taste and the touch of her skin to memory. I knew I would be glad to have something joyous to hold onto as Drakkon and I met our bitter ends. I used to think that would be memories with my father, and to some degree it was. But this was something far sweeter. Something just for us. Something untaintcd. Somcthing good. And in my experience, good things were destined to end. It was better for both of us if I gave her space. She wouldn't be tainted by me, and I wouldn't have a chance to hurt her.

I stepped down the stairs to the lower deck and made my way to the guards' room, next to the dining hall, for our afternoon briefing, only to find it empty. The room wasn't large or well lit. The narrow circular window didn't allow much light in, and the oil in the lantern on the wall was nearly out. The small flame flickered with the remainder of its life before it finally was extinguished into a dark cloud of smoke.

I took a step into the room and looked down at the table in the center. There was a note written in choppy handwriting resting on the top of the table. As I read it, a pit formed in my stomach.

To the Stormson Guards:

A special feast is to take place in the dining room this afternoon to reward the crewmates for their loyalty, sacrifices, and noble efforts aboard the ship. The crew eligible for this reward are posted below. Please ensure they are present for this reward.

~ Rhyker, First Mate

I clenched my fist at my side. If I knew anything about Drakkon, it was that he was slimy and sneaky and would do anything mischievous and malevolent to bring himself closer to whatever it was he desired. In no world would he willingly offer such a reward for anyone on his crew. Not even his first mate.

"Something the matter, officer?" a voice asked from behind me.

I turned around. Waldreg narrowed his eyes at me.

"No, sir. I was just inspecting the instructions for the day," I replied coolly.

"Well then, be quick about it. The captain does not like to be kept waiting."

"Indeed."

I took the paper from the table and made my way past Waldreg. I felt his eyes on me the entire way out of the room, and even when I passed through the door.

I let out a brief exhale and forced myself to take a deep breath. I needed a moment to stop and think without anyone watching me. As I passed several people in the halls, I heard them chattering excitedly about the upcoming feast.

I was just about to round the corner to our room at the end of the hall when I felt a sharp tug on my arm.

Without any warning, I stumbled forward into something invisible. I took several long steps, trying to regain my balance as I entered our room. As I turned around to figure out what had happened, Sybine materialized in front of me.

Sybine pushed me the rest of the way into the room and closed the door. She was out of breath, as if she had been running from or to something for a long while.

"Sybine? Are you okay?" I asked her.

She gulped deep breaths and urgently grabbed at my sleeves.

"I've been looking for you everywhere."

Her eyes were wide and panicked.

"What is it?" I asked her. "What's going on?"

She took another deep breath.

"It's the feast," she said. "It's a trap."

"A trap?"

She nodded.

"I just overheard a conversation between Drakkon and Rhyker. They plan to sacrifice the crew in some kind of ritual tonight."

I frowned and pinched my eyebrows together.

"I know how it sounds," she said, "but you have to believe me."

I briefly wondered if this had anything to do with the chains he was trying to get from Varix. But what could he possibly use the chains for to sacrifice the crew? Surely, this chain was not long enough to bind all of them.

She tightened her grip on my arm.

"Please, Elora. Please. We have to do something!"

"Lower your voice," I told her, and I brought her deeper into the room.

"If this is true, then I don't think there's anything we can do. They have all the guards bringing crew members to the dining hall as we speak. For all I know, everyone is already there and it's too late."

Her eyes were pleading and desperate.

My stomach turned. My mind raced. Was there anything I could do? I supposed I could try to trap Drakkon and Rhyker in a room somewhere, but that wouldn't guarantee anyone's safety. The only thing I could do that would be an absolute solution would be for me to make my move at the feast when they weren't expecting me.

"Okay," I told Sybine.

"Okay?"

"I'll try," I said. "But I can't promise anything. I will evaluate the situation when I get to the dining hall and make my decision there."

"What can I do?" she asked.

I took a breath.

"You need to stay here," I told her. "Getting yourself put on this roster won't help any of us."

"But I want to help."

I placed a hand on her shoulder and gave her a reassuring squeeze.

"You already have. But I really need to go. People are going to start wondering where I am."

"Okay," she said, "be safe."

"I'll do my best."

Every part of me was screaming to run. But where could I run to? We were in the middle of the sea. And there was Sybine to consider as well. No. I had to stay and make sure this ended. I had been waiting years for this moment.

I steeled my resolve and made my way to the dining hall. I stood outside with my back to the door, one hand on my sword, ready to fight my way through. I took a deep breath and counted down from three.

3.

2.

1.

Now.

I burst through the door and unsheathed my sword. I was met with complete silence. My eyes widened at the sight before me.

The tables were lined with people who had their heads sunk in their plates. Many had food in their hair and drinks spilled on their clothes. Nearly half of the chairs were occupied, meaning about half of the crew was here.

I put my sword back in its sheath and walked around, nudging them. Each person was unresponsive and limp. I lifted one man's arm up and it fell back onto the table with a loud thud.

"Come on," I said, shaking him, "wake up."

"Everything is as planned." Rhyker's voice echoed down the hall. They were close.

Shit.

I was too late.

There was no time to hide or leave. All I could do now was wait.

I stood up as straight as I could and held my hands behind my back, trying to look proud and unyielding.

My heart pounded with each of their footsteps as they approached.

"Good," Drakkon replied. "I need everything ready for tonight."

"It will be done."

Rhyker and I locked eyes as they entered the hall.

"You there, just the man we were looking for," Rhyker said to me.

I bowed to thcm slightly.

"Sir. Captain. I have performed my duties and brought the men to your tables. I am at your service."

"Good," Drakkon said again. "Bring in the rest of the guards. I need everyone in this room bound and rallied on deck by sundown."

I bowed again.

"It will be done."

Under the Full Moon

Sybine

"There was nothing I could do," Elora told me.

I sat on the bed, defeated. She made her way over to me.

"By the time I arrived, they were already gone."

"But—"

"They were gone when I got there—" her tone was sharp—
"and I was caught red-handed. I had to make it look like I was
being helpful, or they would have suspected me."

I flinched at her words.

She paused.

"If there was anything I could have done, I would have. But
there was only one of me, and twenty sailors. Whether they
were dead or alive doesn't matter. There's no way I could have

hidden twenty people on board in the time it took for Drakkon and Rhyker to make their way to the hall."

My shoulders slumped.

"I really believed we could save them."

Elora tensed beside me.

"I don't know how to save people, Sybine. I only know how to kill them."

I reached my hand out to reassure her, but brought it back to my lap. I still didn't know where we stood, and even though every part of me yearned to comfort her, I wasn't sure that's what she wanted.

"That's not true, Elora, and you know it. You ran into the flames to save Varix."

Elora tilted her head and dropped her gaze.

"After you goaded me. And she's still dead."

I frowned at her and sighed.

We both jumped when we heard a loud bang from outside the room.

Elora was immediately on her feet, and she made her way toward the door. She cracked it open slightly to look down the hall.

"What is it?" I asked her, scared to know the answer, fearing I already did.

"It's starting," she said, her tone dark and flat.

My jaw dropped.

"But you're...still you," I said, confused and surprised. How was she not being controlled by the same spell everyone else was?

She tensed and spun around.

"We need to go. Now."

Before I could say anything else, she took me by the arm and pulled me out of the room.

"Stay calm, follow everyone else's movements, and whatever you do, don't do anything foolish," she whispered to me as we made our way down the hall.

I swallowed and nodded, unsure of what we would see when we reached the upper deck, and scared of what we would find, or rather, *who* we would find.

The men in front of us walked in a single line down the hall. They looked lifeless and empty and completely devoid of anything that made them human. How was I supposed to fake this?

I fell into step behind Elora, not daring to take another look or make another sound.

Step by step, we ascended the stairs, where the night turned into a blazing inferno. A large fire had been lit in the middle of the deck. There was a black circle drawn around the fire in charcoal. The flames licked at the edge of it but never moved past the barrier. I tried not to gasp or stare as we walked by.

"And just where do you think you're going, Loren?" Rhyker said from behind me.

It took every ounce of willpower not to jump at his low voice.

Elora turned around and gave him a knowing smirk.

"Just making sure these rats knew where they were going." Her tone was sharp and confident.

I wanted to throw up.

"The guards are on the other side of the deck. Let these...rats...take their places. They know where they're going."

I swallowed down the acid at the back of my mouth and continued walking past Elora. All I wanted to do was reach out and take her hand. I wanted to tell her that everything was going to be okay. I wanted her to tell me the same. But more than that, I wanted to believe it.

I caught sight of Harlan from the corner of my eye and tried not to let out a sigh of relief. Slowly, I broke from the line to stand beside him against the rail on the starboard side of the ship.

"Are you okay?" he asked, his voice lower than a whisper.

I gave him a small nod in reply. It was a lie, but there was nothing the truth would do to help us now.

He reached out and took my hand.

"Don't be afraid," he said.

I squeezed his hand back.

"I'm glad you're okay," I whispered.

Harlan tensed, and the air around him changed.

"What is it?" I asked him.

"There's something strange on these tides tonight."

Before I had a chance to ask anything more, the fire in front of us roared, reaching high into the sky. That's when we saw them.

Half of the crew were bound and gagged at the edge of the deck. They were sitting with their hands tied to the railing behind their backs. Some were limp against the rail, but others were alert and frantically trying to break free of their bonds. Their screams were muffled by the fabric tied across their mouths, but that didn't stop their intensity or panic.

The guards, including Elora, stood to the side of the bound sailors. She gave no obvious signs of comfort or distress, except for the muscle that flexed on her jaw every time she clenched her teeth. We locked eyes across the flames. I could have sworn I saw her give the slightest shake of her head. Was it a warning? An apology? Something else? What was I supposed to do?

The rest of the crew circled around the fire, so Harlan and I followed. A few of the guards let out a cheer as the captain and Rhyker made their way up the stairs. Drakkon's black coat was open to reveal his white tunic underneath. The wind combed through his dark curls, and every flash of lightning accentuated the scars across the left side of his face. His face was clean-shaven, which made him look at least ten years younger than he had just the day before. The tails of his open coat dragged behind him, billowing with each step he took. His boots thudded strongly against the wood planks of the deck as he made his way toward the fire. Behind him, Rhyker was holding a large glass jar filled with something black that seemed to writhe and slither. My stomach turned, and I felt my heart leap in my chest.

"What do you think that is?" I asked.

There was only silence beside me. Harlan, it seemed, was just as taken aback as I was.

"I don't know," he finally said, "but I don't like the look of it."

More cheers erupted from the crew as Drakkon raised his arms in the air. A cruel smile spread across his face.

His head fell back, and he thrust his arms in the air. Lightning spread across the sky, accompanied by deep booms like the drums of fate.

"It's time, Rhyker," he said when the gods finally quieted.

Rhyker stepped forward and presented the jar. Drakkon raised it high in the air, which was followed by another round of cheers from the guards. With one swift movement, he threw it to the ground. A thousand shards of glass exploded from the jar, and the black mass that was encased within it emerged.

At first, it was just a small black cloud that writhed and pulsed. Slowly, it began to push and expand. It grew and grew until it nearly reached the bottom of the main mast. Its form warped and shifted, sometimes looking as if it were almost an otherworldly beast, other times as if it were an all-consuming void. There was an overwhelming sense of hatred that emanated from it that threatened to choke the air from my lungs.

A deep exhale from the black mass sent shivers down my spine. I could feel Harlan tense beside me as well. We both squeezed each other's hands and continued to watch from across the flames.

"Dark lord of the depths, I, Captain Drakkon Stormson of the *Vindicta*, free you of your bonds and welcome you to my vessel." The captain's voice was low and commanding. It seemed to echo and creep into every crevice of the ship.

A menacing laugh came from the black mass.

"Fool!" it screeched. "It was humansss who trapped me and a human who ssset me free. What doesss it matter?"

"When I heard of your entrapment, I went searching for you, great lord of the dark. And now, it seems we have finally met."

A hiss came from the darkness.

"As I understand it," the captain said, "you are now in my debt, Keldroth."

The demon shrieked, and its black mass swirled in the air. It was everything I could do to keep from flinching and hold my ground. I wanted to wake up from this nightmare, but every time I blinked, the same swirling darkness was in front of me.

"And what would Captain Drakkon Ssstormssson have as his prizzzzze?" Keldroth hissed.

"I do not ask of anything for free. In return for your favor, I have something to offer."

"And what could you possssibly have that I want?"

Drakkon smirked, and my stomach turned.

"I understand you have been chained for quite some time now, great lord. Perhaps that time has made you weak, and I can't have that affect my favor in return."

"WEAK?" the demon howled. It whirled around the captain in a frenzy. "You think me weak?"

"On the contrary," the captain said, unflinching. "I recognize your power and only wish to feed it."

I felt my breath catch in my throat. Not for the first time, my instincts were telling me to run. Only there was nowhere to run to.

Slowly, rain started to fall. It met the flames on the deck, and I watched as the drops turned to mist and returned to the sky.

The demon expanded in a sudden burst of darkness. All the hope was drained from my body, until all that was left was fear. It was all I could do to shut my eyes and pray to the gods that this horror would soon end.

42

Demon

Elora

There was a chance I could have fought Drakkon, given the distraction in front of us. But against a demon, Drakkon, Rhyker, the rest of the guards, and a crew of brainwashed sailors? Attacking him now would inevitably result in my demise. Instead, I was going to be forced to watch as my bound crewmates were devoured. My stomach twisted. I felt sick. I had a feeling that the sound of their cries would feature in my nightmares for many nights to come.

"Very well. What have you brought me?" Keldroth hissed.

The dark wisps of its body flowed like trapped smoke.

"You may take your share of souls with you down to the depths. May they help ease your hunger. I hope you find them to your...satisfaction." Drakkon motioned his hands toward the crewmates lined up along the side of the deck. "I have no need for them from this point on."

A symphony of muffled screams erupted from the bound crew at Drakkon's words. The hair on my arms rose at the sound.

I locked eyes with Sybine again. She looked back and forth between me and Drakkon. I shook my head, desperately trying to convey my silent message. She needed to stay where she was. There was nothing we could do now. Neither of us were prepared to fight a demon.

I watched in horror as she closed her eyes. I knew that look. She wasn't going to listen. My heart sank. If she made a move, I was going to be forced to make an impossible decision.

To my surprise, her eyes darted open. She flinched and looked over at Harlan, who seemed to be scolding her.

She glanced back at me. I knit my brows together and pushed my lower jaw out slightly. Hopefully she would understand my message. This wasn't worth us losing our lives over. Sometimes losses were necessary, even if they were so painful that they were nearly unbearable.

Keldroth twisted and snarled in the air above us. His red eyes glowed greedily.

"How...deliciousss," he snarled.

I tried not to flinch as Keldroth's smoky mass slowly moved in front of me, as if he were taunting his prey. Two dark

335

tendrils protruded from the black center and reached out toward the first sailor. I watched in horror as the man's skin slowly peeled from his body, exposing the muscles and bones beneath. His liquid flesh pooled around him and leaked out onto the deck. His now completely exposed eyes darted from side to side as he howled in pain. When his gaze met mine, it was all I could do not to empty the contents of my stomach on the spot. The stringy ligaments and tendons at the sides of his face tore as he screamed, until finally they snapped, and his lower jaw fell into the now rotting reservoir of skin in front of him. The whites of his eyes turned gray and shriveled until they were nothing more than two small, dry mounds. They detached from his sockets and disintegrated into a puff of dust in the wind, which was immediately inhaled by the demon. The man's cries were abruptly cut off, leaving only the haunting echo of his screams seared into my mind. The hollow mounds in the man's head seemed to stare at me in silent conviction. I forced myself to look away as Keldroth finally enveloped the sailor in his deathly embrace.

Keldroth moved to the next man and then the next, until one by one, each of the bound crew members was stripped apart and devoured whole. The demon grew more tangible with each victim until he took on a human-like form. Yet, he was twice taller than any man I had seen, and at least that broad. A red glow emanated from within him, matching his eyes.

When finally he consumed the last sailor, his features emerged. He turned around to the captain and the rest of the crew. His forehead was tall and lined with black smoke. His eyes, which at first had been as light as embers, now glowed with a ferocious fiery hue. There was a dark void where his mouth should have been, and his jaw dropped low. Several thick arms extended from his long torso which, too, were covered in smoke. He stood atop two large legs, thick as tree trunks, and hovered above the ground effortlessly.

I couldn't blink. I couldn't move. All I could do was stare wide-eyed at the scene in front of me. Drakkon was far more mad than I ever gave him credit for. Only he would see containing and releasing a demon to be something he could use to his advantage. I shivered, both from the image in front of me and the cold, damp cloth of my shirt that was beginning to stick to my body from the rain.

"It hasss been too long sssince I have tasssted a human mind," Keldroth said through a long inhale. He rolled his head around his neck and stretched out his limbs before settling his crimson gaze back on Drakkon.

Keldroth flashed back to the fire so fast that his motion was nearly imperceptible, save the trail of smoke he left behind.

Drakkon didn't twitch a muscle, even when the demon was close enough to devour him too. A wry smirk spread over his face as he reached around his body and brought something out from behind his back.

A long, thick silver chain clanged in his arms.

The chains. Varix's chains. But why?

The demon flinched back and let out a piercing cry. We all moved to cover our ears with our hands at the noise. Everyone except the captain, who seemed to relish in the demon's pain.

"Where...did you get thossse?" the demon screamed.

Drakkon's smile turned into an evil sneer.

"A little bird gave me a hint, and I had to raise hell to do the rest. True power requires sacrifice. Hers did nicely."

My eyes widened in understanding. Varix. She had been his sacrifice for the chains.

I looked over the flames to find Sybine staring back at me. Her eyes were wide and her lips parted slightly. Based on her expression, I assumed she had come to the same conclusion.

"I paid a steep price for these." With every word, Drakkon stepped closer to the demon, closing the space between them. He rustled the chains in his hands. "But something tells me her price was greater."

The demon hissed.

"That wicked wretch!" he screamed. "I ssshould have devoured the witch ssslowly and watched her sssuffer when I had the chanccce."

"Yes," the captain said, "you should have. But you didn't, and here we are."

He shook the chains again.

"Now, demon. Your freedom for my prophecy. Do we have a deal?"

Keldroth shrieked.

"Yesss. Yesss!"

Drakkon's eyes darkened, and I could have sworn I saw the same fire in his eyes as the demon's.

"Good," he purred.

Drakkon turned around to face the rest of his crew.

"Let you all bear witness to Captain Drakkon Stormson! He who tamed the demon, Keldroth!"

The fire raged higher. Lightning lit the sky, and thunder boomed, seemingly in response.

Drakkon raised his head and arms to the sky.

"The gods have awakened!" he called.

Thunder boomed in the dark night, loud enough to shake the ship.

Drakkon turned around again to face Keldroth.

"Tell me, demon," he commanded, "show me the prophecy."

Keldroth snarled.

"Asss you wisssh."

I was immediately thrust into darkness. It was cold and empty, and...hard? I stood on some kind of rough stone, but I had no control over my body. I turned around against my will and squinted through a narrow gap in the stone. The sea swirled just outside the opening and crashed against it. In the distance, I could barely make out a stone arch that framed the setting sun. Slowly, the dim light fell further and further out of sight until it was barely a pinprick in the darkness. I turned again, and my arm rose out in front of me. I pushed forward through something soft and thick like mud. Slowly, I was sucked in. I sank into the earth beneath my feet. Down, down, down I fell, until my lungs were filled with mud. At last, a glowing light exploded above me and I was transported back to the deck where the demon and Drakkon stood eye-to-eye. Then the demon spoke, his voice low and gritted.

Three shall enter the Sea King's lair,
The first of fire,
The second bound,
The third of water and air.

A weapon made of silver glass,
Many aspire,
But never found,

A Kiss of the Siren's Song

A king transformed to ash.

Below the depths, deep in the dark,

Time is dire,

The king is crowned,

And all is lost to thunder and spark.

The fire crackled. Light traced across the sky, accompanied by thunderous booms.

"I have done what you asssked," Keldroth hissed.

"As you have," Drakkon replied cooly. "Be gone now, demon. I have no more need for you," he said as he turned his back to the demon. "For now."

Drakkon gave Keldroth a wry grin over his shoulder as he threw the chains into the fire.

"No!" the demon screeched.

A low, menacing laugh escaped from Drakkon.

"I promised you freedom, yes. Freedom from your chains, but not freedom from me."

Keldroth's wails filled the air as the fire devoured the enchanted chains. He tried to reach for them, but the flames licked his hands, and his body caught fire. More screams filled the night as the demon transformed from a smokey mass to a ball of flame. Slowly, the fire ate away at the demon until all that was left was a small pile of damp ash on the deck.

"Get rid of it," Drakkon ordered Rhykcr.

"Yes, Captain," he replied.

Rhyker quickly made his way to the pile of ashes and swept them into a small jar. He closed it just as the ashes began to once again take on a smokey form. A series of symbols glowed red around the outside of the container. They rotated around the circumference in increasing speed until they finally snapped back against the glass. Once again, Keldroth's familiar black void filled the container.

I looked over to the side of the deck where the crew members used to be. The only evidence that anything had happened was a small pile of glowing red ash that soon blew away in the wind. It was an empty sacrifice, in my mind. How could twenty innocent lives possibly be worth the price of one prophecy?

Drakkon reached into the pocket of his trousers and retrieved a red ribbon tied in a tight knot. He wrapped it around his first and middle fingers before lifting it to his lips. As he whispered into the fabric, several small circles glowed gold against the crimson satin. When I looked closer, I realized they weren't circles. They were too long, and there were thin lines on the inside that resembled the pattern on the tips of a finger.

Shit.

Drakkon had somehow transferred the crew's fingerprints onto the ribbon. I cursed myself for not realizing it sooner. My right hand instinctively reached for one of the daggers at my back. As soon as my fingers gripped the hilt, I felt the hair on the back of my neck rise. I chanced a sideways glance. The rest of the guards were talking amongst themselves, but Rhyker was staring directly at me. His cold eyes dug into my mind with a ferocity I had only felt a few other times in my life.

I clenched my hand tighter as Rhyker closed the space between us. As soon as he was within an arm's reach, I turned my back to Drakkon and pointed the tip of my blade at Rhyker. He smirked at me.

"Careful, Loren, I would hate to slip and let Keldroth have his way with you."

Rhyker held the jar with only his thumb and forefinger, letting it loosely dangle in front of him.

I swore under my breath and held his gaze with equal fervor.

"That's enough for tonight." Drakkon's voice was accompanied by a series of synchronized footsteps that thudded behind me.

Reluctantly, I pulled my blade back. I quickly re-sheathed my dagger as I turned around so that I could have both Drakkon and Rhyker within my field of vision again.

The mindless crew walked singlefile down the stairs to the lower deck and cabins, with Harlan and Sybine at the end. As soon as they began their descent, Drakkon turned to the line of guards.

"Tonight was a test," he said. He took a few steps toward the stairs before he paused and looked over his shoulder. "You've passed...for now."

I ground my teeth together. The other guards reached around to pat each other on the shoulder, somehow immune to the horrors that had taken place in front of us just moments ago. My fingers itched to rid them of their celebration, but instead, I pushed my shoulders back and put on my mask of indifference.

"Captain, what about the fire?" Waldreg asked before Drakkon walked away.

"Leave it. We'll need it again tomorrow. I trust you not to break the circle—" he gestured to the line of charcoal around the blaze— "and condemn yourselves to drown in the middle of the sea."

The excitement died down slightly. Drakkon gave a slight nod before finally stepping down the stairs.

"Get some rest tonight, Loren," Rhyker said as he turned to follow Drakkon. His eyes trailed up and down my body as he passed me. He gave me a knowing look. "You never know when it might be your last."

43

Stay

Elora

Rhyker's words echoed in my mind over and over again, all the way from the fire to our room.

I was tired of trying to guess their plans. I had trained for battles with swords and strategy, not magic and demons. I was a fool. Both the experience and intelligence I had gained from myself and others had told me that Drakkon preferred to rely on his own strength and abilities. I had been so focused on protecting myself from, and learning to fight against those, that I never considered he would learn magic. How was I supposed to fight something that I had no experience with?

Defeated and exhausted, I opened the door to our room. Sybine was sitting on the bed with her head in her hands. Even from the door, I could tell she was trembling. Her shirt stuck to her back. The wet cloth was nearly see-through. Her hair fell around her head in thick clumps of damp curls. Water dripped down from them into the small pools accumulating at her feet.

"Are you okay?" I asked. I knew it was a ridiculous question the moment it left my lips.

She looked up at me with tears in her eyes.

"How the fuck am I supposed to be okay? I just watched a fucking demon eat half our crew, I was transported into some kind of nightmare, and then I watched the captain of this ship kill the demon just because he could!" Her voice cracked, and she moved her arms around her body in sharp motions as she talked.

I took a hesitant step toward her. A part of me wanted to reach out and console her, but how? It felt awkward and unnatural. There were no words that could possibly erase what we had witnessed tonight, no words to soothe the screams, and no words to bring anyone from the crew back.

You can't change the past, but you can still hope for the future.

I choked down a sob as I remembered the words my father used to say to me. I could almost feel his warm arms wrapped around me, rocking me gently. I met Sybine's teary gaze and hoped that she would find comfort in my father's wisdom like I did.

"I know what we saw was impossible. And I know it was scary. And I know this feels like it is going to change everything. But it's not, okay?" I sat down on the bed beside her and put a hand on hers. "It's not. Because tomorrow, the sun is going to rise, and the seas will still wave, and the wind will still blow. And tomorrow night, the moon will shine again, and the stars will dance in the night sky. And it will continue on like that until long after we are gone."

A tear danced down her cheek, and I wiped it away.

She sniffled.

"I'm scared," she said, looking up into my eyes.

"I know." I brushed her cheek again, and then, finally giving in, I pulled her into my chest. I needed the comfort just as much as she did, even if she didn't know it. "I'm scared too."

It was nearly impossible for me to admit to myself, let alone someone else, but the exhaustion had spread from my bones to my mind, and I no longer had the energy to hold everything in.

Sybine trembled in my arms.

"You should take off your clothes," I told her.

She tensed and pushed away from me slightly. When I looked down at her, I found her eyes wide and alarmed.

"What?"

I scoffed.

"You'll catch a chill if you stay in those," I said. "Take off your clothes and use the extra blanket from the bed to dry off."

She hesitated and looked back and forth between me and the chests.

I sighed, stood from the bed, and turned to look out the small window. The waves crashed hard against each other, causing their white caps to explode. A flash of light coursed across the sky, periodically illuminating the war of the sea.

An awkward tension hung between us. But after the events of tonight, I couldn't push my feelings to the side anymore. Only hours ago, I had been determined to focus solely on Drakkon. Now, all I could think about was her.

"You should take your own advice," Sybine said as she closed the top of one of the chests.

She was right. The burst of energy I had felt from seeing the demon had worn off, leaving me cold and shaky.

I did as she asked and undressed as well. My coat had covered me well enough, but even that couldn't stop the rain from drenching me. I brought my shirt over my head and shivered. The cool air of the night whispered against my exposed back, causing my skin to prickle.

"Here."

Sybine wrapped a blanket around my shoulders. It was still wet from her drying off, but it was much better than my soaked clothes.

"Thanks," I said.

I took down my pants and wrung them out. After I grabbed a new shirt, I hung both articles of clothing across my small wooden chest along the wall and hoped they would be dry by morning.

The frame creaked slightly as Sybine worked her way onto the bed.

"Okay, you can turn around now," she said.

I wrapped the blanket around myself and tucked it under my arms.

My breath caught when I saw her.

Her long hair curled tightly around her face. It seemed to dance around her features and over her pillow. Her eyes glowed with a calm silver green, and her skin seemed to shine in the moonlight. I swallowed hard.

"Is everything okay?" she asked.

As she sat up, her hair cascaded down her shoulders and back in long, dark waves.

I wanted to tell her about the longing in my chest. I wanted to tell her how confused she made me. I wanted to pull the words straight out of my heart. But how could I possibly do that? My tongue caught on the words before I had a chance to form them.

"Y-yes. Sorry," I stammered.

I could feel the heat rise to my face, and this time I knew the energy humming over my skin was all mine. My heart fluttered in my chest.

She lay back down and rolled toward the wall.

"Goodnight," she said.

I removed the wet blanket from my body, pulled the dry shirt over my head, and made my way into the bed.

"Goodnight."

Unseen Energies

Sybine

Every time I closed my eyes, I saw them: the helpless, bound and tortured men. I wanted to feel something else, anything else, other than the chilling and haunting shadow that writhed under my skin.

Elora cleared her throat. She was shivering slightly too.

"We might warm up quicker if we were closer together," she said.

My heart gave a loud thud in my chest. All I wanted to do was curl into her arms. I wanted her to hold me and kiss me and whisper sweet lies of safety and freedom into my ears. I wanted the ice in my veins to be replaced by a burning and unquenchable fire. I wanted every one of my senses to be so overwhelmed by her that when I closed my eyes, all I would see were hers staring back at me through the darkness.

I shuffled toward Elora until our backs touched.

A familiar energy coursed through my body. I shivered again, but not from the cold.

There was a long silent moment between us that seemed to stretch and envelop us both together in an unbreakable bond.

"Would it be okay if I turned around?" she asked me.

My cheeks flushed.

"Yes," I said, slightly out of breath.

Slowly, she turned. She paused for a moment.

"Can I put my arm around you?" she asked.

"Yes," I said, even more breathless.

She carefully placed her arm over my shoulder. Her large frame caged me perfectly.

"Can I hold you closer?" she whispered into my ear.

With that, the spell around us broke. Whatever apprehension and anxiety that had surrounded us before dissipated into thin air.

"Yes." The word came out as little more than a whisper from my mouth.

Her grip across me tightened, and I felt her breasts press against my back. Her hand came up and caressed my face. I leaned into it, taking all of her in. The salt from the ocean rain mixed with her usual wood and oil scent perfectly. I relaxed in her embrace, all parts of me feeling at home in her arms.

"Is this okay?" Her breath fluttered over my ear, causing my skin to pulse and hairs to rise.

"Yes," I whispered again.

All remnants of control left my body as I was completely overtaken by her spell.

She gave a deep chuckle.

"Is that all you can say, Sybine?"

I tried to swallow down the dryness in my throat.

"I thought...you wanted space," I finally said.

Elora hummed slightly, and the vibrations from her chest pushed against my back.

"Not tonight."

My breaths came quick and shallow. My brain was filled with no words, only thoughts of her. Thoughts of her hand in mine. Thoughts of her skin pressed against me. Thoughts of the sweet taste of her lips.

I turned around quickly and took her face in my hands. I pressed my forehead against hers and looked into her eyes.

"Can I kiss you?" I finally managed to ask her.

Her gaze darkened, and I squeezed my legs together.

"Yes."

Without hesitation, our lips met. A thousand strands of lightning raced from our mouths to each other. I felt the energy hum under my skin, through my chest, and down to where our legs tangled.

I rolled on top of her and pulled myself into her, willing our bodies to combine as one. The tip of her tongue made small circles against mine as our bodies moved in a perfect rhythm. I ran my hands through her short hair as hers explored and danced down my back. I arched involuntarily. My head came up, and a low moan escaped my lips.

I was suddenly acutely aware of what we were doing and the sounds I was making.

"What if they hear?" I asked.

Elora groaned into my skin.

"Let them." She inhaled sharply. "I don't care...and they're too...bewitched to tell...anyway," she said as she kissed down my throat. She paused when her lips met my collarbone.

"Do you like this?"

The words rolled off my tongue before I could even think of them.

"Oh gods, yes."

She held me close, and in one swift motion, we swapped places. She looked down from above me. Her eyes glistened in the soft moonlight.

I reached up to stroke her face, and she closed her eyes to lean into my hand.

Her fingers trailed down my sides until she reached the end of my shirt. She gave me a questioning look as she gripped the fabric in her hands. I nodded, not trusting my ability to form words, but needing to feel her skin on mine.

I arched my back as she pulled my shirt up over my body and then finally over my head. The cool air on my skin made me shiver, and my nipples hardened.

Elora looked down at me, her eyes dark pools. She ran a tongue over her lips as her gaze moved up and down my exposed chest. Her fingers interlaced with mine as she kissed my palm and traced the inside of my arm with her lips. I trembled when they hovered over the still healing scar on my forearm. Elora slowly and softly trailed the tips of her fingers from her other hand over my stomach and up to my breasts.

"How about this?" she asked with a slight nibble at the bottom of my ear.

"Uh huh," was all I could manage.

She made her way down my neck again, past the point where she had stopped before, and my breath caught as her tongue traced small circles over my nipple.

"Keep going," I told her.

My back bowed and my eyes rolled back as she traced a trail of kisses down my stomach. I squirmed with anticipation.

I could feel her warm breath on me as she made her way lower.

"You're so beautiful." Elora's voice seemed to swirl around me.

She moved my legs apart and placed gentle kisses along the insides of my thighs. Her teeth nipped at the top of my panties and grazed my skin.

I gasped and squirmed underneath her. It was too much and yet not enough at the same time. It was as if I was drowning in fresh air.

"I need...more," I begged.

Elora took a deep breath and wrapped her fingers under the fabric before pulling my underwear down to my ankles. The sharp movement sent a torrent of sparks under my skin, and I trembled.

She placed a gentle kiss on the arch of my left foot that made my eyes roll back in my head. Every inch of my skin was alive from her touch. She did the same on my right foot before wrapping her hands around my ankles and giving them a strong squeeze. She slowly traced the inside of my legs with her thumbs while her fingernails slightly scratched along the tops, leaving a trail of fire behind.

When she reached my hips again, she leaned down and placed a kiss just below my belly button.

The heat from her breath ignited another spark of flame within me, and I soon found myself begging for more.

"As you wish."

I let out a deep moan of pleasure as her tongue met my sensitive skin. Once again, I was overwhelmed with the energy coursing through me. Each circle she made with her tongue brought fresh waves through my body. I threw my head back and pulled on the sheets under me. Each wave brought new sensations and an ever-increasing urgency. My chest tightened and my breaths came faster. Elora ran her tongue all the way up my core, and my breath caught as she grazed me with her teeth when she reached the top.

"You taste like nectar from the gods...I want to feel what it's like to be inside you," she said, never fully taking her mouth away from me.

"Yes," I whispered again, barely able to form the word.

She gently pushed a finger inside me. Then two. Just when I had thought no extra levels of pleasure could be reached, she massaged upward with her fingertips. Every part of my body buzzed with life. The sound of her fingers moving in and out of me nearly sent me over the edge. I reached down and gripped her hair with one hand while I wrapped my fingers in the sheet below me with the other. Elora moaned against my skin, sending a ripple of pleasure through me. My vision started to blur, and I threw my head back against the pillow. I couldn't catch my breath, and I lost all control over my body. Wave after wave of exquisite euphoria crashed through me, and the urgency racing through my veins climbed until I couldn't take it anymore. My back arched again. Elora's fingers and tongue continued their pace, and my body began to shake. A sound of complete pleasure escaped from my lips as my brain was flooded with light and warmth. My heart leapt so strongly that I thought it might jump straight out of my chest and into her hands.

Elora slowly removed her fingers from me. I looked down just in time to see her tongue wrap around them as she sucked them into her mouth. I thought I'd known pleasure before, but that was nothing compared to my experience here in her bed. She removed her fingers from her mouth and leaned over me to give me one last kiss before kneeling between my legs again.

My breaths came heavy as I gasped for air. My body was still trembling, but not from the cold. I was completely taken with a feeling of peace and calm, and nothing filled my brain except for the sound of the rain outside.

"That was...not like anything...I have ever felt...before," I managed to say between gasps.

Elora kissed the inside of my hand and held it to her cheek.

She smiled gently, and her eyelashes tickled my palm. She brushed a hair from my face, and my body trembled under her touch.

"You're so beautiful."

I smiled.

"You said that already."

"And I'll say it again, Princess," she said, kissing my palm.

We sat there for a few moments, completely entranced by each other.

I finally caught my breath and shuffled back slightly so I could sit up.

I ran my hands down the front of her black shirt.

"What do you like?" I asked her as I tugged at the bottom of the fabric.

She leaned forward and placed a kiss on the tip of my nose.

"This," she replied simply.

I giggled.

"You know that's not what I mean."

Her eyes turned down slightly.

"It's...complicated," she admitted, and a hint of what sounded like embarrassment laced her words.

I let go of her shirt and caressed the side of her face, tilting it back up so she would look at me again.

"What do you like?" I repeated.

She shook her head slightly. "I—"

I cut her off with a kiss. My fingers worked through her hair and gripped around the strands tightly. She moaned against my lips and wrapped her arms around my waist. She pulled me into her chest as she flicked her tongue over mine. She pulled away slightly and pressed our foreheads together.

"Show me," I said, breathlessly, "please."

Elora took a long breath before pulling her shirt over her head, and her underwear down past her ankles. She took my hand and placed it at the bottom of her back.

"Now up...slowly," she whispered, guiding my hand over the small dip of her spine.

I reached a place just a few inches up that made the muscles in her back tense, and a gasp escaped her lips. It was the most beautiful sound I had ever heard.

Her flat chest pressed into mine as she bowed with pleasure.

"There," she sighed.

She reached around to take my hand again. This time, she put it against the soft part of her lower stomach. She closed her eyes and let her head fall back as she moved my hand over her skin until I reached the hollow of her hip bone. Again, she tensed and arched into me. Her breath caught and her eyes flew open.

"And there," she whispered.

Still holding onto my wrist, she pulled my hand up to her lips and placed a kiss on the back of it. Slowly, she took my fingers and trailed them over the chords of her neck that ran from her collarbone up to her ear.

"And there," she moaned.

There was something so soft and intimate about exploring her body this way. It was like her skin was a pattern of stars that only she knew how to read. It was an honor and a privilege to learn their connections.

Elora hummed with pleasure as she ran our hands down her body, past the point near the small of her back, and around across her stomach again. She paused just below her belly button and locked her darkened gaze on mine. My fingers ached to explore and taste every part of her.

"Is that...all...you like?" I asked, suddenly starved for breath.

She shook her head slightly and bit her lower lip as she drifted our hands down toward the warmth between her legs.

"Here." Her voice was dark and rough, and it sent a shiver down my spine.

Elora gasped as she pressed my fingers into her. She pulsed around me, pulling me deeper. She leaned back flat against the bed, and I pressed up gently inside her, searching for the harder ridge that I knew I enjoyed. Slowly and carefully, I ran the tips of my fingers over it.

Elora sucked in a breath, and she tensed around my fingers.

"Here?"

She nodded as she bit her lip and moved her hand to trace small circles around the sensitive point just above. Her other hand reached up to stroke her hardened nipple. She pushed her hips up slightly, and I pressed deeper into her. I stroked in and out of her, keeping the pressure on her upper wall. The sounds she made were like a lullaby to my ears. After seeing her pain and her reservations, it was like a blessing to witness her come undone in front of me.

I leaned over her and placed a kiss on the dip of her stomach by her hip bone. She twitched under me.

"Fuck," she moaned as I nipped my teeth at her skin.

I ran my tongue over the spot to soothe it and whispered my prayer into her.

"I want to know every part of you. I want to taste every inch of your sun-kissed skin. I want to drown in the dark depths of your mind. I want it all. I. Want. You."

I wasn't sure if it was my words or my actions that sent her over the edge, but her walls crashed in around my fingers and spasmed around me. I slowed my pace as she came down, and like she had done before, I removed my fingers and brought them to my tongue to taste her. Elora watched me with hooded eyes as I pushed my fingers into my mouth.

I bent down to place a soft and tender kiss on her lips.

"Are you warm now?" Elora asked me.

I laughed.

"You could say that."

We chuckled together. I lay back down on the bed, facing her. She held an arm out, and I placed my head on her chest. Her hand reached around me to hold me close, and she kissed the top of my head.

"Goodnight, Princess."

"Goodnight."

45

Fang

Elora

The ship was suspiciously quiet all morning. Drakkon and Rhyker were nowhere to be seen and the rest of the crew went about their duties as if nothing had happened the night before.

The weight of the thought of the demon was heavy on my shoulders as I did my rounds. It had only been a few hours since Drakkon's display of power and the delivery of the prophecy. The chill of the darkness still had me shivering at the thought.

I focused my attention on the other events of the night instead. Sybine's words echoed through my mind like the ghost of a whisper that refused to leave. She wanted me. More than I thought. And I would be lying to myself if I didn't want the same in return. There was something so freeing about letting go and allowing myself to be present with her. It was a liberation unlike any I had ever felt before. But it also came with a heavy burden.

"Loren," a deep voice spoke from behind me, interrupting my thoughts.

My skin crawled.

I turned around slowly. Drakkon was making his way toward me, one thick step at a time.

"Captain," I said, giving a slight bow. It killed me to feign respect. I wondered briefly if he would get close enough for me to slit his throat. Unfortunately, he stopped just out of reach.

"Join me." Drakkon's tone was commanding as he gestured to the end of the hall with his head.

Had Rhyker told him about our exchange last night? I studied Drakkon. He held one hand behind his back and the other stretched out to his side in invitation. His dark eyes were emotionless. Nothing in his body language or tone gave me a hint as to what I should expect from our meeting.

A stream of apprehension rippled through me. I had two options: strike now and hope that I would be fast enough to take him down before he struck back, or follow him and hope that there wasn't an ambush waiting for me at the end of the hall.

There was a loud bang, and Drakkon turned his gaze to the sound. This was the opportunity I had been waiting for.

I slowly reached around to my back.

Before my fingers found the hilt of my blade, someone ran into me. I turned to find Harlan muttering his apologies and retrieving his bucket from the ground.

"So sorry, sir. I beg your pardon. It won't happen again."

Frustration coursed through me. This old man had the worst timing. I leaned down and pretended to help him.

"What are you doing?" I whispered harshly.

He scowled at me. His blue eyes seemed to darken in the dim light of the hall.

"Savin' you from gettin' killed," he scolded back.

Harlan stood and adjusted his white tunic before grabbing onto the steel handle of his bucket. He walked past Drakkon, leaving me still crouched down, watching him with confusion. When Harlan made it to the stairs, he gave me a knowing look before ascending to the upper deck.

Drakkon mumbled something under his breath before returning his gaze to me. As he turned his body, the light of the afternoon sun winked across a blade he had hidden at his back.

Harlan was right. The old man, as much as it pained me to admit it, had likely just saved my life.

"My quarters. Now," Drakkon said as he gestured in front of him.

I stood, still slightly surprised that Harlan had noticed something I hadn't. I reluctantly walked ahead of Drakkon to the end of the hall and through the dining room. We passed through the tables, which had only yesterday been occupied by my former crewmates.

There was no ambush, but Rhyker stood where the narrow hall to Drakkon's quarters met the dining room. I clenched a fist at my side. They were always together. It was nearly impossible to catch one without the other.

"Rhyker," I said as we passed him.

His face twisted in a grimace.

"Loren." Rhyker's tone was bitter and unyielding.

He clearly hadn't forgotten last night's events.

And neither had I.

"Enjoy your night?" he asked through a snarl.

I beamed at him as I walked by. I would not give him the satisfaction of seeing me caught off guard.

"Very much so."

The two of them walked behind me as we continued down the hall toward Drakkon's door.

Drakkon walked through first, and Rhyker held the door behind him. I entered the room, which was completely unchanged since the last time I set foot in it. Did the man never sleep? The blankets on his bed looked undisturbed, and the curtains around the frame hung in the same position as they were in previously.

"Sit," Drakkon ordered.

Rhyker brought two chairs up to the desk. Drakkon stepped along the other side. After he took his seat, we took ours.

The air in the room changed as we all studied each other.

"So," Drakkon started, "what did you think of the full moon ritual, Loren?"

I exchanged a look with Rhyker. Had he not said anything to Drakkon? What was this meeting really about?

"It was an impressive display of power," I replied. It wasn't a lie, but it also wasn't the full truth. I wanted to tell him he was probably the maddest man I had ever met for holding a demon in a jar like a pet.

Drakkon leaned forward, resting his elbows on the top of the desk in front of him. He narrowed his eyes, but I held his stare.

"Yes, I suppose so," he said, unconvinced. "And have you figured out why yet?"

I pinched my brows together.

"Why?"

He softened his face as he brought out the book from the drawer to his right.

"Yes, why. Since you broke in and took a look at this for yourself."

I clenched my jaw. He had no proof of that. And anyway, it hadn't technically been me. It had been Sybine.

"I don't know what you're talking about."

The scar above Drakkon's eye twitched as he scowled at me.

"Don't play the fool, Loren. It doesn't suit you." He leaned back in his chair. "Don't bother lying. I know it was you. You're the only other person who has seen the book, aside from Rhyker. And—" he gestured to my side— "you have a key." He raised an eyebrow at me. "What do you say to that?"

Was this really going to be the careless mistake that cost me my life? I swore at myself for being so reckless.

I sat back in my chair, hoping to act as collected as possible.

"Better to look a fool than to be a fool."

The corners of Drakkon's lips turned up at my words.

"Indeed."

Drakkon flipped to a page in the crimson-bound book and turned it to face me. There was a sketched drawing of a dagger on the left page, and a crown on the right. Outlining both pages were a series of interconnected spirals that looked like tentacles.

I knew what the dagger on the left was as soon as I set eyes on it.

"Is that—"

"The Kraken's Fang?" Drakkon nodded. "What do you know of it?" he asked.

I shrugged as if this were any normal conversation, which, of course, it wasn't. This exchange was charged and full of skepticism.

"No more than any sailor. It's a legend. A formidable weapon that any captain would desire, I suppose." The lie swam off my tongue effortlessly.

"You suppose?" He raised an eyebrow at me.

"Forgive me, sir, but I'm not a captain. All I've known my entire life is what it means to hold a sword in my hand. I cannot imagine the skill and power it would take to wield such a weapon." More lies, but if Drakkon suspected anything, he didn't show it.

Drakkon leaned back in his chair and ran his thumb along his jawline.

A shudder ran up my spine. Unshaved, he looked so much like the horror from my nightmares.

"Indeed. It is a quest to find the Fang, and an entirely different quest to understand how to wield it. But I at last think I have discovered the secret."

"Truly, if anyone were to find a way, it would be you, Captain," Rhyker said.

It took all my effort not to roll my eyes at him.

"Great power requires great sacrifice. Tell me, Loren. What would you sacrifice if you could meet your heart's desire?"

I smiled. I had known the answer to the question ten years ago when the man sitting across the desk from me made me consider it.

"Everything," I replied.

Sybine's face flashed through my mind. It was only a moment, but it left a bitter taste in my mouth, and my stomach twisted.

Drakkon smiled.

"I knew there was something about you, Loren, from the moment I met you. You have a keen eye. I can appreciate that. You're a fighter, and not easily swayed by things so trivial as mundane feelings and nostalgia."

On the contrary. My feelings were precisely what led me here. But he didn't need to know that.

"That is a high compliment, Captain."

He smiled.

"Rhyker," he ordered, "fetch us some wine. We have a lot to talk about."

Drakkon wanted the Fang. I should have suspected it from the start, but I never thought he would be mad enough to challenge the Sea King for such a weapon. It still didn't make any sense.

I paced in the hall just outside of our room as I went over everything Drakkon said in our meeting.

Could I do it? Would I really be willing to sacrifice everything...to sacrifice...her? What would have been a definite answer only a few weeks ago was now not even remotely straightforward. Would Rhyker live up to his threat tonight and kill me? Would Drakkon make the final blow himself? Would I strike in time? Would Sybine get caught in the crossfire? Would they use her against me? Or worse, if she saw me take Drakkon's life with my own hands, would she ever view me the same way?

The only way I could keep her safe was to keep her away. The only way I wouldn't be distracted was if she wasn't there. And the only way I wouldn't have to choose between her and Drakkon was if I didn't have to make the decision in the first place.

I knew what I had to do, and I knew she wouldn't be happy about it.

The Dragon's Breath

Sybine

"Believe me, there is nothing more infuriating than your dreams being just out of reach," Elora said.

She paced around the room, her face growing more red by the moment. She hadn't stopped since she returned to tell me the story of her meeting with Rhyker and the captain. A part of me was concerned and wanted to stop her. Another part of me was concerned with keeping my head attached to my body. So I kept silent about that matter.

"I don't have much time," she said. "They're expecting me any moment now."

I stood up from the bed, almost eager to get this nightmare over with.

"Okay," I said, reluctantly. "Let's go."

She stopped her pacing and turned to face me. Her eyes were wide, and a muscle in her jaw ticked.

"No," she said simply.

"But I—"

"No," she said again, this time more forcefully. She ran her tongue over her lips before biting them together. "No." Her voice softened as she wove her fingers through her hair.

She made her way over to the bed and sat down. A long silence stretched between us, and I shuffled my weight from one foot to another, waiting for Elora to explain herself.

"You were wrong about me, you know," she finally said after a moment. "I didn't tell Drakkon and Rhyker about you because I thought it was the right thing to do." She looked at me. Her gaze was hard and unyielding.

My stomach dropped.

"What are you saying?"

She sucked her teeth and took a long breath.

"I'm saying I was going to use you. I *did* use you...I thought you could get me information, or at the very least, steal something for me."

No...no, this couldn't be true.

I shook my head in disbelief.

"Don't lie to me." My voice broke.

"I'm not lying, Sybine." Her tone took on a hard edge again. "But I didn't expect...fuck." She gripped the sheet between us in a tight fist. "I didn't expect to care about what happens to you."

I choked on a sob. Tears stung the corners of my eyes.

"I told myself that I was going to stay away from you to protect you, but I knew that wasn't true the moment that I thought it."

She stood to face me. She placed a hand under my chin and tilted it up so I could look at her. I swallowed as a tear traced its way down my face.

"You were right about one thing, Sybine. I am a coward. I didn't push myself away because I wanted to protect you. I was trying to protect *me*." Her face pinched together as if she were in pain. "I'm still trying to protect myself."

She released me and turned her back to me. I was speechless, trying to wrap my head around everything she had just said.

"I don't understand," I whispered.

She looked over her shoulder at me. There was a deep pain in her eyes that I had never seen before.

"No," she agreed, "you don't." She shook her head slightly. "And I hope you never will."

She turned on her heel and grabbed her black jacket from behind the door.

"You said I could save you. That was your sacrifice, remember? So let me save you!" The words poured from my lips in a desperate plea. I couldn't be left behind...not again.

"No one can save me now, Sybine." She took a long breath. "If I'm going to act, I need to act tonight. Tomorrow will be too late. And if he gets the Fang, I may never get the chance again. I have one last card to play and I have to play it. I have to show my hand, even if it means I lose in the end...I have to do this."

Another tear fell down my face.

"But you don't, Elora. You don't have to. You can stay and we can leave. We'll find a way."

Her hand froze on the doorknob.

"I have to do this. I don't expect you to understand, but I have to. It's all I know. It's all I am."

I stood and closed the distance between us.

"It's not all you are, okay? It's not all you are to me. You are so much more than this vessel of death you make yourself out to be. I...I—"

Elora turned and crashed her lips against mine in a fury of passion. I closed my eyes, and the tears fell down my cheeks. Her hands held my face, and all semblance of control left my body.

"I hope I see you again," she said. With those last words, she walked out the door and locked it behind her.

I stood there frozen for a long time. There was so much unsaid between us. There was so much she didn't know about me, about us, about everything. And she had just walked away.

I slammed my foot against the ground with such a force that it sent a jolt of pain up my leg. I was furious and hurt and scared. There was an ache in my chest that refused to dissipate. It threatened to choke me and overwhelm every one of my senses.

This wasn't real. It wasn't happening again. It couldn't happen again.

My vision clouded, replaced by the image of Gramps walking out the door, a playful, yet pained smile on his face as he looked over his shoulder at me for the last time.

Something in me snapped. Last time, I was barely nineteen. Last time, I didn't know any better. Last time, I thought I was helpless.

I looked over at the mug of water we kept beside the bed and pinched my lips together.

I wasn't a child anymore. This time, I did know better. This time, I wasn't helpless. This time, I wouldn't sit by and wait for things to unfold around me.

I grabbed the mug and made my way back to the door.

You can do this, I told myself over and over until I fully believed it. *You are not trapped. You are not broken. You are powerful, and you can do this.*

I straightened my back and threw the water against the crease where the door met its frame.

I was furious. That was true. But if something happened to Elora, I would never forgive myself. I also knew that if anything were to happen to me, Elora wouldn't forgive herself either. Or me, for that matter. Still, I couldn't just sit here. Elora didn't know what I could do. She didn't know that I could help, that I wanted to help. She didn't know how much it would break me if she died and I did nothing.

I held a hand on either side of the crease and focused on the water dripping down. I closed my eyes and cleared my thoughts.

In my mind, I imagined the water slowly solidifying and expanding. I imagined the crystals growing and pressing against the iron hinge of the lock. I imagined pushing past and enveloping the metal in its icy grip. I imagined it creeping between the boards of the door and splitting the wood in every crevice.

There was a loud snap, and I opened my eyes to find the edge of the door split from the lock. It swung open on its hinges as the ship rocked on the waves.

I had done it.

A mixture of emotions flooded me: pride, understanding, anger, but most of all, fear.

I was out of the door in an instant. Slowly, I crept among the shadows of the hall to where the staircase led to the upper deck. The light of the fire reflected off the wooden panels around me, engulfing me in what felt like a memory of the flame. I took a deep breath and cleared my mind, calling down to the power inside me.

No more fighting, I thought to myself. *Embrace who you are.*

A rush of energy rippled over my skin, and my hand, at first solid and tangible, washed away and transformed into a translucent wave in front of my eyes. As I shifted, the light from the fire reflected off of me like sparks of the setting sun over the sea. I looked around the rest of my body. Every inch of me in the shadows was crystal clear. I swallowed hard as I finally accepted myself for who I was.

I was a siren. Born of the Sea and now returned to the Sea.

As I stood there, an overwhelming feeling of purpose and a sense of home flooded my senses. This was me.

"This is the end." Drakkon's voice boomed from the deck, drawing my attention.

From behind the pillar where I stood, I saw Drakkon, standing in his open, gold-embroidered jacket next to the flames. There was a shorter man standing in his shadow that could have only been Rhyker.

Then I saw her. Beautiful and dangerous in the fire's light. It bounced off of her glowing, golden skin. The soft light cast a series of shadows over her face, making her features sharp and rigid. She looked powerful.

Elora glanced in my direction, and her features softened. At first, I thought she was relieved to see me. But then I realized she was relieved not to. A knot formed in my stomach. I pushed it back down.

Drakkon raised his arms up. The crackling of the fire was the only sound coming from the deck.

I wrapped my fingers around the wooden pillar in front of me as I listened.

Elora shifted her weight. Although she wasn't much shorter, she looked small standing next to him. There was something about Drakkon that commanded attention. He reveled in it.

Drakkon picked up a pitcher from in front of him and downed its contents in a matter of seconds. Then he lit a match and swallowed it. He paused for a moment before arching his head back and letting loose a gully of flames.

The Dragon's Breath.

My breath caught as the flames grew larger and higher. The ends of the flames flicked blue and orange, and the sparks flew high into the air before drifting into the sky with the stars.

Elora tensed, and her hand slowly drifted toward the knife she always held at her back. My stomach dropped as I realized what she was about to do.

I couldn't run to her. The light of the flames would ripple off my body, transforming me into a beacon. At best, it would provide a distraction. At worst, it would get us both killed. So, against the strings that pulled at my heart, I stayed and hoped that she would be fast enough.

"Behold, the Dragon's Breath!" Rhyker yelled. He held his arms outstretched to the captain.

The flames stopped, and Drakkon took something out of his pocket to hold up to his lips. Then, with a sudden movement, Drakkon whirled around, seizing Rhyker's arms to hold them behind his back.

I gasped and then immediately covered my mouth with my hand. Thankfully, the noise from Rhyker's protest masked my mistake.

"What?" The look on Rhyker's face was pure surprise. Even Elora seemed shocked by Drakkon's actions. Her eyes were wide and her mouth was slightly parted.

"You said it would be him!" Rhyker cried out as Drakkon dragged him up to the main mast. His legs flailed from side to side frantically as he tried to regain his footing. "You can't do this to me! You said it would be him!"

Everything happened so fast that I was frozen in place, unable to move or breathe. I couldn't believe what I was seeing. What was Drakkon doing? Was he going to sacrifice Rhyker the same way he had the other crew members? It made no sense. Rhyker was his first mate, his right-hand man. I had seen them...together. I shook my head, trying to make sense of everything.

Rhyker fought and tried to weasel out from the captain's clutches by twisting his body and throwing his shoulders forward and backward. Drakkon's grip never wavered. He tied Rhyker's hands behind his back and wrapped the rope around his body and the mast.

"Is this how you reward loyalty?" Rhyker sobbed. "I gave everything to you."

"It is," Drakkon said simply. "This is an honor, friend." His voice was low, and there was something in his tone that almost sounded as if he were in pain. "Once...long ago...you asked to bind yourself to me." Drakkon finished tying off the knots of the rope that bound Rhyker's body and moved around to face him. Drakkon reached out and brushed one of Rhyker's tears from his cheek. "Consider your wish fulfilled."

Elora seemed to be frozen still in her spot. Why wasn't she doing anything? Drakkon's back was turned, and Rhyker was immobilized. What was she waiting for?

Drakkon raised his voice again.

"Great power requires great sacrifice. Tonight, Rhyker, you will be immortalized, and our wishes will be granted."

"You're traitors! All of you! How can you stand by?" Rhyker spit. "Waldreg? Loren? How?" He thrashed and threw his head hard back against the mast, and I heard the splinters break off. His eyes slightly rolled to the back of his head, and the color drained from his face. A small trail of blood flowed from his nose. Rhyker's voice fell as he sobbed. "And you, Drakkon. I would have done anything for you...but not this." His voice broke. "Please...not this."

There was a long silence before Drakkon finally answered.

"I thank you for your noble sacrifice," Drakkon said as he reached down to grab the next pitcher.

"No...please." The words from Rhyker's mouth were barely audible, like all hope had been stripped from him. He said something else, but I couldn't hear it.

Drakkon leaned over and said something in Rhyker's ear before pushing himself away and bringing the pitcher up to his lips.

My stomach threatened to leap from my throat. My heart pounded in my chest, and my eyes widened as I watched the horror in front of me.

Drakkon lit the match and swallowed it. Rhyker's mouth opened one last time, but the flames reached him before he could mutter another word. Drakkon opened his mouth, and a sea of flames erupted from him. They climbed around Rhyker's body in a flurry of flashes and sparks. Within moments, he was reduced to a pile of ash on the deck.

The night was still and quiet. Elora remained frozen, her lips and brows pinched together in what looked like extreme focus. Everything fell into place as I realized it wasn't that she didn't want to move. It was that she couldn't.

Shit.

I looked back to where Drakkon was standing. He had one hand in his left pocket, while the other traced a pattern in the air in front of him.

Slowly, small golden flakes rose from the ashes where Rhyker once stood.

Drakkon kneeled over the pile and began to chant,

"I bind your soul to mine.
I bind your fate to mine.
I bind your life to mine.
I bind your soul to mine."

At the last line, he threw his head back. Slowly, Drakkon consumed the gold sparks. He lit up with a brilliant and blinding light, and his body pulsed with energy.

I watched in horror as he removed his hand from his pocket to reveal the jar holding the demon captive. A familiar red ribbon fell to the deck, loose and untied. He opened the lid and brought it to his mouth, inhaling the dark contents inside. Then he let out the most horrific bloodcurdling scream I had ever heard in my life.

A flash of white light exploded from his body, and I raised my arm instinctively to protect my eyes. It was several seconds before I could see again. I blinked furiously, trying to clear my vision. Slowly, the dark shadow solidified. He emerged taller and broader, and there was an eerie quality to him that made my skin crawl. His eyes glowed red, and a dark mist followed his breaths.

I was petrified. I had never witnessed something so horrific and terrifying. My head pounded with the sound of my heart racing. Just when I thought the horrors were through, Elora sprang forth from her position and lunged at Drakkon. She flew through the air with her dagger held above her head.

I didn't have time to scream.

Drakkon whirled around impossibly fast. His motion was little more than a dark blur. His arm connected with Elora square in her chest, sending her spiraling backward through the air.

Her body landed with a loud thud, and her skin screeched across the deck. She lay there unconscious in front of me.

All the breath left my body. My heart stopped and my stomach sank. This was her one chance, and it hadn't worked. And now, even if she survived, there was no way she could match his strength and power. He now possessed the power of two skilled warriors and a demon. I doubted even one of the gods could have challenged him and survived to tell the tale.

Powerful enough to rival the Sea King himself. The words echoed in my ears.

"Bring him to me." Drakkon's voice crackled, and his words seemed to possess the men on board.

Several men of the crew made their way toward Elora. Two of them grabbed her under her armpits and dragged her to the feet of the captain. He stood menacingly over her limp body. He nudged her with his large boot and a moan escaped with her breath.

My heart started again, and I let out an inaudible sigh. She was alive. Drakkon had evolved, and there was no way to stop him, but she was alive. She was alive.

He pulled her up by her hair until she was off the ground. Her eyes flew open, and she thrust her fist at his face. A horrible squelching noise was followed by a slight pop as she pulled her hand away.

Drakkon roared. The sound made every hair on my body rise. He threw Elora into the ship's railing, and her head hit a plank with a loud crack. The collar of her shirt caught under her arm as she fell, exposing the tip of the scar on her chest. The sinking feeling returned to my stomach. Her bloody hand fell limp beside her, and a giant eye rolled from her fingertips.

Drakkon screamed as his hand flew to where his missing eye should have been. A line of crimson tears fell down his hand and face. He staggered toward the fire, picked up an ember, and thrust it into his empty socket. Drakkon let out another howl of pain, and his body shook, his arms extended out on either side. When he turned around, the skin around his left eye was black and crusted. Dark cracks spread up his forehead and down his cheek like a shadow of the silver scars. The ember continued to glow red and orange in the place of his eye.

He snarled and whirled around to face Elora. His right eye narrowed at her.

"You!" he boomed. He flew toward her impossibly fast.

I couldn't let him take her. Consequences be damned. My feet finally became unglued, and I took a determined step forward. A hand from the darkness dragged me back.

"No, kid. Not now."

My eyes widened in surprise.

"Harlan? What are you doing?" I tried to wrench myself free, but his grip never wavered. "I can't just stand here and watch this happen."

He sighed.

"Yes. You must. Or I fear you will be lost as well."

A sob started in my chest and bubbled its way up my throat. Before I could make a noise, Harlan pulled me in close to him. My back pressed against his chest as he covered my mouth with his hand.

I flailed and squirmed, but nothing I did was able to break his grip. He was impossibly strong.

Tears poured down my face. And my body shook from my soundless cries.

"Tie her up," Drakkon ordered.

Tie her up...oh gods, he recognized her. Panic gripped me as an icy charge ran all over my body.

Several men of the crew made their way to Elora. They tied her hands behind her back, just as Drakkon had with Rhyker. Then they tied her bonds to one of the rails. She lay there, unconscious and unmoving.

"Ready the boats," he hissed. "We'll leave this one behind for the sea rats."

"Please," I begged Harlan, "let me go to her."

He squeezed my shoulder tighter.

"Not yet, kid. I'm sorry."

The men got to work hoisting the boats from the side of the ship down onto the sea below. Within minutes, everyone was loaded, and the torches were lit.

I watched as the fire in Drakkon's eye finally submerged below the deck. It was several minutes later before his orders to row finally drifted off into the distance.

Suddenly, Elora was on her feet, twisting around, trying to find her way out of the rope. She bit and clawed at her bonds.

Harlan finally let go of me, and I raced up the stairs.

"Elora!" I screamed

She turned around, confused. She still couldn't see me.

"Sybine? Where are you?"

"I'm he–"

A powerful wave hit the ship with a loud crash. Water sprayed up and splashed across the deck. I lost my footing and fell hard.

Elora's scream filled the night air as she stumbled over the railing and down into the ocean.

I reached my hand out into the empty air. There was a loud splash as she hit the water below. I jumped to my feet and raced over to where she once stood. Her hands were poking out of the water and her head was bobbing in and out, gasping for air.

"Elora!" I called. "Hold on!"

I took off my boots and readied myself to jump in behind her. A hand on my shoulder made me turn around.

"No, kid. Let me."

I didn't have time to react before Harlan placed a rope in my hand, ran toward the edge of the ship, and dove into the dark depths below.

The
Siren

A Kiss of the Siren's Song

Sybine

"I can't lift you both!" I cried. My arms shook as I held onto the rope, the force of the wind and the waves both working against me. My legs braced against the railing, and I leaned back to help pull.

Suddenly, the weight at the other end of the rope was lessened, as if something had broken free. I closed my eyes and took a deep breath.

Help me. Please, I begged the power within me.

A familiar rush of energy washed over me and covered my skin. With an astonishing burst of strength, I pulled the rope over the railing one arm at a time until I saw a limp body finally make it over the ledge.

Elora had the rope fastened around her waist, but the rest of it behind her fell limp against the side of the ship. I ran over to her and pulled on the end of the rope. It fell onto the deck with a loud thud, but there was no one else attached to it.

Harlan was lost.

I swallowed back tears as I focused my attention on Elora.

"Shit, shit, shit," I said to myself.

I tore open her shirt and began pumping her chest with my wrists. Her body shook slightly with each press of my arms, but no sign of life crossed her face.

"Wake up!" I screamed at her. "Wake up!"

Tears swam down my face and into my mouth. The salty tang of the sea mixed with my sweat and tears, and the rain poured around us.

A bright flash of lightning lit the night sky, and a loud crack of thunder followed shortly behind. The waves crashed against the side of the ship, and we rocked back and forth. With every pump of my arms, I willed life back into her, but her body remained limp under my hands.

"Don't leave me," I cried. "Don't you dare leave me!"

I took up my fist and slammed it into her chest with one last effort.

Nothing.

No hint of a breath from her mouth.

No hint of movement in her chest.

No light in her eyes.

Nothing.

I took her up into my lap and held her head close to my chest. I rocked back and forth with the waves, sobbing into her hair.

"I'm so sorry," I whispered into her ear. "I'm so sorry."

I kissed her gently on her forehead, then on each of her eyes. Finally, I placed a tender kiss on her lips. They were cold and wet and nothing like how she was supposed to be.

Something deep in my gut pulled at my consciousness. It grew and grew and grew until it became unbearable and impossible to contain. It tugged at me, begging for release like a dam about to burst.

I threw my head back and screamed up into the sky. The energy exploded from within me, sending shockwaves across the ship and the ocean all the way up past the mast and into the sky. The sky lit up completely with strokes of light that rained down upon us. I screamed and screamed and screamed until there was nothing left in my lungs and no song left in my heart to sing.

My head dropped, and I stared down at Elora's cold face. The rain fell on her cheeks, making it look like she, too, was weeping. An icy exhaustion crept into my bones. My heart pounded in my chest and my ears, and my vision darkened. I was so tired. My grip on Elora weakened. The last thing I saw before my head hit the deck was a soft flutter of her eyelids as they slowly opened.

"Sybine?"

Alive

Elora

My head pounded. My vision was black around the edges, and my stomach suddenly rose to my throat.

I rolled over and retched on the deck. It felt as if I was forced to purge my soul. My vision still swam with stars. I fought to catch my breath. I wiped my mouth with my sleeve and tried to blink the stars away.

"Sybine," I wheezed through a cough. "Sybine."

There was a vaguely human-shaped form in front of me. It looked small and frail under the rain and moonlight. The fire was still blazing with life on the deck. The light from the flames reflected in every direction and distorted through the figure. It was like looking through the sea at the setting sun.

Slowly, she returned to her normal state. Sybine's hair cascaded out from her head in dark waves all around her. With one hand, I reached out and touched her cheek. I let out a sigh of relief. She was warm to the touch.

She groaned.

"Ow."

I laughed. I couldn't help it. We were alive and it was impossible and our path was uncertain, but all I could think was that we were alive. We were soaking wet and covered with blood and bruises. But we were alive. We were completely abandoned and without a way of escape. But we were alive.

"Elora?" Sybine's eyes slowly flickered open. They glowed a magnificent green with silver halos around them.

I sighed with relief as I sat up and pulled her into my arms.

"You saved me," I said. I looked down at her and stroked her cheek with my thumb. My laughs had turned into sobs of joy at some point. I had completely lost control of myself.

"Yes," she mumbled, "I think I did." She smiled up at me as a small tear traced its way down the side of her face.

I pulled her into me, wrapping my arms around her. My hand slipped under her curls as I pulled her head to my chest.

"How the hell did we survive?"

She shook her head slightly.

"Sometimes it's better to not ask questions about the Fates," she replied.

I agreed.

We sat together with our bodies intertwined while the rain poured down and the thunder rolled in the skies. I didn't know how she had made it out of our room, or how she'd managed to pull me out of the water, but I would never stop being grateful that she had.

"I'm sorry," I sobbed into the top of her head. "I should have never locked you in that room. I was just...scared. But that was nothing compared to this...to seeing you like—" The words caught in my throat.

Sybine relaxed in my arms and nuzzled her head into my chest.

"Shh.... It's okay, Elora," she whispered as she ran a hand up my back. "I understand...I forgive you."

A warmth spread through my chest. I didn't know if I deserved her forgiveness after everything, but gods was I happy to hear the words come out of her mouth.

"Thank you," I murmured.

She wrapped her arms tighter around me.

"What the hell are we supposed to do now?" she asked.

A memory came flooding back to me. Harlan was in the water next to me, releasing my hands and tying the rope around my waist. There was a sharp tug from the rope, but we didn't move. I lost the last of my breath and took in a lungful of water. Before I finally submitted to the darkness, he let me go, and I watched him drift away deep into the ocean.

"Oh," I said.

My stomach knotted, and an overwhelming sense of guilt came over me.

"What is it?" Sybine asked as she pulled away from me.

I swallowed.

"Harlan...."

Sybine's face fell, and another stream of tears started down her cheeks.

"He jumped in after you. There was nothing I could do, he just...jumped." She took a breath. "I'm sorry, Elora.... It all happened so fast."

My heart broke for her.

"I'm sorry too," I said. "I know how close you two were."

She gave me a sad smile and sucked in a sharp breath between sobs.

"He deserved better."

Sybine nodded in agreement.

I bit my lips together. Sybine was exhausted. I was broken. Harlan was gone. And Drakkon had won. He was far more powerful than I ever could have thought, and he was about to get his hands on the most formidable weapon ever made.

"We can't let him get the Fang, Sybine."

She frowned.

"What even is the Kraken's Fang? Why is everyone so obsessed with it? And why is it so important?"

I bit my lip. The Kraken's Fang was supposed to be a legend, a myth. But if recent events had taught me anything, it was that the myths I knew were sometimes more real than I thought.

"The Fang is said to be the most powerful weapon in the world. If Drakkon wants it, then this mission is about far more than revenge. In the wrong hands, the Fang could do unimaginable damage. In Drakkon's hands..." my voice trailed off.

Sybine hesitated and looked up at me.

"There's something else though, isn't there?"

I nodded and let out a long breath.

"When Drakkon attacked our ship, he was looking for something. I think that, for some strange reason, he believed we had the Fang, or something that he thought would lead him to it? I used to think it was just some made-up story meant to scare kids into obedience, but the more I think of it, the more I truly believe that my father died protecting some kind of secret that had to do with the Fang. Something that he never told me. Something that I will probably never know."

Sybine leaned closer into me.

"Some secrets aren't ours to hold," she breathed.

I gave her a sad smile.

"It doesn't matter anymore." I shrugged. "It's possible that we're the only two who know what he's after that are willing to do anything about it. My father's secrets died with him. But this...this is bigger than all of it."

Sybine let out a soft sigh.

"How are we supposed to stop him, Elora?" There was a hint of despair in her voice. "What can the two of us possibly do against him?"

I shook my head.

"I don't know. But I can't just sit here and wait while he murders more innocent people, and worse...what will he do if he actually gets it?"

Sybine closed her eyes and she slumped in my arms.

"I don't want this," she whispered. "I don't know how to do this. A few weeks ago, I didn't know who I was or what kind of world I lived in. I just thought I was different. I saw things differently, and I felt things differently. I had these strange powers that I had no idea what to do with, and everything made complete, and yet no sense, all at the same time. And now," she sighed, "I'm a liar, a thief, a fool and...a siren."

My breath caught.

"A...siren?"

She nodded and tilted her head up to look at me. Her eyes searched my face for something.

"What are you thinking?" she asked.

I wasn't sure. It made sense. It described all of her strange powers. And who was I to question her? She knew herself better than anyone else.

"I believe you," I said as I reached up to stroke her face.

"You're not scared?"

I shook my head.

"I could never be scared of you, Sybine. Not unless you're planning on dragging me down to the bottom of the ocean and ripping the skin off my bones with your dagger-sharp teeth." I poked my finger at the space between her lips. "You don't have dagger-sharp teeth, do you?"

She pulled her head away, and the skin by her eyes crinkled as she smiled.

"Elora," she chastised.

I couldn't help but smile back.

"No, it doesn't change who you are to me, Sybine," I reassured her. "I just know you a little better now."

She relaxed slightly.

"Thank you."

I looked up at the night sky. The rain continued to pour, and lightning stroked the sky.

"I don't suppose any of your siren powers could magically wash us to shore," I said.

Sybine hesitated.

"That depends," she replied.

I glanced down to see a mischievous look on her face.

"On what?" I asked, unsure of whether I wanted to know the answer.

"How would you feel about another swim?"

49

Breathe

Elora

"Do you trust me?" she asked.

We stood on the edge of the railing of the ship, hand in hand. I could hear the flames rising behind us, devouring the ship. Once we had broken the charcoal line, the flames hungrily consumed everything in their path. The flames grew and grew until they climbed all the way up the main mast. Pieces of the cloth drifted down around us.

I looked at the churning sea below us and swallowed. We had thrown one of the wooden doors overboard to see if it would float and were relieved to see that it did. It wasn't a boat, but at least it would keep us on the surface while we made our way to shore.

"Do I have a choice?" I replied.

She shrugged.

"Not really."

With that, we leapt off the railing. I held my breath and closed my eyes as we crashed into the sea below. I looked over at Sybine, confused. I could still feel her hand in mine, but she blended in seamlessly with the surrounding sea. If I looked carefully, I could barely make out an outline of her body. But it could have easily been mistaken for a ripple in the waves.

I kicked and pulled at the water, bringing us back up to the surface. I took a deep breath, filling my lungs once we hit the open air again.

"Are you okay?" I asked Sybine.

I still couldn't properly see her, but if I looked closely, there were faint silver circles where her eyes should have been.

"I feel...incredible," she said.

The water was even more frigid than I remembered, and it didn't take long before my teeth started to chitter.

"It's fucking cold," I said bitterly as we swam toward the door.

"You didn't have any better ideas," Sybine stated simply.

She was right about that, but she didn't need to point it out. I sighed and climbed onto the door.

"How d-do you want to d-do this?" I asked as I shivered.

"You should stay up there. Try to warm yourself up. I'll kick from the back. It's not far. Can you steer us?"

Before I had a chance to answer, we started moving. I saw small ripples in the water behind us from where I guessed Sybine was kicking.

"Aren't you c-cold?" I asked her.

She laughed. It was beautiful and melodic, which was in stark contrast to the burning ship above us and the choppy sea.

"I can't feel a thing," she admitted, "and it's glorious."

My teeth continued to chitter as the cold seemed to sink into my bones. I had no energy for idle conversation. It was all I could do to keep myself from shivering straight off the door.

After a few minutes, Sybine finally broke the silence.

"How did you break out?" she asked.

"W-what?" I stammered.

"Drakkon's spell. I...saw you," she admitted. "You looked...stuck." She grunted the words as she kicked.

I winced, remembering the feel of the icy phantom grip holding my body.

"I d-don't know. One second all I c-could do w-was watch, and the n-next...I was f-free. I d-don't underst-tand."

"And you still knew what was happening?"

I nodded.

"It w-was like being f-forced to stay as-sleep through a nightm-mare with no c-control on how t-to end it."

How was she not freezing? The cool breeze felt like ice ripping my skin.

She hummed thoughtfully.

"No one else looked like that," she said. "They looked just as lost as last night."

She was right. Looking around, everyone's face was a blank mask. So what else had held me back? The questions were infuriating.

"I d-don't think we have all of the inf-formation to answer our q-questions, S-sybine, d-determined as we are."

She murmured in agreement.

"Have a rest, Elora. I can work from here."

"Watch out...for the...rocks," Sybine grunted.

After an hour of pushing us through the water, the swim back to land had finally taken its toll on her. Drakkon and the crew had steered more toward the south side of the island, so to make sure we put as much distance between us as possible, we had aimed toward the northern point.

I adapted quickly and turned us from side to side, weaving in and out of the rocks. How the crew had made their way through in their small rowboats was a complete mystery to me.

Sometime during the trip, I noticed the rain had stopped. I dared not take my eyes off the environment in front of me, but the soft sound of rain no longer accompanied Sybine's splashes in the night.

The frigid cold that covered my skin had turned to numbness and then to an almost warmth as we made our way over the water. Even my clothes had somewhat dried, despite still being on the sea.

"There, to the left." I pointed. "There's a clearing."

Sybine grunted in approval.

I turned us slowly and continued to paddle until we reached the shore.

We dragged ourselves and the door onto the sand and laid down on our backs. Sybine's body was now clearly visible, and she panted with exhaustion.

"Holy shit," she said between breaths. "I can't believe that worked."

I laughed.

"How do you think I feel?"

"Cold?" she asked.

"It was rhetorical." I rolled my eyes.

We sat on the beach for a moment to catch our breath. Sybine let out a long sigh.

My eyes drifted toward the ball of flames in the distance.

"Drakkon is going to be furious."

I nodded.

"It was the only way we could make sure he would be trapped even if he did get the Fang," I said, repeating the reasoning I had given Sybine earlier to convince her to break the charcoal circle around the fire.

"I know...but now we're stranded too."

I had nothing to say to that. She was right. A part of me was softened by her optimism. But I didn't share in her faith. I never expected us to make it out alive anyway. In the small and unlikely chance that we did, we would have to figure out what to do after. But until then, it was better to focus our efforts on finding and stopping Drakkon. Whatever it took.

We watched as the flames grew to impossible heights and then slowly faded until the only light that filled the night was that of the moon and stars.

I lay down beside Sybine and placed my hands behind my head. She rolled over and put her head on my chest. She draped her arm over my body and held me close. Her breathing, which had been ragged and strained when we'd reached the island, slowly returned to its normal rhythm.

"How are you feeling?" I asked her.

"So...tired," she mumbled into my chest.

"You should get some rest. I'll stay up and wake you if anything happens."

"What about...Drakkon?" she asked as she yawned. "He...recognized...you."

I looked back out at the horizon. My gut twisted as I remembered his words. The way he'd said "You!" like a curse. I pushed the thought away. It didn't matter now.

"I don't think he missed our message, but I also don't think he'll come searching for us. If he hasn't already, he'll realize that you and Harlan both weren't on the boats and assume that you helped me. And since there wasn't anywhere else to go, he'll probably assume we will wash up on shore at some point. But the island is big, and, as you can see, the shore is quite rocky, so it won't be easy for him to navigate. If I see a light from a torch or—"

Sybine's soft snores interrupted me.

I wrapped my arm around her and placed a kiss on the top of her head.

"Get some rest, Princess."

Life After Loss

Sybine

Rhyker was staring straight at me. Except the places where his eyes should have been were black voids that expanded until they took up half of his face.

"Ssssiren," he hissed.

He pointed a finger at me, and his jaw dropped open. His skin melted away, exposing his muscles and bones. Suddenly, he burst into flames. He let out a piercing scream and dissolved into a pile of ash on the deck. I watched in horror as a black, smoky mass materialized from it. As it took form, its arms and legs stretched out until it was taller than a house. It towered over me. I couldn't move. I couldn't breathe. I couldn't scream. All I could do was watch as its red eyes barreled toward me at impossible speed. Its jaws opened, prepared to swallow me whole and—

"Wake up!"

My eyes flew open as I was jarred awake. I patted all over my body, checking to make sure I hadn't been eaten or destroyed by the demon of my nightmare. When I found everything to be in its rightful place, I lay back down on the sand, panting and slick with sweat.

"Are you okay?" Elora asked.

I nodded.

"Bad dream."

Elora grunted.

"I'm afraid to sleep for that reason," she admitted.

I stretched my arms and legs.

"Should we go?" I asked.

Elora looked up at me skeptically.

"Go where?" She gestured to the shore around us and the thick brush behind us. "Even if we knew where we were going, we would still need some kind of light to make sure we didn't hurt ourselves on the rocks. And I'm not willing to risk Drakkon finding us right now. No. I think for tonight, we're better off staying here, or finding a small cave to sleep in. We'll search for them tomorrow."

I looked over at her. She sat with her legs crossed, fiddling with something in her lap. There was a pile of sticks, rocks, and palm leaves in front of her, along with a few coconuts.

"Okay," I agreed, silently thankful that we would have a night to rest. As much as I wanted to put on a brave face, I was exhausted. "What are you doing?"

"Keeping my hands busy," she replied. She sighed and dropped what she was working on in the sand. "I can't stop thinking about him."

I knit my brows together.

"Him?"

"Harlan," she clarified.

"Oh." I swallowed. The weight of Harlan's loss barreled into me like a wave crashing against the rocks. It took my breath away.

Elora moved closer to me and gripped my hand. Her shoulders slumped as if they were holding the weight of the world on them.

"There was something about the old man...." Elora took a deep breath and slowly exhaled. She brought her head up and looked at the night sky. I followed her gaze up toward the stars.

I wished my powers would work on her. Then maybe I would have a chance to help her through whatever troubling thoughts were occupying her mind.

"You look lost," I said. "What's on your mind?"

She sighed again.

"It's complicated...it's been years since I felt this way."

I frowned.

"Felt what?"

Her eyes met mine. They were glazed over with tears.

"Guilt."

I swallowed the lump in my throat.

"It's not your fault," I told her, even though I knew she was immediately going to dismiss it.

She shook her head.

"Isn't it? I got us all into this mess."

I positioned my body to face her and held her hands in mine.

"You did not put Harlan on that ship. You didn't put the rope in his hands. You didn't make the wave crash."

A small tear worked its way down her face.

"But I was so blinded by rage, so consumed by the prospect of revenge, that I lost sight of the consequences of my actions. For over a decade, I have only had to consider what might happen to me. I didn't stop to consider what might happen to you or Harlan or anyone else when I made that lunge."

I smiled at her sadly.

"You're allowed to make mistakes, Elora. You're only human."

She raised her eyebrows and resumed her gaze at the sky.

"Only human," she repeated.

A silence spread between us, like ice slowly freezing a lake.

"Have you ever watched someone you love die for you?"

Her question caught me completely off guard.

I shook my head.

She swallowed.

"I've seen it twice. That's two times more than anyone should have to endure. It feels...strange. Like I owe them something. Like I owe them a debt I could never possibly repay. I hate being out of balance. It's not who I am."

I shook my head.

"It's not a trade, Elora."

She looked at me, confused. Her eyebrows pinched together slightly.

"Love is not transactional. You can't buy it. You can't trade it. You definitely can't own it. Love is a gift."

Her face softened as she considered my words.

"Look, Elora. I won't pretend to understand the weight you feel, but if it helps, I don't think you owe Harlan any more than simply living. And I mean living, Elora. If not for him, then for yourself. You deserve that."

"What if it never goes away...the guilt?"

I shrugged.

"Then it never goes away." I paused for a moment, considering my next words. "When my Gramps passed away, I thought I would never recover. I thought that the pain would eventually be too much and crack me in half. I thought that I would never be able to feel anything else ever again, and that his absence would never leave the front of my mind. Then, one day, I found I woke up and got dressed, and then it wasn't until I went to put my boots on when the thought hit me again. At some point, I was able to go a full afternoon, then a full day without reliving the pain. It still hurts, Elora, and it doesn't go away, but it might get easier. There's no promise of it, but there is always hope. There is still life after loss, even if it doesn't always feel that way."

Elora gave me a sad smile.

I remembered the words she had said to me just one night ago.

"Like you said: tomorrow, the sun will rise, and the seas will wave, and the wind will blow. And tomorrow night, the moon will shine, and the stars will dance in the sky. And it will continue on like that over and over until long after we are gone."

Tears welled in Elora's eyes. She blinked, and a silver trail, illuminated by the moon, fell down her face.

"Thank you," she sobbed. "You don't know how much that means to me.

Ships

Elora

I couldn't help it. Harlan's death reminded me of my father, which only furthered the guilt I was feeling. I wasn't sure that the heavy grief and guilt would ever leave me, but Sybine was right. That was okay. Maybe one day, I would learn to grow around it.

"What did you do?" I asked. "You know, after your Gramps passed away."

Sybine bit her lips together slightly as she looked out to the sea.

"I collected stones from around the lake near our house and threw them into the water. I liked the way it rippled and sounded as the rocks made contact." Her face fell and her eyes saddened. "I know it wasn't much, but it made me feel at peace."

"Why the rocks?" I asked.

She finally looked up at me and smiled.

"He taught me how to jump them across the water when I was young, or at least he tried. I was never very good at it. His stones always made at least ten jumps before they finally submerged. I was lucky if mine didn't sink right away."

I laughed with her.

"It just felt right to honor him in that way."

I nodded. I understood completely.

"I never met my mother," I admitted. "She died just a few minutes after giving birth to me. My father would tell me stories about how she used to build these tiny ships from different things she found either on the ship or on the islands they visited. She was apparently a brilliant engineer. She would even carve unique designs into the wood if she had the time to make them look more realistic. So every year on my birthday, we would take whatever scraps around the ship we could find and try to build a ship out of them. Then, when the sun went down, we would let it free onto the sea."

At some point, hot tears began to pour down my face again. I hadn't been able to find it in myself to make one of the small ships after my father died. Something always felt like it was missing, and it always seemed to tear my heart open to think about it. So I pushed it away and hardened my heart around it. Until now. Sybine had cracked my heart wide open in all the best ways. In all the ways I could never have imagined I would experience. But with that came the memory of the pain. I was terrified that if I wasn't careful, I would drown in it.

Sybine reached over and brushed a tear from my cheek with her thumb.

"That's beautiful."

I smiled. Despite the throbbing in my chest, it felt good to remember. It felt good to share this part of me. A part that I kept tucked away. I used to think it would protect me. I wondered now if that was truly the best decision.

A small sparkle glinted in Sybine's eyes.

"Is that what you were working on?" she asked.

I nodded.

"Would you show me?"

A warmth spread through my chest as my heart gave a strong thud.

"It would be an honor."

"I don't know how to do this," Sybine said while holding up two sticks and a palm leaf.

I smiled at her.

"Watch."

I carefully folded the small leaf extensions over each other, making a slight box pattern. Sybine copied my moves the best she could. There were plenty of gaps in her weaving, but something told me it didn't matter. It was the act, the love that went into it, that was important. Not the quality of the final product.

When she was done, she held it up proudly and beamed at me.

"Now that your mast is done—"

Sybine's eyes widened.

"That was just the mast?"

I laughed.

"Did you think this was going to be a quick task?"

She pushed her lips together.

I shook my head at her and rolled my eyes.

"My father and I spent an entire day making these, remember?"

She flushed slightly under the light of the moon.

"Don't worry," I reassured her. "I won't make you stay up all night."

She gave a slight sigh of relief.

Although it had been years, my fingers quickly remembered how to assemble the mementos for my mother. I showed

Sybine how to weave the palm leaves around the sticks we picked up until they made the base of the boat. Sybine was deep in concentration and made slight tutting noises whenever she made a mistake. Eventually, the noises turned into a hum, and I recognized the melody.

"What's that song?" I asked her.

Even in the pale light of the moon, I could make out the flush in her cheeks.

"Something my Gramps used to sing to me....Harlan...he asked me to sing it for him once, and I didn't. But now, sitting here working on these ships, it won't leave my mind." She let her head fall back, and she rolled her shoulders.

"You can sing it now," I told her.

"Oh." She scratched the back of her head. "I don't know if that's—"

I held my hand up to stop her.

"You don't have to. But if it will help, I'm just letting you know you can."

"Oh," she said again. "Okay."

Only the sound of the sea breathing in and out of the shore accompanied the steady work of our fingers. After a few minutes, Sybine began to hum again, and shortly after, she let herself sing. She kept her voice low and breathy. It was barely a whisper on the wind.

E. A. M. Trofimenkoff

Her skin so pale and eyes of green,

More beautiful than we'd ever seen.

Our hearts so wished

For our Mother's Kiss.

More loved than we'd ever been.

Across the sea of memory,

She called our souls to be free.

Our hearts so longed,

For our Mother's Song,

And its soothing melody.

Behold! What sight had caught our eyes?

A Goddess in disguise!

Our hearts so shocked

By our Mother's loss.

And the courtiers who brought his demise.

The rumors now spread on the sea of red,

Of a creature worse than the dead,

Of our skin that shifts,

And our minds that rift,

Now monsters that sailors dread.

Gone today and reborn on the morrow.

A Kiss of the Siren's Song

Ready to surface, condemned to the shadows.

Now tarried we rest,

In the low, dark depths,

Ne'er to return to the shallows.

A shiver ran through me.

"That was beautiful," I told her. "And haunting. What's it about? It sounds like the Siren's Song, but I've never heard it sung like that before."

She shrugged.

"It didn't have a name in our house," she said. "It was just a lullaby about the sirens that Gramps used to sing to me before bed."

"The Siren's Lullaby?"

She let out a soft laugh.

"I guess so. Or the Siren's Lament. The older I got, the more weight the last two passages held. Even now, it's hard enough to think about them, let alone sing them."

We worked in silence after that. Finally, we tied our masts to their respective sticks and secured them to the base of our ships on either side. Mine stood fine, but Sybine's was slightly unbalanced. It tipped over even on the sand.

"I have an idea," she said.

She placed a few rocks on the right-hand side of the base. When she let it go, it finally stood on its own.

I smiled at hcr.

"Are you ready?"

She nodded.

Together, we made our way back to the place where the sea breathed against the sand.

We both pushed our ships out and let the sea wrap them in her embrace. The pressure in my chest lifted as I watched mine get carried out on the waves.

Sybine's sank almost immediately. She closed her eyes, and a wide smile stretched across her lips.

"I should have known," she said, shaking her head. "My rocks never did manage to skip across the surface."

I smiled down at her and took her face in my hands. Her eyes sparkled as they met my gaze. I placed a soft kiss on her forehead, and she wrapped her arms around my waist. Her ear pressed against my chest.

We both watched as my boat was carried off into the distance. Eventually, it kissed the horizon and was lost to our gazes forever.

Time to Say Goodbye

Sybine

The sea breeze was cool against my damp skin. The waves crashed onto the shore, playing through the rocks and nearly touching our feet. Elora and I stared at the night sky, hand in hand, and a part of me wished I could live in the moment forever. Another, greater, part of me knew there was only ever one choice: to move forward.

I squeezed Elora's hand.

"I can't say I expected this journey to bring me here," I admitted.

Elora squeezed back.

"It's strange. A few months ago, I was no one." I reached down and opened the bag at my side, strapped to my leg. I pulled out the crown and held it in front of me. "This one little thing brought me here to this moment. That feels both inconceivable and inevitable all at once."

"Inevitable?" Elora asked.

I smiled.

"Something tells me we were always meant to meet, Elora." I squeezed her hand. "Call it fate, or destiny, or whatever you like, but from the moment we met, I knew something was right about it. Does that make any sense to you?"

She shuffled in the sand beside me and let go of my hand. For a moment, I was afraid I had gone too far. All of this talk about fate must have been too much. I glanced over to find Elora holding herself up on her elbow, looking down at me. There was nothing except for wonder and admiration in her eyes.

"Actually, Sybine, I think it does make sense. But in a way where it is not supposed to. Sometimes, things aren't meant to be understood, they are just meant to be accepted."

I smiled and let my eyes roam back to the crown in my hands.

"Maybe Varix thought I was a princess because of this."

Elora laughed.

"Maybe. But I think technically you would have to marry the prince in order to get that status. I don't think that literally stealing his crown is enough."

"That's probably for the best. I doubt I would make a good monarch."

Elora shuffled beside me again.

"I disagree. I think you'd make a great leader. I think you could make a real difference."

Elora's words took me aback.

"You're just saying that because you like me," I teased.

Elora's tone went low and serious. She reached over and took my face in her hands so that I was looking directly into her eyes.

"I don't say this lightly, Sybine. You're kind. You see the good in people. I believe in you. I believe in your kind heart and your loyalty. And I think any realm would be lucky to have you as a leader. And I don't say this just because I like you. I say this because I completely and wholeheartedly believe in you."

My heart surged in my chest. It had been ages since I'd heard such a confession. The only other person who had held such a complete faith in me had been Gramps, and I hadn't heard those words from his mouth in years. I found myself at the brink of tears, unsure of how to process the powerful emotions coursing through me.

"I...I don't know what to say." I brought the crown back down and returned it to the bag at my side.

"You don't have to say anything." Elora kissed my cheek and then stood up, reaching a hand down to me. "You are allowed to just accept it, remember?"

I smiled and took her hand. She helped me to my feet.

"Now, we could stay on the beach all night, but I think it would be smarter to find some shelter." She gathered up the coconuts. "Come on. It's late. We have a long road ahead of us. It's time to say goodbye."

I nodded and entwined our fingers together.

I looked out to the sea, and under my breath, said my farewells to Harlan.

Light in the Dark

Sybine

We didn't have to walk too far before the sand ended and the trees began. I took a wrong step and sent my foot straight into a rock that looked like a shrub. I winced and swore under my breath.

Elora laughed beside me.

"I think we found our shelter."

I blinked and let my vision clear. The reason it looked like a shrub was because there were long vines hanging down on the stone. Elora pushed some of them aside to reveal a small entrance to a shallow cave.

"Do you think it's safe?" I asked.

Elora pushed hard on the rock in front of us, and nothing happened. It didn't budge even a hair's width. She shrugged.

"I'm sure I'm not the strongest thing in this forest, but it's probably safer than sleeping on the ground or in the sand."

With that, she brushed away the vines again and made her way inside. I followed behind her reluctantly. I wasn't particularly fond of cramped, dark places, but she was right. We didn't know what was lurking in the forest, and at least in the cave we would have some protection from both the weather and any potential predators.

There was only the dim light of the full moon that illuminated the first part of the cave. After a few steps, everything in front of me was pitch black. I had to stand nearly bent in half so that my head wouldn't hit the top rock. I wasn't sure how Elora managed it. I imagined her crawling on her hands and knees, and the thought sent an odd warmth through my core.

"Over here," she whispered.

I took another step and kneeled down. I tapped on the soft, mossy ground before finally reaching her leg. She grabbed my arm and pulled me on top of her.

"I hope you didn't pay a gold coin for this place," I teased.

I didn't have to be able to see her to know she was rolling her eyes at me.

"Do you think we're safe for the night?" I asked.

Elora's hands moved up from my hips to my shoulders and back down. Her fingers trailed delicate swirls along my spine that made my toes curl.

"I think this is as safe as we are getting," she replied. I had to agree. At least we had some cover here.

I rolled off and lay down on my back beside her. Anxiety gripped me. I didn't want to return to the waking or sleeping nightmares. Images of Keldroth's crimson eyes hovered in front of me. Echoes of the crew's screams as they were devoured rang through my ears. My heart thudded in my chest. I had survived it the first time because I'd had no choice, but I wasn't sure I would be able to live through their relentless haunting. I needed to rest. My body was so tired that even breathing was a labor.

Think of anything else, I told myself.

I cycled through a series of memories and images that used to bring me peace: the rolling hills by our childhood cabin, the meadow by the lake, baking with Gramps...none of them gave me more than a few seconds of reprieve before I cycled back to the horrors of the last few days.

Then Elora's face popped into my mind. She stood beside me at the nose of the *Vindicta*. The warm light of the setting sun played across her bronze skin. The gold flecks of her eyes danced like embers. She looked away from me, but then, to my surprisc, she turned back around and pressed her lips against mine. My core flushed with heat from the memory.

"Tell me what you're thinking," Elora said, bringing me back to my body.

I bit my lip and tightened my grip on her hand that I didn't know I had previously reached out for.

Elora turned her head to the side and placed her lips on my knuckles.

"I can't see your face, so you'll have to tell me." She reached over and brushed my hair behind my ear. She traced my cheekbone with her thumb, and I leaned into her embrace.

"I'm thinking of you," I admitted.

Elora let out a soft sigh.

"What about me?" she asked as she trailed her hand down my side.

A breath escaped my lips as I arched my back.

"Your touch...it's like a thousand tiny fires under my skin."

Elora sat up slightly and reached her hand around to grab behind my knee. She gently pulled me back on top of her so that I straddled her waist.

"I like the sound of that." She hummed while tracing the outside of my legs with her fingers. With a light snap, she released the bag from my side and placed it beside us. "You won't be needing your crown tonight, Princess." She kissed my hands again. "Tonight, you're my Queen, no matter what sits on your head or your body."

My heart jumped in my chest, and the fire spread throughout my body.

"Elora," I gasped.

"Yes," she whispered back to me.

"Touch me."

Elora's arms wrapped around my back and pulled me down. I brought my hands up and twisted her hair in my fingers as I pressed my lips into hers. Her hands traced my spine up and down before she began to explore other parts of my body.

I shivered as her fingers carefully danced down past my back and between my legs. I arched and my head fell back. She placed kisses up and down my neck and made her way to my ear.

Her warm breath and her tongue sent shivers across my skin, and when she nibbled lightly on my lobe, a moan escaped my lips.

"Do you want this?" she whispered into my ear.

"More than anything."

"Come here then. Show me what you want."

I slowly pulled away from her. I sat on top of her, straddling across her hips. Then I pulled my shirt over my head and threw it on the ground, hopefully close to my bag.

Elora's breaths quickened. She sat up and took one of my nipples in her mouth. I leaned my head back and gasped.

She rolled her tongue around before gently brushing her teeth against my sensitive skin and pulling away.

"Stand up."

I did as she asked, one hand over my head so I wouldn't crash against the stone. My legs trembled.

"Is this okay?" she asked as she undid my pants.

I closed my eyes, impatiently waiting for her tongue to touch me again.

"Yes. Please."

She pulled my pants down, and I stepped out of them. She massaged my legs, moving her hands all around as she kissed from my navel down to where my legs met.

Then, just when I thought her tongue would finally meet me, she pulled away. I stood there, trembling. My body begged for her touch.

She lay back down, and I was acutely aware of the absence of her touch on my body.

"Come, sit."

I moved to straddle her again.

"No," she said, gripping the tender skin of my hips and pulling me up toward her face. "Here."

I rotated and kneeled above her head.

"Are you sure I won't hurt you?" I asked.

"I'm quite sure."

She pulled my hips down to her face. When her tongue met my skin, a thousand waves of pleasure coursed through me. Her fingers gripped me from behind and pulled me closer.

My breaths quickened as her tongue flicked up and down. She pulled my hips in close and let her tongue trace the entire opening of my lips.

I dug my fingers into her hair as the familiar heat rose in me. A desperation too hot to snuff out. It was an unquenchable thirst, an insatiable hunger that could only be remedied by her touch.

My body began to tense and pulse, and hers responded in kind. We existed in perfect synchronicity as our bodies became one. A burst of energy exploded from within me. I could feel every stroke of desire and every drop of lust from Elora. I moaned as my mind was overcome with a pleasure so bright and vibrant, it cut off all my other senses.

I collapsed onto Elora, panting.

"How...do you do...that?" I asked breathlessly.

She let out a low chuckle.

"You have your magic, and I have mine."

54

Life

Elora

We woke up the next morning wrapped in each other's arms. It was still dark in the cave, but a hint of morning light played through the vines at the entrance. In the distance, I could hear the waves moving in and out of the shore.

"Good morning, Princess." I kissed Sybine's head.

She pushed her face deeper into my chest.

"I'm no princess," she grumbled sleepily.

I let out a low chuckle.

"You could have fooled me."

That teasing remark woke her up.

She sat up and moved her fingers along the back of my head. "How are you feeling?"

"Surprisingly okay," I replied. "It feels more like I ran into a bar rather than drowned and got my ass kicked by a human-demon hybrid, not necessarily in that order."

"Weird," she said.

I shrugged.

"I've had worse," I lied.

The truth was, I probably shouldn't have survived anything that had happened last night.

"Can I ask you a question?"

"Does that one count?" she teased.

"No." I continued, "What exactly did you do to bring me back once you pulled me up to the ship? The last thing I remembered was watching Harlan float away, then nothing. Then all of a sudden, I was awake and you were unconscious and invisible beside me."

She bit her lower lip.

"I, uhm, pressed on your chest for a while, but you wouldn't wake up. I got so scared, that I might have slammed my fist into your chest."

My hand instinctively rose to the small space between my ribs. It was tender under my touch.

"But then you still wouldn't wake up, and when I had finally given you up for dead, I felt this tug deep in my gut."

I tilted my head to the side.

"A tug?"

She raised her arms in the air as if she wasn't certain herself.

"More of an instinct? I'm not sure, but it was unlike any kind of pressure or pain I had ever known. I had to scream to let it go, and I exploded with light. The next thing I remember is waking up to your voice."

There had been a terrible, empty darkness that had swallowed me after I'd watched Harlan get dragged down to the depths. And there'd been a light. It had been dim at first, less than a pinprick, but had quickly grown upward, as if slicing through the fabric of death. It had called to me. And I had followed. I'd found Sybine on the other side.

I swallowed.

"Weird."

"I said that already."

"I'm just concurring."

We both sat up and looked out at the beach. We paused for a few moments, holding each other's hand and trying to find the will to trudge on.

"You look haunted," she said, peering up into my eyes.

I ran my fingers through my hair.

"I...don't think I can talk about it yet," I admitted.

She gave me a soft smile.

"Okay." Sybine reached out her other hand in front of her. "After you?" She looked at me expectantly.

I stood up and dusted myself off. When I got out of the little rock cove, I stretched and took in a deep breath. Sybine followed closely behind me.

"So...where do we start?" she asked.

I looked south. The sky was a dusty orange above us, streaked with thin white clouds. The sun hadn't yet peeked over the trees that swayed in the morning wind.

"Let's make our way down the coastline." I pointed in the direction I was facing. "We know Drakkon had to have landed somewhere south of us. Then, hopefully, we find him before he finds us."

I heard Sybine swallow loudly beside me.

"And if that doesn't happen?"

I squared my shoulders.

"Then this will be a much shorter trip than we expected."

Tracks of the Enemy

Sybine

Even though time was clearly not on our side, I was thankful we hadn't continued to hunt down Drakkon and the crew last night. In the dark, the trek around the beach would have been treacherous. Sharp rocks pointed out of the sand like spears. I had to keep my eyes focused on the ground beneath me so I didn't accidentally step on one. The larger boulders grew thicker as we made our way around. Eventually, we were forced to climb over them to reach the other side of the beach. My muscles ached from yesterday, but something told me that this was only the beginning of our trials.

We drank the milk of the coconuts and chewed on their meat while we made our way south. As soon as we couldn't stomach any more, we scooped out what we hadn't eaten and placed it in a small woven leaf for later if we needed it.

We were forced to take a break once we reached the other side of the beach. Both of us were sore and out of breath from climbing over the rocky terrain. The sky was much redder than I had ever seen in the morning. Something about it felt deeply wrong. It made my skin crawl.

"What's that?" Elora asked, pointing to something dark floating a few paces ahead of us.

We both stood from the rock we were resting on to inspect whatever it was that had washed up on the beach. I brought my hand up to cover my mouth when I realized what it was.

The tattered remains of one of the crew's tunics washed in and out with the tide. It was torn all the way from the bottom up to the arm and covered in sand and grime from the sea.

A loud crack sent both of us down to our knees. I scanned the beach and the tree line for any movement, but there was nothing, save for the wind brushing through the leaves.

"Do you see anything?" I whispered.

She shook her head.

I was just about to stand up again when something hit the back of my leg.

I jumped and scurried back in the sand. My heart raced, terrified that we had been caught. But no one else was there. It wasn't a person that reached out for me. It was the remains of one of the boats Drakkon and the crew had taken to row to the island.

The boat was split in half; the back was nowhere to be found. The wood splintered on the sides like teeth, as if the jaws of the sea had opened and swallowed the sailors whole.

I sucked in a breath, trying to steady myself.

"We must be close," Elora said, still crouched, as she studied the area around us.

She was right. We kept our eyes on the sand in front of us and the trees beside us, and within a few minutes, we found a trail in the sand and several sets of footprints the sea had not yet washed away. At the end of them was a single boat in perfect shape, seemingly untouched. Another path of footsteps led away from us, facing further south.

Elora moved into the jungle and searched around the boat.

"Keep an eye out for anything that doesn't look like it belongs here," she said.

I turned around to look for any other debris floating in from the sea, when I saw it.

My eyes widened.

"Oh my gods," I gasped. "Does that count?"

I pointed toward a large stone arch resting in the waves.

Elora was beside me again, nearly in an instant. She froze when her eyes landed on the archway as well.

"The prophecy," she whispered. "I thought...gods.... He didn't need the prophecy, he needed the—"

"Vision," I finished for her. "Please tell me this isn't what I think this is."

"I don't think I can do that," Elora replied.

I reached out to grab her hand. She looked down, and after a moment, laced her fingers in mine.

"Do you think they're still here?"

The short waves of her hair shuffled as she shook her head.

"If they were, we would have seen them by now." She tugged on my arm, ushering me forward. "Come on."

As we continued down the shore, we discussed the details of Keldroth's vision.

"What do you remember?" she asked me.

I thought back to that horrible night, trying to block out the screams, and instead focus on the prophecy.

"It was dark...the sun was going down...and it was...hard? I wasn't standing on sand."

"Was it hard for you to see too? Like you only had a narrow view?"

I nodded.

"Yes, it was almost like I was at the back of—"

"A cave?" she interrupted, pointing ahead of us.

A large cluster of rocks sat at the edge of the beach facing toward the stone arch.

Elora squeezed my hand and pulled me in closer to her. She raised a finger to her lips for us to be quiet.

"Are they still in there?" I whispered.

She raised her shoulders slightly and let go of my hand as she reached around her back to the daggers she kept there. She pressed one into my palm and then gestured to her ribs and her throat: the two places she told me to strike at if I had the chance to land a killing blow.

I nodded in understanding.

We approached the cave as quietly as possible. Elora rested her back against the outside as she peeked around the front. She looked back at me and tilted her head. With her free hand, she counted down.

3.

2.

1.

She jumped in front of the cave entrance, holding her blade up in front of her.

Only silence followed.

After a few moments, I turned my head around the corner as well. The cave was empty, save for Elora and four skeletal remains scattered across the stone floor.

I felt my stomach rise to my throat.

"Are those—" I couldn't get myself to finish the sentence.

"The crew?" She pushed a piece of bone away from one of the skulls with her boot. "I don't know. Keldroth didn't leave any bones behind last time, but the gods only know what Drakkon might have done with the same power."

I found myself swallowing over and over again to keep the bile down. It stung the back of my mouth like fire.

"This is it," she said, gesturing around her. "The Kraken's Cove."

She took a few steps further into the darkness and pushed her hand through where the back of the cave should have been. The illusion rippled around her arm. She pulled back and turned to face me.

"Together?"

She reached out for my hand. She knew as well as I did that there was no turning back now. I closed the space between us, pressed my palm against hers, and laced our fingers together.

"Together."

Trial by Fire

Sybine

Together, we stepped into the darkness. When we went to take another step, we found our feet were stuck. Slowly, we sank. The void bubbled up around us. My breaths came faster and faster, and I could hear my heartbeat in my ears. I turned my head to Elora. She had her eyes closed and was holding her breath. She was the face of perfect calmness, but I could feel through her hand that she was trembling.

"It's going to be okay," I said, more to myself than her.

We sank deeper and deeper. I followed Elora's lead, closed my eyes, and held my breath. Then we went under.

The darkness would have been terrifying on its own, but it was the complete silence that unnerved me. Like a complete absence of the senses. We were suspended in a place where nothing existed. I was floating and falling all at the same time.

I could still feel Elora's hand in mine, and I squeezed it. She squeezed back, and together, we continued our descent.

"Ouch."

Elora and I hit the floor on our backs.

"I really need to stop landing like that," she said, rubbing her backside.

I looked around. There was a faint light ahead of us. The floor below us was cold and damp. I carefully stood with one hand above my head like I had in the cave, until I reached full stance. Elora apparently hadn't thought of that, and I winced when I heard her head hit the ceiling.

"I need to stop doing that too."

"Come on, I see a light ahead."

I grabbed her arm and pulled her forward. We crept through the tunnel slowly, watching every step. Elora crouched behind me. The air from her breath teased the small loose strands of hair at the back of my head, sending a shiver down my spine.

Suddenly, our footsteps no longer echoed. The narrow tunnel opened into a brightly lit cave. I stopped and took a careful step forward.

The light in front of us grew ten times the size. The flames from the inferno illuminated a huge spherical cave. I flinched and covered my eyes with my arm.

Everything looked strange and familiar. I had seen something with a fire under a dome before, and a...hand?

"Oh gods," I muttered.

"What is it?" she asked.

"The book." I turned to her. "That day you sent me to find the book. I didn't read any of it, but I saw some drawings before I left, remember? The rock frame with the waves against it? And the hand on the fire? Drakkon wasn't just reading some random book. He was studying. For this."

Her lips parted slightly as she turned to take in the sight around us again.

"Oh gods," she repeated my words.

"What do you think it means?" I asked.

She raised her shoulder.

"I'm not sure.... Do you remember anything else?"

I tried to envision the sketches again, but no extra details came to mind.

"No, it was just a hand on top of the fire."

"Maybe it wants us to put it out," she suggested.

The flames soared excitedly into the air.

I scoffed.

"How the fuck are we supposed to do that?"

Elora pointed a finger below us. My eyes followed, and widened. I hadn't noticed what I was standing on: a narrow pathway to the fire in the middle. Nothing but darkness surrounded the pathway and the pyre.

I gulped loudly.

"You're the one with the water powers," Elora said expectantly.

I let out an exasperated sigh and placed a finger on my temple.

"And I'm supposed to what? Magic us out of this? If you didn't notice, the blazing inferno ahead of us is made of flames, not water." I gestured to the fire at the end of the path.

I stopped and thought about this for a moment. The flames were not water, but they did flicker like light bouncing through waves.

My eyes widened. I turned around quickly and made my way to the fire.

"Wait, Sybine, what are you—"

I cut her off with my hand outstretched and then returned my focus to the flames. Their pattern was chaotic and unpredictable, just like water. They ebbed and flowed, just like water, and yet they were complete opposites.

I placed a hand on the pyre and it sizzled at my touch, but the flames didn't hurt me. I closed my eyes and reached down into the powerful part of me.

"What the...."

57

Thorns

Elora

When I opened my eyes, Sybine's skin was clear again. The light from the fire bounced around her, illuminating her in shades of yellow and orange. She was exquisite. She was radiant. It was as if she were a part of the flames herself. Then she stepped onto the pyre and disappeared.

"Sybine!" I called out.

"I'm here, Elora," her voice echoed through the room, but I couldn't see her.

I slowly approached the pyre until I didn't dare get closer.

"Where are you?" I looked up and down.

"I'm here."

A flame-lit hand reached out and pulled me into the fire. There was no heat from the flames. Like the back of the cave, it was just an illusion. I looked down and couldn't believe what I was seeing. I was on fire, and yet not on fire. The flames licked around my body as if ready to engulf me, but never touched my skin.

Something cracked under our feet, and my stomach twisted.

"Hold on to me," Sybine said.

I could see her eyes glowing bright green amidst the red flames.

The light went out, and we plummeted into the darkness.

Fortunately, we landed on something soft this time. Our fall was cushioned by a damp bed of moss.

Still, the falls and the fights had taken their toll on me. I groaned as I sat up and dusted myself off.

Sybine inched herself toward me.

"So...now what?" she asked.

"This again?"

"It was rhetorical."

Suddenly, three bright orbs appeared in front of us. Each one shone a different color: one blue, one green, one purple.

Just as quickly as they appeared, they disappeared with a slight pop.

"That's not ominous at all," Sybine said from beside me.

"Shhh!"

"Sorry," she whispered.

The room slowly breathed to life as small fireflies, which nestled all along the moss-covered surfaces, glowed. Sybine was completely immersed by them. It was possibly one of the most beautiful things I had seen in my entire life.

We made our way to the end of the room where there were three halls. The one on the left seemed to be similar to this room. The middle one was lit brilliantly, and the one on the right was pitch black.

"This must be the three doors," I said, remembering one of the other drawings Sybine had mentioned.

She nodded.

"Which one do we take?"

"Did the book say anything about them?" I asked.

The exposed curls of her braid bounced as she shook her head.

"Not that I can remember. I was too far away to read any of the words. Maybe we should take a closer look."

Even after walking up to the hall on the right, we couldn't see anything else. It was like a wall of darkness that sucked in any light and extinguished it. The one in the middle was so bright that both of us had to hold our hands out in front of our faces and squint to see anything clearly. The walls were made of some kind of translucent crystal. It wasn't far down before the hall took a turn to the right that we couldn't see past. If we chose that one, at least we would be able to see something.

The hall furthest to the left felt like an extension of the room. More fireflies gathered around the green vegetation that covered the walls. The floor was a soft bed of vibrant moss that, as a child, I would have loved to have run barefoot through. Leaves of all different shades of greens, oranges, and reds sprouted from the thin vines that ran along the archway of the walls and roof.

"Maybe we should try this one first," Sybine said as she started walking into it.

Although it seemed much the same as our current room, the air was cold, and something in my gut was distrusting of it. As Sybine walked through, the walls around her began to twist and writhe.

"Wait!" I called after her. I ran up to her and caught her hand, but it was too late. As soon as my feet crossed the threshold, a metal gate slammed down, blocking our path back.

I took a deep breath, and the air around us tensed.

"Is that supposed to happen?" Sybine asked sheepishly.

I sighed.

"I have no idea...but we're here now. Let's see where it leads."

As we made our way down the hall, the moss turned to densely woven green vines. Slowly, the hall narrowed as the vines thickened. Large leaves tugged at my pants and sleeves with every step. Sybine followed behind me, so close that she ran her foot into the back of mine.

"Ouch."

As I turned to see why she had struck me, one of the vines spontaneously grew across the hall. I ran straight into a thorn, and it cut me across the cheek. I could feel a warm wetness work its way down my cheek.

My hand came up to inspect the wound, and my fingers returned covered in warm, fresh blood.

"Great," I murmured. "Are you okay?"

There was no response, not even a breath behind me. When I looked back, Sybine was gone.

Water to Dust

Sybine

A vine sprang out from the wall and wrapped around my throat. I felt several thorns press against my skin. I dared not move my head or shout to Elora for help. Vines from either side reached out to take my hands. They brought me to my knees. With one leg, I reached out to kick Elora to get her attention. Before she had a chance to turn around, the rest of the vines wrapped around my body and pulled me into their domain.

I froze and closed my eyes. I cursed myself for not thinking more clearly. I had automatically been drawn toward the door on the left, and without thinking of the consequences, had just walked through. Was this what I was to be? Forever lured to danger?

My gut clenched. It was one thing to walk myself into this, and another completely to bring Elora into it.

The vines snaked around me, holding me close. I rolled further into the thicket until I felt an icy wall at my back. An idea came to me then. If there were vines, there had to be water feeding them.

I closed my eyes and dug down into my power again. I felt the familiar tingle across my skin. Slowly, I called on the water, willing it toward me. I visualized it pooling all around me, running through my hair and fingers. With every breath, I thought about bringing it in.

Every.

Last.

Drop.

I was filled with an energy unlike anything I had ever felt before. It was intoxicating and deliciously overwhelming. Every inch of my skin was alive with power.

Suddenly, the vines around me began to scream.

AHH! MONNNSTER! MURDERER! AHH! Their cries rang in my head.

When I opened my eyes, I saw that the once thick and luscious vines had now transformed to mere sticks. I realized with a sickening feeling that I hadn't been drawing water from around me. I had been drawing it from the vines themselves.

DEATH! AHH! PAINNN! MONNNSTER! AHH!

I wanted to crawl inside myself and never re-emerge. It felt like I would never hear a soft word or lullaby ever again. They would forever be tainted by the accompaniment of tortured screams.

PAINnn...MONnnster...Death...death....

They loosened their grip on me, and as they did, they crumbled into dust. I coughed and raised my hand to my mouth.

"Sybine?"

Elora grabbed me by the shoulders and pulled me up so I was sitting. She was coughing too. I tried to blink, but my eyelids were caked closed with dust. I wiped my eyes with the back of my arm, but it was no use. Every inch of me was covered.

"Here."

I heard a tearing noise, followed by the sound of spitting. Then she moved toward me. She took the damp fabric and wiped it across my eyes. I was finally able to open them slightly.

She finished wiping my face and put the handkerchief back in her pocket.

"Are you okay? What happened? One second you were behind me, and the next, you were sucking the life out of those plants."

I hesitated, and my breath caught in my throat.

"I didn't mean to. I thought...I thought I was drawing from the ground around me, not the vines. But then it was too late, and they were screaming and it was horrible." I shuddered, recalling the sound.

Elora looked at me, puzzled and concerned.

"Screaming?"

My brows furrowed.

"It was a sound of pure agony and despair in my mind. It was like the crew disintegrating all over again...."

She knelt on the ground beside me.

"I believe you, trust me. It's just...I couldn't hear anything. Other than your heavy breaths. Then they all crumbled to dust, and I felt like I might follow them. My eyes dried up, and my tongue felt like sandpaper. Even my cut dried shut."

She pointed at the minor cut on her cheek, which had dried blood around it and down her face. It was flaking off with every word she said.

"I felt trapped and I had to do what it took to survive, only that meant that those vines had to die. The water connected us...and that's a bond I don't think I will ever be able to shake."

Elora walked over to me and took my hands in hers.

Tears welled in my eyes as I looked up at her.

"What if...what if I'm the monster the stories always warned of?"

She pushed her forehead to mine.

"Listen to me. Sometimes we have to make impossible decisions, and then we have to live with them. It's what we learn from it that matters. I don't think for a second that you are the monster of this story, Sybine. Nor are you the hero." She brushed off some more dust from my shirt. "We all have our own part to play, whether for the will of good or evil, if they even exist in such a dichotomy. You are who you have always been: yourself."

She wiped the tears from my cheeks.

"I'm scared, Elora," I sobbed.

"You're allowed to be scared," she said as she pulled me into her chest.

I don't know how long we sat there for. But when I next moved, the tears from my eyes had dried and pinched my skin together, and my limbs felt heavy and stiff.

"Should we keep going?" she asked me.

I set my head back and took a deep breath.

"I've got a promise to keep, don't I?"

She smiled, and we worked our way to the end of the passage where it forked in two directions. One was the hall seemingly made of pure starlight, the other dark and damp.

"Maybe we missed something the first time." Elora said.

She moved toward the lighter corridor first, and I followed shortly behind her. We made sure to look without entering either of them completely.

At first glance, the illuminated hall seemed like the safer option. Only the gods knew what lurked in the shadows of the other, but when we looked closer, we could see that the light was so strong because it was being reflected off thousands of glass shards on every surface.

"I think I've had enough of things poking me today," I said.

"I agree."

We moved to the darker hall and stepped in.

To our surprise, no gate collapsed down this time. There was nothing barring our way from going back and choosing the other hall. I was relieved that we had some freedom to move around and escape if we had to.

Just as the thought of escape came to mind, the hall sloped steeply downward. My feet slid underneath me, and I reached out to catch myself. Elora let out a grunt beside me, and her arm connected with my chest, making me lose my balance.

"Shit, I—"

My words turned into a scream as the slope of the floor turned into a free fall, and we cascaded down into the darkness.

Of Minds and Matter

Sybine

We landed in a deep pool of water. Once again, I felt a surge of energy race through me. It was like diving into the lake on a hot summer day: refreshing, calming, and soothing.

Elora emerged first and stood just outside the rippling waves. Her head dropped as she inspected her clothes. Her hair was soaking wet, and it stuck to the sides of her head. Trickles of water poured down her face. She reached up and pulled a piece of seaweed from her hair. She threw it to the ground defiantly and mumbled something under her breath.

The only light in the room came from a silver, glowing fountain in the corner. Silver tendrils snaked down the wall from the ceiling. Every twist of the liquid sent a new glimmer of light through the cave. The sound of the trickling was peaceful, and it was like watching water carve its patterns down a looking glass.

"My ears are killing me," Elora said as she pulled on an earlobe. "It feels like my head might explode." She looked at me as she twitched her head to the side, probably trying to dispel the water caught in it. "Are you okay?"

"Honestly, I feel amazing." I trailed my arms through the water in front of me, embracing it like a warm hug from an old friend.

I wrung out my hair behind me as I walked out of the pool. When I reached Elora on the solid stone of the cave floor, we each took off our boots and poured the water out of them. When I put them back on my feet, they still squished with every step I took. The sound and the sensation made my skin crawl.

"I hate walking around in wet shoes," Elora grumbled, echoing my thoughts. "Shall we see what that's about?" She gestured to the small silver fountain.

I nodded, and together, we made our way over.

The fountain was made of rocks of various shapes and sizes. All of them had smooth surfaces, and they slowly ramped up to form the wall of the reservoir. The light from the silver pool reflected off the rocks facing it, making the light dance all around. The floor was cool and damp, but there was no smell of salt or mildew to accompany it. It was like fresh rain on a warm summer's eve.

"What is that?" Elora asked. Her voice was soft as if she was in awe.

"I don't know...but I don't think it's water."

I leaned over to take a closer look, and Elora did the same. The liquid running down the wall and accumulating in the basin was incredibly thin. It trailed down the wall like illuminated spider's silk and collected at the bottom in small beads that converged together to form the liquid mass.

A strand of my hair fell down and touched the liquid. I tucked it back behind my ear, but a thin layer of light came with it. At first, the tendrils sat there and pulsed with magnetic energy. Then, they slowly traced a trail up through my hair, inching toward my head.

I shrieked.

"Elora!"

Elora turned around quickly, and her eyes widened. She immediately pulled out the knife from her back to cut off the infected hair, but it was too late. I felt the cool tendrils sneak up the back of my head. They snaked their way to my temples, and I felt them move through my skin.

Oh, was all I could think when I felt their presence behind my eyes, tugging me deep, deep inside.

I blinked, and when my eyes opened again, I was back on the *Vindicta*, standing on the lower deck. I could hear boots stomping above me, accompanied by the clashing of blades. I took a few hesitant steps toward the stairs leading to the main deck. When I moved my head around the corner, I could see that most of the crew were crossing swords. Many of them were screaming and grunting. They were cursing each other's names.

I came back to my senses. If I was here, where was Elora?

I took a few steps up to see if I recognized any of the fighters. They were all members of the crew of the *Vindicta*, but I couldn't make out Elora or Drakkon. I let out a relieved sigh, turned around, and slumped against one of the wooden posts.

I leaned my head back and closed my eyes, taking a few deep breaths.

This is a dream. This has to be a dream.

I moved my hands up my arms and gave myself a hard pinch.

"Ouch."

Definitely not a dream.

What was this then? Had I hit my head?

I moved my hand behind my head to inspect for any bumps. I couldn't feel anything, and it came back clean. I looked around, confused. The last thing I remembered was...something silver? The memory felt like trying to see something on the horizon. I could tell it was there, but I couldn't make out what it was.

A hand grabbed my wrist from behind me.

"Don't make a sound," Rhyker's hissed into my ear.

I froze. My heart skipped, and my skin turned to ice.

He held my hands behind my back and led me down the hall. His grip was firm, and I could feel the skin on my wrists chafing.

He pushed me through the dining hall and down through a connecting corridor to Drakkon's quarters. I gulped, and my stomach sank. I could hear my heartbeat racing through my head.

"Wait, Rhyker, you don't have to do this. I haven't done anything."

He gurgled again.

"You're right. You haven't. But you're going to."

I closed my eyes and called to the power within me, but there was no response in my gut. No energy flowing across my skin. No low hum in my ears. There was nothing.

My breaths quickened, and I began to frantically look around for a way to escape.

"Save your strength, Sybine. You're going to need it."

I gasped.

"How do you—"

Rhyker kicked the door to the captain's quarters open.

My breath caught in my throat when I saw what was inside, or rather, who.

Elora sat at the desk with Drakkon. She had her legs crossed, and her hands on a mug. They were...laughing?

"What...what's going on?"

They turned around to look at me.

Rhyker tossed me to the ground in front of Elora.

"Found her right where you said she would be," Rhyker sneered.

He took a step over to me and pressed his foot down on my leg. I could feel the pressure threatening to snap it.

"Here. As promised. The siren bitch." He spat the last word at me.

I could feel my body shudder, and my heart felt like it had been ripped from my chest. How could she betray me?

I had trusted her.

I...cared for her. I thought she'd cared about me too.

Tears welled in my eyes, and a sob caught in my throat.

"Thank you, Rhyker. You've done well," Drakkon said.

With a loud thump, he slammed his mug down on the desk. His chair scraped across the floor as he stood up, and the deep thuds of his boots echoed through my brain. I winced with every step he took. Beside me, Elora stood as well. She looked ravenous. I had never seen her face so warped with an insatiable hunger. Her grin pulled up over her teeth, and her eyes glowed ferociously.

"Elora, please," I pleaded. "This isn't you." The tears flowed down my face. I reached over to her for help, but she kicked my hand away and laughed. She squatted down to face me and tilted her head to the side mockingly. Then she pinched my cheek and tapped me twice on the cheek. I flinched back from her hand.

"Oh sweet, Sybine," she purred. "Looks like you placed your trust in the wrong hands." She stood up and towered above me. She seemed to grow higher than the roof, and her voice dropped. "I am a pirate, after all."

Drakkon laughed and pushed her to the side. He bent down to face me as well. In a final attempt to save myself, I threw my hand up as Elora had to pluck his eye from his head. He swatted my hand away as if it were nothing more than a fly.

"Did you possibly think you could strike me?" he growled. "You are lucky I need you alive, or I would skin you here myself."

Out of the corner of my eye, I saw a slight reflection of light. I looked up, and Elora put a finger to her lips, urging me to keep quiet. I dropped my eyes back down to the planks below me and tried to catch my breath. I shook my head from side to side, trying to make sense of everything. My thoughts raced around my head, and my vision went black at the edges.

"This can't be real. This can't be real," I chanted to myself.

Drakkon laughed loudly in my ear. Then he stood up.

"Pray all you like. No god can save you now."

"We'll see about that," Elora hissed as she lunged at Drakkon from behind.

Drakkon sidestepped so quickly and gracefully that it looked like he flew through the air. Within an instant, he had Elora's striking hand behind her back and her blade against her throat on top of me.

"I am not some fool that can be struck down so easily, lad. You've made that mistake for the last time."

Elora's eyes widened as Drakkon struck her on the back of the head. She collapsed onto the ground beside me, limp and motionless.

"No!" I screamed, reaching out for her.

Drakkon slammed his foot down on my hand, and I heard a chorus of bones snap under the force.

Searing pain shot up my arm. I couldn't breathe. All I could do was watch in horror as he removed his boot, revealing a patch of broken bones protruding from my skin like thorns. Thin trails of blood poured across my hand like a web.

"Rhyker," he called from above me. "Bring her to the mast."

"Yes, sir," Rhyker responded before scooping Elora into his arms and walking her out of the room.

"As for you," Drakkon sneered as he reached down and grabbed me by the hair, pulling me up off the ground, "you're going to watch as I burn your world to the ground."

He pulled me by my braid down the long hall, through the dining room, and up the stairs to the upper deck. It was night, but the fire burned bright against the black sky. The pain at the back of my head and my hand was so intense that stars swam around my vision. I screamed and thrashed, trying to escape his grip, but it was no use.

Drakkon tossed me on the ground in front of him, and I rolled until my back hit something solid. I looked over my shoulder to find Elora, unconscious and balanced on her knees, tied to the center mast.

"Elora!"

Before I could reach out to her, Rhyker towered over top of me and grabbed my injured hand, sending another shock of pain through my body.

He pulled me away from her, one hand wrapped around my wrists, holding me immobile, and the other wrapped around my mouth. I bit down on the fleshy part of his palm, and he wrenched his hand away, shaking it in the air. Just as a feeling of accomplishment began to stir in me, he struck the side of my head.

All I could see was black for several seconds. I was vaguely aware of someone saying, "The Dragon's Breath!" from behind me, but it was muddled, as if I were listening through water. As I blinked, my vision cleared. The dark shapes in front of me slowly took form. I could make out Elora, still bound, and a large black mass in front of her leaning over.

"Time to say goodbye," Rhyker sneered into my ear.

The world lit up in brilliant hues of yellows, oranges, and reds.

This couldn't be real, this couldn't be happening.

My vision cleared to find only a small pile of ash where Elora once knelt.

A numbness crept into my bones. I couldn't blink. I couldn't breathe. I couldn't believe any of this. Elora couldn't be...dead.

I stood frozen in Rhyker's arms, paralyzed with grief and fear.

Gold flakes rose from the ashes, and Drakkon inhaled them, absorbing her the same way he had done with Rhyker.

The thought made my mind go quiet.

That wasn't possible.

Rhyker was standing here, behind me.

What was this?

He was supposed to be dead.

The ship had burned.

And Elora...was by the silver pool. She wasn't here. This wasn't real.

"This isn't real," I said, my voice hoarse and rough. I cleared my throat and said it again. "This isn't real."

Drakkon whirled around, his red eyes glowing against the giant black mass he had turned into.

"What did you sssay?" he hissed.

I set my jaw.

"This isn't real." Every time the words came from my mouth, I believed them more. The memories came flooding back to me.

"Rhyker is dead."

The grip on my wrists loosened. I looked behind me. Rhyker was gone. My gaze returned to Drakkon.

"This isn't real. Most of the crew is dead."

Slowly, the crew surrounding us disappeared like dust in the wind.

Drakkon growled and lashed out to strike me.

"This isn't real," I said, louder. "You're not here."

His crimson eyes flashed as he, too, drifted away.

I looked around the ship. A cold resolve swam through my veins.

"This isn't real. The ship burnt down. And I am in a cave with Elora, who is very much alive."

Nightmare

Elora

"Shit!"

I threw my knife to the ground, and it clattered, echoing all around the room. Sybine's eyes glowed silver and rolled to the back of her head. A trickle of blood ran from her nose. I grabbed each side of her face with my hands and shook her.

"Sybine! Sybine, wake up!" I yelled.

Her body went limp, and I helped her to the ground and leaned her back against the rocks. She slumped against me, her breaths low and shallow. I looked around, frantically searching for something to bring her out of this trance.

I pulled her into my chest and slowly rocked her back and forth.

"Wake up, wake up, please wake up," I said over and over.

Sybine tensed. Her muscles spasmed and she began to shake. I shifted my weight over so she wouldn't hit her head. I accidentally shifted a rock at the same time, and a small drop of the silver liquid landed on my arm.

I held my breath, frozen with horror, and stared at the drop, not daring to move. Sybine still twitched in my chest, and I bit my lip. I could taste blood in my mouth. I had just relaxed and let out my breath when the drop dissolved into my skin. I gasped. I could feel the cold trace as it made its way up my arm and neck and nestled behind my eyes. Then, like an anchor, it slowly pulled me under.

"Hide, Elora."

Dad?

"Quickly, now."

His hands were rough as he pushed me behind one of the crates at the edge of the deck.

"Be quiet, okay? And don't come out until I tell you that you can."

He pulled a blanket over me, smothering me in darkness. Something about the terror and the tone of his voice seemed painfully familiar. What was this? A nightmare?

My heart raced. I heard screams from outside, followed by loud thuds and low cheers. I could hear blades crossing, and I winced with every strike, as if they were hitting me myself.

Then I heard him: Drakkon. I heard his loud roar, followed by the smell of smoke. I coughed and pulled my shirt up to cover my mouth. Soon, the smoke had filled the air under the sheet. I couldn't breathe, but I also couldn't leave. He'd told me not to leave....

My eyes widened when I heard my father scream. A body thudded against the deck beside me.

"Tell me where the book is," Drakkon bellowed.

"Never," my father grunted. "You will never have it," he said through a cough.

A hand rested on the crate in front of me. I could only assume it was Drakkon's. If he was this close, maybe I could do something to help. My father underestimated how strong I was. I wasn't helpless, and I wasn't weak.

I leapt out from under the blanket and reached to my side for the small dagger I always kept there...except for today. I had been practicing my carving last night because I wanted to surprise my father with an elaborate mast to celebrate my mother, and I had left it on the table beside my bed. And like a fool, I hadn't checked to make sure I had grabbed it again before revealing myself now.

Drakkon twisted around and narrowed his eyes at me.

"You," he growled.

I had no weapon, no plan, and no idea what to do next.

Drakkon moved toward me, and without thinking, I reached out and slashed at him with my hand. My fingernails made contact just above his eye. I pushed down as hard as I could, dragging down, hoping to maybe catch his eye on the way. Drakkon flinched back, turning slightly, and instead of moving down his face like I intended, my fingers scraped across his cheekbone, leaving my fingernails cakes with skin, and his eye wholly intact.

My heart sank to my stomach as I realized the weight of the mistake I had just made. With that one impulsive decision, I had likely signed my death warrant.

Drakkon thrust his hand out and gripped me by the throat. At first, I thrashed at his arm, but as the blood pooled in my head and my breath caught in my throat, I focused my efforts on his fingers that were cutting off my air.

He lifted me up, and my feet dangled from the ground. I looked down at my father...only it wasn't my father. It was—

Sybine?

What was she doing here?

Drakkon turned me in the air and pressed my back against his chest. I used my elbows, shoulders, feet, and anything else I could to fight against him. He never budged. He didn't make so much as a grunt as I struck him over and over.

"Rhyker," he called, twisting me to face Sybine again.

Her long dark hair tumbled over her shoulders. Her eyes were round as she watched us, and her lips parted as if she were about to say something.

"Sybine," I croaked, still scratching against Drakkon's hands.

He set me down on the ground and loosened his grip on my throat.

I coughed, trying to catch my breath as Rhyker moved toward Sybine. He picked her up as well, a knife pressed to her throat.

"Please, don't," I begged.

Drakkon reached around to grab a blade of his own, and pressed the tip over my heart.

"Tell me where it is," Drakkon ordered again.

Sybine spat and glared back at him.

"I'll never tell you anything. I'd rather die."

A deep hum rumbled from Drakkon's chest behind me.

"Be careful what promises you make," Drakkon hissed. "Perhaps we ought to...loosen your tongue."

I closed my eyes, unable to watch. There was no mistaking the sound of his blade cutting through her flesh. It was a discorded melody that struck my heart.

There was a choking sound, followed by Drakkon's laughter.

"Have you had enough yet?" he purred.

Sybine whimpered.

Tears ran down my face. I couldn't bear this anymore.

"Show me where it is!" Drakkon ordered again. "Or I'll gut her like a fish," he said, pushing the tip of the blade into my skin.

I winced, and my eyes flew open. I had received cuts before, and although the pain shot through my body in an icy arch, I refused to give him the satisfaction of hearing my screams.

Rhyker held Sybine's head up by her hair. Blood dripped from her mouth, and the color left her face.

With a quick jolt, she shook her head. The unspoken word held in the air between us: *never*.

"You claimed to know my pain," Drakkon said. "You didn't then, but you will now."

Drakkon let out a disappointed breath as he dragged his knife across my body.

It wasn't what I expected. There was no tearing, no resistance, and no pain...at first. It all slammed into me at once as Drakkon let me go and I fell to the deck. I brought a hand up to my chest. When I pulled it away, it was covered in my warm blood. It fell onto the deck with thick drops. The pain exploded all over my body. I couldn't breathe or speak. All I could do was watch as Drakkon moved over to Sybine and held the same crimson-coated blade to her throat.

"You don't want to cooperate? Fine," he growled. "Then die, for all I care. I will walk over your cold, dead body for as long as it takes to find it. I will rip this ship apart board by board. And when I find it, and rest assured I will, I will think of you and this lovely time we have shared together."

With one quick movement, he sliced across her throat, sending a spray of red over the deck.

I squeezed my eyes shut as my heart exploded into a million pieces. I dared not move. I dared not make a sound. All I had to do now was stay alive. And I vowed at that moment that one day, I would make Drakkon curse my name.

I froze on the last thought, the last image. This was wrong. This was all wrong.

An image of Sybine in my arms next to a silver pool flashed through my mind.

"This isn't real," I whispered.

Drakkon twisted around.

"What did you say?"

I shook my head in disbelief.

"My father died, not Sybine."

The image of her body in front of me shifted and transformed to my father.

Oh gods, I thought to myself, *this is a nightmare.*

"This isn't real," I repeated. I looked over to Rhyker and pointed a bloody finger at him. "You're dead."

Rhyker withered away in the wind.

"Sybine is alive," I said, more assured than ever. "This isn't real."

Strength

Elora

At least we were not covered in water when we emerged from the darkness this time. We woke up in the exact same place we had been when we'd fallen into our dreamscapes. Sybine sat up from my lap and massaged her neck with her hand. She twisted her head around, stretching it. My neck was fine, but my leg had been bent in a strange angle while we were in our trances, so my hip felt like it was on fire, and it was like there were a thousand tiny pins poking the bottom of my foot.

Sybine grunted, and it echoed through the room.

"I guess we found out what the hands in the head from the drawing meant," she groaned as she shuffled. "That was horrible."

I nodded in agreement.

"What did you see?" I asked, unsure of whether I wanted to know the answer.

She swallowed and her face blanched.

"You."

The word froze the blood in my veins.

"What did you see?"

I looked at her, trying to memorize every part of her face. I studied her every feature, reminding myself that it was only a nightmare. Sybine was alive.

I let out a low breath.

"You," I echoed.

A muscle twitched at the side of her jaw.

"How do you think Drakkon got past all of these?" she asked, stretching out her limbs.

I twisted my torso, stretching my side.

"Who knows what he can do now that he has Keldroth on his side? And he clearly had time to study the book as well. I doubt it was only pictures in there."

A bright light flashed to our side from where the fountain was. We both twisted our heads. I pushed myself onto my knees and looked over the rocks where the light was coming from. The silvery liquid was gone, replaced by a narrow staircase that led downward.

"Shall we?" I asked, holding a hand out to her.

She took it, and we stood together.

"I'll go first," she said. "I want to be able to see where we're going, and I can't see over your shoulder."

I held my hand out, gesturing for her to go ahead.

Sybine stepped over the rocks and looked down the narrow staircase. She hesitated.

"On second thought, maybe you should go first," she muttered.

I put my hand on her shoulder.

"It's okay. I'll be right behind you."

She swallowed so hard I could hear it. Then she took her first cautious step, then the next. A few stairs down, there was a torch hanging on the wall. She grabbed it and held it out in front of her, then she instinctively shifted her weight backwards.

"What is it?" I called out to her.

"N-nothing!" she stuttered. "Just very dark...and very steep," she added in a low voice.

Slowly, Sybine continued to work her way down the stairs. I followed close behind her, glancing behind us periodically to make sure nothing and no one was following us. Eventually, the light from the cave disappeared, and I returned my complctc attention to the steps under my feet. They were barely large enough to fit my foot on, and they were deep. Before long, I found my legs were beginning to tire and wobble. Sybine was in no better condition.

"Any idea how much further?" I asked her.

Her dark curls swayed back and forth as she shook her head, outlined by the torchlight.

"It just keeps going. My legs are getting tired, Elora."

I sighed.

"I know. Mine too. We've made it this far. Let's keep pushing on. Maybe the bottom is closer than we think." Hopefully Sybine thought my words were true and inspiring. I certainly didn't believe them.

Unfortunately, what felt like a thousand steps later, we were still descending. Both of us had sweat trickling down our faces, and our breaths became more labored. I had stopped feeling the pain in my legs some time ago. It was now replaced by a growing numbness that threatened to buckle my legs with every step. I put my hands against the wall on either side of us. The stair tunnel felt like it was closing in around me. It was suddenly much more difficult to breathe. I paused my steps and held my head back, forcing myself to take in large lungfuls of air.

"Are you okay?" Sybine asked. She paused too, but didn't dare turn around on the narrow steps.

"I'm okay," I lied. "I just need a second to catch my breath."

After that, our pace slowed considerably. Our will to continue faltered with each extra step. I became careless and let my body slump forward slightly. My foot caught the side of the stair, and I accidentally went down two instead of one. My knee made its way up past my hip, and I shot my arms out to my sides to catch myself before I ran into Sybine.

"Sorry," I said breathlessly.

Sybine slumped against the wall to our side.

"This is hopeless. It just continues forever. How are we supposed to know when it will ever end? Are we missing something?"

We both sat on the stairs, leaning against the wall. The flames of the torch danced up into the air. I put a hand on Sybine's shoulder.

"Nothing is ever truly hopeless," I told her.

She exhaled sharply.

"How can you possibly still be holding onto hope?" she asked me, defeated. Her shoulders fell forward.

"Because," I paused, "I've looked into a demon's eyes, took one for myself, and lived to tell the tale." I stood up again. "I refuse to let a simple staircase do what the Dragon Demon could not. Come on, Sybine. We have places to be."

World

Elora

I helped Sybine to her feet and we continued on. We stopped four more times after that to catch our breaths and steady our legs, but we did not speak of hopelessness again.

"Oof," Sybine said from below me.

She moved the torch from side to side, and it disappeared slightly each time.

"Elora," she said excitedly, "we've made it!"

I let out a sigh of relief and thanked the gods that we were finished with these stairs.

I took the last few steps down and joined her on the landing. I patted the dust off the shoulders of my jacket and smiled down at her.

"See? That wasn't so bad," I jested, nudging her gently.

I laughed with her, relieved to finally be on even ground again.

The stone floor was cool and damp. Sybine and I were both exhausted from the descent. My legs felt wobbly underneath me, and each step felt uncertain.

"You know, when I first told myself that I was going to hunt down Drakkon, I never thought that would mean crawling into the dark crevices of the world next to a siren."

Sybine laughed.

"Well, to be fair, you were behind me the whole time."

I rolled my eyes at her, and she giggled again.

"What did you have in mind?" she asked.

I sat with my back against the wall, taking slow, deep breaths. Sybine joined me.

"I honestly thought it would be a simple job. Men die every day for strange reasons."

Sybine massaged her legs as she listened.

"I dreamed about it happening in so many ways. The first time we fought...when he gave me this—" I gestured to the scar at my chest— "I was careless. I knew that if I wanted to actually succeed, I would need to be smart and disciplined. I needed a plan." I rubbed my fingers along my stiff legs as I spoke, trying to work out the tight knots that had formed. "When I was younger and far less strong than I am now, I thought perhaps poison would be the best route, but after a few years on a pirate ship, I learned quickly that no one drinks from a cup they haven't poured themself. I eventually decided that my best chance was to earn his trust and try to catch him off his guard. By the time I felt I was ready, he had already gained a reputation for being a ruthless killer. No one survived his attacks, and he never came back empty-handed."

Sybine watched me, mesmerized.

"I underestimated his cunning. Most men of his strength, size, and reputation have a different brain that runs the ship: a clever first mate, for example. But not him. He always knew exactly what he wanted and how to get it. Rhyker was no more than a pawn in his game, but he led him to believe he was an important piece, critical to his play."

A small door creaked open in front of us. Light poured through, illuminating the frame.

"Looks like we found where we're going next." I stood up and offered Sybine my arm.

She took it, and I helped lift her to her feet.

"How did you get through everything?" she asked.

I turned around and placed a hand on her shoulder.

"Let me tell you something my father once told me. It's all about biding your time and understanding when it's your turn to flow or forge your own path."

She smiled gently at me.

"Your father sounds like he was a wise man."

I took a deep breath and sighed.

"Far more so than I ever gave him credit for."

We turned and made our way to the door. I nudged it open slightly with my arm, taking care to observe everything before jumping in with two feet, especially after what happened with the vines. I shivered.

"Everything okay?" Sybine asked.

"Sorry, yes. I was just remembering one of the last doorways we went through."

"I'll try not to get eaten alive by writhing plants this time." Her calm tone sounded forced.

The door opened into a breathtakingly beautiful cavern of glowing plants and stones that covered the dome roof. Each seemed to radiate its own form of life. It was like walking into a grand hall— an entirely different world that opened up before our eyes.

"It's beautiful," Sybine said beside me as she looked up and around us.

The light shimmered across her face. It danced in her eyes and made her skin look like polished marble. The vision around us was nearly as radiant as she was.

I reached out and took her hand in mine.

"It's unlike anything I have ever seen."

Every part of the cave seemed to vibrate with life, except for a small section at the far end opposite us. As we walked through, it was difficult not to admire every leaf of every plant we passed. The floor beneath us was alive as well. As we stepped, the moss below us glowed with brilliant blues and greens. The roof swam with vibrant plants and stones. A kaleidoscope of colors seemed to accompany every move and every breath we took.

As we approached the other side of the cave, two small sparks of gold began to hum and pulse with energy in the darkness near the ground. With a flash, they erupted about a wingspan apart. They shot up until they reached just above my head before taking sharp turns and meeting each other in the middle. When they collided, it sent a web of spirals out and around the line that had just formed until a brilliantly illuminated door glowed in front of us.

"This is it," Sybine said, her voice soft and low. "There's only one drawing left...the book."

I squeezed her hand.

She turned and looked up at me.

"What do you think it means?" she asked.

"I don't know," I sighed. "Are you scared?"

She let out a shaky breath.

"A little.... Are you?"

I clenched my fist.

"I'm always scared of things that give me an illusion of control," I admitted. "That's why I always work so hard to plan ahead, but throughout all of these tests...I didn't know what to expect. I still don't. And there are few things I hate more than not having all the information I need to move forward."

She pushed her brows together.

"But you always seem so sure of yourself."

I reached out and wrapped my hand around the door handle. Before turning it, I looked back and gave her a soft smile.

"That, Princess, is exactly the point."

63

The Book of Truth

Sybine

A part of me never wanted to leave the fantasy world we had just walked through. I never knew such beauty could exist in the dark. It left my heart feeling much warmer, especially after enduring the frozen nightmare of the silver pool.

As soon as we walked through the door, it slammed behind us. All the light was extinguished, leaving only an empty darkness in its place. We stood there in silence, connected only by our interlaced fingers.

I sucked in a breath, suddenly feeling suffocated by the blinding darkness.

"Are you okay?" she asked me.

I was overwhelmed, exhausted, and terrified. But I wasn't sure voicing those feelings out loud would help either of us. Instead, I focused on the feeling of her holding me in her arms on the beach.

"I'm thinking about us, on the beach, with fresh air in our lungs and sand between our toes."

Elora hummed softly.

"That is a good dream," she said.

"I don't want to wake up."

"I'll be quiet then."

She spun me around to face her. Our bodies pressed together as she placed a hand on my back and drew me in. She tilted my chin up and placed a tender kiss on my lips.

"That's not fair," I said, smiling.

"Shhh." She held up a finger to my lips. "Quiet, remember?" Then she kissed my forehead.

I let out a soft giggle and wrapped my arms around her, letting myself sink into the familiar comfort she now gave me.

She kissed the top of my head again.

Suddenly, Elora was gone. I froze. My arms were wrapped around nothing except the air in front of me. Panic gripped my heart, and a pain rippled through my chest.

"Elora?"

I looked around frantically, but I couldn't see anything in the dark. I reached out for her, but my arms met nothing. Her warm, strong, familiar body was gone. My fingers fumbled in the empty air in front of me.

Two torches lit on either side of me, illuminating the room. The sudden flash of light hurt my eyes, and I brought my arm up to protect them. Water dripped onto the ground somewhere beside me. I turned around, trying to take in my surroundings. To my right was a rushing waterfall. The light from the torches made it look like liquid fire was pouring down the wall. There was a small table at the end of the room with an old, rusted chair.

"Elora!" I called out again.

There was no response.

I blinked and shook my head.

No, I told myself. *Elora didn't disappear into thin air. She is still alive. She has to be alive. You will see her again.*

I took another deep breath. In order to make sure she was okay, I needed to move on. I needed to pass whatever test this was. I needed to survive.

I took one step, then another, until I found myself able to walk again. Finally, I arrived at the table. There was a candle in an intricately decorated stand, along with a book, a long-feathered pen, and a small square jar filled with dark ink on top.

I moved the chair out and took a seat. I stared at the open book. It was completely blank and opened to the middle pages. There was no smoke above it like the sketch in Drakkon's book had suggested. Perhaps that was supposed to represent the torches on the walls. I lifted the book up and inspected the cover. It was bound in black leather. Golden letters sparkled on the cover and swam around the surface, never quite forming words. The spine contained the same golden embossment, and I froze when I made out my name at the bottom: Sybine.

This was...my book?

I quickly thrust it back down onto the table.

As soon as it contacted the tabletop, a dark image emerged from the pages. It billowed up into the air, hovering above the book. Its body was made of smoke, and at first, I thought it might be the demon from the ship. Maybe Drakkon had got stuck here and released the demon into the pages. But something felt different about this creature.

I darted up and moved a few paces back. My heart hammered in my chest. My breaths quickened, and suddenly the room felt much too small.

"Daughter of the Sea," it spoke. The creature had no mouth, and the sound echoed throughout the room as if coming from everywhere.

"Where is Elora? What have you done with her?" I was relieved to hear my voice come out stronger than I felt.

"Fear not for her. Speak true and you will see, or else, be lost to the sea."

The black creature grew away from the pages and wrapped itself around me. I felt a tug at the edge of my mind, like a small rope pulling me up to the light. I felt weightless, soft, and free. I heard the roar of the sea in my ears and smelled its salty breeze. I felt...home.

The smell of the summer breeze filled my nose. I curled my toes in the long, soft grass. My body instantly relaxed. Ahead of me was an old cottage made of pine logs. Small wisps of smoke danced into the air from the chimney. I turned around with my arms outstretched. The familiar flowers of brilliant shades of yellow, green, and blue swirled around me. I was home.

I ran toward the cottage door. The wooden planks of the stairs creaked as I made my way up them. A small wooden chime hung from the porch roof, playing soft music to every step I took. I burst through the door, a wide grin on my face.

"Gramps?" I called out. I turned my body to look at everything around me. Everything was exactly how I remembered it: the small rocking chair by the window, the stone stove, the small table and chairs he helped me carve, and the wooden toy hanging from the doorknob. I took the toy and held it in my hands. The smooth curves were familiar and comforting. It was a small round ball with eight tiny, curved tentacles coming from it. On the bottom side of each one were small bumps. I instinctually ran the inside of my thumb on them. I closed my eyes, and I was immediately taken back to when he had first made it for me. I had been so excited, I hadn't been able to wait to hold it in my hands.

"There's my squiddo."

I turned around to see my gramps standing in the doorway behind me. My heart leapt.

"Gramps!"

I threw my arms around his neck. I was a lot older than I had been the last time we'd been together, but that didn't save me from giggling like the little girl I remembered being with him.

He smelled of lavender and wood. He smelled of home. I held him tight, never wanting to let go again.

"Easy there, squiddo. I'm not as young as I used to be." He stumbled back slightly, catching his balance. Then he wrapped his arms around me and held me tight too.

"I missed you," I said, tears welling in my eyes.

He let out a hearty chuckle.

"I missed you too." He patted my back. "Any chance this old man can take a seat?"

I relaxed my grip on him.

"Sorry," I giggled.

He tapped the bottom of my chin with the inside of his first finger and gave me a cheerful smile. The skin around his sparkling blue eyes crinkled. His light gray hair waved back and forth across his face as the breeze from the door came in. It played in his thick, bushy eyebrows. Like always, he had just a hint of a light stubble on his face that tickled me when I hugged him.

I looked down. I hadn't noticed the basket in his hands when he'd walked in. My eyes widened.

"Are those—"

"Picked 'em this mornin'. Figured you were comin'."

I grinned from ear to ear. He held out the basket to me. I opened up the top, and there they were. An entire basket full of bright red apples. I closed my eyes and took a deep breath until even my stomach was full of air.

Gramps chuckled.

"Easy there, squiddo. You'll pop a lung with a breath like that."

I slowly let out my breath, the smile still stretched across my face.

Gramps closed the lid and made his way to our small table. I took my usual seat, only this time my knees came up to my chest.

Gramps laughed.

"You were a little smaller the last time you sat there."

I sighed.

"Feels like a lifetime ago."

"Aye, it does."

Gramps laid out a cloth over the table and grabbed two dishes and a pot from the counter by the stove. He set down one dish by me and the other by his chair. Then he put the pot and the basket of apples in the middle. I placed the small wooden toy at the end of the table.

"Still remember how to make our famous apple scrumptious?"

I laughed at the name. In my defense, I had learned how to say "scrumptious" at a very young age, and it had stuck. How could I forget? I tried a few times after he passed to make it on my own, but there was something missing every time. Now I realized that it was him that was missing. It would never be the same without him.

I nodded enthusiastically and took the first apple from the basket. Gramps pushed a knife toward me, and I began to methodically chop.

"Now remember—"

"I know, I know—" I mockingly lowered my voice to match his— "watch those fingers, you only get ten of them, and no replacements." I waved my knife at him with every word.

He beamed at me.

We sliced the apples one by one and added them to the pot. When we were done, Gramps stood up and made his way to the counter. When he returned, he had a small jar of sweet honey and some fresh butter. I licked my lips, and my stomach growled.

He poured the honey into the pot. When he was done, he added a few slices of the butter. Then he handed me one of the wooden spoons I had carved as a kid. It was thick and uneven and not at all symmetrical. The spoon part at the bottom leaned to one side. I lifted it up and inspected it.

Gramps smiled down at me and nudged my chin with his first finger.

"It's unique, squiddo. Just. Like. You." He poked my nose with every word. I scrunched my face dramatically. I giggled, placed the spoon in the pot and carefully mixed everything together. When I was done, I looked up at him expectantly.

"One last thing," he said. He walked over to me and kissed my forehead. "Just a little splash of love."

We both blew a kiss into the pot. Gramps lifted it by its handle and placed it on the hook above the fire. Then he came back and sat down at the table.

My breath caught in my throat. The way the sun hit the back of his head, and the way his hair shifted, reminded me of the last day I had seen him.

"What happened, Gramps?"

His expression grew sad. Suddenly, his age was very obvious.

"Where did you go?"

Gramps hesitated. Then he turned to gaze out the window.

"I was called home."

I shuffled in my seat. I wasn't sure when I had grabbed the toy from the end of the table. I ran the inside of my thumb along the curves.

"I tried to look for you." The words caught in my throat as I choked down a sob. "I couldn't find you. I waited...I waited until I couldn't wait anymore. I'm sorry."

He stood up and moved his chair beside me. Then he took his seat again and placed his hand over mine as I traced the small bumps on the toy.

"There was nothin' left for you here," he said. His eyes were also beginning to fill. "But I am glad we can share this again."

"Me too," I let out with a sob. "I missed you so much."

I threw my arms around him again and buried my head in his chest. He rubbed his hand up and down my back the way he used to on my restless nights. My body relaxed.

"It's time to stir," he said softly in my ear.

I sat up and wiped my face with the back of my hand.

He stood up and made his way to the pot, my crooked wooden spoon in his wrinkled hand. Gramps took a large breath, inhaling the sweet scent of our apple scrumptious.

"Careful," I teased, still finding my voice. "You'll pop a lung."

He laughed. When he was done stirring, he brought the spoon over to me. I took it without hesitation and licked the outside of it. It was exactly how I remembered. So sweet and smooth. In a word, scrumptious.

Gramps sat beside me again and placed a hand on my shoulder.

"Tell me, squiddo. Tell me all about your adventures."

I did. I told him all about my professional life as a thief, my run-in with the prince, how that led me to the *Vindicta*, and everything after. I omitted a few parts, of course. He was my Gramps, but there were some details I had to keep to myself.

"This Drakkon fellow sounds dangerous." He wore a look of concern.

I nodded, and I swallowed, trying not to remember the cruelty on Drakkon's face after he burned Rhyker. I shuddered.

"He is, Gramps. But I'm doing what you taught me to do so long ago."

He smiled warmly at me.

"I knew you were special from the moment I first laid eyes on you." He stood up and walked over to me. He leaned down, put a hand on my shoulder, and looked me in the eyes. "I am proud of you. Always."

I immediately put my arms around him.

"Thanks, Gramps. I'm trying."

He kissed the top of my head.

"You're not after this Fang, though, right?"

I shook my head in his chest.

"Something like that should never be in the hands of anyone. Especially someone like Drakkon. I'm just trying to do what's right."

Gramps released me and put a finger to my chin. He beamed at me, and my love for him burned through me like a warm fire on a cold day.

"That's my girl."

Then the world went black.

64

Stars

Elora

There was an empty space by my chest. When I looked down, Sybine was gone, as if she had vanished into thin air.

"Sybine?"

Silence responded.

"Sybine!" I called, this time louder.

More silence.

I closed my eyes and tried to steady my heart rate. I wasn't willing to sacrifice everything for this mission anymore. I wasn't willing to sacrifice her for anything, not even for myself. I had to get through this. I had to find her.

Two torches burst to life beside me, illuminating the small room. To my right was the most spectacular waterfall I had ever seen. It sparkled in beautiful hues of blue and green as the water poured down. The light from the torch flames echoed through it in sparks of red and orange. At the end of the room, there was a small table with an open book on it. I froze. Was this the book Sybine had mentioned from the drawings? There was no smoke around, except for that surrounding the flames of the torches. Maybe I was missing something.

Slowly, I made my way over to inspect it. I was careful with my steps, ensuring there were no traps laying around that might cause the book, or me, to burst into flames. My heart rate settled when I made it to the table without any issue. Oddly enough, the book was empty. I flipped through its rough yellowed pages, only to find them all blank. When I turned the book over, golden letters danced across the black cover. My breath caught when I read my name on the spine.

I carefully placed the book back where and how I found it and took a step away. My nerves were on edge, and the hairs on the back of my head stood on alert.

A dark cloud emerged from the pages, and its voice echoed in my head.

"Daughter of the Sea," it spoke.

I swallowed down my fear and pulled out my knife from my back. Although I was unsure of how I was supposed to fight this monster that did not have a clear form, I was sure that I would do everything in my power to defeat it.

"If you hurt her, I will kill you."

I stood ready to strike.

"Fear not for her. Speak true and you will see, or else, be lost to the sea."

Before I had a chance to lash at it, the dark cloud wrapped itself around me, trapping me. Yet, I did not feel trapped. I felt comforted. Like being wrapped in a blanket and being rocked by the waves of the sea, staring up at the stars on a cloudless night. I could smell the sea breeze and hear the waves crashing against the side of the ship. I was home.

I was no longer in the dark, cramped room. I was on my father's ship. I recognized the small chips in the mast that I had made as a kid. I smiled as I ran my fingers over the dents in the wood. Suddenly, the memory played out in front of me.

It was dark. Everyone had gone to bed. Everyone but David. David was our star reader. He knew the seas best by night.

"The stars are a map, little sword," he would say. "If you ever lose your way, don't be afraid. Just look up."

I saw myself as a young teenager sneaking up onto the deck with my short sword. My father had finally let me use one earlier that day, and he had urged me to practice as often as I could so that one day, I would be the most powerful pirate there had ever been. I couldn't sleep that night, so I'd turned over in my bed, grabbed my sword, and made my way to the deck. I took it out of its scabbard and sliced the air. I loved how powerful it made me feel. I stabbed forward, but I mis-stepped. I lost my balance and fell flat on my face.

David came down from the hull, clapping.

Young me scowled at him.

"What are you clapping for? Are you mocking me?"

He chuckled, but not with amusement. His tone was full of pride.

"No, little sword. I was clappin' because I just watched you grow in front of my very eyes. You see, you didn't fail just now." He reached a hand down to help my younger self to my feet. "No, you didn't fail. You learned."

I smiled as I watched the memory play out in front of me. As comforting as it was, my chest still tightened. In truth, it hurt nearly as much to think of David as it did to think about my father.

The memory in front of me faded, leaving me once again feeling empty and alone.

A hand rested on my shoulder, and I turned around to see David smiling down at me. His golden hair shuffled in the breeze, and his bright blue eyes sparkled with the same adoration and mischief I remembered.

"Hello, little sword."

My eyes widened in surprise.

"David? How? How is this possible?"

I embraced him tightly, and he held me close as well. I felt his chin rest on the top of my head. The nostalgia and comfort overwhelmed me, and I felt tears begin to well in my eyes.

"Is this a dream?" I didn't want to know the answer, but I asked anyway.

David took a breath.

"If it is, then it is a good dream." He echoed the words I had told Sybine less than a few minutes ago.

I was suddenly thrust back into reality.

"Sybine!"

"Shhh," he whispered into my ear. "It's okay. She passed through here a few minutes ago. She's waitin' for you."

I relaxed and let go of him.

He chuckled slightly.

"She's quite somethin', you know. Much like you, I suspect that she does not know how truly powerful she is."

"You've met her?" I asked.

"Oh, yes." He nodded and motioned to the stairs. He took a few steps before taking a seat. I followed him over. We both sat on the stairs to the hull, the same way we used to when I was younger.

He pointed toward the mast.

"I remember the day you almost took that down." He laughed. "I had a hard time explainin' that one to your father. I don't think he ever believed me, but he never asked me about it again."

I looked up to meet his gaze.

"What did you tell him?"

He bent over close to me, mischief in his eyes.

"I told him that a magnificent creature of the sea wanted to make us target practice durin' the night. Which, of course, wasn't quite a lie."

I scoffed.

"I am no great creature of the sea, I can assure you." My eyes lowered to the deck. "I failed to save you two, and I failed to save anyone on the ship when Drakkon trapped the demon. I failed to save Rhyker, and I failed to save the rest of the crew. And now...what if I fail to save Sybine? What if this revenge plot is what gets us both killed?"

David placed a hand on my shoulder.

"Oh, little sword. You haven't failed; you've learned."

The tears fell down my cheeks in steady streams. We sat there for a few moments, my sobs echoing through the night.

"Why do you still dwell on the dead?" he asked.

I wiped a hand across my face and took a breath.

"I've been alone, with only my ghosts to keep me company. It's hard to let them go when they're the only presence I've ever known."

"My sweet child." He squeezed my shoulder. "I am sorry you have felt this burden your whole life. It should never have been yours to bear."

David walked down the steps and took a knee in front of me. He wrapped my hands in his.

"You don't need to live for the dead. You don't need to speak for the dead. And you don't need to act for the dead." He took a breath. "Your life is yours."

My breath caught in my throat, blocked by a sob and a spasm in my chest. I smiled at him.

"I think I'm beginning to realize that now."

He smiled back at me.

"And so what have you learned? What's different now?"

I took in a sharp breath. My heart beat strongly in my chest.

"I'm not alone. I found someone I can trust. And I think she trusts me too."

David beamed at me.

"I think you're right about that."

He moved back onto the stair, and I leaned into him, thankful for his presence. Breath came to my lungs easier. Yet there was still a tense part of me that refused to relax.

"What else weighs on you, little sword?"

I sighed.

"I don't know what to do, David. We've barely survived, mostly on luck. How are we ever going to stop Drakkon?"

I felt him tense beside me.

"Do you know what he's done? Who he is now?"

David sighed and his head fell slightly.

"Yes," he said, his voice low.

"Then you know he's basically a god now. How are the two of us supposed to fight him? We barely escaped last time." I hesitated. "David. I—I don't think I did escape last time."

He placed a hand on my cheek, and I leaned into him.

"Listen to me. You are not here by accident. I heard Sybine's call. And now a part of you lives in her and a part of her in you."

I looked at him. I still couldn't believe he was here. My heart pounded in my chest.

"David, is that...is that what love is?"

"Yes, little sword." He stroked my cheek. "That's what love is."

We sat there for a few moments. I closed my eyes, trying to remember what it felt like before everyone was gone.

David stood and helped me to my feet as well. We walked over to the edge of the ship. I felt the cool breeze on my face, and the smooth wooden railing.

"Elora, you've been searchin' for Drakkon, but he seeks the Fang, so I have to ask you. Is that, too, what you desire?

I considered his question. There had been a moment on the *Vindicta*, during the night of the demon that I had considered holding it in my hand. I had wondered what power it would bring me and how satisfying it would be to slay Drakkon with that which he desired most. And yet, when I had envisioned that moment, it hadn't mattered what I held in my hand. All that mattered was his demise. It wasn't the tool I desired, it was Drakkon's death.

I shook my head.

"No. I never wanted that power. But I don't want to see it in Drakkon's hands either."

He smiled down at me with pride.

"I'm afraid I need to go now."

I opened my eyes, frantic.

"No, you just got here. Can't you stay?"

He smiled gently at me.

"You've already said it. I never left."

He placed a hand on my shoulder.

"Remember, if you ever feel like you've lost your way, don't be afraid. Just look up."

David gave me one last smile, and then he floated into the air like stardust.

The
King

65

Throne

Elora

When I woke up, I was face down on the table in front of me. The book on the table looked as if it were untouched. There was a dull ache in my head. I propped myself on one arm and rubbed the front of my head with the other. I winced. There was a small, tender bump at my hairline. I sighed with relief when I pulled my hand back and there was no blood on it.

My head was whirring like I was caught in a river. My ears were ringing. I held onto my earlobe and gave it a small tug. When I brought my hand close to my ear, I found that the sound lessened slightly. My brows furrowed. I looked down to find a pool of water around me. I spun around. My ears weren't ringing after all. It was just the sound of the waterfall.

My eyes caught on a black fog in the corner of my eye. When I looked back, the book hovered in the air. Gold and black letters began to jump off the page like sparks from a fire. Eventually, they settled together, forming a string of words above the open book.

Only those who speak the truth may test their fate and pass through.

Slowly, the words began to melt and pour back down onto the page like drops of rain. As soon as they made contact with the book, they disappeared back into the yellow pages.

My heart jumped, and my stomach turned.

I stood up and carefully made my way toward the brilliant cascading water at the side of the room. The water was refreshingly cool as I twisted my hand through it.

The words echoed through my brain. Was this a test? I had done my share of lying throughout my life, but I doubted this was an evaluation of the past. No, this must be more recent. I thought back to the ship with David.

I hadn't lied. I didn't want the Fang.

I looked at the waterfall. It crashed down past the ground at my feet. Only the gods knew what was on the other side. This was, in every way, a leap of faith.

I closed my eyes, took a breath, and steeled my nerves. I took a hesitant step into the water and felt the ground shift beneath my feet. I held my breath as I brought the rest of my body through the water. It poured heavy on my shoulders, but I pushed through one step at a time. I hadn't made it this far only to fail now.

You've told the truth, I reminded myself.

I reached my hand out in front of me, searching for a break in the crashing water. Finally, I felt a rush of warm air, followed by a sharp tug on my arm. I fell hard on my back against the rocky floor.

When I looked up, Sybine was on top of me, smiling down.

"It's good to see you," she said.

A rush of relief flooded me.

I pulled her into my chest.

"Oh thank the gods," I whispered into her hair.

"We're okay," she reassured me.

I buried my head into the curve of her neck and wrapped my fingers in her loose hair. She smelled of sea salt and damp moss.

"You're alive," I said through a hushed breath.

She giggled into my ear and pulled up to look me in the eyes again. She embraced my cheeks with the palms of her hands.

"You're real."

Sybine pressed her warm, soft lips against mine in a gentle caress.

When she pulled away, every inch of my body hummed with energy.

She rolled off me and held out a hand. I took it gratefully as she helped me to my feet. It was only then that I took the time to properly take in our surroundings.

The room around us was enormous. The walls were made of crystals of every shape and color. It was the kind of wonder only found by breaking an old stone from the sea. We marveled and gawked at the power each stone emanated. I could feel it in the air like a low hum full of alluring promise.

"This must be the treasure Drakkon was talking about," I whispered to Sybine.

"Too bad most of them didn't live long enough to see it."

I nodded in agreement.

We walked past blue crystals taller than me, and purple ones that would never fit in a chest. At the end of the hall was a dark mass surrounded by black pillars. As we approached it, I saw that they weren't pillars at all. They were tentacles that stretched from the floor to the roof of the cavern, carved of black onyx.

I squinted my eyes. In the center of the pillars was some kind of throne made of the same stone. And on top of the throne sat a man with his head down.

My breath caught, and my steps froze.

"What is it?" Sybine asked.

I pointed my finger to my lips and motioned to the dark figure in front of us.

Her eyes widened in surprise.

"You have proven yourselves to be strong, courageous, smart, and honest. I might have known." The man's loud, thunderous voice boomed and echoed all around us.

He stood and made his way toward us. His figure was tall and lean, and each step he took was fluid, like he himself was made of the sea.

Sybine grasped my hand tight, and I returned it. We stood there together and awaited our judgment. Had Drakkon overthrown the King? If so, what horrors awaited us now? Drakkon had been formidable as a mortal. He would be unstoppable as a god.

My thoughts turned to the dagger at my back. Perhaps if I struck fast enough, we could take him down together. I was just getting ready to brace my position when Sybine let go of my hand.

"Sybine, wait—"

She held her hand up and cut me off. She took a few steps forward and tilted her head to the side. The man lifted his head up, revealing a familiar peppered gray beard and soft blue eyes.

"Harlan?"

The Sea King

Sybine

I couldn't believe my eyes. I was looking directly at Harlan.

"Wait, this doesn't make sense." I brought a hand up to my head and put a finger to my temple.

"I watched you fall. You let go of the rope. You never came back. And now...now you're—"

"Alive?" He gestured to his body. "Please forgive me for my deception."

Elora stood behind me, speechless, still frozen in place.

"But how? How are you...you?" I asked.

"I am me, just as you are yourself, as you've always been."

"Yes, but I didn't jump off a pirate ship only to wash up and be found below even the darkest depths."

"Did you not?" He raised an eyebrow at me.

I held my tongue. That was, in fact, exactly what had happened to us.

"I am so sorry, Harlan. I tried to pull you back to the ship."

He held his hand up to stop me.

"We both know I was lost to the sea the moment I decided to save your partner here." He gestured at Elora, who was still standing still.

She swallowed.

"It's good to see you, Harlan. And thank you...for saving my life."

He bowed to her slightly.

"I would gladly do so again," he said proudly.

Elora's eyes widened as she studied him. The air shifted around us. It was like the calm before a lightning strike.

"You didn't drown," she said.

Harlan tilted his chin down slightly.

"No, I didn't."

Elora clicked her teeth together.

"On the ship, that first night, you said you had been called many names."

Again, Harlan nodded.

Elora hummed as she looked over at the throne at the end of the hall.

"The King of Water," she mumbled. Then she looked back at him. "You pulled the King of Water, and you were barely upset about it."

A smile stretched across his face.

"It was an amusin' coincidence, don't you agree?"

Why was she asking these questions that she already knew the answers to? What was she trying to piece together?

My eyes widened as everything became clearer.

"Oh gods," I breathed.

"You said your home was at sea," I jumped in.

He focused his attention on me.

"It is," he confirmed.

I thought back to our last night on the ship.

"You saw me, even when I was invisible."

Harlan gave me a knowing smirk.

"My child. I see all and know all that swim in my waters. Sometimes better than they know themselves."

I sucked in a short breath.

"But wait, that means—"

Harlan smiled wryly.

"Yes, kid. I am the Sea King."

The cavern lit brilliantly at his words, a symphony of every shade of blue and green echoed around us.

Elora and I were completely shocked. Not only was Harlan alive, but he was here. He was the Sea King. Harlan made his way over to both of us and took our hands.

The joyful look on the Sea King's face slowly faded. His expression turned grim.

"Unfortunately, this is not a completely happy meetin'. There's somethin' just outside of my view in the darkness. I have sensed it, and my suspicions have grown."

He turned around and we followed him to his throne, which was carved from the same black onyx. The legs were tentacles. They flowed down the stairs and turned into the pillars that reached up to the roof of the cavern. The throne itself was the jaw of the Kraken. Rows of large, silver teeth framed the throne. When Harlan sat, the teeth around him looked like they could have either been like an explosion of stars or the jaws of death.

He ran a hand along one of the fangs.

The hairs along the back of my neck stood at attention. I tried to push down the pit that was forming in my stomach.

"Is Drakkon here?" Elora asked the question that we were both thinking.

The Sea King leaned forward, his elbows resting on his knees.

"I believe so."

Elora looked at him, confused.

"You believe so? Did he not have to go through everything we did to get here?"

He pinched his lips together.

"That's not as easy of a question to answer as you think it is." He sat back and folded his hands in his lap.

"Do you remember the two ceremonies he performed on the *Vindicta*?"

We both nodded. How could we forget?

"These were ancient rituals that I believed to have been long forgotten until I witnessed them for myself. That is how I found myself at the Stumblin' Sailor that night. I had heard rumors that Drakkon had a demon in his possession. Then, when I saw an open recruitment into his services, my suspicions were nearly confirmed. I never imagined he would be successful in his ritual of claimin' Keldroth's power, let alone sacrifice his first mate and devour his spirit." He paused and rubbed his wrist with his hand. "Power will drive a man mad. And I fear the unrelentin' will of your captain."

"You fear him?" My voice was wavering and hesitant.

He nodded.

"Only a fool would underestimate him. The two of you have passed every trial to get yourselves here under my watchful eye. Drakkon has somehow found a way to harness the power he has stolen to evade my gaze."

The Sea King raised his fingers to his chin. He rested his head upon them.

"But I know his scent. I know the sound of his movement. I may not be able to see him, but I can sense him. He draws nearer with every passing moment."

67

To Crown a King

Sybine

I swallowed hard. Drakkon's name hung in the air, thick and unmoving. The hair on my arms and neck stood at attention. There was suddenly a darkness to the room that hovered over everything. I shivered.

"You said you can't see him, but you can sense him?" Elora asked.

Harlan nodded.

"He passed through my gate some time ago. The two of you were guided here by my hand, but Drakkon was led through by the demon he possessed."

"But you're a god," I said. "Can't you make him leave?"

Harlan laughed low and gutturally.

"A god?" He laughed again. "Is that what you think I am?"

Harlan stood, never breaking eye contact with me.

"Daughter of the Sea, I am no god." He raised out his arms around himself. His eyes flashed blue. "She is my God."

The dark walls around us were suddenly painted with flowing and glowing blue light. It was like light passed through water. My jaw dropped. I turned around slowly, taking in the spectacle. The light danced all around us. I felt my spirit being called. I looked over to Elora, who was equally struck by its brilliance. I could tell that she too felt summoned. Her chest rose and fell slowly, and the tips of her hair began to gently wave in the air. I felt my long curls move from my back and flow around me as well as if we were both submerged or flying.

The lights faded. The energy in the room slowly dissipated, and we turned to look at Harlan again. There was a crooked smile across his face.

"I am no god. I am merely a shepherd of the Sea. I am, and have always been, Her dedicated, humble servant." He pressed his hand over his heart and gave a slight bow. "I am just a king without a crown, kid. So no, Sybine. Drakkon cannot leave here by my will alone."

Harlan turned and gazed up at the roof. His face fell slightly.

My breath caught in my throat. Something stirred at the edge of my mind. A king without a crown....

Below the depths, deep in the dark,

Time is dire,

The king is crowned,

And all is lost to thunder and spark.

The king is crowned...the king is crowned...the king is crowned.

"The king is crowned," I mumbled to myself.

My hand reached down to the bag at my side. I opened the latch and lifted the top. The prince's crown sparkled as if winking at me.

"What was that?" Elora asked me.

I reached in and pulled out the crown. The sapphire and diamond jewels that adorned it seemed to pulse with energy. The other gems around the room lit up excitedly, matching the pulsing rhythm. Each pulse seemed to have a beat of its own, like a heart that had been returned to its home.

I held out the crown to Harlan. He turned, and his eyes glowed and pulsed with the gems in the room.

"Where did you find that?" he whispered.

I held my tongue. Perhaps revealing that I had stolen it was not in my best interest.

"She stole it off the prince," Elora said, gawking.

So much for keeping that to myself, I thought.

"I didn't steal it, really." I hesitated. "It was more of a borrowing and perhaps selling kind of situation."

Harlan raised an eyebrow at me.

I exhaled and my shoulders fell.

"Okay, I stole it," I admitted. "But it's not like he didn't deserve it."

"Indeed," he said. Then he smirked. "You have no idea what you have in your hands, do you, Sybine?"

I looked at the crown quizzically.

"A crown?"

Harlan laughed.

"Not just a crown, kid. The Heart of the Sea."

Depths

Elora

"It seems you were meant to find me again, kid. I will never understand the games the Fates play. Perhaps that's for the best."

Sybine held the Heart of the Sea to Harlan. He walked over and knelt in front of her, bowing down. Sybine bit her bottom lip and looked at me. I gestured my head at Harlan encouragingly. Sybine took a deep breath and placed the crown on his brow.

A blinding silver light flashed through the room. I held my hand up to protect my eyes a moment too late. I blinked, but all I could see was white. Slowly, the room came back into focus. The Sea King stood in front of Sybine. His eyes were blazing blue, and his blonde curls flew around his face. A black scepter appeared in his hands. It was carved from the same black stone as his throne. It wound in waves all the way up. A single large sapphire rested within the cage of stone at the top. Long black tentacles emerged from the onyx base of the crown. They traced the curves of his eyes, highlighting the brilliant blue of them. They seemed to stretch and grow as if they were alive.

Harlan took a long, deep breath.

"I have searched long and hard for this, kid," he said. His voice was significantly lower now, and his skin rippled with new life. "It's why I came back to land all those years ago. I didn't find the Heart, but I did find you." He took her face in his hand and looked down at her gently. "And to think...it's been right under my nose this whole time."

Sybine leaned into his palm.

"Thank you."

Sybine looked back up at him. Her eyes sparkled.

"You're welcome, Harlan." A single tear fell down her face. He wiped it away with his thumb and placed a soft kiss on the top of her head.

I caught something moving from the corner of my eye. I turned around and squinted into the darkness behind the throne.

I turned to Sybine and Harlan. He moved a finger to his lips.

"We are not alone."

Harlan retreated a few steps back, and Sybine's face washed with fear. I slowly stepped toward the throne as I reached a hand behind my back to grab my dagger. I took light steps around it until I reached the cove at the back, where no light had touched since we first got there.

A silence crept over the room, and darkness began to spread and hover in the air. My heart pounded in my ears like drums. My breaths quickened. I took one final step toward the dark cove.

There was nothing, save more of the black onyx stone. Then I heard two strong footsteps behind me. I turned around with my blade in front of me. The rest of the room went pitch black. I spun in circles, stabbing aimlessly. The black tendrils from the darkness began to creep over my skin, cold and lifeless. My breath caught as a glowing fire-red eye slowly opened in front of me.

"Elora!"

To Slay a Dragon

Sybine

The light was sucked out of the room.

"Elora!" I screamed.

There was no response.

My stomach climbed to my throat. I tried to swallow down my fear.

The darkness suddenly lifted. Elora was on the ground, one hand holding her side, the other reaching for her dagger. I took a step and extended my hand out toward her. That's when I saw him.

Drakkon was cloaked in smoke. He moved impossibly fast. He kicked the blade away from Elora before she reached it.

Harlan placed a hand on my shoulder and walked in front of me.

"You." A low growl resonated from Drakkon's throat. He pointed at Harlan accusingly. Then, as if amused, he tilted his head to the side and laughed. It was a cruel sound that made the hairs on my arms rise. "Rhyker tellsss me you're the Sea King." He laughed again. "On my ship thisss whole time. The Fatesss and their tricksss know no boundsss."

The two of them slowly made their way around the onyx Kraken to the open part of the room.

Drakkon reached to his side and brought out a blade from the shadows around him. Its black edge looked cracked with crimson lines that pulsed through it like streams of bright blood. He pointed it at Harlan. Before Drakkon had a chance to lunge, Harlan thrust out his scepter, the gem glowing a radiant blue at the end. He cast a spiral of water around Drakkon that extended all the way from the floor to the ceiling. A second later, a large gash was torn through it, and Drakkon emerged completely unfazed.

"It is going to take more than magic tricks to defeat me."

My heart pounded in my chest as Drakkon swung toward Harlan. His movements were fluid, and he easily ducked under the blow. When Harlan came back up, Drakkon whirled around and kicked him square in his chest. Harlan flew through the air, and his back hit his throne. He stood slowly and made his way around the corner. Drakkon continued his pursuit.

I took advantage of his diverted attention and ran over to Elora. The color had returned to her face, and her breaths were less ragged.

"We have to do something." Her voice was urgent.

"I know." I helped her to her feet and we traced our way around the edge of the cave.

"You can't hide from me, old man," Drakkon snarled as he lurked around the corner.

Harlan jumped out from one of the tentacles and swung again. Just before it made contact with Drakkon's head, he snatched it from the air. Drakkon tore the scepter from Harlan's hand, and with one quick swipe, he brought his blade down on it.

Nothing happened. Drakkon's sword never made so much as a scratch on it. He roared as he threw the scepter across the room. A black wave exploded from his body, sending Harlan soaring through the air. I flinched as his back hit the throne with a loud crack.

Elora pressed me against one of the tentacle pillars and held a finger up to her lips, urging me to be quiet.

"Stay here," she whispered into my ear. "Wait for my signal."

She pressed a dagger into my hand and fell back into the shadows before I had a chance to ask what the signal was and what I was supposed to do once she gave it. My stomach knotted, and I gripped the hilt tightly.

Drakkon tilted Harlan's chin up with his blade. Harlan's eyes narrowed as he met Drakkon's gaze with defiance.

"Confesssss your sinsss," Drakkon purred. "Tell us all how truly benevolent you are. Tell usss how you live to care for the sea. Tell us your liesss."

Harlan's jaw clenched.

"I live to care for the Sea. She is my goddess, and I am her servant."

Drakkon pushed the Sea King back on his throne and hissed.

"Liesss!" he screamed. Then he whirled back to Harlan. "Confesssss! Tell usss how you took them. Tell usss!"

"I have not taken anyone," the Sea King said simply.

Drakkon growled.

"Ssstop lying. Don't deny it. You took them. You murdered them. My wife. My child. You were supposssed to protect them, not dessstroy them."

His wife? His family? I thought back to the conversation I'd overheard between him and Rhyker.

Not even if I lived for another hundred years would I let another woman on board. The gods will not make a mockery of me. It's precisely because I know their value that they do not sail with us. Never. Again.

"You, of all people, should know that the Sea cannot be tamed, Drakkon. To suggest I was the hand that stole your family is to suggest I hold the reins of power. You could not be further from the truth." Harlan said.

The clouds of smoke that billowed around Drakkon seemed to thicken.

I stayed tucked out of sight.

"I spent decadesss following every trail, every clue. I burned down shipsss and razed villagesss to the ground. I found Keldroth's chainsss. I consumed hisss power. I followed the mapsss and read the starsss. Me! I sacrificed everything! I hunted you down." Drakkon snarled, his eye glowed red, and the ember that replaced the other one flashed as well.

In a split second, Drakkon was in front of Harlan. He pulled out two daggers from behind his back and thrust them down through Harlan's hands, binding him to his throne. The sound that came from Harlan made my skin ripple and my ears ring.

"You didn't think I would get rid of you ssso easily, did you?" he purred. He twisted a blade in Harlan's hand. His scream was piercing and shrill. I covered my ears with my hands.

"I want to bathe in your sssuffering, like you bathed in mine. I want to cherish every sssecond of pain. I want to breathe in every drop of your life." His tone was low and menacing.

"Get away from him."

My heart dropped as I watched Elora emerge from the shadows beside the throne.

"Elora," Drakkon said her name like a curse. "Yesss, I am quite aware of you and Sssybine and your schemes. Rhyker saw through to who you really were once I releasssed him from hisss human bondsss. Once I found a way to communicate with him, he told me everything. You're foolsss to think you could ever defeat me."

Oh gods, if he knew about us, what else did he know?

Drakkon lunged at her, the sharp edge of his sword reflected the light around them.

Elora met his blade with her own, and the clang of metal on metal echoed throughout the room. My stomach sank as Drakkon twisted his sword around, knocking Elora's dagger to the ground.

Elora's eyes widened and my breath caught as Drakkon lunged at her again. Before I had a chance to scream, Elora turned to the side and reached up above Harlan's head to twist a fang from the Kraken's open jaws.

It broke from the stone with a sharp snap, and she thrust it high into the air.

Eight black tentacles shot out from just above her hand. They spiraled through the air before wrapping themselves around her forearm. Elora's head fell back, and she gasped as they made contact with her skin. The air began to ripple and twist around her as the fang extended up and morphed into a blade made of silver glass. The tip of the fang shone in the light of the stones, both glistening and transparent at the same time. It was, in a word, magnificent.

"Holy shit." The words fell from my lips before I had a chance to stop them. I brought a hand up to cover my mouth. "Is that—"

"The Kraken's Fang," Elora said as she lowered her gaze back to Drakkon.

Power radiated off of her in waves. She stood taller, and the toned muscles of her shoulders bulged against the fabric of her shirt. Her cheekbones were sharper, and her eyes looked darker. Her skin seemed to glow with the power of the sun and moon combined. She looked menacing. She looked powerful.

She met my eyes and nodded at me.

Was this the signal?

Drakkon followed her gaze, and his eyes landed on me.

Drakkon flashed forward until he was across the cave, right in front of me.

Ribs, neck, anything, I told myself as I furiously slashed with the knife in front of me.

He rolled his shoulders, easily avoiding my blows, and retrieved a blade from his back. I rolled to the side as he cut his knife through the air, landing hard on my shoulder. It sent a jolt of pain down my arm, and I was filled with terror when I realized that I couldn't feel my fingers anymore.

He snarled at me. Smoke billowed out from around him, and his eyes shone red and ferocious. I stood up and darted away from his path.

Elora raced in front of me, blocking my body with hers. She held the Fang in front of her, pointed toward Drakkon. Her other hand pushed on my chest, forcing me to take a few steps backward.

"Elora, wait!" I cried. But it was too late. Her and Drakkon were circling each other like scavengers around fresh meat, each with a blade pointed toward the other.

"You have no more secrets to tell, but oh how I would love to shave your tongue like I did with your dad," he spit.

Elora's eyes flashed. Her face turned red, and her jaw flexed.

"Hold your tongue, or I'll take it for myself," she sneered.

Drakkon cut his blade through the air over her head. Elora rolled onto the stone and came back up, one hand on the ground bracing her, the other still wrapped in the tentacles from the Kraken's Fang.

She jumped up and unleashed a series of whirling strikes at Drakkon. He met her blow for blow. Their black and silver blades erupted with sparks at every point of contact.

Elora lunged at him, but he blocked her movements easily. They continued to circle. She swiped at his side, lunged low, and then aimed for his legs. Drakkon sidestepped and swung his blade over her head. Elora popped up behind him and kicked him in the back. He took a solid step forward and then whirled around, swiping again. Elora ducked and took a few steps backward.

"Is that everything you have, girl?"

I had to do something to help. I wasn't useless with a blade, but the short training sessions with Elora were nothing compared to the wrath they were unleashing on each other in front of me now.

Think, I thought to myself. *What do you have access to?*

I closed my eyes and called down to the siren within me. A familiar rush of energy coursed through my skin. I remembered back to the vines, and began to call the water to me.

Come to me, I thought. *Come to me.*

I felt the water begin to flow to me. Small tendrils danced through my fingers. My lungs were suddenly full with air, and I felt sparks across my skin. I felt powerful, more powerful than I ever had in my life.

I imagined pulling the water not only from everything around me, but also from Drakkon. I focused on stripping him of everything, of bringing him to his knees, weak and drained.

"Sybine!"

I opened my eyes. Elora was crouched low to the ground. Drakkon took stumbling steps toward her. His movements

547

were slow and jagged, as if he had just finished running across the country. A realization finally hit me. I could do this. I could kill Drakkon.

I pulled harder, feeling stronger with every breath. Drakkon fell to his knees, and an overwhelming sense of satisfaction raced through me. I didn't need a weapon of legend to take him down. I was a force in and of myself.

"Sybine!" Elora cried again. My eyes drifted back to her. I had been so focused on Drakkon, that I'd never even considered there being an effect on Elora. She knelt on the ground. The Fang was under her hand, pressed to the ground, while her other hand was against her chest. She coughed. Elora lifted her head, and I gasped. Her cheeks were sunken, and her skin was gray and cracked. I remembered how the vines began to disintegrate and my heart fell in my chest. I was killing her.

I looked back and forth between her and Drakkon. Maybe she could hold on longer than he could. Maybe—

The tentacles released from her and retreated back into the Fang. It fell from her grasp with a small click against the stone floor.

How many lives would be saved if I had the strength to let her go?

It didn't matter. Not if it meant losing her.

The cost was too great. I released the water I had stolen back to Elora in a wave. I imagined it filling her with life, with power. A tornado of water swirled around her. My heart lurched. Was I too late?

Elora's eyes flashed green through the spiral of water, and she reached out to grab the Fang again.

Drakkon got there first.

The second his skin met the hilt of the Fang, the air in the room hung still. Bumps crawled across my arms and neck. Everything fell silent. At first, nothing happened. I held my breath. Maybe it wouldn't work for him like it did for Elora. As soon as the words passed through my mind, Drakkon's body began to twitch, and I swallowed down the horror welling in me as his frame began to shift and grow. The tentacles slowly stretched over his arms, coiling around like snakes. The muscles along Drakkon's back and shoulders grew, and his eyes shone a fierce red. His head fell back, and he let out an ear-splitting roar that shook the entire cavern.

"That weapon...was not...meant for you." Harlan's voice was low and hoarse.

Drakkon snarled. He tilted his head from side to side as he approached Harlan.

"You're wrong, old man," he hissed. "It's mine."

Elora lunged at Drakkon, pushing herself between him and Harlan.

He blocked her blow with the Fang, and with a great roar, pushed her to the side. Her body fell to the ground with a loud thud. Drakkon's frame turned to black smoke at the edges as he grew. It billowed out from him in waves. But he was only a short distance away. With him distracted from Elora's attack, this was the opportunity I was waiting for. I grabbed the dagger from my belt and launched myself at his back.

70

Vengeance

Elora

Sybine launched off the ground and flew through the air straight at Drakkon. She held her dagger out in front of her. It glistened in the light of the gemstones.

"Sybine, no!" I cried out.

Drakkon turned around impossibly fast. His arm collided with her chest, and he sent her flying across the room. Her eyes met mine as she collided with the stone wall and fell to a heap onto the ground. The dagger landed just outside of her grasp. She reached her hand out to me and mouthed my name before her eyes fluttered closed and her body lay motionless against the wall.

Drakkon roared. I saw the Kraken's Fang in his grasp. His body was filled with its power. I knew that feeling well. I remembered how it felt to touch it for the first time, the spark of life and power it gave. I pulled myself across the floor toward Sybine.

Drakkon was no longer paying attention to me. He took a few steps over to her unconscious body. He bent down and held the Fang to her face.

"Such a beauty," he purred. "Such a wassste."

"Don't touch her!" I screamed.

Drakkon whirled around, his eyes a burning blaze of fire. His face wore a wry smile.

"Oh, dear Elora. Still fighting even though you've lossst."

He stood up and laughed. It was menacing and cruel. The sound echoed off of every wall in the room.

I stood up; every inch of my body was filled with rage. The room turned red in my vision, and he was at the center. The man that had ruined my life.

He grinned at me and let his arms fall to his sides. He was completely open to attack. I lunged at him. His fist came out of nowhere and connected with my chest. I felt the breath leave my body. I collided with the wall and sank to the ground, trying to bring air back to my lungs. I gasped frantically. Out of the corner of my eye, I saw Sybine stir.

"Foolish girl. Did you really think that you could kill me?" Drakkon's words were like acid in my ears.

He closed the distance between us and placed a foot on my chest. I grimaced, and a loud cry of pain escaped from my lips.

Drakkon closed his eyes and took a deep breath, as if inhaling my pain.

"I love that sssound," he purred.

He looked down at me menacingly, his eyes glowing.

"There is no world where you win. You are expendable. You are alone."

The last word seemed to echo all around us, bouncing off the walls. I looked to my side. Sybine was finally awake and facing me. Her eyes were filled with fear. She grasped her dagger in her hand so strongly, I could see the whites of her bones poking up at her skin. I passed a silent message on to her, hoping she understood.

For a moment, I saw her and the betrayed look on her face when I turned around and locked her in the room back on the *Vindicta*. I hadn't thought I needed her then. I'd been wrong. I would be dead if it weren't for her and Harlan, and now I needed to trust her again.

I moved my head back and returned Drakkon's gaze. I sneered at him.

"No," I grunted, "I'm not."

I thrust my dagger into his foot, dragging it down toward my chest.

Drakkon roared and stumbled backward. The tentacles receded. His grip faltered, and he dropped the Kraken's Fang. Before he had a chance to reach down to take it back, a shadow moved over his head.

Sybine jumped through the air and drove her dagger down into his back. He stood up, howling in pain. She dragged her blade all the way down. His flesh tore, and black blood oozed out of him.

I rolled to the side and swiped the Kraken's Fang away before Drakkon could grab it again. A thousand images passed through my head. My father's lifeless corpse, Sybine's motionless body against the wall, Harlan bound to his throne with knives, and finally Drakkon's red eyes filled with rage.

I took up the Fang with both of my hands. The tentacles wrapped around my arms, and I was once again filled with an overwhelming power. With one swift movement, I thrust it into his chest.

"That's for my father, you son of a bitch."

Hero

Elora

Drakkon fell to his knees, his eyes a mask of complete surprise.

I pulled the Fang from his chest, and a spurt of black blood coated the ground.

My heart hammered, and my vision blurred at the edges. Drakkon's mouth gaped. His jaw opened unnaturally wide. I took several steps back. Black ooze fell from his mouth. A giant twisted hand emerged from his throat. Its fingers pushed Drakkon's jaw open further and further until his face ripped. A second hand shot up through his mouth, and Drakkon crumbled into a pile of ashes on the ground, leaving only the crimson-bound book behind.

A dark figure emerged from his ashes, which I recognized immediately.

"Thanksss," Keldroth hissed. "Without my chainsss, I am free." Then he twisted into a dark swirl of smoke and disappeared.

Sybine and I locked eyes from across the ashes and we raced to each other. I grimaced when she embraced me. She loosened her grip.

"Oh gods, I'm so sorry. Are you okay?" She looked me up and down, searching for any visible wounds.

"I'm okay...we did it," I said, panting.

"We did it," she echoed. "But we need to get to Harlan."

We hurried over to the Sea King. I held his head up and looked at him in his pale eyes. The color drained from his face, and his breaths were short and shallow.

"I'm sorry. This is going to hurt."

I tried to wrench the blades from his hands, but they didn't budge.

"Enchanted," was the only word he said in response.

"Use the Fang," Sybine suggested.

I turned around to her. She rested her hands on top of Harlan's and looked at him with wide, sad eyes.

"Use the Fang," she said again. "It can break any barrier. Harlan told me that once, and I believe him. Just try."

I squared my stance and sliced the Fang across the hilts as fast as I could. They shattered as soon as the Fang made contact, scattering into a thousand shards of crimson glass around us. His blood continued to trickle onto the floor. Dark red stains accumulated at the foot of his throne. His eyes rolled back into his head, and he slumped forward. I caught him before he could hit the floor. I pushed him back onto the chair and held him there.

"No," Sybine gasped. She wrapped her arms around him and sobbed into his chest, holding him tight.

"Don't go," her words were barely a whisper.

The Fang hummed with energy in my hand. I looked down to find it glowing a magnificent, radiant silver. Tendrils of light slowly dripped from the blade and swirled through the air toward his hands. To my surprise, his skin began to stitch itself together. Then, after the wounds had closed, the silver strands extended up his arms until they reached his chest.

Harlan's head snapped up, and a ball of silver light exploded from him.

"Harlan?" Sybine asked.

The Sea King was sitting up straight again. The color had returned to his face, and his eyes were bright.

"I'm alright, kid."

She embraced him even tighter.

"Thank the gods," she whispered.

Harlan's eyes met mine.

"No, thank you both."

I gave him a soft smile and leaned against one of the tall pillars. A deep exhaustion crept into my bones. The tentacles from the Fang receded from my arm, until all I was holding was what appeared to be a normal dagger.

"How?" I breathed.

"The Fang," Sybine said. "Harlan, you once said it could heal as well, didn't you?"

He nodded.

I looked down at the blade again.

"But...why *me*?"

Harlan grunted as he readjusted himself in his seat.

"The will of the Sea is not so easily controlled. Drakkon could never have done what you did, Elora. You didn't *want* the Fang." He sucked in a sharp breath. "You *needed* it. But more than that, *it* needed *you*."

I could keep it, I thought to myself as I stared down at it. *It chose me.* No one would ever have the power to threaten us again. I thought about the towns I could rebuild and the people I could protect. My thoughts quickly shifted. Even if I had good intentions, that didn't mean nothing would ever happen. I still needed to sleep and rest. I couldn't keep a watchful eye out for enemies every waking hour of every day. No. This weapon was better off far away from the hands of mortals.

I walked over to the throne and held the Fang up to the empty space where I had retrieved it from.

"Are you sure you want to do that?" Harlan asked me.

I nodded.

"I'm sure."

With a sharp click, it snapped back up and into its place. The blade shrunk down back into the form of the missing fang, and the silver faded back to black.

The exhaustion I'd felt before was nothing compared to the weight that had hit me after the Fang left my hand. I fell to my knees, suddenly unable to stand.

"Elora!"

Sybine was at me in an instant. She wrapped my arm around her shoulder and helped me back to my feet.

"I'm okay," I breathed. "Just need a minute."

Harlan stood and held his hands out to us.

"I'm very proud of you, Elora," he said. He cast his eyes to Drakkon's ashes and the crimson book that lay on top of them.

His body went rigid, as if he were frozen from the sight in front of him. A muscle tensed at Harlan's jaw, and his face flushed.

"Curse that blasted book."

The book? I thought to myself.

In a flash, Harlan crossed the room to grab his scepter and pointed it toward Drakkon's book. I was momentarily blinded by a flash of light that emerged from the sapphire jewel. After several blinks, my vision cleared. The book was nowhere to be found.

"What...." I shook my head, trying to make sense of Harlan's reaction. "What the hell?"

Beside me, Sybine looked equally as confused.

"Harlan, have you...seen that before?" she asked.

Harlan let out a sharp breath and flexed his hand by his side. He turned to face us, his eyes drooped down, focused on something on the ground near our feet. He took five long breaths before he finally spoke again.

"I think it's time...for you both to finally know the truth."

72

Behind the Mirror

Sybine

"There's something the two of you deserve to know," Harlan said as we approached a stone wall behind the throne.

He scratched his head awkwardly.

"But it will be a lot easier to show you."

I looked at the black stone behind him.

"This is just a wall," I stated.

Harlan rolled his eyes at me and gave me a playful smirk.

"This was a gift from someone very dear to me. When I felt lost and like I would never find myself again, She fashioned it for me from fallen stars in the sea. Until now, I am the only one who has laid eyes on it."

He looked over to us lovingly.

"It's nice to be able to share myself with someone else again."

Harlan pressed his hands to the wall.

The stones opened to reveal a large silver mirror. Intricate golden spirals accented the onyx-carved frame. My breath caught when my eyes settled on the inner part of the mirror. It ebbed and flowed as if it were liquid. The light from the gems behind us shone off the small waves, making the mirror appear to be breathing.

"What is that?" I asked in awe.

Harlan moved to stand beside me. His shoulders sank slightly, and his face fell.

"In a way," he said, "this is me in my truest form."

I looked back and forth between the Sea King and the mirror.

"How is this...you?"

He sighed.

"Like I said, it is much easier to show you than it is to explain. Come."

He held out a hand to both of us. We each took one, and he led us closer to the wall.

"There are things I'm not proud of. I don't know exactly what you'll see, but please, try not to think less of me."

I swallowed down the lump of fear piled up in my chest.

Elora and I exchanged a worried look.

"Close your eyes and open your mind."

I gripped his hand tighter as I let my eyes fall closed. As we took our next step, a chill slowly settled into my bones. Thin, icy tendrils worked their way under my skin like roots extending and settling into soil. They reached out to envelop me completely, shooting up my spine and coiling into my mind. The world exploded into a blinding light.

When I opened my eyes, I was no longer in the Sea King's cave. I was in a meadow filled with thousands of blooming flowers in brilliant shades of blues and purples. I curled my toes in the soft grass beneath my feet and took a deep breath of the fresh, floral air. Two people were lying down in the flowers in front of me. I took a step forward to meet them, only to find that my body was not quite my body. I was something between my physical form and my spirit, like a projection of my real self.

"Sybine?"

I turned around to see Elora in a similar state. The places where the edges of her body should have been shifted and flowed.

"I feel strange," she admitted.

I held out a wisped hand to her, and she took it. The sensation was completely foreign. It felt more like a memory of touching her skin, like my mind had every piece of information that said she was there beside me except for the last piece of magic that connected us. Still, the memory of her hand in mine was far better than her complete absence.

"I'm here," I told her. "Come, let's find out what we were meant to see."

We shifted over to the two people lying in front of us. One was a handsome young man. His golden curls shone in the strong afternoon sunlight, and his bright blue eyes twinkled as he smiled at the woman beside him. She was possibly the most beautiful woman I had ever seen. Her ivory skin seemed to radiate the same light as the sun, as if she were a beacon specifically sent to Earth to share its light. Soft black curls framed her face, and the skin around her round green eyes crinkled as she smiled. The man plucked a flower from beside him and tucked it into her hair.

"David?" Elora gasped from beside me.

"David?" I asked.

"That's him, that's David," she said. "What is he doing here?"

"There, now you are the goddess of the meadow," he told her.

She brushed him off playfully, but the creases at the edges of her eyes never went away. She rolled over to face him, both hands under her head.

"Do you love me?" she asked him. Something told me she already knew the answer.

"More than anythin'," he replied. "More than all the stars in the sky. More than all the flowers in the world. And more than you will ever know."

The woman seemed to glow brighter with every word.

"Then when are you going to ask me to marry you?"

David's face lit up with pure, unfiltered joy. He pushed himself up onto her, laughing and kissing her. Their sounds of love made my heart swell. I knew this love. I knew its power. I squeezed Elora's hand, and the small tingle in my arm told me she squeezed back.

David sat up slightly, looking at her seriously. He brushed a hair from her face.

"What about the others?"

"What others, David? There's no one else."

He shook his head.

"You know that's not what I mean."

She sighed and took his face in her hands.

"The other suitors mean nothing to me, David. Their status and power and wealth mean nothing to me. Nothing means anything to me except you. I have nothing without you."

She pulled him down into another long and passionate kiss.

"This must have been before he met my father, but why would Harlan know about it?" Elora asked.

The scene changed. We stood in an old wooden building, not unlike the one I grew up in. A thick woven blanket covered the back of an old chair in the corner near the hearth. The same woman from the meadow sat in the chair wearing a long white dress that seemed to glow in the warm light from the fire. She rocked back and forth, humming a low tune as she stroked her swollen belly.

David walked in the door and placed his hat on the table beside us. He dropped the large bin at his side to the floor, hung his jacket on the back of one of the dining chairs, and made his way over to her. He knelt down in front of her and pressed his lips to her belly.

"I didn't realize he had a child," Elora whispered. "This doesn't make any sense."

"Hello, little one." David's voice was full of tenderness.

The woman scoffed.

"Hello to you too," she said mockingly.

David stood up and pressed a kiss to her lips.

"Hello, my love."

The woman smirked.

"Much better."

David moved back to the bin he'd placed on the floor and grabbed it by the handle.

"I'll just clean these for dinner," he told her. "Don't go runnin' away from me."

"I wouldn't dream of it." She smiled at him as he left again, and she resumed her small circular patterns on her belly.

A few moments later, Elora and I jumped as the door flew open with a loud bang.

Two men held David's arms twisted behind his back while a third came up behind him and kicked in his knees. He fell to the floor with a loud thump, and his face pinched in pain.

"Do whatever you want with me. Just let Kaia go!" he pleaded.

Kaia? Where did I know that name from?

Kaia stood from her chair, and her arms curled around her stomach protectively.

"What are you doing? Let him go!" she screamed.

I wasn't sure if I truly had a heart in this realm, but something in my chest tightened as the scene unfolded in front of us. Once again, I felt the familiar tingle of Elora's hand in mine.

"They're going to kill him," Elora said beside me. "We have to do something." She reached out to grab a knife from the table in front of us, but her hand passed right through it as if she were less than a gust of wind.

"No. David!" Elora cried.

I reached out and brought her back to me. Her form shifted and flowed in sporadic patterns.

"It's just a vision, Elora. It can't hurt us," I tried to console her.

"Shut up, Kaia. You made your choice. He stole you from us. This is the least he deserves." One of the men shoved David onto the floor.

"Please, let her go," David begged again.

The tall man who had kicked out David's legs bent over and spit in his face.

"You don't deserve her, peasant trash." He spit again. David winced, and tears flowed from his eyes. "You call this a home? You call this a life? What a waste."

"Don't do this. Please, we'll leave. You'll never see us again. Just don't hurt him." Kaia's voice was full of heartbreak and pain.

I recognized that pain. I had felt that the moment I'd watched Elora fall to the depths off of the *Vindicta*. It was the same pain I had felt as I'd held her cold, lifeless body in my arms.

One of the men walked over and grabbed Kaia by the chin. She flinched and frantically pummeled her fists into his chest.

"No, Kaia. I don't think I will spare him. You sealed your fate the moment you sealed your lips and spread your legs." He spat the words at her.

He let go of his grip on her, and she fell to the ground in tears.

David looked up at her one last time, his eyes now dark and glossy, as if knowing this had come to its inevitable end.

"I love yo—"

Before he had a chance to finish his last words, a sword slashed down through his back and the light left his eyes.

73

Memory

Elora

If I could have murdered them right there, I would have. I would have murdered them a hundred times over. An ocean of their blood wouldn't have been enough.

I squeezed my eyes shut, trying to block out the image of David dying in front of me. It had been hard enough losing him ten years ago. This felt like that wound had been broken open by a thousand swords. Like my heart had been ripped from my chest.

I still didn't understand why we were seeing him here. What did any of this have to do with Harlan? Who was Kaia? And why hadn't David told me about her? Or his kid? None of it made any sense. Was this after he had left us? Was he...dead?

I sensed Sybine beside me again, trying to hold me and console me. I wished now more than ever that we could truly hold each other. I wanted to feel her warmth, her love, her compassion and her tenderness. I wanted to hold her and never let her go again.

"I'm sorry," Kaia's voice rang around us.

I opened my eyes and found ourselves in the Sea King's cave again. Only neither Sybine nor I were back to our normal forms. This was still part of the dream.

David sat on the throne with his head in his hands.

What was he doing here? And why was he on the throne?

Oh gods. A numbness crept through me. Kaia couldn't be...and he couldn't be...could he? That would make him...thousands of years old.

David's shoulders shook, and I realized he was sobbing.

"Why, Kaia? Why?"

Kaia moved toward him. Her shape, like ours, was more fluid than solid. The warm glow that once emanated from her skin was now replaced by the familiar cold blue hue of the sea.

"It's her," Sybine said beside me. "Kaia, our mother...the Sea goddess."

I swallowed and froze, unable to move.

"Sometimes we must accept the things we cannot understand."

My stomach knotted. I wanted to reach out to David and tell him that everything was going to be okay. I just wanted to help him.

"What about the baby?" he sobbed again.

"She was lost to the sea, David. I'm sorry."

David brought his hands up to his hair and gripped it so tight I thought he might pull his scalp clean off.

"But we gave birth to something else. Something magical. Something far beyond anything we could imagine."

She knelt in front of him and placed her hands on either side of his head.

We were suddenly thrust into a different vision. A beautiful sculpture stood in front of us. The carved black stone showed a woman of Kaia's likeness with a baby held up in the air. Waves embraced both of them, and the joy and love on the woman's face nearly brought me to tears. There was a pool of water between her crossed legs, and lying at the surface was a baby. Her form rippled between solid human and liquid.

The vision snapped shut and we found ourselves back in front of Kaia and David.

"The sirens are the daughters we never had, David. Together, we can raise them to be better than us, to build a world better than the one we knew."

David shook his head violently.

"I don't want this."

Kaia sighed.

"I'm sorry, David."

He shook his head again.

"How are you like this, Kaia? We just lost our child, and you act as if it were passing news on the tides."

Kaia let her head fall slightly.

"I have grieved the loss of our daughter every second for the last hundred and fifty years, David. Not a day goes by where I don't go over every moment leading up to—"

"A hundred and fifty years?"

David's eyes grew to twice their size. He looked around the cave, as if seeing it again for the first time.

"I have been dead...for a hundred and fifty years?"

Kaia swallowed and nodded.

David leaned over and took her hands in his.

"You suffered through the loss of our daughter alone and scared and grieving for one hundred and fifty years?" He took a breath. "Kaia, I am so sorry you were alone for that. No amount of time could ever heal that pain, and I am so sorry for assuming you had simply moved on from it."

Kaia kissed his hands and met his loving gaze.

"But why, Kaia? Why bring me back to this mortal realm of suffering?" His eyes welled with tears again.

She reached up and traced his cheek with her thumb.

"Oh, my sweet love. I wish I could tell you what you want to hear."

David flexed his jaw.

"What are you not telling me, Kaia?"

She let out a long, stuttering breath.

"You are no longer mortal, David. But you're not like me either. I needed help. I *need* help. And you are the only person I could trust. The only one I can trust." Kaia clasped David's hands. "The ocean is in pain. I need you to help me save it. A war is coming. I need you to help me stop it."

A bright flash of green sparked between the two of them, and I squinted my eyes to see past the light. When it faded, two objects were in Kaia's hands. One was a crown made of metal black as night, studded with glowing diamonds and sapphires. Sybine's crown. The other was a dagger that shone like the moon off the waves. Its dark hilt held tendrils that twisted around the handle. I recognized it immediately. The Kraken's Fang.

"I offer these to you, King of the Seas. My Heart and my Will. They have always belonged to you. Always."

Kaia raised the crown to his head but did not place it. David's eyes were filled with love and grief and passion and pain. After a moment, he nodded his head down to her, and she placed the crown upon it. Dark tendrils worked their way around his face, framing his piercing blue eyes. He took the

Kraken's Fang in his hand and held it in front of his face. Again, the black tendrils worked their way up his arm, tracing small spirals over his skin. He seemed to grow in both size and presence, as if some kind of spell had overcome him. He looked every bit the Sea King he was.

He glanced down at Kaia and placed a finger under her chin. She looked up at him, and the moment their eyes locked, there was a familiar spark in the air.

"Will you be my king?" she asked.

My mind raced from all the memories playing out in front of us. My emotions were a complex mess, and it felt like I was slowly losing touch with reality. I felt split between two times, two worlds, two lives, and it was hard to reconcile them.

The scene in front of us shifted. Although he hadn't physically aged, David's posture, expressions, and body language were somehow shrunken, like he had spent too many years holding up the sky so that it would not kiss the sea.

He fell to his knees on the cave floor and buried his head in his hands. For all his power, he looked more like a man defeated.

Kaia gracefully walked to him. Her movements were fluid and purposeful, but gentle all the same. She shrank to the floor with him and placed a finger under his chin, tilting it so he would face her. His eyes were filled with fresh tears of pain and anguish.

"Please," he begged, "take it from me." He gestured to the crown on his head.

Kaia sighed.

"I cannot."

David squeezed his eyes shut, and his body fell even closer to the ground. His shoulders sagged, and his arms fell limp beside him.

"Please, Kaia, please." His voice was barely audible. He was desperate for release. My chest tightened. It broke me to watch him in so much pain.

"I am sorry, my love." She spoke softly, but firmly. "The Sea is not finished with you yet."

David sobbed. He reached his hands up and scratched at his face, leaving red lines down it.

"I can't live like this, Kaia. This isn't life!" He gestured around him, and his voice cracked from the effort. "This cursed loneliness kills me every day. It haunts my wakin' hours just as much as my dreams. Sometimes, I can't tell them apart."

She placed a hand on his shoulder.

"You will grow used to the quiet. There's peace to it, I promise."

He scoffed and wiped his tearstained face with the back of his hand.

"You promise? Kaia, what am I supposed to believe? That you will always be there for me? Where have you been the last twenty years while I have rotted away with no place to decay to? You are everywhere and nowhere all at once. You're not even truly here right now, are you?" David's eyes flashed with anger. He thrust an arm forward, and it went straight through her body.

I gasped, and Sybine flinched beside me.

"It's not that simple, David. I don't have a choice—"

"And you didn't give that choice to me either."

The temperature in the room dropped several degrees as a chilling silence spread between them. Neither of them looked away from each other, as if caught in a trance.

Finally, Kaia let out a long breath and stood.

"I'm sorry, David. I truly am. I'm sorry you are suffering and I'm sorry I can't do more to help. I'm sorry I was the one who put you in this position in the first place." She paused and took a breath to regain her composure. "But I am not sorry for loving you."

She turned and took a step away that rippled her body.

"Wait," David said, his voice soft and gentle.

She faced him again.

"You once asked somethin' of me. I didn't know the cost of this gift-turned-curse." He gestured to himself. "Please," he begged, "let me ask somethin' of you."

"I cannot take it back," she said again.

"I know." He hung his head. "Instead, consider this my one condition for being your king." He looked back up at her with tears in his eyes. "Please, I beg you, don't bring anyone back from the dead ever again."

Kaia's expression hardened.

"Very well. I accept your price." In an instant, she disappeared as if she had never been there to begin with.

David's arms reached out to his sides, and his hands squeezed into fists. He thrust his head back and unleashed a terrible howl that shattered my heart. When he finally ran out of breath, he sank forward again. Then his body shifted. Like a rock had been thrown into a calm pool, he rippled, a distorted image of himself slowly emerged until finally his shape stabilized. He looked down at his hands, which were newly wrinkled and spotted with age. He held them out and turned them in front of him as if seeing his skin for the first time, which, I supposed, he was. When he lifted his face up, his pale hair fell away to reveal the man we knew to be Harlan.

Behind the Man

Sybine

"Holy shit," Elora said, echoing my thoughts.

I struggled to reconcile the idea that David and Harlan were the same person. I could only imagine how Elora was feeling.

The cave collapsed in on itself and we found ourselves back on the mainland of Elandia. We stood in the middle of what appeared to be some kind of fair.

Harlan stood facing us with a hood pulled above his head. The cloak fell over his shoulders, effectively covering his body. Another hooded man approached him.

"Do you have it?" the man asked in a hushed voice.

Harlan nodded, and my breath caught when I saw what he held in his hands.

The Heart of the Sea.

Confusion melted into my brain. What was he doing with the crown? And who was it he was offering it to?

"For this to work," Harlan said, "there must be sacrifice."

The man nodded.

"I understand."

"The will of the Sea is not so easily won, Mr. Whitethorn. It must be earned."

He nodded again.

"And have you earned it?"

The man smiled and revealed a stack of sealed envelopes.

"Every man who swears himself to me will find themself in a position of power, wealth, and privilege. They will be expected to pay this back in kind to those who live both in and on the sea, as well as on land. You have my word."

Harlan nodded and placed his lips on the large sapphire at the middle peak of the crown. It shimmered for a moment before finally settling back to its normal state.

"The crown will listen to you, and only you, Mr. Whitethorn. When your mission is over, meet me back at this dock. Call out to the Sea. I will hear you."

A cannon exploded in front of us. Suddenly, the air was filled with fire and ash.

"Death to the sirens!" A man screamed from beside us. I had to remind myself that this wasn't real. No one was hunting me now, not even this man in front of me who seemed to glow with rage.

Harlan stood behind a building, his back pressed against the bricks. His breaths were heavy, and I could sense the guilt and anguish coming off him in waves. He looked back at the rubble, tears gleaming in his eyes. He winced and shoved his eyes shut. A shimmer ran over his body as he shifted back into David. His shoulders hunched forward, and he walked into the smoke with defeat echoing from his footsteps.

The smoke raced toward us, and when I opened my eyes again, we were in a small wooden cabin. The air smelled of freshly peeled apples and honey. A small girl ran around the living room with some kind of carved toy in her hand.

My heart nearly stopped.

"Dessert is ready, squiddo," the old man said from the kitchen.

The little girl bounced over excitedly and crawled up onto her chair. She closed her eyes and took a deep breath. She hummed with delight.

"Mmmm...scrumptious!"

"Gramps?" The words fell from my mouth like a prayer.

I reached out an arm, but the image in front of us distorted as quickly as it emerged.

A younger version of myself entered the cabin carrying a basket that I knew was filled with apples.

"Gramps?" the younger me called out.

My heart shattered. I knew what this was. This was the day he passed. I never saw him again after that.

Young me dropped the basket and ran down the hall to his room. Something flashed at the corner of my eye. On the other side of the kitchen window stood Gramps. There was a steady stream of tears running down his face. He squeezed his eyes together, and in an instant, the face looking back at us wasn't Gramps' anymore.

It was Harlan's.

Oh gods, I thought to myself, *is this real?*

I felt the hint of a squeeze of Elora's hand in mine.

We were suddenly thrust back onto the deck of a ship. The Sea King was back in David's form, sparring with a partner.

"You're going to have to do better than that," the man said.

Beside me, I felt Elora tense.

"Dad?"

David lunged forward, and the other man twisted around him with ease.

Their blades clashed and their bodies pressed together.

"Do you yield, Lire?" David asked, with a hint of something playful in his voice.

Elora's father smirked, and without hesitation, pressed his lips to David's.

David's eyes widened in surprise, and her father took the opportunity to push him backward. David lost his balance and fell to the deck with a loud thud. His sword landed just outside of his reach, but before he had a chance to move closer, Lire placed a foot on David's chest and pointed his sword toward his throat.

"Do you yield?"

I blinked, and suddenly we were in some kind of study. David and Lire sat on opposite sides of a desk. There was an open book in front of them that David was reading.

"This is how to find me," David said, turning the book around. "Everything here is correct."

Lire gave a slight nod and shut the book. It was bound in crimson leather. I had seen it before.

"That's the book," Elora gasped as she came to the same realization.

"Are you sure you won't leave?" David asked.

Lire shook his head.

"You know I won't."

David looked up at Lire with a pained expression on his face.

"What about Elora?" he asked.

"She'll be safe," Lire reassured David. "Drakkon has his demons, but he won't attack us. Whatever whispers you've heard, you need to forget them. That pirate age died long ago."

The air rippled, and we crashed into the sea. A figure was sinking in front of us, her limp arms stretched up as if trying to make one last embrace. Harlan swam over to her, and I realized in horror that this was the moment I nearly lost Elora forever.

Harlan tied the rope around her waist and gave it a slight tug. Slowly, Elora was raised to the surface, but as soon as her face broke the waves, she stopped.

"I can't lift you both!" My voice called through the dark.

Elora tensed beside me, and I felt her try to console me through the touch of her spirit.

My heart broke as I watched Harlan make the decision to cut himself free so I could lift Elora up alone. Memories of sadness, grief, and uncertainty passed over his face. In a split second, his expression changed. He didn't look defeated or broken. He looked defiant and powerful. Harlan gave Elora one last kiss on the temple, and in one swift movement, submerged himself into the depths.

What Makes Us Human

Sybine

Elora and I stepped back through the mirror and landed on the cold stone floor. My breaths came heavy and sporadic, as if I had just emerged from holding my breath for far too long. Elora coughed and wheezed beside me. She was on her knees with one hand in front of her, steadying her, and the other pressed to her chest as if willing air to come back to her lungs again.

Visions of the scenes we had observed danced behind my eyes. We'd watched hundreds...no, thousands of years of the Sea King's life in a matter of what? Seconds? Minutes? Days? Time seemed to have no meaning to me anymore.

"You," Elora coughed, pointing a finger at him. "Harlan? David? Who are you? What...was that?"

The Sea King let out a long exhale. He moved toward us and offered his hands. Elora and I each took one, and he helped us to our feet.

"Like I said...me, in my truest form."

I looked back at the silver mirror. It continued to ripple and flow as if it were alive.

"It shows me who I am and who I was. When you've lived for as long as I have, it is easy to lose yourself. Sometimes you need help rememberin'. Other people have partners and children and friends and family." He looked over at the mirror solemnly. "I only have myself."

"Gramps?" I asked, finally finding my voice.

He gave me a sad smile.

"Yes, squiddo?"

Tears streamed down my face.

"You're...alive?"

He nodded.

"I know it's a lot to process, but—"

I threw myself into his arms.

He relaxed and held me tight to his chest.

"I'm sorry I didn't say anythin' sooner." He stroked my back.

My heart felt like it would explode. I had prayed and dreamed for this to happen for years. I never thought I would actually be able to live it.

"I don't care. You're alive. That's all that matters." I pulled him closer. "But why didn't you say anything? Why didn't you tell me I was a siren?"

He tensed slightly.

"I thought that by not tellin' you, I was keepin' you safe." He hesitated.

"What is it?" I asked.

He cleared his throat.

"The sirens are...at war with the humans. They have been for over a hundred years. Do you remember the stories I used to tell you?"

I nodded.

"I couldn't lose you. And as you got older, the harder and harder it became to tell you the truth. We had lived a lie for so long that I had almost come to believe it myself." He sighed. "I'm sorry, squiddo."

Elora sobbed behind me.

"David," she whispered.

The Sea King let me go. I turned to see Elora on her knees, sobbing.

"Little sword," he said as he picked her up from the ground. "You're alive."

"I'm alive."

He locked his arms around her in a warm embrace.

"I want you to know that I asked your dad to take you and come with me, Elora. I begged him to run away. By the time he finally agreed, it was too late."

The Sea King's words caught in his throat as he spoke. The twinkle had been in his eyes was replaced by an accumulation of tears beginning to well. He blinked, and a tear traced its course down his face.

"I loved him. And I loved you. So when I heard Drakkon's call over the sea, my heart sank."

Harlan parted himself from Elora and placed his hands on her shoulders. Tears flowed down her cheeks as well.

"I promise I waited as long as I could. But when Lire didn't come back with you...I had to leave before he found me. I'm so sorry, Elora."

I wrapped my fingers around hers under the table.

Elora's breath caught between her soft sobs.

"I'm sorry too, David. I know you loved him."

My heart lurched in my chest. I remembered how it felt when I couldn't find Gramps all those years ago. A small tear ran down my cheek as well. It seemed we were all patrons of heartbreak.

The Sea King chuckled softly.

"I wasn't expectin' to, you know.... I was called back home. Back home to the sea, like I told Sybine. I boarded a ship that would take me far out, hoping to quietly slip away one day. That's the day I met Lire." He returned his gaze to Elora. "That's the day I met you, Elora. Even then you were spirited. You had your arms crossed and a stubborn look on your face. Do you remember what you said to me that day, little sword?"

Elora smiled and let out a small laugh.

"I asked what kind of sailor trades his boots for an old hat."

The Sea King laughed too.

"I hope that man at the docks traveled just as far as I did in them. I didn't think I would need them where I was going. Boy, was I wrong. You kept me on my toes every day."

He shuffled his weight and let out a breath.

"My heart broke again when I thought I lost you and your dad."

My mind was still swimming with the ocean of memories we had just dove through. I couldn't imagine what it would be like to live forever and have no one to truly share it with. He had Kaia, I supposed, but like he had said, she is everywhere and nowhere all at once. My heart broke for him. I struggled to imagine a life where I would always be close enough to someone to sense them, and yet never truly close enough to connect. It would, in a way, be like living in a memory, where everything was only a shadow of what it should be. Every

589

touch, every kiss, every laugh, every smile, every heartbreak dulled and thinned; the magic in them: lost.

My breath caught, and a tear rolled down my cheek.

"I'm so sorry," I found myself echoing Kaia's words. They felt just as empty coming from me as they had from her.

He turned around and took my head in his hands.

"Don't be," he said softly. "Those memories led me to you." He turned and looked at Elora. "To you both." He gave us a sad smile. "I would not change that for the world."

76

Gift

Elora

It was like stepping out of a dream, and not being aware of whether I had entered another or if I was actually awake. I fought to keep up with my racing thoughts.

Until I met Sybine, I had chosen a life of isolation. I chose to be alone, to fight alone, to dine alone, to sleep alone. I chose that life. At least, at the time, I thought that was what it meant to be isolated. Seeing the Sea King in this new light shone an entirely new definition onto the word. Although I thought I had, I realized I hadn't understood what it felt like to be truly and completely alone. My isolation was more of a freedom, and his was a prison.

Those memories led me to you. I would not change that for the world.

I swallowed the lump in my throat. Tears stung my eyes, and I tried to blink them away. The three of us stood facing each other, and the Sea King took our hands in his. He pushed my hand toward Sybine's, palm to palm. Instinctually, we laced our fingers together.

"And I am so glad you found each other."

My heart swelled in my chest.

"What happened to you and Kaia? After, I mean," I finally managed to ask.

He gave me a slight smile.

"That's not exactly an easy question to answer. She loves me, and I love her. I will always love her. I admire her. I always have. Perhaps one day we'll be together again. But, she was right, the Sea is not finished with us."

"Oh," was all I could say.

My mind drifted to David and my father.

"You said you loved my father."

He nodded in agreement.

"Yes, I did."

"But you just said that you love Kaia."

He nodded again. He gave me a confused look.

"Are you really askin' how I could possibly love two people at once?"

Now that he said it out loud, it sounded ridiculous.

He gave me the same look he had when I'd fallen after swinging my sword for the first time. It was full of amusement and pride.

"I think that our capacity for love and our ability to share it is what makes us human. I think that I have seen a lot of death and cruelty and violence in the many years I have lived, but it has never managed to make love any less potent. If I can share it, I will. I should. There is no source I draw from when I extend my love to anyone, and so it will never run out. My love for you does not take away from my love for Sybine or my love for the Sea. Love, little sword, is not a choice. It is a gift."

A Choice of Fate

Sybine

We turned to face the Sea King.

"So, what now?" I asked.

He smiled at us.

"Now, I suppose you have a choice. You can either return to the land, or I can bring you to your siren sisters, Sybine."

"I have...sisters?"

He beamed at me.

"Yes, yes, you do. And I am sure they would be delighted to meet you. You are daughters of the sea, and so you will always have a home here. But I'll understand if you decide to return to land. The choice is in your hands."

I turned to face Elora. She smiled down at me. She brushed a hair from my face and tucked it behind my ear.

"I understand if you want to find them," she said. Her eyes were warm and compassionate.

I raised my hand up to her cheek and pulled her down into a soft kiss.

"That sounds like quite the adventure," I told her. "But I have some unfinished business on land first."

She beamed at me.

We slowly released each other and made our way to the Sea King.

"Have you made your decision?" he asked us.

We looked at each other and nodded.

I thought about returning to Elandia with Elora, hand in hand, ready to start our new lives together, and my chest warmed.

"Could I ask another favor?" I asked.

He nodded.

"Of course."

"You know that crown I stole?" I pointed to the jewels that adorned his head. "I sort of stole that off the prince of Elandia." I bit my lower lip, but Harlan just gave me an amused look in return.

"Do you think you could make me one that looks like it? I'd like to be able to walk around without looking over my shoulder all the time."

The Sea King raised his arms, and I watched in awe as tendrils of black stone, diamonds, and sapphires of all shapes and sizes wound together to form a near perfect replica of the crown adorning his head.

He placed the crown in my hands and gave me a warm smile.

Without hesitating, we both ran to him and threw our arms around him. He was warm and smelled of lavender and wood. I buried my face in his chest. He wrapped his arms around both of us and held us close.

"What an honor it has been to be a part of your lives," he said. "I am so proud of you both. I hope our paths cross again." We broke away.

"Thank you for all the lessons, David. I'll never forget them, or you."

"Farewell, little sword. Until we meet again." He placed a hand on her shoulder, and she returned the gesture. Then he turned to face me.

"I love you, Gramps," I said. A tear slowly fell down my cheek.

"I love you too, squiddo." He reached a hand behind him and pulled out a small wooden toy in the shape of a kraken. My eyes lit up. He passed it to me, and I ran the inside of my thumb along its familiar bumps and curves.

"Farewell," he said, "until we meet again."

78

Elandia

Elora

There was a loud rush of water around us as Harlan twisted his scepter. The last thing I saw of the Sea King's lair was a flash of the sapphire, and the smile that was spread across his face. Less than a breath later, we were standing outside of the Stumbling Sailor. Rain poured down on us, and small arcs of light flashed across the sky. We were back.

I took a deep breath and embraced the sweet scent of the fresh rain. I lifted my face up to the sky. I couldn't help but smile as the light drops tickled my face. Sybine let go of my hand and giggled holding her arms outstretched.

I closed the rest of the space between us and placed my arm around her waist. I drew her close to me. She reached up and wrapped both of her arms around my neck. Her eyes echoed the lightning that flashed across the dark sky.

A wide grin spread across her face. She jumped up and wrapped both of her legs around me. She arched her back and tilted her face to the sky. She opened her mouth to catch the drops of rain. The sweetest sound of joy escaped her lips. She brought her body back up and pulled me in.

When our lips met, it was like the flash of sparks in the sky: bright, consuming, and breathtaking, accompanied by the steady drum of our hearts. I lost myself in her. The feel of her body on mine, the sound of her gentle breaths, the smell of salt water on her skin, and the taste of her sweet lips. Our bodies moved together. Her hands moved to the side of my face as she pressed herself into me.

I took a few gentle steps forward until Sybine's back was against the wall of the tavern. I brought one hand up and danced through her thick curls with my fingers. The next time our lips opened, I made my way down her neck, tracing its curves with soft kisses. She arched her neck and brought her face up to the night sky. I made my way back up her neck and placed one last kiss on her lips. Then I brought our foreheads together.

"We're alive," I said breathlessly.

"We're alive," she echoed.

Cheers erupted from inside the tavern just inside the window. Some men were banging on the glass at us. I blushed and then let Sybine back down to the ground. A carriage pulled by two dark horses approached. We both turned around to examine it. The carriage was black with white curtains that were drawn. They stopped just outside the door of the tavern.

The man driving the carriage tied the reins to the bar in front of him and stepped down to open the door. The inside of the carriage was lined with plush red velvet, but it wasn't occupied.

"Holy shit," Sybine whispered. "It can't be."

I looked down at her, confused.

"Can't be what?"

"Erryk."

"Erryk?" Oh shit. The prince.

I glanced back to the carriage. It definitely looked fit for royalty.

I gripped her hand.

"If he's here, then we need to leave." I pulled on her arm, but she held her ground and shook her head.

"No, Elora. This is my unfinished business. I can't keep living like this."

I swallowed a lump in my throat. Nothing about this felt right. It was too convenient. Too coincidental. And neither of us had prepared for his reaction. Did he have guards with him? Would he lash out? What if we missed something? I didn't know anything about Erryk, except for what Sybine had told me. I felt woefully unprepared.

Sybine pulled herself into me.

"You can't always be prepared for everything," she said simply.

I looked down at her and ran my teeth over my lower lip.

"How did you know I was thinking that?"

She gave me a shy smile.

"I've learned to pick up on a few things. And you always squint your eyes, not a lot, but a little bit, when you're planning something or thinking too hard."

Normally such a statement would put me on guard. But with Sybine, it was different. Her words didn't make me want to recoil. Instead, surprisingly, they set me at ease.

"How perceptive of you."

She beamed at me.

"You taught me more than just how to hold a knife, you know." She nodded her head toward the door. "Come on, let's get this over with."

79

Back to the Beginning

Sybine

Elora kept a hand around my waist as we walked into the tavern. She took an abandoned three-pointed hat from the bar bench and placed it on her head. I eyed her skeptically.

She shrugged.

"Pirate."

I rolled my eyes at her.

I scanned the room for Erryk. It didn't take long before I spotted him a few tables down with three other men. Erryk sat awkwardly on an old wooden chair. His gold embroidered black coat cascaded down his back and collected near the floor. The buttons on his chest seemed to wink in the light. He looked painfully out of place amongst the rest of the patrons. There was no mistaking him for a commoner this time. One of the men he sat with was the one from the first night I was here. He held up the paper with my face on it.

"Yes, yes," Erryk said, his tone bored. He ran a hand through his platinum hair. "But where did she go after she stole your...fortune?"

The man paused.

"I...I don't know. How am I supposed to know?"

Erryk leaned his forehead on his hand, frustrated.

"I rule over a land of witless, worthless worms," he said under his breath. "It's not as if she just disappeared." Erryk slammed his hands onto the table. "I've heard nothing but the same stories for over a week from everyone here. Surely somebody has to know something else."

My hand made its way to the clasp on the bag at my side. I grinned. It was not the Heart of the Sea, but he didn't have to know that.

We made our way over to their table. I cleared my throat.

"If you have something to say about me, the least you could do is say it to my face."

They all looked up at me. Their eyes widened as they glanced down at the paper and then back up. They all stuttered and pointed their fingers at me. Finally, Erryk took a breath and turned around to see who they were pointing at.

"Hello...Erryk."

His eyes narrowed.

"You," he growled.

Erryk stood up and placed a hand on his sword. Elora pushed me to the side and put a hand on her blade as well. Her gaze was dangerous and daring.

Erryk raked his eyes over her body.

"And who might you be?"

Elora bared her teeth at him.

"I'm—"

I pushed myself between them before the altercation escalated any further.

"She's my girlfriend."

I twisted my head to look up at Elora. Her eyes widened, and a few moments later, she visibly relaxed. Something almost like contentment crossed her face.

I turned back to face Erryk.

"Perhaps we should take this outside," I suggested.

He gritted his teeth.

Elora turned to the side, opening the pathway between him and the door. She bowed dramatically as he made his way past her, and I had to fight back a laugh. We followed him out of the tavern.

As soon as the door closed behind us, Erryk flipped around. His eyes were dark and angry.

"Do you know what it is you took from me?" he sneered.

I raised my hands in front of me in mock surrender.

"Look, I'm sorry. But how was I supposed to know you were the prince when you weren't dressed like this?" I vaguely gestured at him.

He balled his fists at his sides, and Elora once again placed her hand on the hilt of her blade.

He scoffed.

"Where is it? Where is my crown?" he hissed.

I reached down into my bag and brought out the diamond and sapphire gemmed crown. His eyes widened.

"Here," I said as I tossed the crown over.

He caught it easily and tightly wrapped his fingers around the jewels.

"Now, will you remove the price from my head?" I asked him.

Erryk's cold blue eyes narrowed at me, but he nodded slightly.

I relaxed and let out a long breath.

"You could have kept it," he said, his voice low. Then in a stronger voice, he added, "You could have continued to run…. Why?"

I looked up at Elora. A rush of admiration, longing, and something stronger coursed through me. Erryk had his crown back, and the bounty would be lifted from my head. I finally knew who I was, and despite it all, Elora was still by my side.

A warmth flushed through my chest. The words perched on the tip of my tongue, sweeter than honey and more intoxicating than any mead. But now was not the time.

Soon, I promised myself.

"I'm tired of running," I admitted. "And I don't need your crown." I took the hat from Elora's head and placed it on top of mine. "I have a better one."

Epilogue

Erryk

I had spent the last few months hunting a ghost, and here she was materialized in front of me.

My vision flashed crimson.

She had taunted me for the last time. She didn't know it, but she had played right into my hand. Sure, I wanted the crown back, but it was her I wanted, her I needed. She was far more important to me than she would ever know. She was mine. Mine. And no other's.

Sybine turned to look up into her partner's eyes.

She should have known better than to turn her back to me. She should have known I would never let her escape from my grasp a second time.

A familiar figure emerged from the shadows behind the tavern. A wry smile tugged at the corners of my lips. She always did have perfect timing.

I took a few quick steps toward Sybine. With one swift movement, my elbow connected with the back of her head, and I watched with satisfaction as her body fell limp to the ground as if she were finally, after all this time, bowing before me.

Do You Want to Play a Game?

I hope you enjoyed reading *A Kiss of the Siren's Song*! There were two games featured in this book that are loosely inspired by real life dice and card games, but with some major differences.

In case you are interested in playing them, I have included the rules and materials you will need here. If you do end up going a round or two, make sure you take a photo and tag me in it! I would love to see who's playing for scraps, and whose lucky number is seven!

Scraps

Materials:
- 1 deck of cards for every 2 people
- Notepad
- Pen

Objective:
- The person or team with the lowest amount of points wins.

Points:
- Ace = 0
- 2 = -2
- 3 – 10 = their respective numbers
- J, Q, K = 10
- Ocean (Joker) = automatic win

Moves:

Choose one of the following:

- Look at the facedown card, but do not reveal it. You may choose to keep this card, or swap it with your opponent (if in a two player game), or your partner (if in a 2+ player game).

- Draw a card. You may choose to swap with your facedown card, or discard it, meaning you keep your facedown card. If you swap the card, your previous facedown card is revealed and placed faceup on the discard pile. The card you have drawn is placed face down on the table. If you choose to discard the card you drew, this card would also be placed faceup on the discard pile.

- Retrieve the top card of the discard pile and swap it with your next card that would be flipped over.
- Once your move is finished, you indicate it by moving the coin onto the back of the card you have decided to lock in.

Rules:

   There is one deck of cards for every 2 players. These cards must include Ace – King in all four suits and an additional ocean card. The ocean card described in the book can be easily substituted with a joker from a typical card deck. Each player starts with 5 cards in front of them face down in a row. There are 5 individual moves per round, one for each card. The possible moves are outlined above. Each player may only choose one move per turn. Once all five moves have been completed, each player reveals their cards. The person (or team) with the lowest number of points wins. If at any point the ocean (joker) card is drawn or discovered through any of the moves, the player is to reveal it immediately and the round is over. If this occurs, all players must reveal their five cards, and all points are counted as if all five turns had occurred. Once the points have been tallied, the cards are shuffled and the next round may begin.

Turns: Each player breaks the deck. The person with the lowest card shuffles and the person with the highest card deals. The person with the lowest card makes the first move for each turn. Once each player has made their move for their card, they place a coin on the back to indicate their turn is over. This continues for all five cards. Once each player has completed their five turns, all cards are placed face up and the points are tallied.

Extra:

In A *Kiss of the Siren's Song*, players are welcome to place bets either for themselves if they are playing, or for others if they are observing. These bets may be anything from cash to objects to favors. The only limit is your imagination. Of course, since we are not pirates (probably), you are just encouraged to play for fun.

Sevens

Materials:
- 2 dice per person

Objective:
- The person with the most number of rolls that add up to seven wins.

Rules:
- Before starting, each player trades one dice with their opponent.
- The preliminary round decides who goes first. Whoever rolls the highest sum is the winner, and the game proceeds from there.
- Whoever won the preliminary round goes first. There are seven rounds that alternate between the two players. The winner of the preliminary round goes first and last.
- Any combination adding to seven counts (1+6, 2+5, 3+4)
- If the opponents are tied moving into the final round, the last roll is the deciding roll. If the person that throws the dice rolls a seven, they win the game. If they do not, the opponent wins.

Pronunciation Guide

(In Alphabetical Order)

Brandor - BRAN-DOOR

David - DAY-VID

Drakkon - DRACK-EN

Elandia - EE-LAND-EE-AH

Elora - E-LORE-AH

Harlan - HAR-LEN

Keldroth - KELL-DROTH

Kraken - CRACK-EN

Laraghan - LAR-AGAIN

Loren - LORE-EN

Navryn – NAV-RIN

Rhyker - R-EYE-KER

Sebastien - SEB-AS-TEE-EN

Siren - SIGH-REN

Sybine - SIB-EEN

Tamarine - TAM-A-REEN

Varix - V-AIR-EX

Vindicta - VIN-DIK-TA

Waldreg - WALL-DREG

Acknowledgements

A *Kiss of the Siren's Song* was a labor of love. I could not have finished it without the support and encouragement of everyone.

First and foremost, I want to thank you, reader, for taking the time to read this little piece of my heart. I hope that when you think of the story, you remember Harlan's love, Sybine's loyalty, and Elora's tenacity. May these be traits that live on through you as well.

This book probably wouldn't have existed without two very important people: Rachel and Cathrine. Rachel, thank you for being my number one fan since day one, and for coming along on this wild journey with me and helping me develop this story into what it is today. You are the friend that everyone deserves to have in their life. I am so immeasurably grateful for you! Cathrine, you are superwoman. Thank you for all of the late-night chats, the encouragement, and the support. You inspire me to be a better person and writer, and I can't thank you enough for that. On top of being an amazing formatter and book trailer maker, you are also, and more importantly, an amazing friend.

Harper-Hugo, Will, Tamika and Josh, thank you for always cheering me on whenever I have a bonkers idea that I need to see through. Y'all have always been in my corner, and I am so thankful to have you in my life. Thank you for listening to all of my excited rambles, and for being the best friends I could ever ask for.

To my parents and grandparents, thank you for helping to raise me to be the person I am. I wouldn't be here without you. And I mean that in both the literal and loving sense. Your unconditional love and support for me has been the greatest gift of my life. Travis, thank you for never judging me for my absurd and outlandish ideas. It's true what they say: the gamer and the book nerd make the best couple. Thank you for being by my side throughout this whole process, and for always understanding me. You are my whole world.

I also want to extend a huge thanks to my developmental editor, Britney. Your feedback massively helped shape this story into what it is today. I also would like to thank Rebecca for being the best proofreader ever. I absolutely loved working with you! And to Brie for doing all of the amazing character art for this book. You are so talented, and I'm so thankful to work with you to bring these characters to life!

To all of my bookstagram fam, THANK YOU! Y'all are amazing. I have been so overwhelmed in the best way. I have loved talking to each and every one of you about the book, your experiences, and everything in between.

I would also like to thank and acknowledge my beta and ARC readers, and street team members. Y'all have blown me away. I didn't know what to expect when I first started on this journey, but I can safely say now that you have made it so magical and welcoming. THANK YOU THANK YOU THANK YOU.

Finally, and this might be a bit unorthodox, but I'm going to do it anyway, I want to acknowledge all of the queer people who came before me. Because of you, I could safely tell this story. Because of you, I can be who I truly am. Because of you, the world is a better place. I hope we continue to grow it in the right direction.

About the Author

E. A. M. Trofimenkoff (she/they) is a Lord of the Rings and cat enthusiast from Southern Alberta. When she's not doing research, writing papers, preparing presentations or teaching chemistry, you can find them writing fiction (obviously), binging TV shows with their partner, re-reading The Hunger Games for the 30+ time, or pestering one or more of their four cats. If it's not any of the above, she's probably sending memes. Good luck catching up on the days' worth of material she's sent you since you started reading this book.

Author photo is by Jordan Tate (jordantatedesign.com, @t.a.t.e._ on instagram).

Made in the USA
Coppell, TX
18 September 2024

37447575R00370